Belladonna

KAREN MOLINE

WARNER BOOKS

A Time Warner Company

Warner Books, Inc., 1271 Avenue of the Americas, New York, NY 10020
Visit our Web site at http://warnerbooks.com

 A Time Warner Company

Printed in the United States of America
First Printing: May 1998
10 9 8 7 6 5 4 3 2 1

Library of Congress Cataloging-in-Publication Data

Moline, Karen.
    Belladonna / Karen Moline.
        p.   cm.
    ISBN 0-446-52318-6
    I. Title.
PR6063.04835B45   1998
823'.914—dc21   97-32285
                                                CIP

Text design by Stanley S. Drate/Folio Graphics Co. Inc.

For Jacki, with love

Cold eyelids that hide like a jewel
Hard eyes that grow soft for an hour;
The heavy white limbs, and the cruel
Red mouth like a venomous flower . . .

Pain melted in tears, and was pleasure;
Death tinged with blood, and was life.

—Swinburne,
"Dolores, *Notre-Dame des Sept Douleurs*"

Belladonna

A Tasty
Little Ditty

Belladonna sounds so sweet
Pretty woman on the street
Pretty woman passing by
Pretty teardrops in her eye
Pretty poison is her cry
Belladonna watch you die

A TASTY LITTLE DITTY

Belladonna sounds so sweet

A whiff of a killer is a potent aphrodisiac.

Sweet sweet poison, they call her, the beauty fresh from hell.

You want to breathe the same air she does, absorb the molecules of her fame as if a sniff could transform your dreary, sensible life. Don't deny it. You know you're desperate for the entire, incredible fable of the incomparable Belladonna—not the fake stories multiplying like hyenas at a carcass, that greedy foraging for shards of gossip among the bones. So be patient. Sit back. Wish you were me, writing poisonously tasty little ditties, spreading a few rumors. All right, I concede: many rumors. I try not to lie, but sometimes I can't help a tiny bit of exaggeration. Why should I spoil the unspooling of my story with the unadulterated truth?

"I don't want truth," says Belladonna fiercely. "I'm not looking for truth. I want *vengeance.*"

La vendetta. Oh ho, how your curiosity is piqued. Naughty, aren't you? Naughty Belladonna sounds so sweet, but she's not, is she? Never was, go the whispers.

"Who wants nice?" she asks with a shrug. "Nice gets you nowhere."

But you don't want her to be nice. Nice is boring. Nice is safe. Nice is not how she got her fortune. "Candy is dandy but lucre is cracker," she says with a bitter laugh. "The power money buys is a woman's only protection against the world. Against men. Against *him.*"

That, and an unforgiving heart.

I expect that many men possess her ruthlessness, but how many would be willing to pursue their passions into her vengeful realm? Do you consider vengeance an unsuitable topic for the women of the world? Too bad, then, for you. *Finita la commedia.*

Allow me to introduce myself. Tomasino Cennini, your most obedient servant. Jack-of-all-trades, master of many. Because I once had the leisure to read the contents of an immense library I am a veritable fountain of arcane information; because I am possessed of such a pleasing personality I am an astute manager of many households; because I am such an officious listener I am a vast receptacle of buckets of gossip; because I am famous for my knee-throbbing hunches I am an uncanny judge of character. I am renowned for my mint juleps served in shiny silver beakers; notorious simply for my proximity to Belladonna.

Don't you forget it.

I am also younger brother to Matteo Cennini, by four measly minutes. I suppose now is the time to tell you my twin and I are not quite all whole. Wholly male, I mean. We were born whole, naturally, but castration is not a topic for polite conversation. In fact, there is no easier way to watch a man's face blanch than to whisper our piteous secret in his ear. Running more to fat than ever, I have been a eunuch so long that I no longer dream of the feel of a woman. But had we not been disfigured so, Belladonna would never have trusted us, and this story would be very different.

Besides, I prefer not to think about my *manhood.* I have so many other wonderful qualities.

"You are my masterpiece of ruined civilization," Belladonna says fondly about me. I am indispensable to her, a man of consummate style and judgment, a delicious comrade for any emergency.

How I love my work!

I came to meet Belladonna when she was nearing the end of the worst of what made her, you see, when Matteo and I were . . .

Botheration. It is too soon to tell you of that treachery, yet surely the purpose of every story is to arrive at a destination.

Let me start again: *This is a story of revenge.*

Pretty woman on the street

Close your eyes and let me conjure a woman of cruelty sublime. You adore her and despise her: The humble are filled with disapproving envy; the wealthy with scornful, grudging admiration—yet still you long to join her world as if to steal the secret of her being and make it your own.

I know you wonder if she has a heart. It doesn't matter, though, because she has enough money to buy one, or anything else she wants.

See her sit, unblinking, cold as frost, yet when she points her fan at you, or talks about everything and nothing in her throaty voice, or smiles, life for a moment seems to go that much faster. And when she laughs—oh ho, *Belladonna,* the very sound of it so intoxicating it could enchant the deaf—you wish you could bottle this sound, genie-like, to uncork and replay whenever you realize that the world without Belladonna is a world without enchantment.

She is not quite real, this magical image come to life in the dark corners of the Club Belladonna.

"What is *real*? What is *useful*?" Belladonna asks one night as she moves among the tables, fingering a bright cerise ringlet of her wig. "What is more boring than a *useful* person? Flowers are useless, but we love them, we nurture them, we can't live without them. So don't talk to me of *useful* unless you understand the kind of usefulness I need."

Which, of course, no one understands. Except me.

People believe almost anything about Belladonna. That, for instance, she uses dilute drops of *Atropa belladonna* to enlarge her pupils and make them gleam. No no no—it is a glimmer of disdain and vague amusement, tempered by her preclub ritual: a glass of watercress juice and a diluted vinegar chaser to start the blood flowing.

Her otherworldly eyes and hint of a smile under her masks petrify your imagination, and render you nearly dumb like my brother Matteo, the silent sentinel at the club's door, with the dog Andromeda at his side. Belladonna's devastating beauty—or rather, what you imagine it to be—is of such power as to arouse even the impotent.

And I should know, shouldn't I?

Pretty woman passing by

Ask yourself this: What is concealed behind that glorious facade of the impenetrable Belladonna? She may appear to be a woman of beguiling ease, but how easily she can seduce your senses into confused bewilderment. She's had too many years to perfect this talent. It started, quite unwillingly, under a very *particular* kind of tutelage. It continued under another, where she learned how to play at concealment like a game. One of the few she could win.

Yet, I warn you, she has an uncanny radar for deceit; lie to her and she'll turn that green gaze upon you, freezing the marrow of your bones. In *her* club she knows all the secrets. And the truth is, you never had a clue what Belladonna looks like, really. I'll tell you this much: If you see her walking down the street, you'll say, "Now there is a fine figure of a woman." Her hair is long and thick and very wavy, a lustrous dark reddish chestnut, with hints of gold running through it; the firmly shaped planes of her face are slightly tilted; her lips like chewy cherries; her chin strong, like her nose; her neck long and lovely; her body of only medium height, curvy and strong, held ramrod-straight so that she seems taller. Her movements are impossibly quick; she is agile like a puma, lithe and fastidious.

Blink and you'll miss her. No, Belladonna *doesn't* trust anyone. Why should she? I wouldn't, if I were Belladonna.

Pretty teardrops in her eye

The absurd juxtapositions life presents: One moment you pick up the telephone and overhear your husband telling his mistress how much he desires her, and the next you're looking at toothpaste in your bathroom, spit into a marble sink as turquoise as the tiles of a pool glistening in the gardens underneath the tower window of a Tuscan palazzo.

Women started flocking to the imperious Belladonna in desperation, you see. They decided she might be a sympathetic ally, and they began to write pleading letters. In the early years of the 1950s, we lived in a twilight world of unjust verdicts; courtrooms were ruled by fools, by men, where new money and old connections bought freedom for the guilty willing to pay any price.

But Belladonna has more than enough money to buy them all. And now all those women have Belladonna.

Pretty poison is her cry

See what she has become: the octopus of revenge. How these women plead, hoping to be admitted to her secret lair in the Club Belladonna.

For them, she is a modern-day oracle of vengeance. Her voice, they say, is low and sweet, and when they tell her what they want she lights the fire and burns the incense, her calm movements evoking a primitive eeriness. She makes these ladies repeat their desires, and it is then that her voice changes, only for the briefest of seconds, into a shape as brittle as the mahogany skin of a roasted suckling pig dug steaming out of a pit of glowing coals.

Oh ho, a whiff of Belladonna is wafting their way.

So much in so few words! I didn't say Belladonna is nice, did I?

She prefers the *Atropa belladonna,* of course. Deadly night-shade, lovely purplish-red flowers shaped like bells, berries black and shiny as a cocker spaniel's coat.

I prefer *Nerium oleander.* So delicate, fragrant, and touchable, so bitterly toxic. It's not from the dogbane family for nothing. Brush that glossy coat of pretty poochie all you want before he laps the pond water where a few sweet leaves and branches of oleander float, innocently rotting. Kiss pretty poochie good-bye.

Belladonna watch you die

There she sits in her secret lair, the toughness of her shell invulnerable to criticism and jealousy. A deliberate cipher, since no one can see her face. Yet the fire burns inside her, propelling her on.

She changes all those other women profoundly, but for her they are a mere diversion, a crochet hook and yarn to keep her hands busy while her mind frets in its quest for the men who wronged her.

The members of the Club, she calls these men. Not the Club Belladonna. The *other* one.

And the worst of them is known as His Lordship.

Yes, the women in the Club Belladonna are only a small part of my story. But like everyone else who meets Belladonna, they long for acknowledgment, the smallest token of her love and esteem.

Don't hold your breath waiting.

It's not that my darling Belladonna is immune to love, even if the landscape of her heart is full of hardness and chill. She lives to plot, you see. The plotting, like the fire of her rage, will not leave her. She will reshape her world; she will remold herself; she will create her own destiny. How she suffered—but she will not let fate squash her down and kill her spirit.

"You can become anything—if only you know what you want, which most people don't," she was told. "If you think you can't fail, you won't. If you think you're going to lose, you will. If you avoid the truth, you pay for your lies. A lie will always do the most harm to the person who tells it."

That, she learned too well. But at the bottom of every conquest is a little worm, snaking in the dirt, looking to feed itself. A little worm, a little bit of poison to spoil your fun and cut a jagged edge in your hopefulness.

It keeps her ever vigilant, and she knows how to protect herself. We were introduced to a man who taught us the best way to shoot: Stand in a perpendicular stance to expose less of your body, take a deep breath, exhale halfway, swallow, then squeeze—never pull— the trigger before your target knows what hit him. Shoot steady.

Aim for his heart.

Belladonna sounds so sweet

Are you still with me? Of course you are. I know where you want to go, but you haven't yet earned the right to cross the exclusive portals of the Club Belladonna. It's time to go back, years and years, to the beginning of what molded her.

It was 1935, early spring in London, the trees just beginning to bud, and she was only eighteen and knew so little of the world. She was visiting her cousin June, free at last from the boring burden of her upbringing. Life was a pleasingly empty road of vague dreams and girlish hopes stretching before her in the mist of a March twilight. It was then that she had the misfortune to meet a man named Henry Hogarth. At least that's what he said his name was.

Henry Hogarth. How the sound of his name conjures a flood of memories. How the thought of him and what he started leads me to this tale of the incomparable Belladonna.

Oh ho, the sweet sweet poison!

The Diary

(1935)

—*All* women are whores, Hogarth was saying. He'd come to their little flat for tea.

June's eyes got as round as the saucer of milk they put out for the cat, when she heard that. Her cousin, sitting in a corner of the flat, looked up from her book.

—Henry Hogarth, June said, giggling, you are too shocking. You say the most unbelievable things.

—But it's true, my dear June, he said, whorish behavior begins when a little girl bats her eyelashes at daddy. He becomes putty in his wee darling's hands, does he not? The more affectionate she is, the more loving he becomes. Aha, she says to herself. This is progress; this brings me presents. Then she begins to work her way through the other masculine members of the family. As putty, they become as well. And so it goes, on and on from there until she hooks them all.

—But what has that to do with whores? June's cousin asked.

Hogarth flicked off an infinitesimal speck of lint from his jacket. He was fussy about his clothes. He was always complaining about his tailor. Then he smiled.

—It has everything to do with whores, he said. Girls learn that flaunting a few of the feminine wiles may very well bestow upon them what they think they desire. A husband, a house, whatever. They are willing to sell themselves in exchange for security. And this they've learned at darling daddy's knee.

—I didn't learn that from my father, her cousin said.

—Your father was a drunk, June said. She didn't understand this conversation, which meant she didn't like it. It had nothing to do with her.

—Women are afraid of their own desires, Hogarth went on. They're simply too overwhelming. Sexual desires, I mean. Therefore, they sell themselves short; they sell the possibility of their freedom for the allures of security. He shuddered. Quite a dreadful concept, if you ask me.

—Is that why you're not married? June's cousin asked.

—One of the many reasons, he replied. Always on the move. Must *remain unencumbered. "A man has missed something if he has never woken up in an anonymous bed beside a face he'll never see again, and if he has never left a brothel at dawn feeling like jumping off a bridge into the river out of sheer physical disgust with life." Flaubert, of course.*

Hogarth was always quoting things. Especially quotes from Frenchmen. That made June impatient. She didn't know who Flaubert was or what Hogarth was talking about.

—Had I indeed taken the fateful plunge toward the matrimonial state, Hogarth went on, I should never have had the pleasure of meeting the delicious June Nickerson.

—Oh Hogarth, June said. You say the nicest things.

—I don't think what you've been saying about women is nice at all, said her cousin.

—No, I don't suppose it is, Hogarth replied. You shall learn that sometimes, my sweet, nice gets you nowhere. Nor does conventionality. Or conformity.

June's cousin had the feeling he was talking directly to her, testing her in some odd way, bypassing June because he knew she was too feeble to understand.

—What would you do, for example, if you had a chance, if something remarkable and splendid could be handed to you if only you dared reach out to grab it? Hogarth asked, looking directly at her. A chance to change your life, utterly. All you'd have to do would be to agree to take one step into the shadows.

She felt a chill. A premonition. Don't be absurd, she told herself. It's just talk. Hogarth talking to two impressionable American girls pretending to be sophisticated in his London world.

—I'd grab it, June said. Of course I'd grab it.

—Yes, my dear June, I always knew you were a brave darling, Hogarth said. And you?

—Oh, she doesn't know what she wants, June protested. You won't ever get a straight answer out of her.

Hogarth knew her answer, she decided. He gave a tiny nod only she could see. And he didn't like June at all. The sudden realization struck her like an afternoon downpour in Kensington Gardens. He tolerated June because he was interested in her. She didn't like him like that; nor was he interested in seducing her. It was something else. She had no idea what. She'd never met anyone like him before in all *her young years. But the knowledge that she intrigued a man like Hogarth pleased her very much.*

—A touch of the forbidden sharpens one's focus, Hogarth said.

June frowned. Honestly, the most ridiculous things sometimes came out of Hogarth's mouth.

—Yes, a touch of the forbidden, he went on. My roundabout manner, dearest June, of inviting you to a very exclusive costume ball. A house party in the country. It will be the most splendid event of the season.

—Oh, what fun! June said. London's been such a bore. It's always raining and gray and damp and so boring. Ever since I got here; ever since she got here last month. But does she have to come with us? Look at her, always got her nose buried in some dumb book. So boring.

—Of course your cousin must come, Hogarth said. We couldn't think of going without her. Those lovely green eyes will dazzle everyone there.

June really didn't like hearing that. She pouted. June had a tendency to pout, when she wasn't complaining. But she needed her cousin with her in London, even though June didn't think she was showing enough gratitude. More opportunity to go out, meet people, when she had another girl her age with her. People like Hogarth were much more interesting than dusty old statues and boring old things in museums. Who would you ever meet in a museum besides boring old tourists?

Her cousin should be grateful that June had already met Hogarth at a dinner party a few weeks before. Hogarth knew everybody and got invited to everything. Hogarth took June and her cousin to the most fabulous places, tea at the Café Royal and dinners at the Gargoyle and the 400 and the Ivy, where everyone looked at them, because they were jealous. Swanky parties in mansions full of servants and lots of young people, interesting people who were wearing fabulous clothes, women in silken gowns with fluttery chiffon sleeves. And the jewelry, huge things that left June speechless with desire. People didn't wear jewels like that in Minneapolis. Ropes of pearls. Chunks of emeralds and sapphires, and oh, those diamond tiaras. June wanted a tiara. More than anything, June wanted a husband who was rich enough to buy her a tiara.

June also wanted her cousin to go away, back home, but people seemed to like her. Even Hogarth. Especially Hogarth. It was terribly aggravating.

June looked in the mirror, preening after Hogarth left. Her dull blue eyes stared back at her. Everyone talked about her cousin's dazzling green eyes. Men, handsome and strapping young men, who should be paying more attention to June. After all, June had all the money and the letters to society people that her mother had finagled for her. Her cousin had nothing. Well, June'd show them. She'd go to this fabulous costume ball and then go back to Minneapolis with a tiara and a handsome and strapping young husband with a title or something and a swanky accent. A husband who knew how to shoot and ride and had a big house in the country with lots of dogs and servants, a house that June could invite all her little friends to and they'd be so jealous because their own lives were so boring.

But June couldn't go to the very exclusive costume ball. Something was terribly wrong with her stomach and she wasn't getting any better. She was still too sick to get up out of bed, except to run to the bathroom. Must have been something she'd eaten the last time they'd all gone to the Ivy or the Café de Paris. She accused her cousin of poisoning her so she could go to Hogarth's party all by herself.

—I'll never forgive you, June screamed from her bed. You did this on purpose.

—I won't go if you don't want me to.

June was torn. What if her cousin went and met someone interesting and he had an older brother who was even richer and more handsome and he'd take one look at June and fall madly in love with her and—

—Oh, I don't care what you do, June said, pouting. I don't care if you ever come back.

PART I

The Oracle
of the Fountains

(1947–1951)

Belladonna doesn't know
What to think or where to go
Who can teach her, who can tell
Where is heaven, where is hell
Wander blindly, hold your breath
Belladonna walks toward death

1

The Secret of Perpetual Youth

"*H*e's staring at you again. That one, over by the fountain."

Belladonna looks at a chubby man sprawled on a chaise and dismisses him with a shudder. She tucks a soft pink mohair shawl tighter around her daughter, Bryony, napping peacefully in her lap. "He looks like an overboiled chestnut."

Matteo smiles, pleased she can joke about a man. As long as the man doesn't come anywhere near us.

Wait. This is not quite right. I beg to interrupt already. She is not yet Belladonna; I am not used to thinking of her as what she had once been, frightened and weak.

No—I must remember to call her Ariel. Her given name once upon a time was Isabella Ariel Nickerson, and her traveling name, written neatly in one of her several fake passports, is Ariel Hunter. I am using the false name of Thomas Smith, and my brother is calling himself Matthew. I can thank my training in the Resistance for the development of one of my many talents: the very particular art of forgery and counterfeiting.

"Yes, he does look like a flabby chestnut, especially with those lovely bulging eyes. I hereby christen him Mr. Nutley," I say, not wanting to think of the Resistance. "And look, all the regulars are out today."

Ariel closes her eyes, but I know she is alert to their presence in the limpid spring air. My blather distracts her, because she is easily spooked by the few passersby, casually curious about the fragile lady with the seven-month-old baby and the two men with luxurious dark curls; smooth, pale, hairless skin; and soft, round bellies.

"Signora Mange is in fuchsia today. She appears to have had her hair fluffed again," I report about the plump matron in the too-tight capris and clattering mules topped with—what else?—powder pink poufs, smothering her revolting ratball of a shih tzu with smooches. "And let's see . . . Madame Twenty Carats has exchanged her tiara for a simple parure of cabochon emeralds. From Woolworth."

"Is the other one there, too, the Count of the Sorrows?" Ariel asks, her eyes still closed.

"Yes, in his usual spot," I tell her. This is what we call the slim, elderly gentleman with the full head of white hair, slicked back sleekly, and the shapely Roman nose, who walks with a beautifully shaped mahogany cane topped with the golden head of a lion. He bows to us with the utmost courtesy every morning but never says a word. Nor do his lips curve into the semblance of a smile. I respect him for that, lost in his melancholy as we are in our own.

"He must be someone important," I say. "All the staff shower him with a special sort of deference."

"Do you think the waters will cure what ails him?" Ariel asks.

Matteo looks at me. There is no cure for what ails us—only time, and plotting. Meticulous plotting. Careful planning. The thought that someday, perhaps, we really shall find the men we are looking for.

The necessity of revenge.

She loathed Matteo and me at first, not understanding who we were or why we were in that house in Belgium. She couldn't stop herself from flinching in either terror or revulsion when, laden with her meals on a tray, either of us entered the large room we'd painted the color of clotted cream, lined with books, a baby grand piano near the window. And she responded with a more tangible fear to anyone closely associated with the man we'd been instructed to call Mr. Lincoln. This included the dreadful Moritz, "cousin" we were told, of the dreadful Markus, the keeper of the locked gates. Equally taciturn, squat, and broad of face as Markus, reeking of cheap damp tobacco, Moritz patrolled the grounds with a shotgun tucked lovingly under his arm and gleefully hunted down the rabbits spoiled by easy accessibility to the lettuce in my vegetable garden.

When she first arrived, Hogarth had said her name was Doula, that she was a "special companion" to Mr. Lincoln, and instructed us to stay out of her way. To keep her doors locked. Or else. Especially not to talk to her. Or else.

Or else we'd risk the wrath of the dreadful Moritz, who always seemed to be underfoot, shotgun in tow, watching us and waiting for the slightest infraction.

She had been there for several months before I dared even to say hello. But I couldn't help it when I noticed her belly growing large and the lavender circles under her vivid green eyes deepening.

"Do you need anything?" I risked asking her one day as I tip-toed in to pick up her tray.

She turned away from the window and stared at me, her eyes flashing emerald orbs of fear and disdain. She opened her mouth to speak, but had to clear her throat first. I got the wild idea that she wasn't used to speaking. "You're not supposed to talk to me," she said.

"I don't care what I'm supposed to do," I mumbled. I couldn't yet tell her about the tiny peephole in her room, hidden near one of the Corot landscapes Hogarth gloatingly showed up with one day, and that Markus and Moritz sat there for hours. On Mr. Lincoln's instructions, no doubt. That day, Moritz was hunting and Matilda was browbeating the shopkeepers in the village, so Markus was guarding the gates, and it was safe to have an unspied-upon conversation.

"Is that so? Who are you, anyway?" she said. Her voice was foggy, rusty almost.

"Tomasino Cennini. My brother is Matteo."

"You sound American."

"Haven't been there for a long time. Doesn't matter," I said quickly. "I'm still worried about you."

"*He's* not, and you work for *him,* don't you? Why else would you be here?" she asked, her voice trembling. "Do you belong to him?"

"Belong to him? What do you mean?" I said, taken aback.

"Can't you get away?" she pressed.

"We owe him our lives. Besides, Matteo can't cope with people yet, and I don't know if I can, either." Only when I said it did I realize how true it was. "You've seen Markus. And Moritz. Try getting past them—and that gate is the only way out. There's barbed wire the entire length of the fencing around the property. We've checked. They've even rolled it into the hedges. The charming Moritz enjoys skinning all the animals that get caught in it. He'd kill us in a second."

"Markus and Moritz I understand. The rest I don't."

Oh ho, take the plunge, Tomasino. She'll be the first person you tell the embarrassing truth to. What does it matter? She despises us anyway.

So I told her. To my surprise, the world didn't stop turning and come crashing down on my crimson cheeks. I watched her eyes soften slightly as she rubbed her ring, a dazzlingly large emerald flanked by two yellow diamonds. At least she didn't laugh.

"You can't . . . ?" she began.

"No. I can't even try. There's no desire to try. And Matteo's even worse. His tongue scarred over badly and left him with a peculiar lisp. He hardly ever says a word, not even to me."

"I see. But why—" She stopped abruptly and sighed deeply. "I don't know how to carry on a normal conversation anymore." She sat down and stared at the hands she'd clasped over her belly. "Why don't you try to escape from this hell?" she asked, in such a low voice that I had to strain to hear her. "Don't you want revenge?"

She puzzled me exceedingly, but I was too leery to ask more, for fear she'd never talk to me again. "I don't know who did it exactly. Someone betrayed us, but we never saw the faces of the Fascisti. Besides, they're all dead. Mr. Lincoln killed them. That's how we got out."

"Who's Mr. Lincoln?"

"*Him.* You know—the master. He said to call him Mr. Lincoln because he freed the slaves. Meaning us."

Her eyes widened in astonishment and she burst into peals of hysterical laughter so deep they quickly turned to hiccups. I wanted to pat her back to make them stop, but she cringed as soon as I took a step toward her.

"Oh thank you. I can't remember the last time I laughed like that," she said sarcastically between gasps, calming herself. "But how do you know Mr. Lincoln didn't set it all up because he needed new houseboys?" She smiled thinly, humorless again. "Now get out."

I bowed and left, troubled. But the next day when I brought her lunch, she was holding a slim volume bound in morocco leather. I glanced at the title: *Secrets of the Ottoman Empire.*

"According to this book, in the harem they called it being 'shaved' for duty," she said, clearing her throat and opening to a page she'd marked. "The Romans invented a special clamp, so that a man would be locked in position, and the serrated edges would cut him cleanly in a single stroke. Did you know that?"

No, I didn't know that. What a thrill you've shared that tasty tidbit with me.

"Easier to heal, less mess. They often carved lions on the hilt of the clamp, as a cruel joke about some poor soul's *manhood.*"

Oh ho, my darling not yet even Belladonna, that was such a Belladonna moment.

I didn't say she was nice, did I?

She turned to another page. "It says here that some eunuchs became overly sensitive, some excessively affectionate, some withdrawn and hostile. The quick-witted ones often became effective administrators in the harem, because they owed no clemency to anyone who spurned or mocked them." She looked up at me, her eyes questioning. "Do you think you might become an effective administrator?"

I tried to smile, and failed.

"Here's something," she went on, "Juvenal wrote: 'There are girls who adore unmanly eunuchs—so smooth/So beardless to kiss, and no worry about abortions!' "

She smacked the book shut, then handed it to me. "Maybe this can help you."

"Maybe the Romans knew something I don't," I told her, and she gave me the ghost of a smile, this time for real. With that, the molecules in the air seemed to shift, and the smallest smidgen of the fear and bitterness melted from her eyes.

Each day, as I brought and carried away her trays, we talked a little bit more. Once my tongue loosened, it was not difficult to tell her about myself and my brother, and, eventually, she grew to believe Matteo and I would not betray her. We became allies, friends forever, confidants of the heart. I realized I'd found my true calling.

Especially when she showed me the diary she'd scribbled, stashed inside a hollowed-out volume of Gibbon's *Decline and Fall of the Roman Empire,* to keep from going mad. I told her the little I knew about Mr. Lincoln—she called him His Lordship—and I tried to keep my hand steady as I copied over the diary at her request so it was legible. I told Matteo as much as I needed to, and we started to plan our escape. We didn't know how we were going to get away—only that we had to.

That's what brought her back to life, she once told me. Forcing herself to think again. Plotting. Being able to envision a future in a world that had nearly destroyed her. Being able to have her baby. Being able, somehow, to hope.

Not that she could ever be able to live a normal life. Not that she ever wanted to, not after—

I love her, even though I can't love. I love her more because I can't.

What can ever take the place of a woman?

Of course for me that's a bit of a problem.

*N*o, there is no cure for what ails us. Merano had never been as chic a spa as Montecatini, and is now neglected and quiet. There are few guests, and they have, until Mr. Nutley's arrival, kept to themselves, as we do. Signor Goldini, the loquacious manager, is thrilled with our long booking and my extravagant tipping, and is obliging with any particular requests. He makes sure we have privacy when Ariel is feeling poorly, which is more often than not. He sent us a lovely grandfatherly pediatrician who lived near the closest village, for Bryony. Merano has become, after several months, a sort of safe haven, as unlikely a place as any for us to hide in plain sight after our escape from Belgium.

No no no, enough about *that.* I've got so much to tell you, and our escape can wait. Right now, I need my afternoon constitutional.

Castrati, and all the wounded, have always been soothed by the waters, you see. We sit in the sunshine, and each day is slightly warmer than the last, and we are grateful for the dulling, pleasurable sameness of the hours, the unobtrusiveness of the staff, and the thin plink of the water in the fountains. We get up with the sun to drink the hot, brackish water in the pump rooms, water full of radon and, I think, a hint of arsenic to improve the digestion.

To kill what remains of the clientele, more likely.

Matteo gets up, points toward the formal gardens, and strides away. He's lost his feel for speech, although he babbles softly to Bryony when she fusses, soothing her. I know when she starts to talk she will imitate his lisp when she says "Tomathino."

"He hasn't said a word in two weeks," Ariel says, watching him recede, his shoulders hunched.

"There's a woman with the Count of the Sorrows," I tell her as a distraction. "Blond, pretty, expensive-looking. She's crying. No, wait. Now she seems to be yelling. Hmmm. What can this mean? How can a woman be so sad and so imperious at the same time?"

"How should I know? How old is she?"

"Younger than she appears." When she got up it looked as if the lines on her palms had been imprinted on her face, buried in her hands for too long. "Maybe it's his daughter. Or a young wife he deserted who's come to beg him to return home. Or a mistress who pawned all the jewelry." I watch her walk away. "She doesn't look at all like him. And he doesn't appear to be the mistress type. Although you never can tell."

At that moment Mr. Nutley decides to saunter by. He tips his Panama hat, then abruptly turns on his heels and plops down on the chaise next to Ariel. She stares at him and freezes, and there is a sudden heaviness in the air around her. He has startled her so much that she's too scared to move. He is after something; I feel waves of craving rising from his damp brow like mist on the fountains at daybreak.

Mr. Nutley wipes his face with a starched handkerchief. It is the only part of the beige linen ensemble sagging on his dumpling body that is not wrinkled. Why he chooses to wear a cravat while taking the waters is beyond me. It reminds me of Hogarth, and I don't like it.

"Good afternoon. I do believe it is getting warmer," he announces, oblivious to the stormy look on my face. He licks his pinkie and lifts it to the nonexistent wind. "Quite stultifying. How lovely it would be to have a storm. A terrific onslaught. Oh yes. How lovely indeed." He leans back, waving his hankie. I notice the initials J J A.

"Jasper James Adlington," he says. "Businessman. *Homme d'affaires.* At your service."

"Thomas Smith. And this is Mrs. Hunter."

"How do you do. And where, may I ask, is the enchanting infant?"

"With my brother, Matthew."

"I see. A male nanny. How divine. How I wish I'd had one. Ah, well." He heaves a contented sigh. "Have you been here long? I must confess I do adore this place. So decrepit, so outré, so horribly Italian. They are masters of bumbling incompetence, I must say, losing one's things or disappearing just as one needs them. And the food—all those noodles! Quite wearing for the digestion."

He is fussing with his handkerchief as he babbles, but I catch him looking askance, for the briefest of seconds, at Ariel's magnificent emerald, the same color as her eyes, flanked by two yellow diamonds set into a golden band so thick it reaches up to her knuckle.

Oh ho, Mr. Nutley, you sly jewelry-loving little devil, working the spa circuit of lonely rich ladies. He must have realized the pickings at Merano are very slim indeed.

"Who *are* you?" he says suddenly to Ariel. "Why are you here?"

She absolutely starts. "What?" she asks, her voice rising in panic. "*What?* Why did you say that?" She rises so quickly that her chaise tips over with a loud thunk. "*Why did you say that?* What do you want? Who sent you?"

Both Mr. Nutley and I leap up to help her, but she steps back from us, her skin deathly pale.

"Get away!" she screams at him. "Get away from me!"

He stares at her, taken aback by the desperation in her voice. The fountain tinkles on, oblivious.

"I do beg your pardon," he says, and slopes off, replacing his hat and tucking his hankie in his pocket with a flourish.

Of all the stupid phrases in the world, he had to pick those words. I'd like to clobber his fussy fat ass. Now she is going to want to leave this place, just as I thought it was having a truly calming effect. Botheration. How could she not be teetering on the edge? Tomasino, you are a fool to think otherwise.

Who are you? Why are you here?

Ariel has sat back down on another chaise, her skin ashen, shivering uncontrollably in the warm air. I kneel down, careful not to touch her.

"Let's find Matteo," I say.

"Make him go away. Make him go away," she is whispering over and over, her arms wrapped tightly around herself, rocking back and forth.

"He's gone. Don't worry, he's gone."

A shadow falls over my shoulder, and I look up, to see the Count of the Sorrows. His fingers, I notice, are as slim and finely shaped as his cane, and his eyes are a peculiar hazel, dotted with flecks of gold. "Might I be of assistance?" he asks, his accent unmistakably Italian.

"She's had a shock," I tell him. "I can't explain now." I don't know why I feel I can say anything to him, but I do. I have one of my famous hunches. He seems trustable. Perhaps it is the expression in his eyes, with no hint of any ulterior motive save compassion. "Would you find my brother? He should be in the gardens with the baby."

He bows, then quickly walks away. I start talking to Ariel, about nothing, really, just words to calm her down. Thankfully, Matteo hurries over within a few minutes to put Bryony in her arms. Ariel is still deathly pale. "You can go up to the rooms now," I tell her gently. "Matteo will take you upstairs and you'll be safe."

As they start to walk away the Count of the Sorrows hands me his card, engraved with his name and an elaborate family crest. Leandro della Robbia, it reads. "He is an odious little man, that *inglese*," he says. "It is a pity. One comes to the waters to be undisturbed. The war has changed everything, you see. Now there are so few clients, only the vulgar foreigners, it seems."

"I suppose we're vulgar foreigners, too."

"Foreigners, yes. Vulgar, no," he says. "The young lady who has arrived to join me is also *inglese*, but I am hoping to keep her from the attentions of Signor Adlington. Perhaps you might care to join us tonight for dinner."

"It would be a pleasure," I tell him. "But I'll have to see. We're not very sociable at the moment. I'll leave you a message at the front desk."

"I quite understand," he says.

Once I made sure they were safely ensconsed upstairs—Ariel will be sitting on the balcony with Bryony in her lap for hours, Matteo standing guard, I know, staring out at the bright wide vista of the Adige Valley stretching out into the mist, perfumed with the scent of apricot blossoms and unencumbered by walls and darkness—I went in search of Signor Goldini, inviting him to tell me over a glass of grappa what he knew about Leandro. I had a feeling my dear signor would relish the opportunity to gossip, and he did not let me down.

"*Il conte?* Ah, he is such a gentleman. So kind of him to come here," Signor Goldini says. "The word will spread that il Conte della Robbia was here, and they will flock back like before." He beams. "So many of the rich, they left my country during the war, but not *il conte.* The *contadini* he protected, the property he saved in his estates—a miracle! And such a fortune he has still—more than the Medici. Shipping, you know. The Greeks have bathtubs compared with *il conte.* Ah, he must be one of the richest men in Italy. Because he never trusted anyone. Those who were trusting with their money—poof! *Arrivederci!* Of course il Duce tried to— how do you say—confiscate what he could find, but *il conte* was too clever for that baboon. He sailed the ships away. They destroyed two of his houses, but not the biggest one, in Tuscany. It is called Ca' d'Oro."

The house of gold.

"Never try to separate an Italian from his money, or his pasta, *sì?*" he goes on. "Or from *l'amore.* Ah, it is such a shame. Such a tragedy. First his wife died just after the Great War, and they had only one daughter, Beatrice."

I love the way Italians say that name: *Bay-a-tree-chay.* Like some exotic flower.

"But no son to carry on the family name." He sighs deeply, offended no doubt by this insult to Italian manhood. I'd hate to tell him what happened to me and my brother.

"His Beatrice died during the war, when she was giving birth to a *bambino.*" He sighs volubly again. "The *bambino* was—how do you say—not breathing when he was born. *Che tragèdia!* The young lady here with him was a friend of the young Beatrice."

I thank him for the illuminating conversation, and he smiles proudly, thrilled to be of service. I scrawl a note asking Leandro to meet for a drink after dinner. I'm curious. All right, I confess: I love to snoop. Snooping is ever useful, when done properly. And a bit of snooping will help me deal with the peculiar questions of one Jasper James Adlington, our precious Mr. Nutley.

When Leandro joins me by the fountain a few hours later, I notice his ring, set with a large stone of a strange greenish yellow hue, the color of thick raw honey. I wonder how I could have missed it earlier. Well, I suppose I was a little agitated.

"This is a chrysoberyl," he explains when I ask him what it is. "Most usually called a cat's-eye. The finest have a perfectly centered eye—you see—and when the light hits a certain angle it resembles the iris of a cat in bright sunlight, widening and narrowing as if it were alive. They are mined in Ceylon, where they are considered a formidable charm against evil spirits, as well as a preserver of fortune and good health. In this respect, it should very well protect me against the likes of Jasper Adlington."

"We've nicknamed him Mr. Nutley," I say. "We've not yet found an animal to describe him."

"How appropriate."

"I've decided he likes sparkly things. Have you noticed? You'd better watch your back. I'm sure a stone of this size and translucence is very rare."

"Yes, it is. But I am quite certain I can take care of myself." He jabs his cane, topped with the lion's head, into the tiles of the terrace, and a thin, sharp blade slices out. He jabs it again, and the blade slides swiftly back in. It couldn't have taken more than a second. I decide I like this man more and more. Yes, my dear Tomasino, you can always trust your hunches. The stiffly erect Leandro has an unmistakable aura of hypervigilance. And those lips are just a little too thin: they're the giveaway. I'm certain he could be ruthless when need be, bless his conniving little heart, yet he is an impeccable gentleman with us. I don't suppose a man can run a shipping empire without developing the instincts of a barracuda.

"How useful," I tell him.

"One never knows," he says, "when one is safe."

"One never is."

"No," he says simply, gazing out at the fountain. "There is no protection from fate. Or from age. Few people know how to grow old. Because our hair is white and our faces lined, does that mean we are enfeebled or no longer able to be ourselves? I am not yet tired, although my heart is weary." He looks at me and sighs.

"Please do forgive me. I have not felt the need for speech since my arrival, I fear. Much like your brother."

"You are very observant."

"One cannot help but watch when one is silent."

We sit in companionable calm for a while, listening to the water and the laughter of the other guests as the wine continues to flow. The water may be healthy for the body, but a little vino is even better.

Oh ho, things are about to shift for us. I *feel* it. My knee is throbbing pleasantly.

"You may have noticed the young lady who has joined me," Leandro says. "Her name is Laura Garnett, and she was the closest friend of my daughter, Beatrice, who died several years ago. School friends, from Switzerland. Now, it is not a happy time for her. She asks for advice yet does not want to hear it. She is so young. Around her, I feel my age."

"You are not so very old."

"Well, my legs are good. This much I can say. I sleep well, and I still have my legs. The secret of perpetual youth is perpetual motion."

I laugh. "I hope you're right."

"I doubt it, but one can only hope. I'm afraid that since the death of my Beatrice I no longer care. For a man to lose his power and his expectations, take away that which he most loves. All I can be deprived of now is the present, and one cannot lose what one does not own."

We are interrupted by a burst of raucous laughter from Madame Twenty Carats's table. I am surprised to see Laura sitting there with Mr. Nutley, both of them downing martinis. Leandro sees them, and the only sign of his unease is a slight shifting.

"How unfortunate Merano has been appropriated by imbeciles," he says, his eyes on Mr. Nutley. "It was once more luxurious. My wife, Alessandra, and I used to come here in the summer, for the breezes. But that was in another lifetime, before the Great War, before she died. What, I wonder, shall historians call *this* war?"

"A masterpiece of ruined civilization." I smile. "At least that's what Ariel calls me."

"She is very afraid, your Ariel, is she not?"

"Is it that obvious?"

"No, I am sure it is not. As you have said, I have been observant, simply because I am here and you are here, and she is as
lovely as she is afraid. *La bella donna, pazzo di terrore.*"

There is a faint barking of dogs in the hills.

"She is a *bella donna,* isn't she?" I say. "And to tell you the
truth, I am also afraid. For her. It is a horrible story, one I fear I
am not at liberty to discuss."

"May I ask why you decided that Merano might help you?"

"We never thought he'd find us here," I say, before realizing
even a hint of His Lordship is not wise. "Now I'm not so sure. I
think we must be going."

"I see."

"The only thing is, I don't know where we might go that will
make Ariel feel safe. Maybe you could advise me."

There is another burst of laughter, and we see Laura getting up
with Mr. Nutley, linking her arm in his. Leandro lights a Montecristo with a slim gold lighter encrusted, I note, with another
chrysoberyl. His eyes narrow, not from smoke but from following
Laura's disappearing backside. He offers me a Monte, but I decline. I used to enjoy a good puff now and then, but a cigar is
simply too phallic for me to hold in my dumpling fingers.

Oh ho, another pastime extinguished.

"She does not want to go back to her husband, you see," Leandro explains. "There are two children . . . it is most unfortunate.
She thinks she is punishing me because I warned her not to marry
him, but in truth she hurts only herself."

"The martinis, you mean," I say, "and Mr. Nutley."

"One could not endure the latter without the former."

"Most men are exceptional bastards."

"Yes. Even I. And I have been called worse." He exhales in
perfect rings. "Not lately, of course. My age, you see, and the end
of the war. I have delegated much of the business, and so I have
been at liberty to wander from one spa to another. Stabiane, Ag-
nano, Sibarite, Montecatini, Saturnia, Recoaro. The water heals the
body, yes, and my presence stirs up a bit of gossip. It can't be
helped, but it is good for the locals. And now I am weary. I want to
go home. Perhaps . . ."

I sit, waiting. My heart starts thumping along with my knee, confirming my hunch. This could be just what we need. I will have to assess the situation, many more details about him, the site of his house, the accessibility, the privacy, but it may be the perfect place for Ariel's shattered nerves to bake themselves clean and hot as she sits in the sun, away from the Mr. Nutleys of the world.

"Perhaps I may be so bold as to extend my hospitality," Leandro goes on. "Despite her unhappiness, Laura will return to her family in England, and I have none. My palazzo in Tuscany is too large, and the rooms echo with quiet. There are several guest houses, and my staff has been with me for many years. To hear the laughter of a baby would do their hearts good. And mine also. Yes," he says to himself, "it would do my heart good. You would be doing me a great kindness."

"It is you who offer us kindness."

He waves his cigar in dismissal and rises. "I must see to Laura," he says.

"Thank you," I say. "I will talk to Matteo and Ariel tomorrow."

He bows and walks away, leaving a faint trail of smoke in his wake.

I broach the subject as we're eating melon for breakfast the next morning.

"Are you mad?" Ariel says to me. Her eyes are hard, flashing emeralds. "What are you trying to do to me? Stay in the house of a strange man? Never."

"He's not a strange man. Everyone in Italy knows who he is. He's one of the richest men in the country. Ask anyone in the village and they'll tell you stories about him."

"Worry about what they don't say," Matteo says.

"I wish you could have heard what he said to me." I am not going to let this drop without a fight. "I know it'll be okay. I just know it."

"Spare me your hunches."

I ignore that. "He's getting old," I say. "He's sad, he's lonely, and he wants company."

"Oh, so now he's your new best friend, after one conversation," Ariel says. "I didn't think you were such a fool."

"There are several guest houses and a large staff," I press on.

"I despise staff. Especially large staff."

"Here's a photograph Signor Goldini gave me. See. It's a tourist brochure. Visitors can't go to the palazzo itself, but they can view part of the gardens. Look—they're amazing. He's not hiding anything."

"How can you be so naive?"

"I don't know. I just trust him. Can't explain why, but I do. He *feels* trustable."

"So did Hogarth, when I first met him."

I am surprised she can bring up his name. Maybe part of her is starting to get better after all.

"That was a long time ago," I tell her. "You are no longer naive. You have us now. We have money. We are beholden to no one, and we don't have to stay. But I don't like Mr. Nutley, and I think we should be off, away from here. We've been in one spot long enough. Should we stay, there'll undoubtedly be another Mr. Nutley before long. I'd rather go someplace less public, and we can see what happens once we get there."

"I won't go to a house I don't know. Private houses have locked doors and secret places. I hate them. You know that."

"We can check it out thoroughly before we decide to stay. I asked Signor Goldini if he knew about it, and he told me a cousin of his wife's best friend works there in the kitchens and the count is a very kind master. Servants like that are not shy about complaining. I'll speak to her directly."

"And he has no ulterior motive, I am sure."

"Listen, he is very rich. He's connected. He can help us."

"Help us? How do you know?" she asks.

"Well, he must know important people. Other rich people, not just in Italy. He's in the shipping business, so he must have global contacts. Company men, businessmen, diplomats, even spies— they all communicate. Who knows?"

"Why would he want to help us?"

She is starting to waver, just slightly. Let me worm my way in. Keep going, Tomasino, don't let up now.

"You can help each other," I say. "His wife died more than thirty years ago in the influenza epidemic after the war. He never remarried. His only child died in childbirth a few years ago, and so did her baby."

I finally see the hard green glint in her eyes lessen somewhat. It's only because of the baby.

"Who's that woman with him?" she asks.

"An old school friend of his daughter. She is having a bad time with her husband and came here to get away. She's leaving soon to go back home, to England and her family. Surely the fact that he cares about his dead daughter's friend is a good indication of character."

"Maybe it's more than *character*," she says.

"Not every rich man is bad," Matteo says.

"We have to start trusting someone if we're going to get the help we need," I go on. "As you trusted us. No one will find us there."

"Unless he's one of *them*."

"He's not one of them. Talk to him. He doesn't smell like one of them." I kneel at her feet, humble supplicant that I am. "Listen to me, my darling, if you are going to start to live again you must heal in a place where you feel safe. I know how hard this is to say or think, but there are a few people in the world who are generous and kind and wish one another no harm. Let him try to help you, please. Whatever good you do for him will come back to you in a way you most need."

"I wish no forgiveness," she says simply. "I need no pity. I have none."

"Ah, but Leandro does. I know I can learn a lot from him, if he is willing to teach me. Matteo, too. Besides, if we don't like it at his palazzo, we can leave. Just talk to him. We'll all be there. See what he says. See if you like him. Then we can decide."

She pushes me away with an annoyed swat. "Get up," she says, "before I change my mind."

The next day, we are all sitting near the fountain, drinking the bitter water and soaking the heat into our bones. Laura is nowhere to be found, and when Leandro walks by I'm afraid to ask if she's still seeing Mr. Nutley. I gesture to him and he bows as usual, then sits down on the chaise next to me. He reaches into his pocket and extends a round yellow ring made of rubber.

"It is from the mechanic's wife in the village," he says. "She tells me it is good for the teething."

Ariel looks at him in surprise, and I reach out to take it so she doesn't have to worry about touching his fingers. I'd left a note telling the count not to make any sudden gestures. Then she nods her thanks.

"It is nothing," he says. "Once your child is born you never escape the weight of love on your heart, even when they keep you up all night screaming with their teething."

She clears her throat, but is unable to say anything.

"Tell us about your daughter. If you don't mind," I quickly say. I know that's what Ariel would have said, had she been able.

"Only if it would give you pleasure," he replies, glancing at Ariel.

She looks very small and lost, and my heart flops with compassion. Leandro leans back and closes his eyes.

"Her hair was very nearly the same color as yours, but her eyes were such a dark brown they were nearly black," he says. "She liked to take the waters, too. Her favorite spa was at Stabiane, because it is closest to Pompeii. She was entranced by the ruins there; she was convinced we are descended from the house of Menander, because of the gold coins and small statues my father had given me when I came of age. Things that his father had given him. She was a historian, my Beatrice, always telling stories. She loved the Greek stories about the oracles, for that was how she met Laura, even though she was five years older. They were both at boarding school in Switzerland, and my Beatrice took pity on this girl who was shy and lonely and crying for her mother. Every evening, she went to this girl's bed, little blond Laura, and told her stories and gave her courage. She was a wonderful child."

Ariel gets up suddenly and walks over to Leandro, holding Bryony out to him without a word. I am astonished. She's never let anyone hold her baby but Matteo and myself.

He looks up at her, speechless, and takes Bryony in his arms, kissing the soft whorl of strawberry blond hair on her head as she settles easily in his arms. If he were not such a self-contained gentleman, I know I would have seen tears in his eyes.

Ariel is wrong. She can still take pity on a man.

*M*atteo and Bryony are on their daily search for butterflies in the gardens, and we sit talking in our usual spot. "The oracles never explained," Leandro is telling Ariel. "They spoke in riddles. It was the responsibility of the listener to interpret the words, and then act."

My hunches never explain, either. If I trust them, they never lead me wrong. I must be the reincarnation of an ancient, wise priestess. Just my luck to land a vestal virgin.

"I have a sculpted marble panel in my hallway, of Achilles on his way to Troy. There was a battle, and Achilles wounded the local king with his spear. This wound refused to heal, so Achilles consulted an oracle for advice. She told him he would reach Troy only if the king he'd tried to kill would consent to guide him." He fingers his cane. "The king also consulted an oracle, you see, and was told that he, the wounded, could cure what had wounded him. That is the essence of the story. The wounded could cure the enemy who'd wounded him."

"I think I understand," Ariel says slowly. I notice that she has grown pale in the sunshine. "Are there still oracles anywhere on this wretched earth?" she adds, as much to herself as to Leandro.

"I can't answer that," he replies. "But my housekeeper, Caterina, is a *strega,* what you in America might call a witch. I bow to her advice on all matters of the spirit."

Now I imagine most people would have been flummoxed by this conversation, but to us it is somehow perfectly of this place, with the tinkling of the fountain and the wind in the cypress trees and the bizarre nature of our lives. In fact, I decide it is exactly what Ariel is needing to hear.

It is, at least, until Laura suddenly appears, flushed and panting under the broad brim of her straw sun hat, pulling up a chaise and plopping down with a melodramatic sigh. She has that classic creamy English rose complexion, white and unfreckled: her cheeks pink from the heat, her large blue eyes fraught with coy disingenuousness, her wavy blond hair swept back in a simple ponytail. There are perfect pearl drops, edged in diamonds, dangling from her ears. She kicks off her espadrilles, unbuttons the top of her blouse, and smooths the wide sweep of her skirt with a flourish. Botheration. Its red and white polka dots give me an instant headache, and so does she. She catches a glimpse of my face and frowns.

"It's rude to stare," she says.

Ariel and Matteo exchange glances. Sometimes they are tele-pathic, those two, and I must confess a twinge of jealousy. I do all the talking, and he gets all the credit for understanding her every need. But what are siblings for if not to set your teeth on edge!

They both stand up, Bryony in Ariel's arms, bow a thank-you to Leandro, and walk away without saying a word. Serves the stuck-up Laura right.

"Well, I see I've interrupted," she says to Leandro, "but I need to talk to you. Now. I'm afraid it's quite awfully urgent."

"You have interrupted," he says calmly, "and I should think you owe my friend an apology."

"Sorry." She shrugs. "Now if you will excuse us . . ."

I get the hint, but for some reason I don't feel like budging. No one has bossed me around since we left the house in Belgium, and no snot-nose Brit bitch is going to tell me what to do.

Leandro has better manners than I do. "We shall discuss this upstairs," he tells her, and walks off into the gardens.

Laura sulks as she slips her shoes back on. She'd be awfully pretty if she wiped that pout off her face.

"I suppose he told you the sob story about Beatrice," she says. "Why don't you ask him who the father of her baby was? Not such a paragon of virtue after all, was the lady Beatrice. No, no. Not so very nice as her darling papa would like to believe."

"I thought she was your best friend."

"She was."

"I'd hate to be your enemy," I tell her.

"Drop dead," she says, and sashays off.

"*I* do believe I owe you an apology," Leandro says to me later when we meet for a nightcap.

"I do believe you don't," I retort. "Hardly your fault that she's such a mess."

"Yes, she is. I think the simplest explanation is that so many whom she's loved have left her. It's much easier for her to remain angry than to confront her grief."

"You're still here."

"Yes, but it is hard to listen to a surrogate father, especially now that Beatrice is gone. Laura married the first man who said he loved her, even though she knew in her heart that he was after her money. Andrew's become even more arrogant and domineering since he had an heir. The children are quite young, and I assume she feels trapped."

"How old are her children?"

"Rupert is three, and Cassandra is two."

"Why aren't they with her here?"

"Oh, they're quite safe at home with the nannies. The English way, is it not?" He calmly unwraps a Montecristo and lights it, and we glance over to the table where Laura is sitting with Mr. Nutley. When they notice our attention they raise their martini glasses in a mock salute.

"Men like that are entirely predictable," Leandro says. "Clinging to their rituals, making themselves into a breed apart, and creating what they think is a manner of behaving that is a law unto itself. One would think that men who have been properly educated and have every advantage might possess some notion of proper conduct, but they're never quite strong enough alone. There always must be people around, if only to echo the paltriness of their opinions."

"Their secret little groups, you mean."

"I have not had much experience with them *nel gruppo,* fortunately. I prefer to take them on one at a time."

I heave a huge inward sigh of relief. Ariel will be pleased to hear this, his last comment especially. No, he cannot be one of them, the members of the Club. It's not possible. He is too self-contained. He cares too much about the women he's loved. He may be a shark at sea, but there's too much compassion in him to have been one of *them.*

I knew it all along. Ariel is going to have to believe me.

"But the worst is that they play dirty, and they know nothing about women," he goes on.

Naturally, Laura and Mr. Nutley choose that moment to join us.

"Lovely evening," Mr. Nutley says, snapping his fingers at the waiter for another drink.

This blubberball really gets on my nerves. Before we leave Merano I'm going to test my hunch about his slick fingers and watch him squirm.

"Yes," I say, "the sky is the color of a milky sapphire."

Mr. Nutley smiles to himself.

"It reminds me of a story I once heard about a famous courtesan," I go on. "She had a lover, a repulsive masochist and impotent to boot—undoubtedly you know whom I mean; he was an English earl—but whenever she could manage to rouse him he would reward her with her choice of jewels. Well, one day he was feeling exceptionally pleased with her—who knows what she had to do for *that*—and summoned the jeweler to his home. Instead of showing a simple strand of pearls or a ring or two, the enterprising jeweler emptied what seemed like the entire contents of his safe on her bed. There she sat in her silk negligee, dazzled, running her hands through the treasure—sparkling tiaras, ropes of gems, turquoises and aquamarines as big as goose eggs, rubies and emeralds the size of your eyes, you name it—like a pirate with his booty. 'Ah, my darling, I cannot possibly decide!' she said to her loathsome lover. 'You choose for me.' So her lover went over to the bed, shoved her down, tied her wrists to it with the two longest diamond chains, and said, 'It's all yours. All of it.' Well, the jeweler didn't bat an eyelash. He packed up his now-empty cases and quickly departed. What splendid generosity! What a gentleman! Well, perhaps he was a bit of a rogue, but can you imagine! What a bill he had to pay!"

Mr. Nutley is no longer smiling. "No, I have not heard that story," he mutters.

Of course he hadn't—I just made it up.

"My dear sir, you needn't be shy around me," I say. "Surely a man of your experience would have heard this tale. The splendid lover went bankrupt six months later and threw himself off Big Ben."

"Cigar?" Leandro offers. I suspect he knows I'm pulling a fast one.

"Speaking of jewels," I say to Laura, "I was greatly admiring your pearl earrings earlier. I hope you didn't lose them rushing off like you did."

She instinctively puts one hand up to her ears, flashing a look of cool disdain. Tonight she is wearing clusters of crystals, nothing terribly valuable. But don't say I didn't warn you.

"Shall we have a stroll in the moonlight?" Mr. Nutley asks her, standing up and proffering his hand to lead her away.

"When does Laura return home?" I ask Leandro.

"In two days' time."

"Then I'll wager there's going to be a scene tomorrow," I say. "Just wait and see."

Sure enough, Laura comes up to me in a huff as I am sitting in the garden the following afternoon. "All right," she says, "where are they?"

I assume my sweetest blank look. "Where are what?"

"My pearl earrings. You made up that story last night to disguise the fact that you stole them."

"Let me see if I understand you," I say slowly. "We have had the very briefest of encounters, yet you dare accuse me of stealing your ugly little pearls. Back where I come from, namely Benson-hurst, Brooklyn, that is a hanging offense."

"I don't give a toss where you come from—I just want my earrings back."

"Then I suggest you have a word with your precious Jasper James. He is a much more likely suspect. Perhaps they fell off during one of your moonlit strolls."

"You bastard," she hisses. "*He* is a perfect gentleman. I'm calling the authorities."

"Please, be my guest. I'd love to discuss your appalling behavior and false accusations with them."

"How dare you!" she says, and flounces off.

Delightfully pleased with myself, I decide it's time to pay a visit to the lair of Mr. Nutley. Another one of my many talents is the ability to deftly pick my way into any lock, so when I spy the lumpen sod consoling Laura on the terrace, I sneak up the stairs and into his suite. What a surprise to see his valises neatly packed at the foot of the bed. What a surprised look on his face when he enters his room a short while later and finds me sitting in a chair, fanning my face with his train tickets and passport.

"Leaving us so soon?" I say.

"Of all the . . ." he sputters. "Get out before I throw you out."

I laugh. If I sat on Mr. Nutley I'd squash him. I may be a bit pudgy, but, frankly, I am still an imposing figure and I still know how to fight. It's in my body language and glinting in my charcoal black eyes. Don't let the cherubic cascade of dark curls that Bryony loves to tug lull you into thinking I am remotely cherubic.

"First we need to have a little chat," I say.

"I think not."

"I think so," I retort. I pull Laura's pearl drops out of one pocket.

"Where did you find those?" he says, astonished. "So you did steal them after all. You've come here to blackmail me. I knew it from the moment—"

"Oh please. I've had quite enough of you." I pull a small black velvet jewelry roll from another pocket, and his eyes practically bug out of his head. "We have several options. I can go to the authorities and report you for the light-fingered fool that you are," I say, waving the roll containing a delightful assortment of other ladies' earrings at him. "I could, on the other hand, turn these over to Leandro and let him deal with you. These options both involve— how shall I put it?—a certain amount of pain and distress. Or I can deliver everything to Signor Goldini and tell him they were found on the gravel path by the fountain. In which case, you will already be on the next train to parts unknown and will, I might add, owe me a rather considerable favor."

"I knew it." He sighs melodramatically but relaxes nonetheless. "Which is . . . ?"

"The answer to a question."

He looks at me, confused. "The answer to a question? That's all?"

"That's all. And a promise never to set foot near Laura Garnett or any of us ever again in your unnatural lifetime, or I shall be the first in line to happily wring your neck. I know where you live, I know who you are, and, should you continue to misbehave, I'd be looking over my shoulder in the dark, if you catch my drift."

He barely hesitates. "Oh bloody hell. You have my word." For what it's worth. "Now ask me the question and bugger off. I've got a train to catch."

"Very well," I say. "Why did you ask Mrs. Hunter, 'Who are you? Why are you here?' "

"What are you talking about?"

"The day you first sat down with us, you used those very words. She became upset. I want to know why."

"I've no idea. They're perfectly innocuous questions, I should think."

"That's all it was, simple curiosity?"

"Of course it was." He looks genuinely perplexed. "What else could it be?"

My pathetic Mr. Nutley, thank you for your stupidity. I believe you. You're too dumb to be one of *them*. What a relief not to have to worry about this pudgepot ever again.

"Nothing," I tell him. "Nothing at all."

That evening, Laura stayed in her room, and Leandro joined us after consoling her for the untimely exit of her holiday beau.

"What will she do now?" I ask him.

"I hope she will visit me with the children in August," he replies. "With my invitation she will know there is somewhere to go if she is tired of home."

I hope the sound of that makes Ariel feel safer.

"Why doesn't she ask your witch to make the husband go away?" Ariel asks.

"That is not the way of the *strega,*" he says.

"Then what does the *strega* actually *do?*" Ariel asks, almost to herself. "Do you think she could help me?"

"She helps those who are in need, yes, but not everyone who comes to her finds her message to their liking."

"Can she find the disappeared?"

Leandro looks puzzled.

"I need to find someone," Ariel says.

No no no, not this. Not yet.

"My baby."

Leandro looks at Bryony and seems even more puzzled.

"He stole my baby. Bryony has a twin. A boy baby. His name is Tristan." Ariel's hands are clenched together so tightly that her knuckles are dead white. "They told me he died, but I know he's still alive. I *know* it. I want my baby back."

"I am very sorry—"

"I can't explain now," she says fiercely, with more energy in her voice than I think I've ever heard, "but he's gone. I've got to find them. My baby, and the man who stole him. I am going to get my strength back, and I'm not going to stop until I find them."

"I see," Leandro says.

"I must go." Ariel stands up with Bryony and hurries off, Matteo following, worried. I am stunned that she confessed this terrible secret to a man whom only a few days before she said she'd never trust.

"Well," I say, "she is full of surprises."

"*Una sorpresa della bella donna.* Yes. A grand surprise. I do not know what to say."

"Your address might be helpful."

Leandro nearly smiles.

"You have said more to help her than you know," I tell him. "I hope that we can be there in a week or two. I'll sort it out. We'll drive a circuitous route, just to be safe. I'll tell Signor Goldini we are leaving for America, and then we'll disappear again."

"I shall be waiting."

For the last time in Merano, he bows and walks away, and as he leaves I swear I see the cat's-eye winking.

2
The House of Gold

"The fine points must come from within," Leandro is saying to Ariel.

"You know I shall be pleased to help you, however well I can," he goes on. "But that does not mean I should tell you precise details of how and what to do." He takes a sip of grappa, distilled from his most recent harvest. "If you are sincere, you have much work to do. Once you begin, you must suppress the instinct to want to lash out for immediate results, and learn how to bide your time. Even if it takes years."

"It has already been years."

"Then it will be years more. There is plenty of time for all of it. You, my dear, are in far more contact with your need for revenge than you might imagine. I sense there is an unspoken fury within you threatening to explode."

"Yes. I want *out*," she says. "I've said it to Tomasino already. I want out of myself. I want to become someone else. *La bella donna.* I want to be the Belladonna you think I am."

"That is good. It will keep you fighting." He plants his cane firmly on the terrace and stands up. "Please, come with me, all of you. I want us to share a small something."

Leandro withdraws inside, then soon returns with a tiny vial, a tea towel, and a small bowl clutched in one hand. Beckoning with a large flashlight, he leads us down in the deepening twilight to one of the trees sheltering the stage of his outdoor theater. As he shines the beam up, we notice an owl carved into the bark. I'd never have noticed it in the daylight. Obviously, it's not meant to be noticed.

"Why an owl?" Ariel asks.

"Why do you think?" Leandro replies.

"Symbol of mortal wisdom," I say. "Unblinking and exact."

"Yes," he says. "And . . ."

"Of nightly prowling, of the killer instinct," Ariel says. "Waiting to pounce."

Leandro smiles broadly. We so rarely see him pleased like that. He turns off the flashlight and leads us back to the fountain of a laughing Dionysus. He pulls out several handkerchiefs, uncorks the vial, sprinkles some powder on his wrist, and quickly inhales it. I am taken aback, wondering if it's snuff, or a strange drug. This is most unlike Leandro. I notice that Ariel has paled even in the dark. She takes a step back, ready to flee.

Leandro sees our faces and smiles once more. "It is merely a little bit of snuff that Caterina mixed for me," he explains. "You see, the gods are appeased only by ritual. We must soothe them if they are to believe we are sincere. This is a sneezing ritual, a story described by Casanova, told to me by my grandfather. To perform it correctly, Casanova's lover gave him sneezing powder similar to that which I have here, and it caused both their noses to bleed. They put their heads together over a basin, so their blood could mingle together."

He gestures to us. "Like so." He sprinkles a bit of powder and I snort it up. Matteo does the same. It tingles all the way down my throat and makes me want to giggle. Ariel slowly holds out her wrist. Please, my darling, trust him. It's not a drug. He'll do you no wrong.

Once she and Matteo have inhaled, we follow Leandro's lead and bend our heads down. Within seconds, our noses are dripping. Leandro passes us the bowl, and our drops of blood mingle with his. He scoops a palmful of water from the fountain and adds it to the bowl.

"And now to Caterina," he says, handing Ariel the tea towel so she can wipe her nose.

I don't want to know what Caterina is going to do. It doesn't matter. We are partners in plotting, preparing ourselves for battle, bound in blood.

*H*ouses have souls. You can tell as soon as you walk inside whether they're happy or miserable or neglected. Or maybe even haunted. I knew the minute I saw the rows of floppy straw hats hanging on marble hooks in the hall by Leandro's kitchen that this was a safe house, despite its daunting history and grandeur.

I still feel safe a year and a half later as the moonlight gleams on the wide terrace outside the library as we wait for Leandro to join us, preparing to toast in the New Year, 1950. Year of the Tiger, according to the Chinese. Yes, I should say we have much to be thankful for: a protected palazzo to hide in, a thriving child, adoring servants, and the daily company of the most charming embodiment of nonprying discretion, the Count della Robbia.

This year is going to be different. We've been quiet long enough. Something's coming. I feel it. Call it a hunch, and not just in my psychic kneecap.

"Come on," I say to Ariel as I fill her glass with a spicy vintage Brunello. She refuses to drink champagne. "Make a wish."

"That's simple," she says. "I wish I were a man."

"I wish that when I die I will know that I would come back as a man," I say. "A *whole* man."

Matteo smiles wryly. "I wish I could come back as a dog," he says.

"Oh really?" I ask. "What breed?"

"Neapolitan mastiff, maybe. Or an Irish wolfhound."

"I'll get you some one day," says Ariel. "Protectors. But you already are my protector. For that, I toast you, my Matteo."

She has a peculiar look on her face. I close my eyes and conjure her as a sleeping form inside a chrysalis, cocooned in darkness, gathering her strength. If that chrysalis were crystal-clear, I'd see her hunched over and hardening inside it, laying the foundation for the fortress of her psyche; the fearful quivering of the woman in Merano disappearing, bit by tiny bit.

But looking at such a thing isn't so clear, is it? What we wish for never is.

That's because down there in the blackness the little worms are gnawing. But leave it to my darling. She is making friends with the crawling creatures of the dark, so that she can conquer them and bend them to her will. Soon she will burst forth like the butterflies hovering over the honeysuckle under the kitchen window.

And then you'll wish that nice, quiet little Belladonna back again, won't you? Once you know the truth.

Too bad if it's taking a bit of time. She can't be rushed; no creature can emerge without a struggle. That would be as tedious as listening to the spoiled rich kids from the neighboring villas chattering about squandering their inheritance on gold-plated steering wheels and lazy months in Sardinia.

Not that I should talk, pampered slug that I have become. At least I have superior taste. Leandro has been teaching me. We talk for hours nearly every day, about life and love and art and history and the Machiavellian conniving it takes to run a shipping empire and stay one tub ahead of Niarchos and Onassis. We talk, too, about suffering, and sometimes about Ariel. He always calls her Belladonna, so Matteo and I have taken to calling her that, too. Ariel will be no more. Once, though, I made the dumb mistake of calling her Bella.

"Don't *ever* call me Bella," she screamed.

"Why not?" I was taken aback by her fury.

"Because that used to be my name," she hissed. "Isa*bella*. The pathetic little Isabella Ariel Nickerson. The sweet, docile thing who disappeared off the face of the earth. Or have you forgotten already?"

"No, I haven't forgotten. It was just a stupid mistake. And I'm sorry. I won't ever do it again."

"Isabella's dead. She died a long time ago. And Ariel is getting on my nerves. Ariel sounds nice, and airy-fairy, and *pleasing*. I don't like who she is, either. I don't want to be *pleasing*."

"Doesn't Belladonna bother you?" I venture to ask.

"Not the way Leandro says it," she mutters.

Don't try to distract me from the scent of this path, my darling. I've seen you having more and more surreptitious little chats with Caterina Mariani, the *strega* cook, whose pasta is as toothsome as her potions.

It's about time, too.

Even before our New Year's toast, Belladonna had started coming up more regularly to the big house, to our regular Sunday lunches with Leandro. He'd sit at the other end of the immense wooden dining room table, and we'd talk of pleasant nothings, of the beauty of the gardens and the state of the harvest. Leandro did not visit our quarters, and as the months went by, Belladonna began to stroll

away from the security of her room, and the anxiety finally started
to seep out of my heart.

When we'd first arrived, Leandro put us in one of the guest
cottages, where Belladonna retreated in a state of near catatonia
for months. Perhaps because she was freed from worry about her
surroundings, she allowed herself to regress emotionally, and was
in a far worse state than she'd been in Merano. She took comfort
from no one save Matteo, who'd communicate with her in some
sort of pidgin sign language, and Bryony, for whom she'd try to
rouse herself into some form of essential mothering. And from the
radio. She'd asked only for a powerful radio, and she listened to it
all the time. Often I heard her talking softly back to it, at all hours.

At night, I used to hear Belladonna crying softly in the dark, her
radio turned down low, but she wouldn't let me near her to wipe
her tears. During the day, when I brought her meals in on a tray as
I used to do in Belgium, I'd catch glimpses of her pacing, scribbling
in notebooks Leandro had given me for her use, talking to the
voices on the radio. Plotting something, in her way, to keep herself
from going completely mad.

This is how she's mourning what's been lost, I told myself, on
her own terms. Let her be.

At least she felt safe in her room: Its windows were too high
and too narrow to be breached. It was reached only through a passage hidden behind a hanging tapestry in the room I shared with
Matteo, and opened out onto a small terrace with a sheer drop on
all sides, shaded by tall hedges with thorns on top, planted in fat,
deep terra-cotta pots. We have made it safe for her and safe for
Bryony, but impregnable for intruders.

Here, she imprisoned herself. All we could do was watch, and
wait.

Our little cottage used to be a retreat for the abbot of the monastery, which is what Ca' d'Oro once was. Perched on a steep hill,
its descending terraces overlooking the village below, surrounded
by acres of sunflowers, grapevines, and olive trees, the immense
palazzo is approachable only by one narrow, curving road. It looks
frighteningly austere from below, but every time I approach it after
a jaunt to the market I still feel a frisson of pleasure that this is
what we can call our home. Maybe it's the comfort we've found
inside the solid ring of its thick stone walls, where there are wood

ceilings decorated with painted zodiacs in the living room; multi-colored tiled floors in the halls, cooling our feet in the summer swelter; busts from Pompeii lining niches in the long corridor on the second floor, where the monks' cells have been turned into bedrooms; and fantastic frescoes of dancing nymphs and satyrs painted on the walls in Leandro's bedroom. Naturally, I gravitate to the kitchen, where copper pots hang over marble sinks and Caterina is bustling, chopping tomatoes with her husband, Roberto, but I also love to retreat to the reading room in the bell tower near the staff wing which overlooks the central courtyard, or to the turquoise swimming pool, which appears carved into the hill. From there it seems that the ground itself is the same color as Leandro's ring.

Where we all feel most at home, though, is the library. It is far more marvelous than the one in Belgium, which we never speak of, and I often find Leandro in it. Unless he's gone off on one of his business meetings in Rome or Florence, but this is rare. His shipping empire seems to be run by capable lieutenants, and he leaves most of its aggravation to them. I suspect he's been looking for leads to help us in our search, but so far he's uncovered nothing. We don't talk about it, and I'd never mention it to Belladonna. If it seems fruitless now, it may stop her before she is ready to leave our hidey-hole and start her hunt in earnest.

At the end of the day Leandro and I often walk to the goldfish pond dappled with shadows from the cypress trees, past the fountain of Dionysus spurting water instead of wine, past the chapel and the family vault, down the winding path where the owl sits guard, to the theater with its open-air stage shaded by two giant trees, their branches intermingling over the boards. There, we often discover Belladonna sitting on the carved granite steps, watching patches of sunlight chase one another over the ancient stones.

Sometimes we sit in the terrace off the library and watch her swinging slightly in a hammock strung between two gnarled apricot trees, sipping from the glass of watercress juice laced with Caterina's tonic herbs, to strengthen her blood. Leandro is patient, waiting for her to harden. He knows she'll come to him when she's ready, the way I do already. In the meantime, he is content to instruct me in the ways of his world. His staff does, too. Naturally, they all love me because I speak their language, with a few Brooklyn gems thrown in for spice. And because I am so deliciously charming.

Every morning there is a heated discussion about who will be allowed to watch over Bryony that day. Her favorite is the plump Roberto, probably because he always comes to her with a *biscotti* he baked specially for her, which good-naturedly infuriates Dino and Renaldo, who tend the horses; and Pasquale and Guido, the chauffeurs who tend the cars; and Bruno, the head gardener; and all the maids. Carla Fantucci, the head housekeeper, is most likely singing lullabies to Bryony. Even her taciturn husband, Mario, the butler, had been seen to crack a smile when Bryony grabbed onto his legs for balance when she was learning how to walk. It's as if this laughing little girl with the strawberry blond ringlets and immense blue-green eyes has brought the house back to life, just as Leandro had hoped. Nowadays, the staff always seems to be singing: nonsense songs for Bryony, and folk songs and arias for yours truly, who has succumbed to instruction by Carla, who does not remark on the unnatural pitch of my voice. Belladonna diligently practices the piano and harpsichord, and once in a while I hear Matteo tripping over exercises and scales. It's to keep his fingers nimble. He'd rather practice his card and juggling tricks and disappearing acts with the rabbits and his top hat, rehearsing for the children of the staff, who are less fearful of him now that he can amuse them. I guess he's decided to be the world's first silent magician.

If only he could conjure the lost bits of himself.

Still, Bryony is his delighted main assistant; she toddles around, trailing colored handkerchiefs and Roman coins, and Roberto gives her lettuce, which she loves to feed to the bunnies they keep in a hutch near the vegetable garden.

I wasn't too surprised when her first word was *neelio,* short for *coniglio,* the Italian word for rabbit. Belladonna bit her lip to keep from laughing when she heard it. When Bryony didn't say the word *Mama,* I guess she was relieved it wasn't *puttanesca.*

To all the staff, Belladonna is simply who Leandro said she is, a friend who'd been ill for a very long time and who needs to be left alone to soak up the fresh Tuscan air. They'd no more dream of prying than judge any of us, and hope only that she feels a little bit better every day. They have more important things to worry about, like tending the endless expanse of gardens and the vines and the horses, or fixing the plumbing in the fountains, or painting the proscenium arch of the theater before a concert given by the local brass band. Matteo and I lend a hand whenever we can, and the days float by in a pleasant haze.

*I*n the meantime, I am worrying about my seat. Riding, that is. I've decided to become an expert equestrian, and Dino is trying to teach me. I'm pretty hopeless; I can't get the balance right.

"That's because you're unbalanced," Belladonna said when I complained about it.

"Oh really? Well, I'd like to see you try."

She frowned and said no more, so I was surprised when she woke me up early a few days later. "Come on, get up," she said. "I want to get on a horse."

I groaned. I am not what you call a happy morning person. "Let me sleep."

"No. You have to come with me. I don't want to be alone with Dino."

Dino, mind you, is probably about seventy-five, and a great-grandfather several times over. Rinaldo can't be much younger. No one really rides anymore, and I suspect Leandro keeps the horses and their keepers on because, where the staff is concerned, he's an old softy. To him, they are family, and he can't bear to let them go.

As I threw on my riding gear, Belladonna sat on the edge of my bed. Matteo was still snoring slightly. "I want to be strong. I *need* to get strong," she whispered. "I want out of myself."

I had been wanting to hear this for so long that I forgave her for awakening me. And as soon as she entered the stables, the horses all nickered. Botheration. I pretty much gave up my riding prospects right then. Belladonna was about to discover the pleasure of talking to and caring for animals, as well as learning from Dino. His grizzled face came to life every morning when he saw her, thrilled to be of use to Leandro's special friend. He was quietly patient, and she was such a quick learner, surprisingly fearless, recognizing that mastery of a large horse could give her a sense of power she'd not felt before. I don't know how she did it, but even the most recalcitrant nag seemed to adore her. Her thinness and pallor were soon replaced by firm muscles and a glowing tan the color of butterscotch.

It was then that Leandro brought us Orlando Pitti, a big brawny Venetian with more black hair than I thought possible on a grown man, a bashed-in nose, and lots of crooked teeth. He smiles often, but his dark brown eyes are watchful, like Leandro's. An accomplished black belt, he specializes in all matters of security. He'll be living in the big house, staying close to teach us whatever skills we want to absorb.

Our routine is simple. We get up, and Belladonna rides for an hour. We eat melon and bland toasted Tuscan bread for breakfast; then Orlando takes us to target practice before the heat becomes too much for our concentration. We alternate among rifles, shotguns, pistols, even a bow and arrow.

"Shoot steady," Orlando says. "Breathe carefully. Aim for his heart."

Every other day, we have a lesson in self-defense, and practice our falls and throws in the sweet-smelling piles of hay in the stables. Bryony mimics us, running around as we trip each other, dripping with sweat, pulling the horses' tails as she screams *Hiyaahh!* whenever we do. After lunch, I lounge around, reading my way through the library; Matteo rehearses his magic show, or disappears on the grounds. He's become friendly with the equally taciturn Marcello Rolandi, who works on the fountains, and they often tinker with the mechanics or stroll down to the village with Orlando for a glass of vino. Belladonna studies Italian and French, practicing with the staff, or she meanders through the gardens, stopping to pull a handful of weeds or prune a rosebush, a camera slung around her neck. Whenever Marisa Columbo arrives—she's the fresco expert who drives down from Lucca every few months to check Leandro's walls—she gives Belladonna a lesson in light and composition with the beat-up Leica I found in a drawer in the bell tower. I have been given the task of developing the film, for Belladonna panicked when we first went into the darkroom Leandro set up near the root cellar. Dumb, thoughtless Tomasino: I should have known better than to take her down anywhere in confining darkness.

When the daylight has nearly faded, we meet Leandro on the terrace, and talk into the night.

It is an endless botheration trying to keep up with all of them.

Especially watching Belladonna effortlessly gallop her horse, Artemis. If she can ride that creature, she can ride anything. She proves it when an ostrich arrives one day, a joke gift from Leandro. Dino throws a rope around its neck, Belladonna hops on, and off they scramble. She bounces along and hangs on for dear life as they zigzag through the tomatoes and green peppers. Caterina tries not to wail in distress as the rest of us are nearly collapsing with laughter. Bryony names the revolting creature Fluffy, and when Pasquale and Guido build an enclosure for him downwind of the horses, he becomes the talk of the village. We try to tame him so the local kids can ride him, but Fluffy has fallen hard for Belladonna, and a one-woman ostrich he remains.

Oh ho, the magic touch!

We go up every afternoon to hear a different story from Leandro, fanning ourselves as we sit in the shade of the grape arbor on his terrace, the valley below us shimmering gold and brown. I've got to be very careful of the sun here—I don't tan anymore; I blotch.

Like Scheherazade, Leandro enchants us and instructs us. He talks *around* the topic *del giorno,* and this way we are far more likely to remember what he says.

"I no longer wish to impose my will, to tell people what to do," Leandro said to us one sweltering afternoon just before dusk. "I have done that for too many years, and paid the price for it. Now I am content to watch others instead. They must figure out the answers for themselves."

He makes us think. Belladonna is observing and absorbing his manner and wisdom, his vast store of knowledge, his charming facade, which belies a core of steel. His pain. And, of course, his ruthlessness. He occasionally shares with us snippets from his catalog of professional dirty tricks. Personally, I live for those moments. Of course I'm not going to tell them to you now. What manner of fool must you think me!

Besides, I expect you'll figure out which are his soon enough.

"Tell me about your childhood," Leandro says to Belladonna one day. "It will help me to understand you."

I am curious myself. Not once has she mentioned her family.

"I grew up in small-town America, just outside St. Louis," she says after a long silence, staring out over the sunflowers drooping in the heat. "Webster Groves, Missouri. A million miles from here. My mother's full-time occupation was getting drunk and doting on my father. He was a banker, all puffed up with the power it gave him in our little world. William and Maria, the infamous party-mad Nickersons. I was an only child, which is why I'm sometimes so jealous of you and Matteo," she adds, turning to me.

"Jealous of us?" I am stupefied.

"Jealous of your twinness," she says. "Jealous that you grew up with family around you."

"Yes, well look where it got us."

She ignores that. "My mother stayed busy with her bridge parties and the country club and serving my father's every whim. I was starved for attention, so when they shipped me off to boarding school I kept getting into trouble, hoping somebody would notice me." She ventures a rueful grin. "Fighting for the underdog. I got expelled from one school because I cut Sally Simpson's pigtails off and then flushed her head in the toilet. She was bullying the little kids and I couldn't stand it."

"I'm sure she deserved it," I say.

"She did, but my parents were furious. They were terrible snobs, and manners were all they cared about. Appearances, one-upping everyone at the club with the biggest car, the driest martinis, the new decorator with the horrible overstuffed sofas. All I really wanted to do was please them, of course, like any child wants to please its parents. I wanted to please everybody. I just didn't know how.

"And then, my mother's drinking got out of control," she goes on, her face and her voice both far away. "Her gambling, too. As soon as my father went to work she pulled out the racing form and snuck out of the house—she walked to her bookie so no one in town would see her driving and wonder where she was going. I suppose that's how she stayed so slim. She hid all her bottles underneath the rosebushes in the garden. I'll say this—she had great style. For a lush."

She sighs and is silent again for a long time.

"Where are they now?" I finally venture to ask.

"In Holy Spirit Cemetery. Side by side forever," she says. "They crashed the car when I was fifteen, driving home drunk from the club. At least they died together."

"What happened to you afterward?"

"I went to live with my uncle Paul and aunt Blair and cousin June in Minneapolis. Well, for the summers. It was easier to stay at boarding school and milk all the sympathy I could get as an orphan. I gave up my tantrums and became excruciatingly polite. My teachers loved me, but I was hiding behind my impeccable manners because it kept me close to something that had been important to my parents. And then, when I graduated from high school early, I went to stay with June. She was living in London, pretending to study art."

"Husband hunting, you mean."

"Exactly. For the first time in my life I could breathe. I was just starting to figure out what I could do, when—I mean, that's where . . ." Her face shifts and becomes hard and, in the shadows, cruel. "That's where my manners took me. To a place where I could be tricked."

Leandro sighs. "I am very sorry," he says.

"Where is June now?" I ask.

"I have no idea." Belladonna's voice is full of bitterness. "When we were in London she was busy looking out for herself. I don't know how she knew him, but she introduced me to Hogarth, and that was the beginning of it."

"One cannot foretell the future, whether in relationships, with children, our livelihood, our friends, our homes," Leandro says eventually. "One can only *imagine* it. There will always be catastrophes and calamities. One must not yield. One must go on. You, my sweet Belladonna, you must fight, and create your own world, your own rules, despite everything that has happened to you. Wherever the path leads you, you must not give in."

"What you really mean is that I should find June," she says. "If only to satisfy my curiosity."

"What makes the world go round is tension," Leandro says. "Tension between men and women, man and wife, parent and child, lover and beloved. Between the master and slave."

Belladonna shudders.

"Control is at the heart of all human relationships." Leandro twists his ring around and I see a gleam of color. "Control and the resistance to it. Seeking or refusing to let someone or something dominate us. Now, my dear child, your own will is always within your control. Nothing can stop you unless you let it."

"Nothing can stop me," says Belladonna. And we all believe her.

"This story is most likely apocryphal," Leandro says to us the next day, "as stories about notorious women often are. Ninon de Lenclos was a fascinating courtesan in France; she established a salon, was the lover of kings and dukes and princes, friend to Molière and Racine and countless others. It was said that when she was of a certain age, a young man fell in love with her. Despite the decades between them, he saw only a delectable and charming woman. Unbeknownst to him, she was, in fact, his mother; he had been born of a liaison with a duke more than twenty years before, and educated far from Paris, as young nobles of that era often were. When she divulged the unhappy truth and rebuffed his declaration of undying passion, he threw himself on his sword. In front of her."

That is a bit melodramatic, even for me.

"One must learn how to fail. That is what the son of Ninon never understood," Leandro says.

"I know how to fail," Belladonna says fiercely. "And I won't, ever again."

"Well, then, how you create your world is by the way you think. Obviously, you cannot alter the physical circumstances of what happened to you, but you can change the way you think about it. For your purposes now, it is not so much what happened, or happens, but how you allow yourself to react to it.

"You, my Belladonna, must train your thinking with concentration and discipline. Think of revenge, not forgiveness. But you must realize that you will be forever captive to the revenge if you let yourself remain obsessed by it."

"I don't want to be free," she says, "and captivity I understand. The only thing that will make me free is finding my son, and the man who stole him from me. And all the other members of the Club. I want them to wake up in darkness. I want to smell their terror, to read it in their eyes. I want to hear them beg."

"Very well," he says. "I see we are making progress."

"I am," she insists. "Every day I feel myself changing."

"Change is not a burden once one learns how to embrace its opportunities. And the result is rarely what one presupposes."

We sit in the deepening darkness and watch the stars come out. A whiff of basil floats past us as the leaves rustle in the slightest of breezes.

When we arrange ourselves on the terrace the next day, Leandro waves a letter at us. "It is from Laura Garnett," he says. "She is arriving soon. By herself. The children are with Andrew's family. She says she is looking forward to seeing all of you."

"I'll bet," I say.

"Do not be unkind," Leandro says, chastising me. "Poor Laura was mortified by her folly with your Mr. Nutley. She writes often, and I can divine from her letters that she is still unhappy. I would have liked to have seen her children once more." He sighs.

"What do you mean, 'once more'?" I ask, a fluttering flag of panic waving in my gut as Belladonna and I exchange glances. He looks the same as ever, but I worry about his health. He is seventy-one this year, and the effort of hiding so much of his grief and rage from us cannot ease his worries. Sometimes I wonder if he is willing himself to stay alive until he knows Belladonna is ready to leave.

"Only that sometimes my bones ache, and Laura's children do me good," he says. "It would be nice for Bryony to have playmates her age."

"She has plenty of playmates her age," I retort. "Carla's children, Caterina's children, Bruno's children, all the children here. And she has Sam."

Sam is her boy doll, which she insists on dressing in girl doll clothes. He's got no hair and a glazed dumb look in his glass eyes, and Bryony forbids him to wear underwear under his lacy frocks. She also insists on discussing this with every person she meets. Poor Sam must be a transvestite. Gender problems seem to run in this motley group, don't they?

"Not English children," Leandro says.

"You're right," I say. "And I am trying to feel nothing but pity for Laura. Really."

"She laughs and acts the fool to protect herself from hurt," he says. "Surely you understand that."

"How can I not?"

"Ah, well," Leandro says, sighing. "One can never understand relationships or the strange bond between lovers. But I have watched Laura, who was lovely and curious, become a docile puppy."

What a thrilling visit we have to look forward to. Besides, Laura never struck me as particularly docile.

"Dependency is not love," Leandro says, leaning back, his eyes closed. "That is a mistake I have made."

"I won't make that mistake," Belladonna says fervently. "Never will I let myself be dependent on any man. *Never.*"

Leandro opens his eyes and smiles at her gently. "Ask Laura to sing for you," he says, stifling a yawn. "That would please her very much. She possesses a voice that could melt a glacier."

"If it pleases you," she says softly, "and only you, I will."

He is teaching her well.

3

The Cascade of
the Contessa

"If only he were more discreet."

Discretion is not a word you'll see often in *this* saga.

Leandro is, however, discussing Laura's husband, the reason she is not here with us after all. Some family emergency, the cable read. One of Andrew's mistresses threw a fit or something equally charming, I expect. Frankly, I'm glad she's not here. Who needs her? Not us. Not me.

Certainly not Belladonna.

We are walking in the gardens, past the neatly sprawling plots of rosemary and lavender. The wind is heady with their scent, and fat bumblebees, drunk on nectar, fill the air with a low buzzing.

"Why doesn't she leave him?" Belladonna asks Leandro.

"Leaving is never simple. Perhaps it is a situation that, though unpleasant, is habitual." Leandro gives the most imperceptible sigh. "But I fear that as long as she remains with Andrew, she will not know what it is to be loved by a man."

"Nor do I. Nor will I ever."

"My dearest Belladonna," Leandro says, stopping to kiss her hand. After all our time here, it is the only gesture she can bear without automatically flinching. "I will not let you believe it so. There is a Greek word, *metanoia,* which one could say denotes a change of mind. Stopping in one's tracks. One's mind turns around, and one no longer thinks as one once did. The ancients saw this as a gift, as opening oneself up to the possibility of grace."

"I don't want to hear it."

"It is possible to rant and rage and fume and then turn one's mind around."

"That may have worked for you," Belladonna says savagely, "but I plan to rant and rage, and my mind will not be turned around. I will *never* let go. You can't make me."

"No, my darling, that has not worked for me. Nor can I make you do anything. Or even wish it so. Quite the contrary. If one thinks about it, throughout history men full of rage have been lionized as heroes, as warriors and prophets. But a woman full of rage, she can only be a demon or a witch. Like the Bacchae: When they were mad, they would tear men's flesh to shreds."

"So you could say that the world actually needs more enraged women," I offer.

"That, I understand," Belladonna says.

"Yes, but what I have learned all too well is that if life is to be bearable, then you must regard it as something quite insignificant," Leandro tells her. "I have not let go—I will not ever. I am old, and I hide my thoughts better, that is all. Still they exist. One can acknowledge them and continue to live without being tyrannized by them. That's what the death of love has taught me."

She looks at him, her eyes soft.

"Forgiveness is a gift," he says. "It is the only thing that can free us from the weight of hatred."

"But you have chosen not to be freed from it. And you aren't listening to me," she protests. "I don't want to be freed from it, either."

"Then you accept that as long as we fail to forgive, we're holding the hand of our offender. That will always be the hand pulling us backward."

"I don't care. Let it pull me; I must do it. I just don't know where to start."

"Start at the beginning."

"The beginning. Who got me there, in other words." Her eyes narrow. "You mean June, my cousin. You've meant her all along."

"I mean whatever it is *you* think is the beginning. There are no rules. Trust yourself, and you will know what to do. All I will say is that you can become anything, but only if you know what you want. Which, of course, most people don't. If you think you can't fail, you won't. If you think you're going to lose, you will. If you avoid the truth, you pay for your lies. A lie will always do the most harm to the person who tells it."

"I don't have to tell lies to find the truth."

"Perhaps not, but you must accept the possibility that your plans may not end as you might wish them to. You must focus, and stay true. There will always be some little spark of doubt, a tiny little snake creeping deep down inside the dark places. You must turn your head away from it."

"This I know," Belladonna murmurs.

"The surface is that only: a facade. This is why your plotting must be meticulous. Only with much digging does one find the treasure—or lack thereof—underneath. Which is why jealousy and envy are so often futile. They are a mere response to the facade."

Yes, but it's so much fun to make snap judgments about awful, stupid people! Not all the wisdom in the world will keep me from rushing in where Belladonna is too cautious to tread.

"No wise man is always entirely wise; and no evil man is always entirely evil," Leandro continues in a matter-of-fact tone. "Even a monster will have some moments when he forgets the horror of his own soul. That is his weapon, his appeal to your weakness. You must not falter in the face of it."

Belladonna's face is pale, but her mouth is firm. "I will not falter," she says. "I will not succumb to the weakness. I will not turn my head away from them. Too often, I wake in the middle of the night and I feel *him;* I can feel his eyes staring at me even though it's dark and I can never see him. He's still watching me and he won't let me go. I *will* find him. All the rest of them. And I *will* make them suffer."

"*Per amore o per forza.* Then you shall start at the beginning. You will find June Nickerson, whoever and whatever she is, and you will do whatever it is you feel you have to do, and then we shall see. Prepare yourself carefully. Remember, it may take longer than you think."

We will practice and refine our methods with the hapless cousin, I think Leandro is too circumspect to say. Then we shall see. We shall see very far indeed.

"I've told you before," Belladonna says. "I have nothing but time. I can wait. Don't you think finding them is worth waiting for?"

To that, Leandro has no answer.

* * *

"You know, the world is a brute of a place," Belladonna says to me several months later, handing me an airmail letter from one Mr. Jack Winslow, P.I. Those initials are supposed to mean private investigator, yet to me they stand for pathetically incompetent. Perhaps I am just being my usual impatient self, but he's dug up nothing worth mentioning so far, so I think he's useless.

Leandro had given us the name of a former detective chief superintendent at Scotland Yard named Harris Pritchard, who before that had been some high muckety-muck in the Special Branch, a hotshot he'd used to crack a smuggling ring years before. That was before our cheeky chappy had discovered how many vitamins there were in a pint of Guinness. On his first visit down to Ca' d'Oro, the Pritch, as I called him to his obvious disdain, told us he often worked with an American based in New York, the one and only Jack Winslow. Meticulous, tenacious, strong, and determined, he claimed our fair Jack to be. Ex-spy and ex-cop, who wouldn't suck up to the old-boy network of bribe-ridden brass. Fine, we said, how saintly. Do whatever you have to do. Fly wherever you have to fly. Trample whatever alleys you have to trample. You, Pritch, calling yourself an Enquiry agent, inquire away. Stoke your beer belly up with as many pints as necessary; plonk your bowler hat back on your thinning ginger hair; poke around in dusty dank corners with your umbrella and your rheumy brown eyes and our boy Jack—as long as you deliver.

So far, *niente*. Botheration. Now that we've actually started to look for a real person, we are alarmingly anxious, although we pretend not to be. We hide it from Leandro, who, as usual, asks no questions. The days slip by in a hazy blur. Bryony is growing strong and fair, her hair delectable ringlets of strawberry blond and her blue-green eyes holding the same penetrating gaze as her mother's. I tell myself it doesn't matter, and I don't know how on earth it could be when I am so utterly fascinating, but at this stage Bryony prefers Matteo to yours truly. Perhaps because I spend so much more time with Leandro.

Or perhaps it's because children so often want things they can't express. This the silent Matteo understands. His patient ingenuity in communicating with little speech and the playfulness he is rediscovering with the magic tricks he now performs seamlessly, conjuring sprigs of rosemary directly under Caterina's nose to tickle her with, is awfully endearing. For such a rough giant, he is artfully gentle with Bryony, especially when she balks at bedtime, wanting to stay out on the terrace with the grown-ups long into the night. "Sam is yawning," he tells her, "and he needs you to put his nightie on." This works like a charm. She starts yawning, and is soon out like a light.

Sam will wear only the finest dainty lace nightgowns, like his mistress. But as soon as she wakes up, Bryony is off racing around the estate, playing with the staff's children, laughing and talking with them in Italian. Dino gives her rides on the pony Leandro gave her for her fourth birthday two weeks ago; Roberto still spoils her with sweet biscuits. Like her mother, she could have charmed the feathers off Fluffy, if Fluffy hadn't croaked a few weeks ago. Except for Bryony, we are all secretly glad, even Leandro. The silly thing got loose from its pen, trampled the tomatoes, squashed the basil, then invaded Caterina's private herb garden and scrabbled up one of her prize mandrakes. If a few bites of the plant hadn't killed it, Caterina surely would have. She's been nurturing the twisted roots for years. Her mouth set, Caterina sewed Fluffy's feathers onto a mask as a rather unusual reminder of the price paid for willfulness.

In the meantime, we try not to wait too anxiously for the mail or for the phone to ring, if, of course—this being Italy—there is even a dial tone. June Nickerson can't be that hard to find.

Unless she's dead.

It is with great relief that we wake one morning to see the Pritch's bowler hat on the terrace table and the great man himself, fanning his florid cheeks with a rolled-up copy of the London *Times* and dunking one of Caterina's hard rolls in a bowl of cappuccino.

"Morning, Pritch," I greet him. "Lovely day, isn't it?"

"Hmmph," he says. "Too bloody hot."

"Yes, and we're glad to see you, too. I bet a lot of your clients are equally happy to see you, considering your line of employment."

He ignores me. Smart guy. I don't know why I'm ragging him. Maybe I just don't like Brits. Or ex-coppers. Or licensed snoops. I am, of course, a highly unlicensed, unprofessional snoop.

Guess I must be jealous. Try, Tomasino, to keep it shut for once in your life.

"I once locked up a man whose mistress rejected him. It drove him right round the bend. He wouldn't let her alone. When he disguised himself as a postman, delivering registered letters she'd have to sign for, well, that's when she called me," the Pritch says, slurping down his coffee and helping himself to a grappa chaser. Maybe I could learn to like him after all.

"He was a right proper shirty fellow," he goes on, "ringing me up—mind you, he thought he was contacting the Yard—to inform me that she was suffering from a serious opium addiction and was a very disturbed woman. Opium . . . disturbed woman indeed. Hadn't thought of that in donkey's years till you mentioned it."

"I mentioned it?"

"Always happy to see me, she was." He smiles, then wipes his mouth with surprising daintiness and pats his sparse ginger hair. "Now, shall we set down to the business at hand?"

"Let me find Belladonna." Then I look up. She is standing on the edge of the terrace, waiting. I wonder how much she's heard.

The Pritch attempts to get up, but she hastily waves him down as she seats herself. "Please," she says. "Enjoy your breakfast."

"Yes, mum," he says, instantly deferential. It isn't just that she's the boss; it's her immediate effect on people. Her otherworldly aura, as if she were lying still, a coiled cobra waiting for the right moment to pounce. Even a hardened professional like Pritch easily falls sway to the spell of Belladonna.

If I could bottle her essence I'd be one rich and happy fella.

"Right." Pritch clears his throat, and I pour him another grappa. "Mr. Winslow has found your Miss June Nickerson," he says, pulling an envelope out of his briefcase. "Her name is now Mrs. George Hauxton and has been since—let me see . . . May 1936."

"A year later," Belladonna says to herself.

"She resides at Two six five Cedarhurst Lane in Kansas City, Missouri, with the aforementioned husband, George; their daughters, Helen, age fourteen, and Caroline, age thirteen; their dog, Rover; their cat, Sandy; and their maid, Tallulah," Pritch says, continuing to read. "George Hauxton is proprietor of Hauxton Enterprises, a firm started by his grandfather, dealing in cattle futures and other highly speculative ventures, et cetera et cetera. Not surprisingly, it seems that Hauxton Enterprises is leveraged, as Mr. Winslow says here, up the wazoo." He grimaces at the slang. "In other words, should one choose to approach and thereby infiltrate Hauxton Enterprises with the offer of financial assistance, one may be fairly certain of a welcome." He wipes his face, then resumes reading. "Mr. George Hauxton is a staunch Presbyterian, Republican, Rotary Club member, treasurer of the Groveside Country Club—what one might call *exclusive,* or so Mr. Winslow says here."

"Busy beaver," I say.

"Hmmph," says Pritch. "Mrs. June Hauxton is an avid golfer and bridge enthusiast, member of the Planning Committee at the Groveside Country Club. Et cetera."

"Eager beaver." I can't help myself. "What about her parents?"

Pritch consults his notes. "Parents . . . parents . . . ah. The mum and dad. Yes. Paul and Blair Nickerson, residing at One one five Miller Lane, Minneapolis, Minnesota. He retired in 1949—bad ticker, allegedly. . . . The grandchildren usually spend their vacations up there in Minnesota at . . . it says here, a summer camp. Camp Minnetonka."

There is not a puff of a breeze. I am afraid to look at Belladonna. Pritch glances up at her, then quickly away. He clears his throat again, wipes his hand on a linen napkin, and resumes reading.

"Mr. Winslow has chosen to represent himself as a potential investor in cattle futures, using the sums you've allocated for this purpose. In such capacity, he has met quite often with Mr. and Mrs. George Hauxton as their guest at the aforementioned Groveside Country Club. During the course of their conversations, he has elicited that the then June Nickerson does indeed remember her youthful jaunt to London in the spring of 1935 and the disappearance of her cousin, one Isabella Nickerson, at that time."

"Don't say that name again," I warn him.

He nods without looking up. "Mrs. George Hauxton claims her cousin had run off with a prominent gentleman introduced to her at a costume ball in the country by an acquaintance of June's named, ah, Henry Hogarth. After receiving several letters from her cousin, then residing happily, she was told, in a rather inaccessible corner of northern Scotland with her new husband, Mrs. Hauxton returned to her parents in Minneapolis and thought no more of it."

"The letters were forged," I say.

Pritch's eyes flicker at me; then he goes on. "As a matter of fact, Mr. Winslow notes here, Mrs. George Hauxton was rather peeved on the topic of her cousin. She was still angry that her cousin had found herself a 'prominent,' as she put it, man of the landed-gentry persuasion, and had disappeared to the fresh country air without so much as a by-your-leave or an invitation for a weekend visit. Mr. Winslow adds that June thought her cousin had, and I quote, 'poisoned her with something so that she, June, was unable to attend the costume ball in the country and get her tiara.' "

"That's it?" I ask.

"That is, I am afraid, *it*. Very much *it* indeed."

"Never contacted the police, or wondered why she never heard from her cousin again."

"It seems there was this matter of youthful jealousy at play, one might say."

"After nearly twenty years she's still pouting about a tiara."

"It appears so."

"They're all living the American dream, right there in Kansas City." Soon to be the American nightmare, if you ask me.

"Mr. Winslow is awaiting any further instructions, mum," Pritch says.

"Give me the papers," Belladonna says. He hands them to her. "Thank you and Mr. Winslow for your diligence. You will be contacted when your services are once more required." She gets up and whispers in my ear, nods good-bye to Pritch, and walks off into the morning haze.

Pritch knows better than to ask any questions. He downs his drink with a smack of satisfaction.

"I'll be right back," I say, and hurry off to the safe in the closet of the tower reading room where we keep a stash of cash. Belladonna has instructed me to double their fee. They've earned it, and now will be more than willing to drop everything next time we need them. Pritch looks at me with his usual bland expression when I hand him the wad stuffed into an envelope. If he says *aforementioned* one more time, I'll choke him with it.

"We do not expect more than the agreed-upon fee," he says.

"Take it," I say. "You've earned it."

"Very well." He's no dummy. "It's been a pleasure."

"And thank Mr. Winslow for me, as well. No doubt we shall have the pleasure of his acquaintance someday."

"Someday soon, I gather."

Like I said, he's no dummy.

"They found her. June, I mean," Belladonna is telling Leandro later that afternoon on their usual walk past the lavender. "What do I do now?"

"If you do not know what to do then you are not ready to do it," Leandro says soberly.

Belladonna bites her lip. For all her plotting in private, it appears she may not be as ready as she wants to be after all. "I should talk to Caterina," she mumbles.

"You talk quite enough to Caterina. She has taught you everything you ever need to know about roots and herbs and medicinal cures."

Permanent cures for breathing, he means.

"I don't want to go to Kansas City," she says eventually.

"One can hardly blame you," he says. "You've not left my home in three and a half years. Before that, you hid in Merano. Before that, well . . . There is a world outside and you have chosen to live without it. My darling, your first journey back to life should not be to Kansas."

"Where, then?" Her voice is ragged.

"A small village not far from here. If you are willing, we shall go the day after tomorrow. Bryony will quite enjoy it. And then, should you agree, we shall go to Firenze."

He means to take us to Saturnia, the Cascate del Gorello. The whole family, and Orlando, so Belladonna feels safe out in public, Pasquale and Guido driving us in two cars. I've heard of it, the stream meandering from the spring through fields of sunflowers, gushing in heated, furious cascades, reeking of sulfur, in a waterfall over rocks stained a coppery green. The locals sit in it for hours, bathe their babies in it, cure their gout and whatever else ails them.

What is still ailing us. The waters helped us once before, brought us together. The waters will help us again.

* * *

"The Etruscans discovered the spring," Leandro tells us as we eat dinner on the piazza of our hotel in the village of Saturnia, "and the Romans had a rule that the waters were available to all warriors. Here, the most bitter of enemies laid down their swords together in order to heal."

"So they could go out and fight one another all over again," I venture.

"Of course."

"I could never lay down my sword next to my enemy's," Matteo says.

"Nor I," Belladonna says.

"They will come to you if they don't know who you are," Leandro says. "Besides, the Roman Empire is no more."

As usual, there is no arguing with his logic. I wouldn't try, anyway. He looks tired, and I'm worried about him. Perhaps the waters will ease the aches concealed behind that facade of imperturbable confidence and vigor. I feel a pang of deep affection for this man who has turned us away from what could have been a life of nothing but bitterness and confusion. Yes, Belladonna is still full of bitterness and confusion, but under Leandro's tutelage she is in the process of transforming her life and herself. She is learning precisely how to use her—how shall we say—emotional deficits with skillful perfection.

That night, while Orlando and Matteo stay with Bryony, I drive Leandro and Belladonna to the waterfall. It is a short walk from the road, down a slight hill, and we hear only the rush of the water and the crickets chirping. The warm summer sky is alive with the constellations. As we sit on the rocks and let the steamy current rush over us, I feel as if the stinging force of the water is a baptism of sorts, pounding the rage and the fear out of my neck, and out of my darling Belladonna, washing away the fears and doubts and the pain of her self-inflicted torture.

The scent of sulfur is so strong that this could be the water springing straight up from hell. Sent by the devil himself to strengthen the resolve tightening around her heart.

We stay there for days, taking the waters. It is a difficult cure, and we do little more than read or laze around during the day, or perhaps take a drive on the Montemerano road through the countryside. Belladonna does not seem to mind being away from home, perhaps because we interact so little with the locals. She doesn't notice that they treat both Leandro and herself with grave deference, or that they call her *la fata,* "the fairy." With her piercing green eyes and chestnut hair spilling down her back like Rapunzel's and her aura of odd remoteness, she seems conjured straight out of the imagination of an old granny telling a bedtime story to a little child.

She has lived so long away from the reality of the world that she no longer seems a part of it.

As soon as the night grows dark we go to the cascade, sitting in silence under the stars, the water pummeling our shoulders. It is not like Merano, but rougher, more vital somehow. Our skin is glowing and I swear my hair has grown an inch. We all exude a faint odor of sulfur, no matter how much we bathe. I've never been so exhausted and exhilarated at the same time, and I am keeping a careful eye on Leandro. His color is improving, I'll say that, so when he asks us if we are ready to leave for a day or two in Firenze, where he has business, I shove my anxiety aside and quickly agree. Belladonna hides her reluctance, but when Orlando tells her he won't let her out of his sight, that she will be safe, she cannot bring herself to disagree. I think she's relieved, after all this time.

She needs to visit a proper city; she needs to move among people. She needs to realize that to strangers she is but another woman, strolling through the streets, of no importance to their lives. Hidden under a broad straw sun hat and large tortoiseshell sunglasses, she trails behind Matteo and Bryony, Orlando and myself at her side, window-shopping on the Via Tornabuoni. No one is looking for her or at her. No one cares. No one can see her face, even if they try.

It is very reassuring to see her shoulders relax, to murmur politely at shopkeepers when I am deeply engrossed in some serious shopping accidents, glutton that I am, scooping up the finest lambskin leathers, wallets and notebooks and shoes. I find a tiny shop crammed with scented inks in the oddest colors and fat marbleized lacquer fountain pens, and I buy reams of handmade paper, just because it is so lovely. I make her handle the money and hail a taxi and order her meals in restaurants, like a normal person. She hasn't done so in sixteen years. It must be a bit of a shock, standing on concrete as traffic whizzes by. But Firenze is a small, beautiful city, and its scale is not overwhelming. The locals are friendly, and she understands their language. She has already found a favorite place in the Boboli Gardens, the big Oceanus Fountain surrounded by a moated garden, down at the end of what Bryony calls "the cypress street."

"Look, Matteo," Bryony says, running down to it, her curls flying. "This is our star. You have to stand in the middle, there. Stand on it and make a wish." She dances near the leaping waters, then calls to me to be the timekeeper in her race with Matteo around the pond. He always lets her win. Smart guy. He's certainly learned how to manage a female.

"It's the wishing star," Bryony says, running into her mother's arms.

Later that night, we are sitting on the roof terrace of our hotel, hoping for a breeze. Everyone else in the city is sleeping but Leandro and Belladonna and me, it seems. He wants to talk to her; I feel it.

"Bryony is obsessed with her wishing star," Belladonna says, eventually breaking the silence. She, too, feels that Leandro wants to say something, and she isn't quite sure what it is.

"I have a wish," he says, and pulls out a small ruby velvet box. "I wish to marry you."

Belladonna looks at him in amazement. "You can't be serious."

"I am very serious."

Her face changes, and she pales. A fear I haven't seen for ages is creeping into her eyes. No no no, my darling, I want to say, save yourself. Do as he asks. You can trust him.

"Why do you ask this?" she asks. "You can't love me. I don't want you to love me—not that way."

"You are quite wrong," he says, perfectly calm and collected. "I do love you. I have grown to love the sight of you every morning, every day. I love how your face looks when I speak to you, no matter what I say. I love the colors in your hair, the shape of your fingers, the way you hold your child, the hunch of your shoulders when you are troubled. I do not expect you to love me, but my love is simple. I have not asked for it; it exists. That is all. Despite what you say, I believe in you."

"Believe in me? How can you?" she asks, her eyes blazing. "Look at me—I am *nothing*. Certainly not a *woman*. I've done nothing for anybody, been nothing, since you met me. I no longer know how to exist in the world. I feel nothing but hate."

"That is also quite wrong," he replies. "You are very much a woman, and you feel many things. I will not hear you deny the love you feel for your child and your friends, or your caring and compassion for the people around you."

"That's not the same."

"Of course it is. You can burn with hatred and rage for one creature and yet still love another."

"But why?" she cries. "Why change things? Why ask this of me now?"

My darling Belladonna, please, look at this man. He is dying before your eyes and you refuse to see it.

"I am tired," he says, "although my heart is not yet weary."

He said something like that once before, in Merano. Except then it was the other way around.

"But I can't touch you," she says. "I won't ever let any man touch me. You know that. I could never be a *wife* to you. So why bother?"

Honestly, sometimes she is so obtuse I want to shake her.

"My dear, that is of no consequence. I doubt the possibility should arise, even if you so desired it."

Oh ho, impotence. Fidelity's dearest friend.

"There should be no reservation in your mind that my intentions are honorable," he adds.

Her face is troubled. "Then what do you want? I've never known a man to say that."

"Your experience of men has not been the usual."

She throws me a sharp look. "What else has Tomasino told you?"

"Nothing more than you have already told me yourself. Which is why I want to protect you. I have no direct heirs, and it is my wish that Bryony have a name and a father. No one will ever know of whence you came, unless you choose to tell them. To me, you will always be *la bella donna,* but to the world, you will be la Contessa della Robbia."

They will come to you if they don't know who you are.

"Should you choose to become my wife," he adds, "there will be fewer problems with my will when I die."

"Stop it, please. Just stop it. You're not going to die," she says.

"Just before my great-uncle died, he complained that there was not enough room for his feet in the sarcophagus. *Allungare!* He said it must be made longer. He refused to die until the stonemason cut him a new one."

"That isn't funny."

"I have no plans to die at this precise moment," Leandro says with the slightest smile as he rises to go in to bed. "However, it is an inevitable condition of life."

"Leandro," she says. "Please."

He ignores her. He knows her better than she knows herself.

"If you so wish, I shall draw up papers, if that would make you feel safer," he tells her. "There will be no changes once we return home. Should you prefer, the ceremony itself will be conducted with the utmost discretion. It is strictly a formality. No one need know until after I am gone." He places the velvet box on the table. "There is a ring inside, similar to the one I gave to Alessandra. That one I wear round my neck so a piece of her is close to my heart." He bows, then disappears inside.

"I hope you're going to do the right thing," I say after a long silence.

"This is your idea, isn't it?" she says.

"*Al contrario,* dearest. I'm as dumbfounded as you are."

"Don't play coy with me."

"It's hardly coy to tell you to marry him, you fool. If only for your daughter's sake. Then she will have a father she can be proud of."

"Instead of His Lordship, you mean. Instead of a monster."

I shudder involuntarily at the sound of those two words. I've not heard them in many, many months. They don't belong here, not tonight, hanging like a curse in the limpid night air.

"It's not Bryony's fault," I say.

"It's not mine, either."

"Or June's. This isn't about June Nickerson, or whose fault it is. This is about Leandro. Your friend. My friend. *Our* friend. He's not indestructible. He's asked for so little from you, and his generosity should not be repaid with fear and unkindness." I'm really on a roll now, but Leandro means too much to me. "I swear," I go on, "sometimes I think it is his will alone to see you healed and back in the world that is keeping him alive. He *needs* you. You are just too selfish to see it. Besides, what's the worst that can happen? Show it to him."

"Show him what?"

"What you wrote and I copied, once upon a terrible time. That book. The *diary*."

That book. Every last grotesque detail is in it, and I know she's got it stashed somewhere. I've searched all over, but she's hidden it without a trace. Clever girl. She knows what a snoop I am.

"I can't," she says after a long pause.

"Why not?"

"You know perfectly well why not."

"What's he going to do? Tell you to leave? You don't think he suspects something like what he'll read anyway?"

"I don't want him to know the worst of it." She wraps her arms around herself and shivers, even though it is still sweltering.

"Don't be ridiculous. Who do you think he is, having taken care of us for so long? He *saved* us. He knows he saved us from something awful. But, most of all, he saved us from ourselves."

"What if he's one of them?"

"Oh come on." I must be harsh. "You know he's not. This will be your final proof. And it will help us. Perhaps something in the diary will jar his memory."

She laughs bitterly. "You drive me crazy sometimes."

"Good. Then do something about it."

*H*appily, she swallowed her fears and did do something about it. She married him in Firenze a few days later. A friend of his, a retired judge, performed the ceremony. No one was invited. Not Matteo, or Orlando, or Bryony, who would have loved to have been the flower girl. No one knows but me. When we return home, nothing changes. She hands Leandro the diary, but he adamantly refuses to read it, and she returns it to its hiding place before I have a chance to find it. The only difference is the ring she wears on a slim gold chain around her neck, set with a sapphire very nearly the same color as a Tuscan sky. And, thankfully, a willingness on Belladonna's part to spend nearly all her days with Leandro, walking with him in the gardens, sitting with him for lovely tranquil

hours on the curved stone steps of the theater, watching the butterflies dance in the sunshine.

As the grapes ripen and swell later that year, Leandro takes a
chill and withdraws to bed. We visit him every afternoon, trying to
hide the fear in our eyes. He is only seventy-two, and too young,
too energetic still, at least in my mind's eye, to die. I won't let him.
And to tell you the truth, I think he almost enjoys being sick, since
it brings Belladonna closer to him. She is actually fussing over him,
tucking in his blankets, shouting at Caterina for a hot herbal infu-
sion. She reads to him, or they sit and talk about nothing and everything.

Late one evening, after Bryony has kissed him good night and
gone to bed, Belladonna shoos me away. Naturally, I sit outside,
hidden off the terrace, and listen to everything.

I hear her reading the end of *A Midsummer Night's Dream,* and
then the thunk of the book on the table.

" 'Give me your hands, if we be friends,' " Leandro says to her.
"Ah, that is better. Your hands are so cold."

"I *am* cold," she says, even though the night air is still and close.
She is speaking so softly that I have to sidle up closer to the door
to hear her properly. "I want to give you more, Leandro, I really
do. You've done so much for me, everything you've taught me,
letting us live here, safe from the world, and taking care of Bryony.
I want to—I just—I *can't.* You might not think that I do, but I
think about it every day, what's wrong with me. But I can't. I don't
think I can, ever."

"Shhh," he says. "Lie down here beside me. Lie down and be
still."

"I don't want to do without you," she says after a long silence.
"I never thought I'd say that about a man, but it's true. I don't
want to be like this, but I don't know any other way. It's too deep
in me to undo."

I've never heard her so tender, and my eyes fill with tears, sentimental softy that I am. Under the hardness of her facade a woman's heart is still beating.

"It doesn't matter, my darling," he says. "Truly. You are here
with me now, and that is all I need."

"But—"

"Shhh," he says again. "Sleep. We need to sleep."

After that, she reads to him every night, and then she lies down beside him, and he puts his arms around her, and they sleep. It is comfort, pure and simple, as if he were a father embracing his child.

That kind of security is not anything she has ever known, and, of course, given the nature of my story, not anything that could last.

One stifling late-August morning, I put their breakfast tray on the terrace table and open the door. Belladonna is sitting up in bed, her arms clasped around her knees, rocking back and forth. No no no. Her face is deathly pale, staring out at nothing, and my blood freezes. Leandro looks peaceful and handsome as ever, as if the years had suddenly been erased from his face by a glimpse of heaven. For a fleeting second, I wonder if he saw Alessandra and Beatrice before his eyes closed for the last time.

I turn and run for the kitchen. Caterina takes one look at me, drops her spoon to the floor with a crack that sounds louder than a cannon blast, and starts to wail. She knows. Not any of her potions would work now. Roberto comes running, and suddenly the house is in an uproar. "Get Matteo, quick," I say to him, "and Orlando." I run back to Leandro's room, and nothing has changed. Belladonna still rocks back and forth, unseeing.

When Matteo hurries in, he puts his arms around her and lifts her up as if she weighed no more than Bryony. She doesn't blink. I almost wish she would start screaming, or thrashing around in grief like Caterina and the rest of the maids, whose howls can be heard from the other end of the house. Shock has stilled her senses, and hardened her heart once more.

Belladonna refuses to leave her room, even for the funeral. Few of Leandro's business associates are invited; only the staff and their families, and most of the townspeople, weeping as they brush his coffin with branches of laurel before it is taken into the sarcophagus in the family vault.

I walk to the outdoor theater afterward and stare up at the owl hidden in the tree, remembering the night he'd shown it to us. My longing for his calm gaze and cryptic comments fills me with such pain that I throw myself down on the stone steps and sob for a good long while, until Matteo comes to fetch me back. He sits beside me until my shoulders stop heaving, then hands me a linen handkerchief.

I take it and blow my nose before realizing it's one of Leandro's. I start to weep all over again.

"You look awful," he says. "Come. We need you."

Such a request always gets me where it works, appealing to my munificent nature. Besides, my eyes are all puffy and my shirt is wrinkled and damp.

Belladonna is still nearly catatonic several days later when the will is read. I shall spare you the scene of utter astonishment when the will reveals that she and Leandro had married. I fancy I see a small twitch at the corner of Caterina's lips, but naturally I can't be sure.

As I'd expected, Belladonna is to inherit the vast bulk of his estate, with a sizable trust established for Bryony, and an equally gigantic sum provided for Laura and her children. All the staff are given extremely handsome payments, and it is Leandro's express wish that they and their families stay on for life, if they so wish, to run Ca' d'Oro as it has been run for years.

He wills me his collection of canes with the lions' heads and the hidden blades, and any of the books from his library that I so desire. And his cat's-eye, though I don't wish to wear it. It's too much a part of him, but the gesture fills my eyes with tears. The lawyer then hands me a note sealed with crimson wax, addressed in Leandro's bold handwriting in a blue-black ink I'd found for him in Firenze. "Thank you, Tomasino" is all it says on the card inside. *"Perduto é tutto temp che in amor non si spende."*

All time not spent in loving is lost.

He also provides for me and my brother, and when Matteo and I hear the figure, we look at each other in amazement.

Too bad all that money can't buy us what we need most.

*A*nd so the Contessa della Robbia is stupendously rich beyond even my own wild imaginings. Not that she cares, staring out from her terrace in silence. She barely eats, barely nods to her daughter. I notice that she is now wearing Leandro's sapphire ring on her right hand, and she twists it around and around till her skin is raw and Caterina whispers at her to stop.

Leandro's money is not real to her. All that is real is what we found in a numbered account after we escaped from Belgium, but I haven't told you about that yet. Don't think I've forgotten. You're just going to have to wait.

Please, have some respect for the dead.

Nearly a month later, Belladonna comes up to the terrace outside Leandro's room and sits down next to me. She is holding one of the leather writing pads I'd bought in Florence, and when she opens it I see a stack of papers covered in her tiny slanted script.

"Here," she says, pulling out a sealed envelope and handing it to me. I recognize Leandro's handwriting in the blue-black ink. I can't imagine how she could have endured a month without reading it. I'd have gone mental with curiosity.

"He meant it for you," I say.

She shakes her head. "Just read it."

"Very well." I slit it carefully, clear my throat, and read:

"My darling Belladonna—

"You have been chosen to break the bonds set by the world, and I have faith that you will not falter in your quest. Once before I said to you: If you think you can't fail, you won't. This I know you have learned. Stay true to your path, for the vengeance will conquer you if you do not conquer it.

They will come to you if they don't know who you are.

Yes, and you shall find them.

I did not think the stoniness round my heart could ever be crushed and obliterated, but you, my angel, have done this for me. Remember this when the nights are black and the dark thoughts are gnawing. Do not, my beloved, ever forget how much your Bryony loves you and needs you. As do your faithful Tomasino and Matteo. Sorrow must not be allowed to become woe. Do not, I beg you, let the loneliness freeze your soul.

I bless you, my most cherished Belladonna, for the love you have given me.

Your Leandro"

Belladonna's cheeks are wet with tears, but her eyes are sharp, piercing emeralds. I look at her closely and I see that her face has shaped itself once more into that impenetrable mask. I get one of my bad feelings behind my kneecap. That mask is set in inviolable stone.

"There is nothing else to lose," she says. Her voice is harsh.

"What are you talking about?"

"Don't you understand? He was my last chance."

I don't want to be like this, she'd said to him, *but I don't know any other way.*

Chance for love, she means, chance for a life not shaped and shifted by the worms digging their shadowy holes of revenge.

"Well, there's me, and Matteo, and Bryony," I offer, trying to keep my voice conversational. "And everyone else here who loves you."

"Don't ever talk to me of love. Love has nothing to do with me."

"Don't be ridiculous. You love your own child."

"That doesn't count."

"*That* is not what Leandro would have wanted."

"Say whatever you want to say, Tomasino. You will anyway. It doesn't matter."

A sense of futility makes the words die in my throat.

"I am ready to leave this place," she goes on. "It is Leandro's home, and without him I no longer belong."

No no no, I think. I am awfully spoiled by the lush life here. "Where do you want to go?"

"I want to go where I can find the members of the Club," she says fiercely. "I want to find them all, and I want them to suffer and rot, and I want to watch them begging me to ease their pain before I'm through with them."

"You won't find them in Italy."

"No."

"Where, then?"

"New York. You are going to New York right away, and you are going to find us all the space we're going to need. I don't care what it costs. He'd said it to us before, and he just said it again. Make them come to you. Therefore, I must create a place so desirable that everyone in the world will come to me. Here"—she hands me the sheaf of papers—"are my ideas. For a nightclub. The Club Belladonna."

I look at her in sheer amazement. This woman, hidden away from the world for more than sixteen years, is about to open her arms wide to it.

She looks back at me, and I summon all my strength not to shudder at her expression.

"Don't worry," she says. "I'll never let them see my face."

I am still amazed, but a shimmering picture is starting to form. Yes, I see it now. I know what we have to do. I will go to New York and scout out the perfect location. We will set the trap, and spring it shut. Once again, and for the very last time, Leandro has saved her, and given her purpose.

No one will ever think the Contessa della Robbia is Belladonna. Not anyone. Certainly not the members of the Club. We will find them, and crush them all.

Oh ho, Belladonna, the sweet sweet poison!

The Diary

(1935)

*H*ogarth asked for her exact measurements so he could have her costume made. She protested, but he insisted. His treat, so she would be the most beautiful creature there.

—Don't tell June, he said. She's jealous enough as it is.

She liked him even more for saying that.

Hogarth told her to pack enough clothes for a long weekend and to take the train up to York and he would fetch her there. A bit of a drive, he said, but it'll be fun. Your costume will be waiting for you at the house. A surprise. He can't wait to see her in it.

On the drive, though, Hogarth was not his usual talkative self.

—You seem preoccupied, she said.

—Oh, I was just thinking about my great-uncle, he said. He used to lie in his great carved bed, with an elegant long pistol in hand, shaking with hangover, sans doute, and from his bed he would shoot flies that had gathered to eat the jam he made the footmen smear on the ceiling. The footmen stood by with strong black coffee, a bottle of champagne when my great-uncle was feeling up to it, several rounds of ammunition, and several pots of orange marmalade and strawberry jam.

She laughed. Why are you telling me this now?

Hogarth smiled sweetly at her. Because, my dear, I must confess that I am descended from barbarians. The Goncourts said that savagery is necessary every four or five hundred years in order to bring the world back to life. Otherwise, we would die of civilization. I do believe we're all pagans at heart, descended from raving hordes of slobbering maniacs worshiping druidic stones and tearing hearts out of virgins in glorious sacrifice.

—Sacrifice to what? she asked. I don't understand. Their own desires? Or their own fears?

—My dear girl, you astonish me. I can't quite decide. However, whatever extraordinary circumstances may befall one during one's life, whatever sacrifices and adventures, it should be possible for one to remain who one is, at heart. Despite everything.

He pulled out a spotless handkerchief and wiped his nose, though he hadn't sneezed. Forgive me, he said, I am in a bit of a mood. I shall get over it once we arrive, I assure you. Do let's have a drink.

He opened a picnic basket and handed her some wrapped cucumber sandwiches. Eat up, my dear, it will be a while before dinner. Then he pulled out a bottle of champagne and two glasses and twisted off the cork.

—_To the evening's entertainment, he said soberly. I am delighted it is you here with me, and you alone._

—_Thank you, Hogarth, she said. I think June is never going to talk to me again._

—_If I may be perfectly frank, dear girl, that would be no great loss._

She laughed. I'm so glad you think so. Poor June.

—_Why, may I ask, must you stay with her?_

—_My aunt and uncle, her parents, sent me over to keep her company. I don't have much choice at the moment._

—_What about your own parents? He didn't tell her he knew all about her parents already. That her orphaned state would make her an even more desirable guest at this costume ball._

—_They died three years ago in a car crash. My aunt and uncle took me in, although I stayed in my boarding school for most of the year so they wouldn't find me too much of a burden._

—_I expect that June's parents are quite similar in personality to June. He shuddered. Say no more, my sweet. Parents can be such odious creatures. Children can be such odious creatures._

He drained his glass of champagne and poured another.

—_Procreation is not my cup of tea, he said melodramatically. Did you know that Balzac thought so highly of his sperm that he quite hated to waste it. He always pulled out just short of, well, you know what I'm talking of, dear girl. To him, tiny replicas of his brain cells were located in his precious sperm; therefore, to lose himself was to drain away all his creativity. Once, after he had gotten carried away and forgotten his philosophy in the heat of the moment, he was quite inconsolable. "I lost a book this morning," he cried to his friends._

—_Hogarth, you really are too much._

They smiled in contentment and the car drove on through the darkness. She leaned back and dozed. She had no idea where she was or where they were going, but she didn't mind.

It was all going to be a grand adventure.

Finally, the car turned and drove up a crunching, winding road. Nearly there, said Hogarth. We'll go in the back way.

The house seemed awfully dark and quiet. Where is everyone? she said.

—Oh, this isn't where the party's meant to be, Hogarth said. It's the neighbors' nice quiet house, where we'll be changing and sleeping. I expect everyone's gone to the great house already. Starting on the champagne without us, the naughty buggers.

He took her into the kitchen, where a frowning, heavyset woman, stirring a big pot of something pungent, nodded to them. That's Matilda, Hogarth whispered. She's dreadfully unpleasant. But efficient. Peasant stock, you know. Limited imagination.

They hurried into a hall and up the servants' staircase, pushing open a door leading into a wide, dimly lit hallway. Where are the bloody lights, Hogarth muttered. Bloody useless.

He opened the door of a bedroom, finally, and switched on the light. There, spread carefully on the bed, was the most exquisite ensemble she had ever seen. She gasped at the glorious sight of it.

—I'll send Matilda up to lace your corset, Hogarth said. Unless you'd like me to help you. He winked lasciviously.

—Don't you need to change? she teased him.

—Yes indeed. I'll be just down the hall. Do come fetch me if you need anything. Let's see. I'll send the lugubrious Matilda up to you in about forty-five minutes. Plenty of time for a bath and to start dressing. How does that sound?

—Lovely.

He kissed her cheek and left.

The dress came in two parts: the sleeveless bodice of emerald green satin the color of her eyes, with flowers and leaves embroidered with golden thread; the skirt was of the same green satin, full and heavy, with gold and silver flowers edging the hem. There were several layers of stiff taffeta petticoats to go underneath the skirt. She fingered the delicate lace on the smooth silk underthings. There was a pale pink corset with thick gold lacings. She held it up to her body to see how it would fit, running from just under her breasts to her hipbones. She'd never worn such a thing. She'd never seen such clothes. There were sheer silk stockings and golden garters and shoes of the same embroidered green silk, that fit her perfectly.

What fun she was going to have tonight!

She ran a bath and soaked luxuriously, humming with pleasure. There was an entire array of makeup already set up for her in the bathroom, everything she needed for her face. An intoxicating bottle of perfume and matching body lotion. A finely knit cap so that her hair could be contained under the wig. There was the wig itself, of shiny blond curls, piled high in intricate patterns and looped with pearls.

It was all too fantastic.

She slipped on the underthings and struggled into the corset. Matilda knocked on the door and came in. She didn't say a word, gesturing to her to turn around. Matilda pulled the corset strings so tight that she cried out. Then she pulled them tighter still.

—I can't breathe, she gasped.

Matilda said nothing, merely frowning even more severely as she picked up the bodice and slipped it on. Then she fastened the skirt in the back. The wig was placed carefully over the cap, with several minute adjustments. Then Matilda went into the bathroom, fetched the wet towels, and left.

She was trying to catch her breath and step into her shoes when Hogarth knocked on the door and announced himself.

—Come in, she said.

—My word, you look magnificent, he said. Positively breathtaking.

He was dressed like a courtier of the seventeenth century, in a bright white satin frock coat with silver buttons marching down the front, and matching satin pants that came to his knees. His stockings were also spotlessly white. His shoes were embroidered with silver curlicues and his silver-white wig came cascading down over his shoulders. He'd rouged his cheeks and his lips and put a black beauty mark on his cheek. He had a silver-topped cane in one hand and his other hand hidden behind his back.

—I can't breathe, she said.

—Matilda is a beast, he said. But your outfit fits you most perfectly. I can loosen your corset if you wish. It would be my pleasure.

—I'd laugh if only I could breathe.

—You'll get used to it, he said. Now close your eyes and hold out your hand.

—What is it?

—Close your eyes.

She closed them, then felt a long, thin box being placed in her hand. She opened her eyes, and then the box. Inside was the most ravishing necklace she had ever seen, a thick choker that must have been laced with hundreds of emeralds and diamonds.

—*I can't possibly wear this, she said.*

—*Why ever not? Hogarth asked as he fastened it. It's as divine as you are.*

—*I feel like a fairy princess, she said.*

—*You are, my darling. A fairy princess for the evening. The most entrancing creature in our kingdom. He stepped away and examined her with a critical eye. Yes, I think you'll do. You'll do very well indeed. Now come with me.*

He took her hand and led her down the hall, back down the stairs to the kitchen, where Matilda was nowhere to be found, and into another hall. Then he pushed open a door, and she gave a little cry of delight.

They were in a huge empty ballroom, lit only by candles burning in dozens of candelabra lining the mirrored walls. The mirrors reflected the light in crazy patterns, and she felt as if she'd stumbled into an enchanted world.

Hogarth went over to a small table in a dark corner and turned on a phonograph there. A waltz started to play, and she laughed. Then he came back with two glasses of champagne and beckoned to her. He was standing with his back to an immense marble fireplace.

—*Drink it all at once and make a wish, he said. Then he threw his champagne glass over his shoulder, toward the fireplace. Close your eyes and make a wish.*

She drank it all, closed her eyes, and threw her glass. She laughed again in pure pleasure at the sharp sound of it breaking.

—*May I have this dance, milady, Hogarth said. He offered her his hand and they began to waltz, dwarfed by the immensity of the empty ballroom. Slowly at first, Hogarth turning her carefully, as if she were made of crystal as fragile as the glasses they'd just smashed. Then faster and faster. He was a smooth dancer, Hogarth. Of course he would be, the dapper thing. She was so excited, so happy, so thrilled to be alive. This was going to be the most wonderful night of her life.*

They were whirling faster and faster around the ballroom. The room was spinning, and she stopped suddenly. She couldn't catch her breath, she was so dizzy. Her skirt was terribly heavy, pulling her down. Her feet felt frozen. Her legs, frozen.

Hogarth had a worried look on his face. What is it, my darling?

She looked at him, perplexed, but didn't reply, then swooned into a dead faint.

PART II

The Red Toenails
of Andromeda

(1951-1954)

Belladonna had a dream
Smiling like a cat with cream
Smiling oh so satisfied
Followed by her secret spies
Belladonna watch you die

4

The Mask of Black Lace

"*D*id you see her nails?"

"Whose nails?"

"Andromeda's, of course."

"What about them?"

"They're a bright, shiny crimson, you fool. The color of blood. It's a disgrace."

"But, my dear, I don't understand. Look at my nails—they're a bright, shiny crimson."

"Not those nails. Her *toenails*."

"My toenails are crimson, too."

"You don't know anything, do you? The *dog*. The *dog's* toenails are crimson. So is the drink."

"What drink is that?"

"The Belladonna, of course. The house drink. It's a blood-red martini."

"The martinis have blood in them?"

"Can you ever stop being a fool? Of *course* not. They're colored red, like the dog's toes."

"Whose dog?"

"*Belladonna's* dog."

"Andromeda is a dog?"

"Well, who else could Andromeda be?"

"But why does the dog have nail polish on her toes?"

"Unbelievable. You are *hopeless*. Andromeda is the dog outside the Club Belladonna. The only club anyone ever talks about. The most exclusive, wonderful club in the whole world, and it's run by that damn dog."

"What kind of dog?"

"How should I know? Some horrible, hairy, slobbery, overgrown mutt. They say her collar is real, all those diamonds on a *dog* collar, but nobody'd dare steal it because the dog would take your arm off. If those *awful* doormen next to her didn't first."

"No."

"The dog's always out there with those *awful* doormen, with the masks on. *She* always has a mask on inside, so they're just the warm-up to get you ready for *her,* if you can catch my drift. All you see are their eyes, those *awful* doormen, and a hint of their lips. They hardly ever say a word to anyone, on account of that dumb dog. Especially the chubby one. He gives me the creeps; you feel him *looking* at you from behind his mask like you're some blithering idiot, but he never says anything. Just *stares.* Anderson told me it's because he's only got half a tongue."

"Poor thing."

"Anderson says he got it chopped off when some duke surprised his wife by coming home early, walked in on him when he was . . . you know . . ."

"No. That's ghastly."

"He stands out there, rain or shine, next to the dog. If she barks, you can't get in. Why, she barked at the Duke and Duchess of Windsor—can you imagine! He used to be the king of England! And to top it all off, the bitch had the nerve to bark at us last night—I was with Anderson and Digby, and it was *most* annoying. My evening was absolutely ruined."

"Maybe if you brought her a nice bottle of pink nail polish she might like you better."

"Who?"

"The dog."

"Unbelievable. You really are *pathetic.*"

*H*ow I love the delectable smears of gossip clogging my very pores! Poor Andromeda. She really is a nice, well-trained poochie, discriminating and patient. She barks only in response to nearly invisible hand signals from Matteo, ones I'm certain none of our socially obsessed patrons would recognize even if they were biting the hands that fed them. They are fearfully preoccupied with mounting an assault on the door. It's not marked; there's no brightly lit sign on Gansevoort Street saying THIS WAY, WORLD, THIS IS IT. There's only a dark crimson door. Two taciturn doormen, one small, one large. One barking Irish wolfhound. And several hundred people on the street, desperate to get in. They simply must, darlings! How dare the police shoo them away! How inconceivable that they can't bribe their way in, so accustomed are they to buying everything they want. Why, that damn dog barks at the merest sniff of a well-palmed Franklin. The *bitch*!

Naturally, anybody who is somebody has already stepped over the threshold into the enchanted realm of the Club Belladonna. Anybody who is somebody who hasn't, well, having to deal with them is so boring. It's their sense of entitlement that gets up my nose. I watch them sometimes through one of the peepholes and laugh and laugh. Deprive them of their expected evening's entertainment and watch their tongues flap as wildly as the wings of Petunia, our parrot, when she gets startled. I'm training her to say a few select phrases for their benefit.

First, of course, they have to make it past the divine Andromeda. I'm sure she's the only wolfhound in New York with Cherries in the Snow on her nails, but it's a dog's life, isn't it? Soon all the bitches we meet will be crimson-colored and barking, if they aren't already.

And why not? Serves them all right.

I find the location three days after I arrive in New York. Or rather, I find the block. Down where the nighttime revelers are not prone to crawl nor respectable rich contessas likely to live; only burly cigar chompers with bloodstained aprons shouting to one another as they haul huge dripping slabs of beef from cold rooms to waiting trucks. Around the corner from the desolate cobblestoned streets of the meat district is a huge FOR SALE sign on what used to be the Kiss-Kiss Kandy factory, taking up nearly all the block of Gansevoort Street between Greenwich and Washington streets. Even better, there is a row of derelict brownstones around the corner on Horatio Street, whose back windows face the factory and are no doubt encrusted with the grimy remnants of spun sugar.

We make the arrangements and buy all the buildings—an entire square block. The few tenants in the houses on Horatio gladly accept our hefty cash buyout of their leases, as well as moving expenses. We buy much of the property across the street as well, just to be safe. As ever, we are clever, and very cautious. We take our time. Leandro had taught me well, and the lessons continued after his death. He had already set up several offshore corporations for us, which I discovered months after the reading of his will, when the paperwork was all in order. There were tax shelters and diversified portfolios and accounts, annotated files chock-full of letters and the names of colleagues in New York. Once I saunter in to their hoity-toity offices, sweep past the secretaries and the underlings, drop his name and show them the letters of introduction, divulge the nature of some of my assets, and watch their jaws drop, I become a valued member of the investing public. No questions asked and all deference paid. It is a game, and I rather enjoy it. Matteo and Belladonna and I read financial journals and prospectuses and shareholder statements after Bryony's nighttime fairy tales, and we discuss what to buy and what to sell. It is almost frightening how stupendously rich Belladonna is. We have so many companies that even the firm drawing up the contracts and completing the purchase of our many parcels of prime real estate has no idea exactly for whom they're working.

The renovations about to begin, linking Kiss-Kiss to some crumbling houses, are barely noticed, in a part of the city of no consequence to anyone but butchers and hookers.

I expect you've guessed why all this subterfuge. Of course. So that once the club is up and running no one can trace it back to the source: the Contessa della Robbia. *She* hasn't decided to show her face in New York yet. There's no need. We enroll Bryony in kindergarten at the Little Brick Schoolhouse, the best private school within easy walking distance for us, and none of the parents of the other children will ever realize that the bilingual and bubbly Bryony Rose Robbia is the daughter of the masked marvel. Who will think that the soon-to-be notorious Belladonna in reality lives Kiss-Kiss close to her infamous den of celebrity? Who will suspect that at the end of an evening all she has to do is pass through one of the secret doorways into the narrow passageway built between the club and her row of houses?

As far as the records go, she doesn't exist.

*   *   *

One of Leandro's architects comes over from Italy with his team, and the scaffolding goes up. We are paying him so handsomely that he asks no questions about some of our more bizarre requirements, making sure only that everything is up to code. The foreman is well versed in the fine art of greasing palms for the necessary permits. Luckily, Manhattan bureaucrats are still reeling from Mayor O'Dwyer's resignation a year or so ago, as well as the allegations of the Kefauver committee, and they pay absolutely no attention to us. The demolition and heavy work crews are hired in Chinatown, work around the clock, and are rotated after a few days so they have no basic idea what the final results will be. No one who speaks English hammers in a nail.

After only a few weeks of furious activity, the vast space is beginning to resemble a club. Marisa Columbo, who tended to Leandro's frescoes in Ca' d'Oro, arrives with a team of painters to decorate the walls with scenes from Venetian carnivals. Around the corner, the row of brownstones has several interior walls on the ground floor knocked down, combining five houses into one, though you'd never know it walking down the street. Why, we are so paranoid, we have letters delivered to the so-called tenants in each house so the lazy local mailman won't be suspicious. The floors are stripped and the walls painted a bright apple green, like a leaf about to unfurl in the spring. We buy comfortable overstuffed furniture and colorful Orientals; we hang pictures and Belladonna's photographs of Italy and heavy velvet curtains. We install a piano and a harpsichord. The terra-cotta tiles and the pots of herbs on the windowsill in the kitchen remind me of Caterina. It is starting to feel like a home.

Belladonna and Bryony settle in the middle house, although Belladonna always uses the door closest to Washington Street, the one farthest from the entrance to the club door around the corner. Bryony's nanny, Marisa's widowed aunt Rosalinda, sleeps in a room on the next floor up. I have the entire second floor of the house on Belladonna's right to myself; Matteo takes over on the left. Farther down, Orlando sets up an exercise area near his own room, and at the other end, our cook, his cousin Bianca, takes care of the kitchen. Two of her distant cousins, Fabia and Donatella, come in during the week as maids. They barely speak a word of English, and are so grateful for the work and the opportunity to be near their family that we don't have to worry about them spying. When the house rings with the lovely lyrical sound of Italian, it makes us feel as if we have brought a little piece of Leandro with us.

Especially when we go up on the roof. We turn the top of the second house from the left into a haven, a lushly planted roof terrace. We lay down a carpet of grass, line the sides with terra-cotta planters, plug in a small fountain, and hang Petunia's huge wrought-iron cage out for her to squawk her pleasure to the sunshine. We even add a large fake marble fireplace that Bryony loves to hide in, with a gilded baroque mirror hanging from a stand above it. The effect is theatrical and ridiculous, and we love it.

Yes, we are getting closer. The club space is shaping up nicely. Now we need to find the right people to put into it.

It is, in other words, time to have a nice long chat with Mr. Jack Winslow.

*H*e meets me in a midtown coffee shop, and he doesn't look like I thought he would. I figured he'd be whippet-thin and highly strung, but our boy Jack is of medium build and moves with deliberate assurance. When he takes off his fedora I see that his dark brown mane is slicked back with pomade, not a hair out of place. His white shirt could practically walk by itself, it is so crisply starched. His tie is dark brown with subtle red stripes, and his trousers baggy and cuffed; his cuff links are plain gold disks. He is a perfectly pleasant-looking American man in his late thirties, of no noticeable ethnicity. His eyes are brown and his nose is straight and his cheekbones are only moderately chiseled. I guess that's the essence of a good detective: one whose demeanor is so innocuous that he could blend into a crowd anywhere and not call attention to himself.

I notice a Masonic ring, and he sees my quick glance at it. He doesn't miss a thing, this one. Leandro was one to watch carefully, yes, and I can tell that Jack is equally vigilant. He hardly blinks, or moves, but it's as if he is absorbing the very molecules of information swirling around him so he can fit the pieces together later.

"Cigarette?" I offer.

He shakes his head no. "I need my sense of smell," he says, "in this line of work."

"Of course," I say. "How did you meet the Pritch? Mr. Pritchard, I mean."

"During the war."

"Intelligence, I suppose."

If he had a cigarette he'd be exhaling in a rush. "Where did you fight?" he asks.

"How did you know I did?"

"I guessed."

"Italy. The Resistance. Till 1943."

"What happened to you?"

I try not to blush. He can't possibly know what happened. "Betrayal," I say with what I hope is an offhand shrug. "Torture. The usual."

He nods. The imaginary cigarette would be stubbed out now. I'd like to tell him everything, I decide, but now is not the time.

"Who brought you to Mr. Pritchard?" he asks.

"Leandro, the Count della Robbia. He took care of us in Italy until he died. I'm sure the Pritch told you some of the details."

"Yes, Harris said he was a man of hidden talents."

"You might say that, yes. He was very good to us. Saved us, as a matter of fact. He taught us—me, my brother, Matteo, the Contessa—all about planning, and patience. Which is what brings us to you." I flash one of my devastatingly charming smiles, which he ignores. Oh dear, what a bore. This one's all business. Not an unnecessary word will be crossing his lips.

I plow on nonetheless. "We have a slightly unusual project for you. The Pritch told us you are indisputably the best man for us, a man who is trustworthy beyond reproach. Are you?"

He looks at me soberly. "Yes, sir," he says, "I am. Trustworthy. I can't speak for the rest until I hear more."

"Do call me Tomasino," I say. "I am no gentleman." He nods. "This project," I continue, "will involve all of your time and many of your contacts. Cost, as you may have already guessed, is not going to be an issue. The utmost discretion *is*."

"Go on."

"We're trying to find some men the Contessa was introduced to in 1935. Nearly seventeen years ago. Members of a peculiar kind of club in England—at least we're fairly sure it was England—of a reprehensible nature." I sigh. This is not as easy as I'd like it to be.

"Then why are you here and not there?" he asks.

"The Contessa doesn't want to be there. The thought of it is too much for her," I explain. "The Pritch is working on it from his end, of course, but the complicating thing is, we don't know any of their names. She never saw any of their faces. They wore masks. All she knows is their voices, their hands, if you catch my drift. I can't say any more right now."

He nods again. Now I'm glad he's the taciturn type. Not one to pry unless necessary, although he must be bursting with questions.

"So you have no idea how many of them are still alive," he asks.

"No. But I'm sure most of them are. They're too mean to die. Especially the worst one. The one she came to know only as His Lordship."

I shudder at the thought of him, even in broad daylight, then take a deep breath and go on. "Finding them—especially His Lordship—and then, well . . . At any rate, it is our life's mission, you might say. It keeps her going. The Contessa, I mean. Coming here was inspired by something Leandro said—that we should reel them in. So we've decided to create a place that is so unique and so spectacular that everyone who is anyone will want to come to us. We're going to call it the Club Belladonna, which is named after what Leandro called the Contessa. Here, in New York, where it's much easier to blend in. And where we can absolutely control the environment."

"I see."

"That's where you come in. Since the Pritch has vouched for you, and you've just said we can trust you, I want you to see the space, now, while it's under construction. I'm sure you'll have lots of suggestions."

"Explain."

"Well," I go on, eager to spill the beans, "the entire club and everyone in it is going to be rigged. Two-way mirrors, hidden cameras and microphones, the very latest tape-recording devices, peepholes tucked away in the frescoes, you name it. So even if the Contessa's not there, she'll be able to listen to the voices later, if need be. We want many, if not all, of the staff to be your kind of professionals. Professional people watchers, that is. People you know and trust, moonlighting cops, leftover spies from the war who are bored, perhaps. Whatever. Those who are adept at overhearing conversations and reporting on them later."

He nearly smiles. I know this whole idea must strike him as only slightly preposterous.

"How long do you foresee the surveillance lasting?"

"Until we find at least one of the members of the Club. After we're done with him, he should be able to lead us to the others."

"And then what?"

"Then we see. A swift getaway, most likely. Always leave when you're having a good time, that's my motto."

Jack eyes me thoughtfully. Clearly, I have tantalized him. "I need time to consider the ramifications," he says, "and to see the club as it is right now."

"No problem."

"And I must meet with the Contessa."

I frown. "That might be a bit of a stretch. She's not up to seeing anybody right now."

Jack shrugs and stands up. "Suit yourself."

"Sit down," I say. "Let me speak to her. You have to understand she's not a very social creature."

"Then how will she cope with running a club?"

"Well, for one thing, she's not going to be there every night. No one will ever know whether she'll show up or not, so that will make them keep coming back in anticipation. And she'll always be costumed, in disguises. A facade to hide behind. Naturally, that will make her seem more exotic and unreachable. I needn't tell you there's nothing men love more than the challenge of making a conquest."

But of course I have to tell him anyway.

"The Contessa is going to be like the Mount Everest of hostesses. We're working out the details now, having the dresses and wigs and her masks made. The decor of the club," I go on, with cheerful confidentiality, "is going to be Italian carnival. You'll see soon enough. And we're planning to have masked balls. Theme parties. Bring in the rabble from around the world. Spy on them all." I smile broadly. "Frankly, I can't wait. If it's not fun, what's the point?"

"Set up the meeting," he says. "If she's worried about my trustworthiness, I'll be happy to sign a confidentiality agreement beforehand."

I eye him carefully. "Do you think I don't trust you?"

"I know I can trust myself," he says, "and no one else."

"Well, then," I say, "what would you do in our position?"

"Hire me."

We meet for tea at the Waldorf-Astoria, just in case Jack doesn't work out. Then he won't know where we live, even though the club's address will soon be no secret. We take a table against the back wall, where we can scan the room. Matteo and Orlando come along for protection. I make the introductions.

"Thank you for taking the time to meet me," Belladonna says. "I expect you've quite a lot of questions."

Jack nods.

"About trustworthiness," she adds.

He looks at her. She does look ravishing, if I do say so, wearing a wasp-waisted black crepe suit, with large red buttons down the bodice and matching red leather gloves. She has high heels on so she seems taller, although she sits so erectly that she often seems to loom over anyone else present. Her lips are stained nearly the same red, setting off the piercing green of her eyes. Or would, if you could see her eyes clearly. There is a small black velvet hat perched on her hair, which she's twisted into a neat chignon, with a veil nearly obscuring her face.

Oh ho, how I love a lady with an air of mystery!

"Although," she continues, her voice low and mellifluous, "I should think I'm the one who should be asking you if *you* are trustworthy."

"In which way?"

"In the way I need."

"Explain yourself."

"As a detective, and as a man."

He frowns. "As a detective, assuredly, Contessa."

"Please, call me Belladonna. Just that."

He nods. He doesn't yet know that few have that privilege. Of course, few actually talk to her as Belladonna, do they? Their loss.

"And as a man," she repeats.

"As a man? I don't follow you."

"Women. Are they your weakness?"

His face becomes blank. "Not at the present. Not anymore."

"Good." She takes a sip of tea, Lapsang souchong. "Tomasino told me he has explained the scope of our project to you."

"In brief."

"You'll be working nights. You'll be on call even when you're not working. If you had a family and responsibilities of that nature there would undoubtedly be conflicts."

"I work alone," he says, for him a little too quickly.

He doth protest too much, our Jack, I say happily to myself. She's zoomed right in on what is probably his only weak spot, poor thing. So he is human after all. I'm very relieved. No one needs a sourpuss running the club. Hmm, I start to wonder, if we didn't have so much for him to do, I wonder if he might like Marisa. She's got to get her head away from those frescoes before the fumes do her in.

"I was hoping you'd say that," Belladonna goes on. "You'll be responsible for a large staff of people who must know how to keep their mouths shut. Who are incorruptible."

"No one is incorruptible," I say.

"Are you incorruptible, Jack?" she asks, throwing me a sharp look. "If what we have in mind works, there will be many, many people offering bribes to the staff to uncover our secrets. Even now we're taking a calculated risk talking to you. But we have to find someone. Mr. Pritchard has nothing but praise for you, and my husband told me that Mr. Pritchard's word has always been good. We've got nothing else—no one else here—to go on."

"I hope to serve you to the best of my abilities," Jack says. "No one can bribe me, if that's what you mean. You have my word."

Belladonna gets up suddenly. She means to sit next to Jack, I realize, and we swap seats. A faint hint of her perfume, a strange mélange of yellow jasmine and lily of the valley and other exotic flowers, wafts by. I smile, blissful at the scent of it.

Jack doesn't move a muscle, but he is already falling under her spell, I can tell. Desperately curious, our boy, but he's a real pro. He's burning with curiosity; I can smell it on him.

Like he said, a sense of smell is indispensable in this line of work.

"Give me your palm," Belladonna tells him.

"What?"

"Your hand." She tries her best not to flinch at his touch. "Hmmm," she says, tracing the lines on his palm with a red-leather-clad finger. This is something Caterina taught her. Jack is mesmerized, despite himself. He can't help it. "Analytical, but your fingertips show a decided creative streak." She turns his hand over. "Heavy knuckles; that means you cut to the chase. And need constant variety." She turns it back over. "Aha, a triangle on the mount of Saturn. You wonder about your place in the universe, and it's hard for your brain to shut off. You ask questions until you get the answers you seek. Good."

He nearly blushes, and worries that his hand is starting to sweat. What is she doing to him? How can her eyes remain limpid and yet so focused?

"Your mound of Luna is normal," she goes on. "That means you're resourceful and self-motivating. And your Venus here—a strong and durable constitution. Yes, and a double head line. Duality of nature. That's very rare."

She drops his hand abruptly and takes the seat I quickly vacate.

"Do I pass the test?" he asks.

"You'll do."

"So will you."

She freezes. Matteo and Orlando look at me with consternation. "What do you mean?"

"You're very good," he says.

"I beg your pardon?"

"The other day, I followed you."

"You followed me?"

"You were with your daughter. She was skipping down the street and back, around the corner from all the scaffolding, and you were singing to her. Both of you laughing. It was delightful."

"How did you know who I am, and where I live?"

So much for tea at the Waldorf.

"I'm good at my job."

Her face pales visibly under her veil.

"Also," he hastens to add, "you look a bit like June. A very small bit. She's a little taller, but hardly svelte."

Belladonna is still frozen, not mollified at all. Being followed by an unseen stranger has got to be one of her worst nightmares. Jack, bless him, sees that she is upset, though she's not moved a muscle, and quickly tries to undo the damage. Yes, he is absolutely the right man for our job. I'm going to send Pritch the biggest keg of Guinness ever brewed. He's earned it.

"I'm sorry," Jack says. "It was wrong of me to do that."

"Why did you follow me?" she asks.

"Curiosity. To see where you were going."

"Where was I going?"

"Macy's. At least that's where I lost you."

I see her let out her breath with a small sigh.

"I didn't know you were there," she says. "You have no idea how upsetting that is to me."

"But you walked as if you did."

"Did what?"

"Knew that you were being followed. I've never seen a woman walk with such elusive deliberation before. Fast, and purposeful. Dodging cars. Cutting corners, doubling back. Pretending to slow down to look in a window, then speeding up. Hurrying into a department store with hundreds of people and dozens of corners. I was sure you knew I was there, that you were trying to shake me."

"I like to travel incognito," she says slowly. "Since we arrived here I've trained myself."

"Ah. Who is he, then?"

"He?"

"The person you're trying to avoid."

I thought this question would bother her, but she answers it nonetheless.

"I don't know exactly who he is," she says. "That's the problem. Trying to find a shadow."

"More like the devil himself," I mutter, thinking of His Lordship.

"What if he's dead?"

"He can't be dead. I refuse to believe it. So we have to work from that premise." She looks to me and nods, giving me permission to divulge a few necessary details that she is unable to describe herself.

"His face was masked," I explain. There's no reason to elaborate, to tell Jack that she was blindfolded, too, every time His Lordship came near her. Every time, except the first time. "She saw his hands, once, and he wore a peculiar ring, with intertwined serpents and a ruby. All the members of the Club have them, we believe. Even though we don't believe they'd wear them in public, at least not often. They have their rules."

Jack sits, waiting for more. He is staring at her hands. She hasn't taken her gloves off.

"She heard his voice, obviously. So did Matteo and I. He couldn't disguise that. And there were other voices, too." I sigh. Belladonna looks like death. "Once you hire the employees I'll show you a drawing we made of the ring."

"You haven't got any names at all?" Jack asks me. "Faces? Peculiarities?"

"No," I say, "only voices and accents." I think of the ring on Hogarth's finger, splattered with blood. I'd thought of taking it with us, so we'd have one as evidence, but that would have been too much of a clue for—

No no no, Hogarth's blood will not stain this conversation. Not here in the Waldorf. Not at teatime. Hogarth belongs to the darkness.

"I see," he says, although I don't quite think he does. I sure wouldn't if I were Jack. "What, may I ask, is the connection to June Hauxton?"

"Belladonna was with her—they're cousins, as you know—in London years ago when they met the man who was responsible for taking her to His Lordship," I tell him.

"Entrapment, you mean," he says. "By Hogarth, that man June mentioned."

"Yes. And now we're going to set the trap for him, and the rest of them. As I've said to you, all we need is one, and then he should be able to lead us to the others."

"I will leave you to Tomasino and Matteo to discuss the preliminaries, as well as your salary," Belladonna says. She has regained a bit of color in her face, although I can tell she is aching to leave. "Take your time to iron out the particulars, how many employees you'll need, their training, any special equipment. It's imperative, as you can imagine, that as few staff as possible know anything about what we're really doing. Tomasino will take you down to the space whenever you like, and you can make your suggestions before the final touches are completed. And sign your contract. I believe that's an issue for you."

"As well it should be." He would probably smile if this were some other client. But she's not like any other client.

"Quite right," she says. "Any other questions?"

"What else did June do?"

Belladonna sits as motionless as the statue of Aphrodite we've placed in the back garden. "She left me there," she says, her voice low. She flips one hand in a dismissive gesture, but then curiosity gets the better of her. "Tell me a little bit about her. Is she aging well?"

Oh ho, the girlie details. Does she dye her hair; how fat is she; how much of a bitch; how can we make her pay?

"The only word for June is *boring,*" Jack says. "She's a lot rounder than she'd like, always trying to lose ten pounds. I pictured her squeezing herself into her girdle with a grimace. She's still devoted to the New Look. Her daughters are just as round and spoiled and boring. The husband is loud, and he gets louder with each successive highball. Here, I've got pictures." He pulls a sealed envelope out of his jacket pocket.

"The Old Look by now," I say, taking the snaps. Of course, Kansas City is not Manhattan. Or London. Belladonna shakes her head slightly. She doesn't want to see them. Not here, not yet. Probably not ever. "Would she come here, I wonder?"

"Once the buzz filters out, I expect she would," he admits. "Bragging rights to her bridge club. I'd settle in first. Invite her to one of your theme balls later. Perhaps with her parents, if you can bear the thought of it. Perhaps not. Make sure everything runs smoothly. It'll be too irresistible. Because," he says carefully, "you don't know how you'll react when you see them."

"What do you mean?" Belladonna asks.

"I mean that seeing June in the flesh will most likely take you back to a place where you'd rather not go. It's unavoidable. See her as a practice run, a guinea pig. That way, when you find the others it'll be easier to deal with the reality of their presence."

Well, what a clever dick, our boy Jack.

The temperature in Belladonna's corner drops another ten degrees.

"Thank you, Mr. Winslow," she says, tucking her veil under her

chin and sauntering away with Orlando and Matteo. Every eye in
the room is watching her leave, wondering who on earth the veiled
creature is.

Botheration. She might not like what he said, but she has to
admit that he's right.

We send crimson Venetian carnival masks trimmed in black lace,
along with massive bouquets of blood-red roses, to the best columnists at the more important newspapers, to magazine editors, to
theater and movie stars, to the biggest social-climbing blabber-
mouths, and to several select politicians and prominent businessmen. Attached is a simple note card that reads "Club Belladonna.
Gansevoort Street. June 11, 1952. Nine o'clock in the evening.
Festive dress."

No one had heard anything about a Club Belladonna, much
less Gansevoort Street. There is absolutely no information about
the owners to be had, so we soon receive several indignant visits
from the city's top two gossip columnists, L. L. Megalopolis at the
Daily Herald, and Dolly Daffenberg, his rival at the *New York Re-
porter.* With their noses turned up so high at the derelict neighborhood that you could practically use them as vents, they pound on
the door underneath the scaffolding and demand a tour. We ignore
them, so they decide we are unworthy upstarts before we've even
opened. A snub from a stranger—why, how dare we! They make
up reams of copy in desperation—all nonsense, but readers believe
them. Then I call in a few tales about the mysterious owner. "Belladonna," I say, "naturally you've heard of her. In Europe, she's already notorious. Beautiful woman. Lovely poison. *Belladonna
sounds so sweet.*" I recite several of the ditties I'd "heard" about
her.

You can imagine the rest, although nothing they write rivals reality. Let them be caught in their own lies, and choke on them. As
opening day grows closer, the buzz is louder than a horde of cica-
das emerging after seventeen years of sleep.

We are ready for them. All of us.

When it came time to hire the staff, Jack'd had few problems.
He put the word out to his contacts and brought the lucky ones in
for an interview. We let him do his job, and we got along fine.
Matteo and I reviewed their credentials and asked a few pointed

questions, then briefed them on their duties. Mostly, they are retired cops and former agents who left the FBI in disgust over the
blacklist and the Rosenberg fiasco. One, an ex-fireman named
Geoffrey, is so adept at karate, although slightly built, that he can
actually flip both Matteo and Orlando. He is slightly more effeminate than you'd think a fireman would be, which is probably why
he was harassed out of the department, but we ask him no questions and take him on as assistant doorman. Even better, he has
lovely green eyes, practically the same hue as Belladonna's. "We
must have been secret twins," she told him, thus earning his undying devotion. And then Jack found a bandleader, Richard Lascault,
who'd been in intelligence with him years back. That was a lucky
break, because he'll be sure to keep the musicians in line. The
money we'll be paying them is too good; the opportunity to snoop
on the world's celebrities far more enticing than the drawbacks of
a nighttime schedule and wearying hours to be spent on a small
bandstand in a nightclub. No bribes, no secret asides to L. L. and
Dolly and all the others desperate for a tidbit, will unseal their lips.

Unless we want that tidbit planted.

Remaining incorruptible will be too much fun for these straight
arrows. Even Richard's lovely young wife, Vivienne, gets into the
game. She will become our cigarette girl, walking around the club
with a tiny Minox hidden in the front of the box slung over her
shoulders. Honestly, if I were a professional in this line of work a
gig here would be a dream come true. Of course, I am what you
might call highly unprofessional.

But I always get the job done.

"Can you believe the inside of that club?"

"Whose club?"

"The Club Belladonna, of course. The one run by the dog."

"Yes, but everybody knows about the dog. What they don't
know is how it looks once you get past the dog."

"Well, let *me* tell you. Once Andromeda approves of you—and
what a struggle that is—you have to pay twenty dollars to get in.
No exceptions, can you believe it! Why, even Clark Gable had to
pay! And Rita Hayworth! Nobody—not Hollywood celebrities, not
royalty, not reporters, no one gets in for free. And then everything
has to be checked—coats, hats, umbrellas, purses larger than your

palm, practically—with this really nasty lady who is built like a brick shithouse, if you'll pardon my expression. I bet she used to work for the KGB. Makes you fork everything over and gives you a blood-red ticket for it. Why, you're afraid *not* to tip her, the old bag."

Yes, our so-called Russian coat-check lady is actually the very nice Bronx-born wife of our club accountant, but she never lets on to anyone. A paragon of discretion is our Josie. She told me that this job was just about the most exciting thing that ever happened to her, getting to see all the lords and ladies and stars and hangers-on trooping in, chattering in nervous excitement that they'd actually made it through the door.

Josie mans that spot with an eagle eye. Whenever she hears a man with a thoroughbred English accent, she presses a small buzzer to alert us, and that party would be seated at tables where it is particularly easy to spy on them.

Then the guests are patted down by one of the tuxedo-clad moonlighting cops. All of them. No hidden camera or notepad is ever going to be snuck into *this* club. A picture of what the club and its proprietress really look like would be worth a fortune. This is so much of a hoot for our cop employees that they beg to do it—it's much more exciting than the dreadfully boring street patrol and crowd control—and we won't let them at it for longer than a week at a time.

Divested of all nonessentials, frisked and flummoxed, the club guests quickly recuperate and walk in, their senses heightened with expectation. A desperately hoped-for invitation into the Club Belladonna is like falling down Alice's rabbit hole into an enchanted realm. Through the thick purple velvet curtains, past the stoic Josie in coat check; down a long, curving corridor where the carpet is so thick your shoes sink into it—which conveniently helps muffle extraneous noise from being picked up on the tape recorders. This hallway is lined with mirrors: for ladies to pat their hair and check their lipstick and their hemlines; for men to strut; for us to sit behind the two-way glass and watch them, trying not to roll our eyes at their preening. They can't help themselves, and we're glad. We set it up this way intentionally, of course. To snap their souvenir photographs for our files, neatly dated and cataloged. Nervous giggles ensue as the guests push through two sets of swinging soundproofed doors, each time into a still-curving yet progressively narrowing corridor lined in sparkling mirrors.

It is like Belladonna herself, an exotic facade constructed only to lure you in and suck you dry. All they can see is what we want them to see. A perfect illusion of fun and excitement.

Finally, they push open the last door, and there is the club itself. At last.

It's not gigantic, seating only about three hundred. The room itself appears to be a large square, with a soaring ceiling held up by thick painted plaster pillars carved with dancing satyrs chasing horrified nymphs. More mythological scenes of gods and goddesses dressed improbably for a carnival in Venice decorate the frescoes shimmering on the walls, seemingly lifelike whenever the spotlight on the stage shifts onto them. There is a long bar against one wall, a small dance band up on the stage opposite, and a huge shiny dance floor glistening under a massive skylight. No, nothing could possibly be more romantic than dancing in the Club Belladonna with summer rain pelting the glass of the roof.

But who really cares about the dancing? Everything else pales next to the possibility of snagging a seat at the U-shaped banquettes flanking the back wall. That's because Belladonna herself sits at the one in the middle. If, naturally, she shows up the night you are one of the chosen few. No one knows whether she'll be there or not. There's no pattern to it. Sometimes she's in the club every night for two weeks, and then not again for days. Then she'll appear for an hour, and as swiftly seem to vanish again.

Sometimes the club itself closes for a week or two, just because we feel like shutting it down. But tonight, that's not anyone's worry.

Please oh please oh please let her be there. Please. Just tonight. Just for me.

That's the club mantra, muttered under the breath of all our hopeful dancing, booze-swizzling patrons, smug and oh so satisfied that they've breached the ramparts outside, yet soon to be socially bereft if the evening ends without a visit from the supreme being herself. They try not to complain to the Ringer. He's the host who leads them to their tables. Actually, his name is Phillip Ringbourne, and he is very tall, very lanky, and very unhelpful to the clientele. I gave him the nickname because under his imperturbable club facade beats the heart of one of the world's great worriers. Everything must be perfect: the flowers just so; the band in tune; the drinks promptly served; the guests seated and mingling as Belladonna wants them. Ever since I caught him wringing his hands in the kitchen on one of his breaks, I think of him so. I mentioned it to Jack, and he told me not to worry, that the war frazzled his nerves a bit, but that Phillip's memory was so photographic he could remember the shape of a flea that bit him on March 8, 1945, in a bivouac somewhere in the German countryside as his battalion was approaching Berlin. As well as all the rest of the fleas on all the rest of the soldiers.

Luckily, the nickname suits him. Lucky for us to have him. He knows all the repeat customers, all the English snobs who've come for a visit, and he pulls their photos from the files, so Matteo and Geoffrey can be vigilant about letting them in.

Yes, the excitement is palpable inside, the guests trying not to glance at their watches as the minutes tick by without a sign of Belladonna. They're not hungry, no, and besides, there's not much to eat. Earlier in the day, a caterer brought us racks of trays of cold snacks, delicate sandwiches, and an assortment of desserts. We didn't want a full kitchen. Too much space, too much mess, too many unsupervisable employees to hire. No one comes to the Club Belladonna to eat. They sit at their tables, nervously kicking at the blood-red taffeta table skirts, the color of the house drink. The Belladonna, naturally. Really, it is just a simple martini made with gin stained red with food coloring and two drops of bitters replacing the vermouth, turning it the same scarlet as Andromeda's toes.

Silly cows. That's as close as they'll ever get to her, slurping down an intoxicating concoction. No one can have the real Belladonna.

No one knows how to try.

"*D*id you see what she looked like?"

"Who?"

"Who else? The only woman everyone in New York is desperate to see. The woman everyone is talking about. Belladonna, you fool."

"Oh, I thought you meant the dog."

"Honestly, I don't know why I bother talking to you sometimes."

"Did she have a diamond collar on, too?"

"Who?"

"Belladonna. I already know about the dog."

"No, she had diamonds on her *shoes*. I swear. She was wearing high heels studded with diamonds, so she glowed from behind. You couldn't *not* see them, because she had a very thin strand of diamonds around her ankle, too. *Plus,* she had the most enormous pearl necklace I've ever seen, *hundreds* of pearls. And her rings. She was wearing them on the outside of her gloves. On both pinkies and her thumbs. Giant pearls and rubies looped with these thin chains dangling from them. Unbelievable. But there's more."

"What can compete with diamonds on shoes and ropes of pearls all over the place?"

"Well, first of all, there was her clothing. Not clothing—it was a costume. She must have had it made specially. Totally outlandish, like she was Marie Antoinette or something. I mean, her bosom, you should have seen it. It's the corset underneath, I suppose, pushing her up. It was practically obscene. And the ruby, at the end of her pearls, dangling down between her breasts. Now, *that* jewel wasn't as big as the aquamarine she was wearing one night. Anderson says it was the size of a robin's egg. No matter. You could practically hear every man in the room salivating. Not that they got near enough to her even to say hello."

"I suppose I should get a corset and an embroidered bodice. Brocade would be nice."

"Can't you ever have an original idea in your head? That's what *she* was wearing. A gold-and-red brocade bodice, tightly laced up the back. And a long brocade skirt over all these petticoats, but not so long that you didn't see her shoes and ankles. But it's not just the dress that's so amazing."

"What? Tell me."

"It's the whole package, I guess. First, there are her eyes. Why, Rhonda dared to ask her what she used for eyeliner, and she told Rhonda that she used an ultra-fine nib of a calligraphy pen dipped in India ink."

"I never thought to do that for eyeliner."

"It can't be, silly. How would she get it off?"

"Maybe it's really just plain old Max Factor."

"Oh, you drive me crazy! Belladonna's just too, too much. Too much dress, too much jewelry, too much eyeliner, too much wig—"

"Really? What color?"

"Honey. Ringlets of honey, and loops of pearls braided into it."

"It must have weighed a ton."

"Don't be so silly. How much can a wig weigh? She certainly didn't seem bothered. Of course it was hard to tell, because she had that stupid mask on. So no one can tell what she really looks like."

"Black velvet?"

"No, you goose, it was lace, the same gold as her dress. It was fastened on somehow under her wig. She simply doesn't want you to see her face."

"Maybe she's missing a nose or something."

"How can you be so stupid? She's not missing anything. All you can tell is that she has piercing green eyes. And lips the same color as her rubies."

"Like the dog's toenails, you mean."

"You really are hopeless."

$\mathcal{A}$lmost immediately, she starts a mania for rings worn on the outside of kidskin gloves of the softest colored leather. Not that most of the patrons of the Club Belladonna can afford rubies like hers. They copy the pearls with the dangling chains, and the clever rings she likes to wear, rings with tiny golden-hinged boxes, their lids pierced with tiny holes so she can wave them under her nose for a waft of scent.

My favorite is the fountain ring. If someone tries to kiss her hand, she'll let loose with a fine spray of perfume. It is an ingenious thing, filled like a fountain pen. Soon copies appear in boutiques all over town.

But nothing comes close to the original.

The joke is always on everyone else. That's why we decide to create a unique perfume, one made from the essences of plants that are toxic if ingested. Called Profumo B, it is an intoxicating concoction of lily of the valley, azalea, iris, black locust, yellow jasmine, and hyacinth, with a hint of oleander. It is poured into bottles of dark crimson glass, cut cunningly to resemble multifaceted pyramids, and a tiny golden *B* for Belladonna is etched into the stopper. It is sold by the dour Josie to guests as they file out, reluctant to leave this fairyland behind to pick up their coats. One bottle only, one hundred dollars, cash, thank you very much, and goodbye. Practically everyone buys one, whether they like the highly unusual scent or not. They simply have to display it on their living room cocktail tables to prove that they have indeed been worthy, and lucky enough to breathe in the same delectably scented air as Belladonna herself.

Oh ho, how Belladonna radiates such a strange mixture of fire and ice. She terrifies everyone in the club, fascinates them, renders them dumb with amazement and envy. She sits masked, her melancholy most exquisite, as if she'd risen straight from the grave, exhumed after a long burial and powdered with the pale mold of decay, seemingly untouched by feeling.

Yes, Belladonna inspires awestruck admiration more than pleasure, doesn't she, sitting at her table like a colossal fallen face of a statue, sublime at a distance, terrifying in her stony unblinkingness up close, carved of cold marble, unreal, yet breathing.

She is both passionate and frozen. You can't melt the ice round her heart, because she won't let you close enough to try.

Yet when Belladonna disappears from sight, she never gives any one of the club's revelers, glowing with smug happiness that they'd actually made it inside, another thought. To her, they no longer exist.

She is waiting. She has patience. Think things through, that's what Leandro taught us. Be cunning, be crafty. Plan, plot, keep it direct. Do not stray from the path.

We are going to find them.

Sooner or later, one of them will come crawling, and she'll open the beautiful golden-hinged top on her ring, and a whiff of sweet poison will invade his senses and he'll swoon in delirious pleasure.

Pretty poison is her cry.

5

The Night of
Public Tenderness

*N*ow I suppose you're wondering about a few logistical kinds of things. For one, how does no one discover where Belladonna lives? Aren't there the lingering curious, waiting after the club closes every night, hoping for a glimpse of her? Usually. That's why we hire a body double to wear near duplicates of her costumes and wigs and masks. It is a good-paying gig—less than an hour of work each night "Belladonna" makes an appearance—to dress up and walk out into a waiting car. A different car each time, so the license plates can't be traced. These cars are driven by a professional, our conductor, Richard, who could lose any tail in Manhattan. That's why Vivienne, our cigarette girl and Richard's wife, usually plays Belladonna. And when she can't, Geoffrey, Matteo's assistant doorman with the lovely green eyes, is happy to fill in.

Don't people lurk around the club all day? Hardly. The musicians and staff are expected in no earlier than an hour before the club opens. Delivery people are allowed only in the late afternoon, grumbling that they have to carry everything through the narrowing hallway in the front. There is always a hopeful crowd waiting as soon as Matteo pushes open the crimson door at 9:00 P.M. sharp. But during the day, few come by. When the wind blows the wrong way off the Hudson, a few lungfuls of eau de rancid beef fat wafting over from the meat packers in the neighborhood send most hurrying on their way.

The truth is, nobody really wants to know the true identity of Belladonna. It's much more delightful trying to decipher her mystery. People are starting to throw Belladonna parties all over town, expecting their guests to show up in masks and costumes, with exotic hounds straining at jeweled leashes.

What about our own exotic hounds? Simple. They have the run of the interconnected backyards behind our brownstones and so don't need to be walked. Whenever they get too rambunctious and deserve a proper romp, we bundle them into a van that pulls into the former loading dock of Kiss-Kiss, then drive them up to a park in Westchester or across the river to Hoboken. Around the house, we call Andromeda "Dromedee," which has always been Bryony's name for her. When Andromeda is devoid of her diamond collar and her nail polish—we always take it off at the club so Bryony won't see it and inadvertently say something to one of her class-mates—she really looks like any other Irish wolfhound.

And what about Belladonna's ring? Not the cherished sapphire ring Leandro had given her, but the other one, the huge emerald flanked by two yellow diamonds that's fastened on so tightly she hasn't been able to get it off for years. She can't bear to look at it one more minute, she confides to me one day, so Jack finds us a jeweler in Chinatown. The jeweler doesn't ask any questions. He turns on a strange-looking power tool and deftly cuts the ring off with a hideous whir and display of sparks. She's always hated that ring; she still hates the sight of the stones, unmounted, in my hand, and she makes me promise to throw them into the Hudson. They're evil, she claims. I do as she asks, of course.

She's never asked me what became of the emerald necklace. The one that—

Botheration. I am getting distracted again.

The expression on her face at the sight of her finger frightens me. Belladonna is staring at the circle of dead-white skin around her finger; it hasn't seen the light of day in seventeen years. The ink of the tattoo is as horridly black as ever. She shudders, then slides Leandro's ring over the tattoo and says no more about it.

Of course this particular point is really a bit immaterial, because she always wears gloves in the Club Belladonna. Brilliant-colored skintight kidskin, fuchsia or teal or citron or aqua, coordinated with her gowns, the pearl and golden rings dangling from the leather. Her fingers remain invisible to all in the club, the guests, the staff. No one touches her, and she touches no one.

This, our staff knows well. Trust me, it was hard to find an all-ex-and-current spy band, but Richard is well connected, especially with many of the Europeans who established themselves in New York after the war. The band members have only a small dressing room, but they don't complain. They need little. Like all the employees, they work fixed hours, and that's it. The club opens at nine, and shuts at two in the morning, so we don't have to worry about the 3:00 A.M. entertainment curfew in the city. We never open on Sundays and Mondays. Five days a week, five hours a day. No exceptions. Sometimes, as I've already told you, we close just for the hell of it, continuing to pay the staff's salaries, naturally. The staff have been instructed to come in through the front, and they leave that way as well. They are given a lovely cold platter of food and any drinks they want when they arrive. They are paid exorbitantly well and warned not to gossip, to come to us immediately if and when approached with bribes. Like I've said, it's such a good gig that no band members snitch, or louse up. None of the waiters do, either. They're making too much money from the tips palmed off from desperate guests, and having too much of a blast hanging around with the world's best and brightest, dazzling and dumbest.

And we are all masked. Don't forget about that. The band members, the waiters, the busboys, everyone. We wear simple stiffened silk masks, colored deep crimson. They cover only our eyes and nose, so they aren't too hot, and we get used to them quickly. Masks are great equalizers, I soon realize; that's why they were so popular in centuries gone by. They let the nobility mingle with the rabble.

That's what we're doing in the Club Belladonna. Or rather, the rabble are trying their best to get close to *her*. They will try anything to mingle with her serene highness. I say that because those lacking in imagination compare Belladonna to that appalling creature down in Argentina, Eva Perón. What, my darling Belladonna bleach her hair? Never.

When it is bitterly cold outside, Matteo and Geoffrey wear cloaks of darkest crimson wool, with hoods shadowing their faces. Belladonna tries to avoid seeing them clad so. I actually thought she was going to faint when I showed her a prototype.

They remind her too much of His Lordship.

We had worried, you see, that by some bizarre coincidence someone might recognize us at the door. Well, we needn't have fretted. The costumed doormen and the jeweled dog have become part of the mystique of the Club Belladonna. It starts from the moment you see and hear the crowd on the street, hoping for a passage into paradise. It grows as you inch your way closer, hoping that you will not be one of the rejected, still milling around aimlessly in disbelief if indeed you are. It spreads into your very pores as Andromeda sits silent and, by some major miracle, you are admitted into the secret world.

"Don't you know who I am?" they scream when the dog barks. "Yes, I know perfectly well who you are," Geoffrey says calmly as Matteo stands hulking, the dog at his side. "According to Andromeda, you are a spoiled, rude, mannerless twit. Andromeda is never wrong." *"I'll get you,"* they screech, *"you and your blasted dog! You'll be sorry."* Geoffrey rolls his eyes, and that's when one of the off-duty cops—"the shadow bouncers," we call them— appears as if by magic to escort the twits gracefully to the corner, where they are thrown into a cab. Then the shadow bouncers palm the driver a large tip so he won't be insulted by the babbling belligerents in his backseat.

The cabbies love the corner by the Club Belladonna.

One night, a reject is so astonished by Andromeda's bark that he's practically frothing in incredulity. *"Don't you know who I am?"* The same old same old. They are always so original. *"I can break you. I can break you in two. Do you have any idea who I am?"*

Geoffrey turns on the microphone, which is kept there for crowd control at the police's request, and picks up a powerful square camping flashlight usually kept hidden in the dark corner. "Ladies and gentlemen, may I have your attention, please," he says, tapping the mike and turning his light on to sweep over their expectant faces. The crowd is instantly stilled into a thrilled silence. What can this mean? Will they, perhaps, be admitted en masse? Or will Belladonna herself be making an entrance onto the street to see them and comfort them? Or will—

No no no. Of course not. *Fools.*

"Your attention, please," Geoffrey repeats. "I have a gentleman here who seems entirely baffled that he doesn't know who he is." The light sweeps the crowd to land on the face of the belligerent

would-be guest, whose eyes squint painfully shut against it. "If anyone can help him find his identity, please come see me immediately."

A loud ripple of laughter sweeps through the crowd. The man
shouts something, which can't be heard over the merriment, and
slinks off, the light following him to the corner where he hurriedly
hails a cab. He'll wind up in some less exclusive watering hole more
sympathetic to the color of his money, where he can nurture his
grievances and mutter about his identity crisis.

Oh ho, just another night at the Club Belladonna!

There are many things you notice about human nature when you
open a nightclub. For one, society might occasionally be delightful
if people actually listened to one another. Or if they had something
interesting to say. For another, there are those who have more dinners than appetites, while others have more appetites than dinners.
They're the nervous eaters, even though we serve only cold snacks
to keep the drinkers' bellies full.

You can imagine what Belladonna does to these fools. When
she wants to wind them up, she orders a luscious basket of fruit.
She helps herself to a succulent bunch of grapes, plump, juicy cherries, dozens of blueberries, carefully slicing each in half with devastating precision with a petite fruit knife studded with emeralds,
flashing like her eyes. Then she gets up, plate in one hand and
knife in the other, and walks around the room, dropping a grape in
a drink here, a berry in a drink there. Or she trails the shimmering
hilt of her knife along a guest's shoulders. Sometimes she does this
without saying a word; other times, she murmurs a greeting or a
remark about someone's jewels or Balenciaga gown or the color of
their gloves.

She comes close enough to make you shiver.

This perfect fastidiousness sets a trend at dinner parties all over
town: to serve a cold supper, accessorized by gem-encrusted knives
and forks with delicate tines. I'm sure you understand which parties I mean—the ones devoted to endless discussion of the club
the guests aren't allowed into at the moment.

Other evenings, Belladonna will stroll by the tables, fan waving
languidly. Sometimes she sits down to play a hand of poker or
move a cribbage peg at one of the tables reserved for games. Every-

one holds their breath, hoping beyond hope that she'll stop to talk to them. She's as completely capricious with her movements and her conversations as Andromeda is with her barks. Both inside and outside the club, the rich and famous, movie stars and moguls alike, are ignored for the shop girls and obvious unsophisticates nervously fussing with their rhinestone earrings and too-tight waist cinchers.

On the rare occasions when she bestows a genuine smile upon her guests, they feel as if they have been kissed by the very breath of heaven.

Quite often, though, Belladonna sits at her center banquette, watching. If the mood strikes her, one of the waiters will deposit a pile of blood-red chips on her table, and she'll point her fan at a lucky guest, who blissfully scurries over for a game of cribbage or poker. To be chosen to play a game with the goddess herself is simply, utterly, too divine. Unnerving, too; her prepossession makes her partners flub their moves. Still, they can't say a private game with Belladonna isn't worth it. Worth their losses; worth all the waiting outside with other desperate hopefuls; worth the creepy stare of the big man at the door.

After we've been open for a few months, our evenings have settled down into a not-unpleasant monotony. On one particular night, Mayor Impellitteri is playing backgammon with the police commissioner as a handful of New York City Ballet dancers, giddy from that evening's performance, crowd around his table. The ballerinas start flirting with the guests nearby, not knowing they're butchers from the meat markets around the corner; movie stars trawl around the room, expecting to be noticed as they mingle with jazz musicians and subway-token clerks and society swells and artists and a prince and a priest or two.

Belladonna ignores them all. She is wearing a simple multifaceted ensemble, "her drink jewels," she calls them. Her bracelet, earrings, and rings are all studded with diamonds the colors of cocktails: Rémy Martin, Dubonnet, Lillet, Chartreuse. And of course the Belladonna. Blood-red, the color of vengeance.

We are sitting at our regular table, silently wishing that somebody useful might show up. A large party of Europeans is installed at the next table, boisterous with joyful proximity to Belladonna. The men drink too much, and the ladies try not to stare too overtly.

They are blabbing too loudly, making sure we can hear them. This is their little fantasy act; they think that if their wit is somehow so dazzling, Belladonna herself will lean over and say, "Darlings, please, do join me. Tell me all about yourselves and we'll become the best of friends, forever and ever."

As if!

Finally, one of the men leans toward us and says confidentially, "How delighted I am to have met you, *la bella* Belladonna. It is such a pleasure to see you at last." He looks to his friends for moral support, and they all grin and nod their heads. "Tell me," he goes on, "what can I do to give you pleasure in turn?"

"To give me pleasure," she says. They are in raptures that the divine creature has actually addressed them herself. The sound of her voice! The sparkle in her eyes! "Would you really like to do that?"

"Yes," he says, slightly surprised at the strange tone in her question.

"But really?" she presses. "You would do anything I say?"

"Of course." Now he is licking his chops.

She signals to the Ringer, and as the band stops playing the spotlight from the stage is turned on our table. "Cherished guests, ladies and gentlemen," she calls out, standing up, "I should like you to meet one of my most beloved patrons here at the Club Belladonna. For, you see, this gentleman has generously offered to give me *pleasure*. Indeed, he has offered to give me enormous pleasure this very minute."

She laughs, and the other guests sigh, intoxicated with happiness, before they start clapping and whistling. Then she holds up her hand, pointing her fan at the man who's spoken to her, and the crowd is instantly stilled.

"Ah, *pleasure*," she says. "How splendid *pleasure* can be. And this gentleman is goodness personified, offering to bestow pleasure upon me. To do anything I say. Anything whatsoever." With that, she laughs again.

The man is beaming, basking in adulation. "Whatever you say, my dear," he says loudly.

"You would do anything I say?" she repeats. "To give me pleasure?"

"Anything. Name it. Whatever you say."

"Very well." She pauses for effect, the light shimmering, hot and bright, so that her jewels seem lit with a secret fire. "Leave my club."

She snaps her fan shut and sits down. The light remains on the man's face, which is suddenly flooded with color, until he slowly gets up and walks out of the hushed room, banished from paradise. His friends soon follow. As soon as the spotlight goes off, everyone starts talking all at once, delirious with delight that they've been witness to such a scene in the Club Belladonna.

Besides, this will give the humiliated man's companions something delectably vicious to gossip about and spread all over town until it sounds as if Belladonna had practically poured poison down their throats before they departed in a panic.

No no no, boredom in the Club Belladonna simply will not do. Our routine is suddenly seeming too, well, routine. Rosalinda gets up when we are all fast asleep and takes Bryony to the Little Brick Schoolhouse. The rest of us roll out of bed by noon, eat a light breakfast, read the papers. Belladonna listens to the radio; she must have one on and near her at all hours. We watch the dogs romp. We have three trained wolfhounds now, although we call them all Andromeda at the club. Bryony names the other two Froggy and Tinkletime. I'm sure you can imagine how Tinkletime got *her* name.

No matter what or how she feels, Belladonna ties a scarf around her head, puts on oversize dark sunglasses, and picks up Bryony from school. It is only a few blocks away, and she relishes the task. The other mothers know her only as Mrs. Robbia, that she is a recently bereaved widow and is quiet and pleasant but prefers to keep to herself. The thick sunglasses are tinted a brownish hue, so the famous eyes of Belladonna look more hazel than green. But she needn't have worried, because there is absolutely nothing in her demeanor to suggest that she ever sets foot in the Club Belladonna.

Bryony is thriving in kindergarten, and has lots of little friends to play with on weekends. She takes ballet classes twice a week, and often practices around the house, sliding on the highly polished floors. At home, surrounded by the familiar faces of those who are as likely to speak to her in Italian as English, she feels secure and loved. Our odd schedule is all she knows, and she is young enough not to think our lifestyle anything out of the ordinary. Orlando gives us all judo and karate lessons, and Bianca often whips up a mean pesto from her kitchen pots of basil. She isn't quite Caterina, but our neighborhood is weird enough without us having to worry about spells and potions.

For the moment.

When we have some free time and feel like roaming, Matteo and I busy ourselves with exploration of the city, which has about as much in common with our childhood streets across the East River in Bensonhurst as Siberia. We walk by the lot at Gansevoort and Hudson where college students are playing lousy basketball and head for lunch at Louis', a short walk away in Sheridan Square. There we eat the house special of spaghetti and meatballs and salad for sixty-five cents and listen to the proto-beatniks discussing J. D. Salinger and Jackson Pollock and free love and atomic testing and how broke they are. We doze in the sun to indescribably horrible poetry readings by scruffy and bearded perpetual students in Washington Square or snoop on conversations by budding Freudians befuddled by the baloney spouted by their analysts. If possible, we dash uptown for matinees. On evenings when the club is capriciously closed, I like to check out the other bars in the Village. Mostly, they're dives, like the San Remo or Minetta's or the White Horse Tavern or Marie's Crisis, whose singer I wished we could appropriate for gigs at our club. Chumley's, a dark and dusty former speakeasy on Bedford Street near Bryony's school, is one of my favorites, because the door is unmarked like ours and locals like to hang out in it. Matteo and Orlando love to slip out to Eddie Condon's jazz club or the Village Vanguard or the Five Spot in Cooper Square to hear Charlie Mingus and Miles Davis and John Coltrane. They come home, eyes glowing and clothes reeking of stale tobacco, after hours spent enraptured by the music and the hep crowd so unlike the overstuffed and coiffed guests of the Club Belladonna.

The men we are looking for don't go to jazz clubs, unfortunately.

All is calm, too calm. The cameras click, the recorders hum, the files grow. The Club Belladonna is more popular than ever. But we've been open for months, and haven't yet spied a soul who has sparked any sort of memory in Belladonna. She is beginning to fret, Matteo and I decide, although she never breathes a word of her anxieties. Instead, she tells us it's time to start having theme balls. She hands us a list of ideas. What a dope I am; I'd forgotten I'd mentioned them to Jack, when we'd had tea at the Waldorf.

On ball nights, we'll bend the rules and draw up a select list, sending out only a few dozen highly coveted invitations—on our thick lemon-colored cards with Club Belladonna engraved in ruby ink at the top—to a quixotic selection of people from all over the world. From all professions, all strata of society. Especially society people from England.

Surely someone will have a connection to the members of the Club.

In the meantime, at least we'll be amused deciding how to decorate our club for each party, and whom to ask to it. All the staff add their ideas to Belladonna's list. And the prize for best costume—complete with mask, naturally—is to sit with Belladonna herself, so our guests will outdo themselves.

Indeed they do. For the Circus Ball, we cover the floor with sawdust and bring in performing poodles and clowns; there are enough costumed ringmasters and tutu-clad trapeze artists to start our own troupe. Even more fun is the Coney Island Carnival, where we have fire-eaters and tattooed bearded ladies and a miniature merry-go-round on the dance floor. The prizewinning costume goes to the man who comes as the owner of a peep show. He's literally fitted a large box on his body, covered with black silk, and when you peep through a hole you see two tiny figures, carved of ivory, inside, locked in an embrace.

At the Zodiac Ball, the masks people wear are fantastical creations representing each of the twelve signs; when we do the Garden Ball, we lay sod down on the floor, haul in huge potted ficus trees with trained doves cooing in the leaves, and stretch a painted twilight blue sky with twinkling stars across the ceiling. Each table sports a miniature landscape of ferns and mosses, like the floor of some primeval forest.

We all have lots of fun at the Animal Ball. Belladonna is wearing the mask Caterina made from poor dead Fluffy's ostrich feathers, with fanciful matching wristlets. She especially likes one woman who comes with her face rouged, red claws attached to her gloves,

and a red turban cunningly tied so that she looks like an imperti-
nent lobster. Guests are instructed to bring their house pets, and
the boring ones arrive with little lapdogs choked by jeweled collars
like Andromeda's. (She, poor dear, has to stay home that night, or
there would have been far too much barking at the door.) Those
with slightly more imagination bring costumed teddy bears, and
iguanas on leashes. I let loose Petunia, the parrot I've diligently
trained to talk. Only a few select phrases, mind you, would she say.
When I give her one of her favorite peanut butter crackers, she'll
let rip with a special sentence.

We have long been fed up with Dolly and L. L. Megalopolis,
you see; we nickname him "Loose Lips." We don't mind write-ups
in their columns, of course, but we object to constant lying, vague
innuendos, and slandering of people who've done nothing to harm
us. And they are always pretending they've been in the club, when,
in fact, Andromeda won't let them get close unless we want them
to be. Dolly is worse than Loose Lips. Matteo compares her to a
giant snail, leaving a trail of slime in her wake. A vile gasbag who
thinks Hedda Hopper and Louella Parsons have class, she is so
feared in society circles that no one raises a voice to challenge her.

Except us, of course. The night of the Animal Ball, Dolly Daffenberg finally gets a dose of her own medicine. I calmly wait for
the perfect moment, when the club has quieted after laughing at
one of Petunia's particularly loud squawks.

Vengeance is like comedy; timing is crucial.

And then Petunia says to the hushed audience, "Dolly's a bigger
whore than her mother. *Dolly's a bigger whore than her mother!*"

She repeats it so many times the whole club is in stitches.

Can you sue a parrot for slander? Dolly wouldn't dare try.

One night, our guests seem drunker than usual, as if they are
forcing themselves to be merry. Perhaps it's because it's summer,
sultry and stifling in the city. Perhaps they're bored with the world,
and crabby. Perhaps they sense that Belladonna is not herself that
night, that the snaps of her fan as she wanders among the tables
are harsh and angry. Her odd state is infecting the club.

She returns to her center banquette, and we begin snooping on
the conversation at the next table only because we're temporarily
too lazy to do anything else.

"Oh, *her*," one of them says. "Claudia. He took her to bed, on his famous black sheets, and he said she was so fat she resembled a stranded dead fish."

"He's a horror," says another.

"Not Luca! He's like champagne."

"More like gin."

"Gianni, do you know Claudia?" the simpering guest asks.

"Of course I do, Sylvanna. Don't you remember all the dreadful things we said about her yesterday?" says this Gianni. "My poor dear Claudia, how she talks and talks and talks. She's not a woman meant for men. She doesn't know anything about how to serve them, or how to amuse them. All she can do is bore them."

I have taken an instant dislike to Gianni, this voluble Italian so unlike Leandro, with his eyes like Portuguese oysters, glinting and oily as the pomade in his hair. Still, hearing him, I am overcome with longing to hear Leandro's voice, and I wonder if Belladonna misses him even more. She rarely speaks of him, or of anything that happened before.

Every night, we hope. We wait. And we leave with headaches from the noise and the babble and the wondering.

"If I have to talk to a woman for more than twenty minutes I stop wanting her," Gianni is boasting. "Besides, most females are shameless, heartless, or dull."

"Gianni, you are terrible," says Sylvanna with a giggle.

"*Basta*," he replies, pouting. "Why is it that everyone is always talking about how terrible I am and how many women I've seduced, but no one ever says how good I am in bed?"

The entire table bursts out laughing. Except for Gianni's hapless date, who's becoming less enchanted with each passing moment. He sticks his tongue in her ear, then grabs her hand and places it underneath the table. How exquisitely subtle. I glance over to Belladonna. She hasn't missed a thing, her mouth set. All of a sudden I know what it is—he reminds me of Mr. Nutley. I never thought that damp pudgepot would come to mind again, and certainly not in the Club Belladonna.

"You, sir," Belladonna says to him, rapping her fan on her wineglass. On this fan is a painted scene of the Trojan horse, with Helen looking down from the city walls at the men come to steal her away. What a coincidence—she looks just like Belladonna.

Everyone at the next table stops talking, and Gianni perks up, having been flattered into provoking the attention of the great, secretive hostess. If he were a canary, he'd be preening.

"Do be so kind as to share the no-doubt delightful comments you were lately whispering in the ear of your lady," she says to him.

The poor date blushes with mortification. She looks like an unfortunate minnow trapped in a tank with an unwieldy whale.

"For you, signora," he says, "I was merely remarking on the delectability of her . . ." His voice trails off.

"Of her, yes?" Belladonna's eyes are darkening into a dangerous green, the color of a pond teeming with algae.

"Of her earlobes," Gianni says.

"I see," Belladonna says. "How quaint. How romantic."

Gianni downs a glass of champagne, then looks to his friends for support, laughing. "Yes, all American women have delectable earlobes," he says, expansively throwing his arms as if he were sweeping the room with his embrace. "But they know nothing about tenderness."

"I see. American women know nothing about tenderness." Her voice sounds like a steel trap clanging shut. "And what brings you to this momentous conclusion?"

"Because, *cara,* they know nothing about pleasing a man."

"Ah."

There is a nervous silence at their table. Everyone is starting to look this way. One of our waiters, bless his cunning little heart, signals to the band to finish their song. Something is about to happen in the Club Belladonna. Another scene. How marvelous!

Belladonna whispers to me. I go to the bar, and come back with our house cocktail, then offer it to Gianni. "With our compliments," I say. "A particularly unique Belladonna, one replete with tenderness."

He is not duped by my dazzlingly charming smile. He's heard all those ditties.

Pretty poison is her cry.

"My dear Gianni," Belladonna says. Her voice is low, yet dripping with savage charm. Everyone in the club is straining to hear what's going on, but her words are for Gianni only. "As we have taken the trouble to concoct an especially *tender* cocktail for you, I shall be most insulted if you do not join me in a toast. A toast to *tenderness*."

Reluctantly, Gianni raises the drink to his lips and takes the smallest-possible sip. Belladonna's smile widens as she drinks from her own glass.

"I should like to ask you, my dear Gianni, to explain to me the difference between a steak of some tenderness and a woman's flesh," Belladonna goes on, her voice lower still as she leans close to him. Lucky boy, the other men are thinking, watching this, to be so close to Belladonna. Whatever can they be talking about? "If she does not succumb to your advances, does that make her not tender?"

Gianni hasn't quite understood her implication. He is nervously wondering if he's about to die. Boor that he is, he makes a dismissive gesture with his hand. Naughty boy.

"What precisely do *you* know about tenderness, Gianni, darling? What regard have you for the sweetness of a woman's body or the pleasuring of her *tender* needs? Hmmm?" Belladonna continues, fanning herself as if she hasn't a care in the world. "When has her satisfaction been more important than yours?"

"I hardly think—"

"Quite right. You hardly think," she says in a fierce whisper.

Gianni's lips narrow. He is angry, but also panicking. For once in his life he doesn't know what to say. How could any man know what to say to the imperious Belladonna at such a moment?

I realize you could hear a pin drop in the room as Belladonna stands up suddenly, snaps her fan shut with a harsh click, and walks over to the bandstand, her peach-colored brocade skirt swaying gently. Her wig is towering high, honey-colored this night, interwoven with strands of pearls and opals to match her necklace. Her gloves are also peach, and each finger sports an opal, glistening like magic iridescent beads of milk in the spotlight. Everyone is entranced, wondering what is about to happen. She has spoken to the crowd before, but not from up on the stage. Some of the women are trying hard not to bend over to see her fantastic diamond-studded shoes as she passes by.

"Good evening, ladies and gentlemen," she says, taking the microphone from the bandleader. "Welcome to the Club Belladonna."

There is a large outburst of applause.

"I take it you are happy to be here tonight." More applause.

"Thank you for joining me," she continues, waving away the clapping. "I should like to initiate what may very well become a tradition in my club. You see, I often hear comments from my guests that leave me, well—how shall I say it?—*perplexed.*"

"Not you, surely," someone calls out.

If they could see her face under the mask, she would almost be smiling. After all, Belladonnas are made, not born.

She opens her fan again and begins to wave it languidly. "Yes, even me," she says. "For instance, this evening we have a *gentleman* who has pronounced to me that American women know nothing about tenderness." Heads swivel to look over at Gianni, whose temper is barely kept in check. "Ladies and gentlemen, I throw the floor to you. Do American women know nothing about tenderness?"

There is dead silence for a few seconds, everyone too astonished to speak. And then one stalwart woman calls out, "We know too *much* about tenderness," she says.

"Brava," says Belladonna. With that, the floodgates open.

"It's men who know nothing—"

"But she's only tender to me when she wants a mink stole."

"Our children teach us about tenderness."

"My dog teaches me what sweetness really is."

"The dog outside is more tender than most men I know, and certainly my husband."

General hilarity all around.

"We would always be tender if we got tenderness in return," one lady says.

"But men need tenderness, too," Belladonna says.

How true. Look at me, what a sensitive bunny I am. Look at my shy, silent brother, how he suffers. Look at Jack, at the Ringer, at Geoffrey.

Think of Leandro.

"That's right," shouts one man inebriated enough to be foolish. "I don't know what you're all complaining about. All the tenderness you'll ever need is in this!" He holds up his lovely crimson Belladonna in its crystal martini glass.

"How intriguing," Belladonna says, then starts to laugh. Oh ho, the luscious sound of it, so divinely intoxicating! Except to this drunk, of course, and dear Gianni. He has just gotten a very sharp stabbing pain in his stomach, and beads of sweat are forming on his brow.

Belladonna steps off the stage, the spotlight following her and reflecting dazzling shards of light in the eyes of the guests as she approaches the drunk. "Do share your tenderness with me, kind sir," she says to him, pointing to his drink. He looks befuddled as she leans over him to pick up the glass. Then she takes a sip and sighs melodramatically. "Quite right, you are, kind sir, quite right indeed," she tells him. "This drink is indeed bursting with *tenderness.* Yet I believe it can be improved upon." She twists the opal of one of her rings, and it pops open. Then she sprinkles a bit of what seems to be a fine powder into the drink and swirls the crimson liquid around for a few seconds. It bubbles slightly. She takes a sip and laughs again.

"Much better," she says. "Much more *tender.* Here, you try it, and tell me."

The color drains out of the dumb man's face. He has rather instantly sobered up, and he shakes his head no.

"I said, try it," Belladonna says calmly, but her voice has changed. It is no longer full of merriment.

There is dead silence in the club. Gianni nearly cries out, to tell him not to do it, but he is wracked by a sudden cramp. Strictly psychosomatic, I assure you. The powder in Belladonna's rings is nothing more potent than plain old baking soda. A little in-house joke.

Belladonna stands motionless as the man looks up at her. Ever so slowly, he reaches out for the drink, his hand trembling. He is more terrified to disobey her than to swallow whatever it is she's concocted, so he takes the tiniest sip, his hand now shaking uncontrollably, then puts the glass down so quickly most of the liquid sloshes out.

He'll be thinking he was poisoned till the day he croaks. And not a moment too soon.

Pretty woman watch you die!

Belladonna slowly puts her hands together, as if she is about to pray, but instead she starts clapping, the sound muffled by the leather of her gloves. "I salute you, kind sir," she says to the man, who is now as pale as the white linen handkerchief he's using to dab his lips, "for now you understand the true nature of tenderness."

She returns to the stage, and her wide smile is visible under her mask. "We are all here to enjoy ourselves, are we not?"

No one says a word. They are afraid this may be some sort of trick question.

"Yes, of course we are," Belladonna goes on, unperturbed. "Therefore, since this is *my* club, and, as you obviously have recognized, I am a fairly strong believer in *rules* in *my* club, I am pleased to inform you of a new rule."

Nervous hand-wringing. Will she make all of them sip from a cocktail laced with a mysterious powder? Could all of them be banned forever for breaking some unwritten code they knew nothing about?

"As of this moment," she announces, "there will be no more disparaging comments about tenderness in my club."

There is a collective sigh of relief, and the spell is broken. Amid tumultuous applause and laughter, everyone seems to start talking all at once. Belladonna waits for the nervous chatter to subside, then holds up her hand.

"Is there anything else any of you, my cherished guests, would like to say to me?"

Of course there is. Did you really poison that man? What were you whispering to the other one? Please, can we see your face? Can you come sit with me, for just one blissful moment? Can your dog let me in whenever I want? Can you be my friend? Where have you come from? Who are you?

Who are you? Why are you here?

Don't ever ask her *those* questions.

Yes, there are a million things her cherished guests would like to ask Belladonna. But they wouldn't dare.

"Drinks are on the house. Enjoy your evening," she announces, and all in the room think they're the luckiest persons in the world, even though none is going to take a sip from any drink. Except Gianni, who still has an awful stabbing pain in his gut, and the other man, who is shakily getting up to leave.

How tragic. Well, I wish both of them nothing better than they deserve.

Although we don't know it yet, Belladonna's performance is only a warm-up for what Loose Lips Megalopolis will soon call the "Night of the Necklace."

The night of the Ball of the Elements.

6

The Ball of
the Elements

Sometimes things don't quite go according to plan. And then the plan is revealed to be something else entirely.

But after all the work we'd done setting up the Club Belladonna, where would be the fun in predictability?

Let me tell you about the elemental ball of October 23, 1952. The Ball of the Elements, I should say; people are expected to dress up as fire, air, water, earth. Actually, what makes this ball so extraordinary was set in motion a few nights before. It started out as a perfectly forgettable night, and we were about to finish our drinks when Matteo · suddenly materialized at our table. He wouldn't have left his post unless something was wrong, and Belladonna and I immediately followed him into the kitchen. Through the kitchen to a locked door, leading to a corridor, another locked door, and then Belladonna's office. To one side, through another door, is her dressing room, which has racks of her vividly colored costumes sent to us from seamstresses in Hong Kong, boxes of her bejeweled shoes, dozens of wigs hanging on hooks along one wall; stacks of kidskin gloves and lacy masks; a lighted theatrical mirror and pots of lipsticks and eye shadows, though only a glimmer of them will be seen from behind her mask; and a large three-way mirror so she can inspect the laces in the back of her corsets and bodices before entering the club itself. She keeps her rings in blue velvet boxes on her desk.

This is her private retreat, and it's more like the sultan's throne room in a harem. The walls are upholstered in pale green silk; a long, comfortable chaise is covered in deep pink velvet, flanked by thick cream-colored church candles in tall wrought-iron stands; and a large rectangular divan, draped with luxurious velvets, rests along one wall, heaped with embroidered pillows that resemble some of the more ornate bodices of her dresses. A gilded wooden fan lazily rotates on the ceiling. There are several gilt chairs with thick cushions near her Louis XIV desk, where she attends to paperwork, and piles of books stacked neatly on the floor. Framed prints of photographs she took of the Tuscan countryside decorate the walls. It is a room meant as a safe haven, a soundproofed place to stretch out when she is tired from listening to the endless chattering inside the club.

Belladonna sat behind her desk, fiddled with her pen, and waited for Matteo to speak.

"A woman at the door," he said. "You should talk to her."

"Why?" I asked.

"A feeling."

Botheration. This was so out of character for Matteo that something extraordinary must have touched him. I was usually the one with the hunches, but would naturally be inclined to take one of his very seriously.

"Is it safe to let her in here?" I asked. We have fire exits, of course, and many side passages, but no guest, or even a staff member, has ever been let in behind the scenes. This office is strictly off-limits.

"I don't think so. And it's not that I don't believe you, Matteo," Belladonna told him with a small frown, "but I don't want a strange woman in my office."

"I understand," he said, looking very disappointed.

"May I talk to her?" I asked my brother, and he perked up a little bit. Belladonna sighed, then let me go. Matteo went back to his post, and I took my mask off and changed in her dressing room. No one would pay any attention to me in my normal street clothes. To them I am no more than a slightly rotund man with surprisingly smooth skin for someone my age and a lot of jet black curly hair.

I slunk outside via the dim and dank side entrance, the old freight platform of the Kiss-Kiss Kandy factory around the corner on Washington Street. One of the shadow bouncers was waiting for me, alerted by Matteo. He took me to one of the off-duty cop cars, where a woman was sitting in the backseat. I tied one of the waiter's masks back on—I didn't yet want her to know that I was the man always sitting near Belladonna in the club—knocked on the car door, then slid in next to her.

She was wearing a beige raincoat slightly too large for her petite frame. Her light brown hair was pulled back in a careless ponytail, and she wasn't wearing any makeup. Her pale blue eyes would have been pretty if they hadn't been swollen from crying. She would, in fact, have been very pretty if she hadn't been so disheveled and upset. She reminded me of someone. Double botheration. Who could it be?

Laura, that's who. Laura Garnett, moping around Merano with Mr. Nutley. Laura, friend of Leandro, who never came to see us after he died. I'd nearly forgotten about her in all the bustle of the Club Belladonna.

Now I knew why my brother had a feeling. Just that second, Matteo knocked and sat in the front seat. Because of the masks, the woman couldn't tell that Matteo and I are twins. He looked at me. I knew what he was thinking; we were both thinking of Laura. And Leandro. How Leandro helped us when we needed him.

My psychic kneecap began thrumming pleasantly. There was a reason this woman had appeared, an important reason. Something bigger than whatever she was about to tell me. I'd figure it out soon enough.

"Tell me your name," I said gently.

"Annabeth," she said, her voice hardly louder than a whisper. "Annabeth Simon."

"You wished to speak to Belladonna."

She nodded. "Thank you, whoever you are," she said. "Thank you for seeing me. I don't know why I thought I'd be noticed at the door. It's insane, really, I've never been here before. But I didn't know where else to go or whom else to turn to, and he's . . ." Tears welled up in her eyes again. "If your doorman hadn't seen me, I don't know what I would have done."

She fiddled with her buttons and I saw that her hands were trembling. Instinctively, because I am such a naturally sympathetic kind of guy, I took them between mine and rubbed them. "They're like ice," I said, even though it wasn't cold out. In fact, it was an unusually balmy October night. Then I pulled out my handkerchief and gave it to her. She blew her nose and wiped her eyes.

"You're so kind. I was going crazy," she said. "It's my husband, you see. He's going to be coming here in a few days. Or nights, I mean. At the Ball of the Elements. With his mistress."

"How do you know that?" I asked.

"Friends of his have also been invited, and he's been boasting to them that he's bringing her, and telling everyone what she'll be wearing because he's convinced her costume is so clever she'll get to sit with Belladonna." She took a deep breath, calming herself. "You must think I'm a madwoman, the wronged wife who's so pathetic she has to follow her husband around when he's invited to a party."

"I think nothing of the kind," I told her. "Go on."

"I wouldn't have come, truly, I wouldn't, but my husband, Wesley, he—" The tears were falling again. We waited, calmly.

"It's not my husband who's the problem right this moment, what he's doing to me," she added. "It's the necklace. He took it."

"Took what exactly?" I asked.

"The necklace belonging to my mother. It was given to her by her mother, and it's all I have left of her. And it's meant for my daughter, Charlotte."

"He stole your mother's necklace?" Matteo asked.

She nodded again.

"He stole it so he could give it to the mistress he's bringing to the ball?" I asked. "To impress her? And because he's too cheap to buy her another one?"

Annabeth tried to smile. "Exactly. I'd never have discovered it missing, except the insurance was due and I needed to take it to be appraised. It's a very valuable heirloom, you see, late Victorian. Everyone who's seen it has always said that it's as delicate as spun air. That phrase must have clicked in his head when he heard 'Ball of the Elements.' Look." She opened her purse and frantically scrambled through it, fishing out a photograph. A family portrait. "See, here I'm wearing it. That's Wesley, and my children, Marshall and Charlotte. I brought this so you wouldn't think I was making it up when you see him here with her."

"How, may I ask, was he invited?" I said. This was serious. If scumbags like Wesley were being invited to our parties, our guest list was in need of a very serious overhaul.

"Wesley? He's a prominent lawyer," Annabeth explained, "and very connected socially. But I believe someone at his firm was invited, or his wife was because she knows somebody, and they had to go out of town. Wes was owed a favor."

"Why doesn't he want to take his own wife?" I asked.

"I don't know," she said, biting her lip. "Perhaps I'm not glamorous enough for a ball."

"That's absolutely not true," I said indignantly. "Do you still live together?"

"Yes. I mean, I guess so. He usually comes home most nights, although he often stays at the club near the office where he's working on a big case. Or so he says."

"He doesn't know that you know about his mistress?"

"Her name is Linda. Linda Jerome. No. He doesn't think I'm clever enough to figure things out. When I told him I thought he was having an affair, he got incredibly angry. He threatened me, saying he'd have me followed with a private detective so I can see what it feels like to fall under suspicion."

"So you can assume that he's been lying for quite some time."

"Yes," she said. "But I don't want to upset the children. He's a powerful lawyer, remember, and I've got nothing. We've been married since college, and I worked as a secretary to support us when he was in law school, but after he passed the bar and I had the children, well, I really don't know what to do. I can't believe I'm sitting in a car here and telling this to perfect strangers." She smiled ruefully. "I think I snapped when I realized the necklace was missing. I got a baby-sitter and ran out the door. Your doorman"—she gestured to Matteo—"was kind enough to listen. I don't know why he bothered to notice me." Matteo leaned over the car seat and kissed her hand, and she looked so bewildered at the gentleness of this imposing masked stranger that I felt a sudden sharp pang in my heart.

Unlike other employees, Matteo almost never interacts with anyone at the club; he prefers to remain the silent sentinel, guarding the door. The power of his position hasn't gone to his head, no no no. Mostly I think he is bored, or disdainful of the pathetic specimens he sees groveling before him on a nightly basis. He's never shown a particular interest in any person, much less a woman, since we moved to New York. I still couldn't for the life of me understand why Annabeth had him so *personally* interested, but I was glad for it. He'd been too much on his own. Hopefully he wouldn't need too much of the encouragement we would start subtly shoveling his way.

This entire situation was most improbable. We were meant to stay detached from the rabble while waiting for one man, and one man only. One of *them*.

But my brother and I were both working on gut instinct right then. A hunch, whatever—we had to trust it. Matteo took the photo from Annabeth and we scrutinized it.

"Why do you think we can help you?" I asked. I knew I'd have plenty of time to get to the root of Matteo's unusual behavior later.

Annabeth looked at me in some astonishment. "Because she's . . . because she's *Belladonna*. She can do anything."

Well. What do you know.

Belladonna sounds so sweet.

Annabeth stared down at her hands. They were trembling again, and I felt an intense wave of pity for this woman, desperate and afraid. Helpless while her louse of a husband gleefully planned his evening, basking in the superiority allowing him to attend an exclusive ball in the Club Belladonna. I bet he was planning to screw Miss Linda Jerome all night long, while she was still wearing the necklace delicate as spun air.

Belladonna would not be pleased, but my knee was screaming that we should help Annabeth. One glance at Matteo's face, and I could tell he was thinking the same thing.

"I'm terribly sorry to do this to you. I've never been here before," Annabeth said again. "I was afraid the dog might bark at me."

"I don't think she would," Matteo said. "She can tell who's worthy."

I thought of Leandro once more. He, too, had been *worthy*. I remembered how, whenever I'd had a problem and asked for advice, he'd never given me a direct answer. He'd driven me crazy, because I had been so impatient and wanted an answer, right that moment. Instead, he'd talked *around* the problem, as it were.

"Do you know the story of Medusa?" I asked Annabeth. She

looked at me as though I was a bit touched and shook her head
no.

"The god of the sea, Poseidon, tried everything to seduce Medusa, an innocent, beautiful virgin. But she was afraid, and she
refused him," I said. "He raped her anyway, in the temple of the
goddess Athena. Then Athena was so enraged by this violation that
she blamed the victim, and turned poor Medusa into a hideous
dragon, her hair a nest of vipers and her gaze so strong and evil it
would turn men into stone. How Medusa suffered, trapped in that
monster's body, abandoned and desperate. The only thing that
saved her was when the brave Perseus cut off her head."

Annabeth sat, puzzled, not knowing how close this myth mirrors
the life of my darling Belladonna. That was what saved Medusa—
death?

"By cutting her loose, he set her free," I explained. I was fervently hoping that Leandro would be proud of me as I told this
tale, that Belladonna would be proud of me when I related everything to her later. "Even in death Medusa kept her power, for it
was said that if you touched the blood from her right side, it would
bring you sadness and death; and if you touched the blood from
her left, then life would be restored to you."

"You're telling me that I can choose sadness, or I can choose
life," Annabeth said cautiously.

"Are you willing?" I asked her. "We will tell Belladonna everything, and I can assure you," I offered, vastly overstepping our
bounds and praying that Belladonna would not chop off my head
and my brother's as well, "that she will help you. Only you can say
the word."

I rummaged around in my pocket for one of Belladonna's
golden coins that I always carry with me on club nights as a good-
luck charm.

"Shall we flip?" I asked. "This coin is from Pompeii. It survived
fire and ash and centuries of burial, hidden away from the world.
This way, we can blame it on Vesuvius."

It fell on heads, as I had hoped: This meant Belladonna would
figure out what to do, and Wesley would get no less than what he
deserved.

* * *

We drape yards of gold lamé on the walls and the tables; we make place cards in gold leaf as souvenirs. Blocks of dry ice are placed in copper buckets to cover the floor in a sea of silver fog. All the staff have masks of bright silver and gold, for a change, and gloves and bow ties of bronze leather.

Naturally, this ball means lots of jewels. Belladonna comes as diamonds and ice: her gown seemingly made of spun silver, dripping with shiny paillettes that flicker reflected light, dazzling all who see her. Silver dewdrops glisten in a wig the color of molten copper, and her gems are so big you could use them as perfume stoppers. One on each finger; two more dangling like miniature chandeliers from her ears; giant black pearls marching down her bodice.

She is an unearthly apparition. Of course, she always is. But tonight she outdoes herself.

The show begins as the guests stream in. Women have painted their bodies and clothes in bronze, gold, copper; while others, dressed as air, are wearing diaphanous gowns with floating streamers of gauze in blue and white. Fire sprites are clad in red and orange stripes; a fiery lady seemed to have singed her leather cowgirl gear like a demented Dale Evans. Several water bearers are carrying goldfish in glass bowls to match the color of their gowns; one overheating slob has a snorkel as a mask. One man, evidently slumming as a peasant, is wearing a rustic shirt under his white dinner jacket and rough corduroy trousers tucked into scuffed boots, and he has smeared his lapels with dirt. It is probably as close to the earth as he's ever gotten in his life. The pitchfork is a nice touch, but we still make him check it at the door.

I like his clever simplicity so much I seat his party at the next table while Belladonna has temporarily retreated to her office to adjust her wig. Peregrine Burrell, he says his name is, and he introduces us to his friends: Celeste Lucaire, the editor of the fashion magazine *A la Mode;* another editor, Bettina Barrone; their top photographer, Johnnie Mink, and his little pal, Scottie Tannahill, who both sit with what seem to be permanent smirks of superiority on their faces. And another friend, Guy Lindell. No peasants these. Botheration. Fashion people get on my nerves, so smug and sanctimonious and sure of the perfection of the hemlines they tell their readers to change on a monthly basis. Really, who cares? We are so

used to having our own tailors and seamstresses make anything our
hearts desire that I wouldn't know how to set foot in a department
store, much less buy anything that some stupid magazine tells me
is an absolute must.

I have to say this about Celeste, skinny thing that she is: Her
dress is beautiful—it must be Jacques Fath peasant wear. She looks
like Marie Antoinette on a feed-her-flock day, in a bodice laced
with gold ribbons, and yards and yards of skirt made from gaily
colored ribbons sewn together. Even better, her necklace is made
of tiny cigarette lighters strung together on what seem to be cigar
wrappers. Bryony would love this getup, yet I have an irresistible
urge to smear some of Peregrine's dirt on Celeste's lovely white
stockings, even if she'd probably kick me with one of her ballerina
slippers. Bettina is not quite so elegant: Having drenched her
nearly transparent ball gown in the style of Napoleonic masochists,
she'll probably go home with a bad chest cold. Johnnie and Scottie
are trying not to sweat in their matching fur vests. That getup took
a lot of deliberation. No wonder they call Johnnie the Mink. I think
I'll have to remind him that minks are rodents.

Then I realize they're talking about someone they're calling the
sociopathic squire, and I perk right up. It may be a lead. Only an
inherently sadistic Brit would dump such an outlandish name like
Peregrine on his child, I decide. Guy, too, has an English accent.
Yes, this may be *that* kind of international group, so I signal one of
the waiters, ask him to bring Jack over, and have him tell Belladonna to join us sooner rather than later.

"The last thing he gave her was a custom-made black leather
corset from Rigby & Peller, studded with diamonds," Peregrine is
saying.

"And they all said it would never last," Bettina says with a smug
smile.

"That's because she turns a blind eye, Michaela does. Like the
time she came home and found a young woman tied to the bed, in
hysterics. He'd left her there when he popped out to have a drink,
and forgot all about her."

"Michaela *likes* it," Celeste says. "*She* bought the handcuffs to
use as napkin rings." She takes a delicate sip of her Belladonna
cocktail. "But, Perry, darling, I really don't understand how you

endure them. Sometimes I think your friends are a little too stupid for you."

"They're not stupid," Perry protests. "At least Squire Simon isn't. He's just a tad eccentric."

"What do you mean?" asks the Mink.

"For one thing," he says, "he's never so much as set foot in Germany, but he insists on being called 'Schultzie.' He swears his favorite film is *Heidi.*"

"*Triumph of the Will* is more like it," Guy mutters. His only concession to our theme is a bronze leather mask, and his brightly colored bronze silk cummerbund and bow tie. He actually could get up and mingle with our waiters, if he were so inclined. Although I don't think service is a concept that has much appeal to him.

"Schultzie loves lederhosen," Bettina goes on. "And he hums 'Edelweiss' whenever he ties his hapless lover to the bed. Then the poor girl's forced to look at the trompe l'oeil scene of the Alps he's had painted on his window shades. Guy, surely you've heard that."

"No, I hadn't heard that," Guy says. "All I can say about Schultzie is that his pug eyes remind me of the spigot on a sink."

I try not to laugh.

"But he's been nothing but nice to me," says Bettina.

"After all you've done—or rather, what your magazine's done for him—why shouldn't he be nice?" Guy asks. "But what rich man is nice? Or rather, what rich man is nice to his wife? If she's smart, she knows she must be nastier to him—in her very own special *nice* way, mind you—than he can ever be to her. That's her only leverage when he's controlling everything else.

"Take her jewelry, for example," he adds, opening a silver monogrammed case and tapping a cigarette on the table before fitting it into a mother-of-pearl holder. He leans over to Celeste and lights it from her necklace. "She must hold out for the best, always. Why should a man buy his woman a piece of real jewelry if she shows herself willing to wear fakes?"

"The only time it's permissible is if the real jewelry is in the vault and the copy is better than the real thing," Bettina says.

"No copy can ever be better than the real thing," Guy retorts.

"It can be nearly as good," she says.

"Good like a man is good?" Guy asks sardonically. "Nothing is so bad for a woman as a man who says he's good."

"And you ought to know," Celeste says. "After what people say about *you*."

"Oh," he says, languidly blowing smoke rings in our direction. He knows we're listening, and I admire his self-control. He never once looks at us. "I know full well what they say about me. That I'm filth. Real filth. Filth *totale*."

I can see why he says that. I bet lots of women in the room would like to pounce on this Guy. It's the posture that's so seductive, the air of casual, expensive ease, the way his tuxedo is cut close to his body in a style that's more reminiscent of Noël Coward than of Nathan Detroit. He likes to be looked at, this one, and he knows he's worth it. That's why he's pushed his mask up on his forehead. He's got black hair, slicked like Jack's, deep-set dark blue eyes, a nose that could be slightly too big on any other face, and an expressive mouth. His skin is deeply tanned and his figure is trim. He fairly reeks of sex. Filthy, sweet sex.

Oh ho, those days are long gone. Now I can only look at Guy and dream of his conquests. Belladonna has slipped into the banquette beside me, and I can sense her gaze. Then I feel her fingers lightly on my sleeve for the briefest of seconds. Sometimes I swear she can read my mind. I wipe the melancholy off my face and smile brightly, directing my attention back to the bits of conversation swirling in the air like cigarette smoke, and I'm almost beginning to feel bad that the infamous Schultzie couldn't have been here tonight. We do, after all, have a special treat in store for our guests.

The happy couple is sitting at a table near the center of the room, cooing like lovebirds. Wesley is dressed as a balloon seller, and Linda's clad in a Jean Harlow–like charmeuse nightgown, topped with a diaphanous robe fairly dripping layers of chiffon. Hardly what I'd call an original concept. She looks like a ball of airy pink fluff. A necklace of hundreds of diamonds strung on gossamer threads sparkles beautifully at her throat.

It will look particularly fetching in the photographs being developed right this instant.

Belladonna stands up and moves through the club, pausing to compliment one couple's costumes and asking them to move to her table. They've come as the Tin Man and the Scarecrow from *The Wizard of Oz*. Metal and straw are pretty elemental, and these are much simpler costumes than the fanciful froufrous most others are wearing. The couple practically swoons with pleasure. I see Linda shrugging as Wesley leans over to whisper in her ear.

"Ladies and gentlemen," Belladonna says when she reaches the stage, tapping on the microphone with her fan rimmed with crystals. She seems a veritable apparition, glistening and sparkling, as evanescent as sea foam. The club is instantly silent, dazzled. "Thank you for joining me here tonight, at our Ball of the Elements."

Applause crashes all around. "This is indeed a special occasion," she continues, "for it seems that there is a saga unfolding before us. It is an earthly saga, particularly fitting for our elemental theme." The crowd ooohs and aahhs. "Here, in my club, sits a man of particular sensibilities, and his very entrancing lady friend. In other words, this *gentleman*"—she says this word with particular sarcasm—"is here with his mistress. Obviously, I know who he is, but he doesn't know *how*. I shall, therefore, refer to him as Mr. John Doe. Is that satisfactory?"

There is a much smaller smattering of applause, because many of our cherished and invited guests are here with their mistresses, and they are starting to get a rather uncomfortable squirming feeling.

"Yes," she continues, her voice smooth and mellifluous, "Mr. John Doe is here with, hmmm, I think I shall call her Madame X. She is wearing a most exquisite necklace, among other things." The hands of all the mistresses instinctively rise to cover their jewels, and we hear a few nervous titters. They can't help themselves. "The problem is, this particular exquisite necklace belongs to Mr. John Doe's wife. Furthermore, it was given to Mr. John Doe's devoted wife by a dearly departed member of *her* family. In other words, its value is sentimental, and therefore entirely priceless." She opens her fan and begins waving it languidly. "I hasten to assure you that Mr. John Doe's wife is undoubtedly sleeping at home, and she has absolutely no idea I am speaking these words on her behalf." Which is true, if you think about it in a Belladonna kind of way.

But then Belladonna's voice darkens, and even I shudder. "Nor is this the time to judge the morality of whether the lady's husband should be lying beside her in their marital bed, instead of flaunting his broken vows in my club."

There is dead silence, and when Belladonna snaps her fan shut with a violent click nearly everyone in the room jumps.

"Do I detect a whiff of a guilty conscience?" she asks as she steps off the stage. The spotlight, as usual, follows her as she imperiously walks around the club, stopping before each and every woman wearing a necklace.

"How lovely," she murmurs, examining a diamond dewdrop. She points her fan at a pearl choker. "Soak them in seawater," she says, "to renew their luster."

Around the room she moves, in no particular order, until she reaches our own happy couple. Wesley's mouth is pinched in rage, while Linda's cheeks are flaming circles. Elemental indeed!

"Magnificent," Belladonna says, trailing the fan along Linda's shoulder blades as she flinches and tries not to be sick. Then Belladonna moves on to the next table and Wesley sighs in relief. Linda is too terrified to get up and run to the ladies' room.

Belladonna returns to the stage. "My most welcome guests, I ask you this," she says in sugared tones. "Should Madame X be allowed to keep the necklace, souvenir of her lover's feckless desire? Or should she return it—surreptitiously, of course—to its rightful owner, and demand in its place an even finer piece of jewelry as proof of his devotion? Applaud, if you will, when I ask you again.

"Should she keep the necklace?"

There is not a sound.

"Should she give it back?"

The applause is deafening.

"Thank you," Belladonna says, her voice still sweet. "I am very pleased that you have restored my faith in the value of those worthy of entry to my club. The verdict is in. To protect the identity of the guilty, we are going to dim the lights. This will give Madame X the opportunity to unfasten her necklace under the cloak of darkness. There will be a small box in the coat check as you leave, so I ask her to deposit the necklace there. No questions will be asked. I can assure you the necklace will be returned to its rightful owner, and we shall hear no more of it.

"And now, Richard is going to lead the band in a luscious song for all the duplicitous, the lovelorn, the weary, all you splendid liars among us. Ladies and gentlemen, 'Love Is Here to Stay.' Drinks are on the house. Enjoy your evening."

She curtsies, and the lights go off abruptly. Nervous tittering again flits through the club, and when the lights go up a moment later, Belladonna is nowhere to be found.

All at once, the club erupts in noisome conversation. Several couples get up to leave, but Wesley and Linda are still with us, he stony-faced with fury and she trembling with mortification. I almost feel sorry for the girl, who is no longer wearing Annabeth's necklace. She couldn't have known her sweet lover was such a cheap scumbucket.

Our waiters keep an eagle eye on the table, then surreptitiously follow our happy couple to the coat check when they finally get up to leave. Linda looks around to see that she's not being watched when Josie is fetching her things, then takes the necklace out of Wesley's jacket pocket and quickly drops it into the box.

"I'll kill the bitch," Wesley is saying as he hands Linda her coat and they step outside. "This is all her fault."

They walk quickly to one of the waiting cabs. As Wesley opens the door and Linda slides her fluff into the backseat, he feels a tap on his shoulder. It's Jack, who wordlessly hands him a manila envelope. The label is addressed to Wesley's law firm.

Wesley tears open the envelope and pulls out the freshly printed evidence of his duplicity. Ever so flattering, I must say, although Wesley clearly doesn't think so. His face, previously enraged, is now positively apoplectic.

"You son of a bitch," he says, and takes a swing at Jack, who quickly steps out of the way. In a flash, Wesley is flat on his back. Geoffrey has karate-flipped him and is now standing with his shoe poised over Wesley's neck. One of the cops on street duty hurries over.

"Everything under control?" the cop asks. "Shall I book him?"

Jack shrugs and steps back. The cop nods and goes back to his post as Linda scoots out of the cab, helps Wesley up, and brushes off his coat. Then they both get in and speed away.

Geoffrey has a broad, goofy smile on his face. "I've wanted to do that ever since I started," he tells Jack with smug satisfaction.

And at the end of the night, when we take the box from the counter of the coat check and empty its contents in Belladonna's office, we are astonished to find a dozen necklaces, glistening in a colorful heap of sparkles on her desk.

7

The Oracle
in the Office

That's how it starts, the rumors spreading like crabgrass on a golf course. The gossip in Loose Lips's column doesn't hurt, and for once he doesn't have to provide a lavish exaggeration. We receive a tearstained letter at the club, then another, and another. From women begging for help, women too scared to sign their last names or put a return address on the envelopes. Just phone numbers. *I'd do anything if only you'd call me, Miss Belladonna, please, during the daytime only. I don't know what else to do,* they write in large, nervously slanting letters. *Please, can you help me.*

You're the Belladonna, they write. *You can do anything.*

Belladonna make them cry.

When taking nightly breaks in her office in the club, Belladonna starts reading the letters. As the pile grows larger, she gives them to us—her inner circle, I guess you could call it—to read, as well. Then she calls a conference one afternoon, asking Matteo, Jack, and Orlando to join her for tea, making sure Bryony is playing at a friend's house so we won't have to worry about her overhearing anything. Bianca bakes a huge tray of scones, and we nibble them slathered with fresh butter and ginger marmalade. Andromeda, Froggy, and Tinkletime, the shaggy sentinels, doze in patches of sunlight on the glossy wooden floors. Petunia nibbles on sunflower seeds and lets out an occasional squawk. Noises from the street are muffled by the thick velvet drapes, and the outside world seems very far away.

In this saga, the outside world will always be very far away. The

Korean War is winding down but there's squabbling in Indochina; McCarthy rants about Communists and many of our clubgoers find themselves blacklisted. Dior is about to raise hemlines and cause a ruckus; atomic hysteria is in full sway; children practice bomb drills at school. We care not a whit. We are on a quest.

Nothing else has mattered. Not really. Not since we opened the Club Belladonna.

"What are we to do with these letters?" she asks when we're through stuffing ourselves. "We seem to be in no danger of them stopping."

"Why don't we start calling the ladies who wrote them?" I ask. I've been thinking hard about this. Belladonna needs something to occupy her time while we wait. I fear that she's like a well-oiled machine that breaks down only because there's nothing for it to do. Our business is thriving. Belladonna already gives so much of her money away; I won't bore you with the names of our pet causes and donations and foundations, set up and administered with the help of some of Jack's contacts. All the funding is anonymous, of course, and often unlooked for and dazzling in its generosity. Yet no matter how much Belladonna gives, it barely makes a dent in her fortune. Maybe if she becomes more engaged in the particulars it will somehow help us get closer to what we're looking for.

Or maybe I should stop thinking so hard about Belladonna. I don't want to get wrinkles in my baby-soft and hairless skin from worrying. Instead, I'll concentrate on the positive. About how much I love the delicious possibilities of *la vendetta*!

"What I mean is, this will give us something else to focus on while we're waiting for certain people to show up. We have the energy, don't we," I go on, "as well as the money and the knowledge. After all, the club is running smoothly, and this will fill the downtime. It could be fun."

"We'd need to implement some sort of screening system," Jack offers, "to make sure the requests are legitimate. Once they've seen you the first time—if indeed you do want to see any of them—they'd no longer have to come here. We could set up another office somewhere, with phone numbers that'll be billed to one of the dummy corporations. Actually," he adds, "for now we could have anyone you wanted to talk to come in through the Kiss-Kiss freight entrance on Washington. No one goes there."

That's because we've planted some moonlighting cops dressed as decoy hookers there, and on most corners near the club. They're the biggest joke in the precinct, and have been ever since our monthly contributions for the upkeep of the station house and for the Patrolmen's Benevolent Association started rolling in. In fact, there's a waiting list of dozens of cops who want to earn some extra cash lolling about in feather boas and stiletto heels, moaning about how much their girdles pinch. These guys are so ugly you'd have to be blind and beyond desperate to want to go near any of them.

"Might do you good," Matteo says. He's the only one who could say something like that to Belladonna and get away with it.

"Might do all of us good," I add, seeing her frown.

"I know that some of the staff would be happy for more work," Jack says. "There's no shortage of competent detectives who can investigate the claims. They could start their investigations as soon as we contact any of these women. Do the legwork and the paperwork, tail whomever, make whatever phone calls and follow-ups are necessary. This way, your actual involvement will be minimal. Piece of cake."

Belladonna's face is troubled. She doesn't like the thought of having to deal with strangers, even if she'd be helping them. Annabeth Simon's case was a fluke, and she did it more for Matteo's sake than anything else.

Matteo took her necklace to Annabeth the next day, as we knew he would. Wesley also moved out the next day and into a small private hotel with Linda, which was probably best for all concerned. His lawyers have already been in touch, and we've assured Annabeth that ours are better. Besides, she has nothing to fear. Jack has a team on twenty-four-hour surveillance of their hotel and Wesley's office, and the photographs in his file are not something I'd like to show my colleagues. Wesley's bank account is about to show a huge deficit, if we have anything to do with his divorce proceedings.

All this we know because Matteo has suddenly become a rather regular figure in the Simon household. If it weren't such a surprising turn of events, I might almost say he is falling in love. I didn't think it possible. You know, the hormone problem, the too-ashamed-to-talk-about-it problem we both share. But Annabeth hasn't asked him anything remotely probing so far, and she's especially grateful for the attention he pays her son, Marshall. The little guy is entranced with the nearly silent man who comes to visit in the late afternoon and teaches him card tricks. Only after Marshall's done his homework, naturally.

I must admit I haven't talked very much about my darling big brother, have I? Bryony adores him, especially when he plays with her or takes her on window-shopping expeditions after school. We couldn't run the club without him. It's as if he's a living embodiment of our shadow bouncers: present, yet seeming to belong more to the hidden darkness than to the light. He and Orlando, who is by nature not a voluble talker, are great friends, and often disappear for long walks all over the city or to their favorite jazz clubs. They are both reliable to a fault, and ask for nothing. I've always worried about Matteo more than I've let on, because he does say so little. We never discuss our difficulties.

I, on the other hand, have learned to occupy myself with gregariousness, and, as you know, absolutely adore sticking my busybody self in lots of places it shouldn't go. I mingle with the crowd in the club and positively revel in their sucking up. Belladonna laughs at me sometimes, how at home I am there, but she knows that my fussing and bustling are shields to stave off the loneliness that can creep unbidden into our lovely house at night. How must it be for Matteo? His life is even lonelier. He has chosen to stand guard outside, no matter what the weather, with only Geoffrey and a dog for company. He doesn't complain. Yet he and Belladonna have always seemed to share an almost psychic connection, one that has made me plenty jealous.

It is the shared language of pain.

Matteo simply is. He doesn't speak of his needs, or his dreams, or his fears.

Nor do any of us. If we did, I should think we'd all go quite mad. But who's to say we're not all mad already?

And who are we to be surprised, after all, if Matteo finds the courage in his heart to look for love? Of course, Annabeth is in for a bit of a surprise should their relationship progress, but I don't think Matteo is quite ready for that conversation. *This* conversation is turning out to be difficult enough.

"I need to think," Belladonna says eventually. She looks at all of us, reading the answer she doesn't want to see in our faces. She sighs.

"Let's see what happens, and take it one step at a time," Jack says to her. "It could turn out to be a huge mistake, and a waste of our time and energy. If so, we'll stop immediately. We must be as meticulous in our preparations for this as we were with setting up the club."

He's juiced, I can tell. Once a snoop, always a snoop.

And I have a funny little hunch that Jack is happy to be doing anything that might bring him closer to Belladonna.

We start with ladies who have relatively simple problems, ones that have somehow piqued Belladonna's interest. I call them our "warm-ups"—useful to perfect our skills and potential scenarios. These ladies are contacted by Jack or one of his assistants, and if they pass the Theodora test—I'll get to that soon enough—they are met on the corner of Washington and Gansevoort in the late afternoon and led through bewildering dark passages to Belladonna's office. They all look as if they're expecting her to pounce on them suddenly and whisk them away, never to be seen again. They nervously smooth their clothes and sit up straight, hats on heads and gloves in laps and handbags at their sides, darting glances around the sumptuous luxury of the room. They are desperate to pull out their compacts for one last inspection, patting the sweat away so they can look as perfect as possible for Belladonna.

When she enters the room quietly from a door hidden behind a large painted screen behind them, they invariably start. The air seems to shift imperceptibly. Poor ladies—they are almost fainting from nerves when they see her in full regalia, her face masked. She projects no air of friendliness or concern; she says little. Women who are rattled will talk more and reveal things they meant to keep secret, making our task easier. The air is so heavy, aromatic with scent, the spectacle of the real live Belladonna in front of them, listening to them, unbelievable and more than a little frightening. It's as if she isn't real, but some vaguely sinister fairy godmother conjured up straight out of their subconscious.

Belladonna goes over to a side table and lights a cone of jasmine incense on a silver-glazed plate, puts a small ceramic pagoda over it so that the fragrant smoke will waft out its windows, then sits

down behind her desk, placing her fan near her inkwell. I sit on a
gilt chair near the door, trying to look inconspicuous, which isn't
easy considering how imposing my persona, and am not surprised
when the ladies don't seem to see me. Belladonna is much more
interesting.

She picks up the letter *del giorno* and scans it once more. She
puts it down and looks at her blushing lady, who is near tears from
worry or disbelief that she is actually there, I can't tell which. Probably a combination of both.

"How can I help you?" Belladonna asks. Her voice is low and
melodious, yet remote. The woman cannot read her expression
from behind her mask.

"Well," she says, clearing her throat. "Thank you for seeing
me."

She nods.

"I've heard . . ." The woman is really nervous now. "I've heard
that you—"

"That I what?"

"That you help women," she whispers.

"And who told you that?" Belladonna asks. It is a ridiculous
question, really, because the woman has already written to her and
been contacted and screened and brought to the bowels of the club
itself, and, well, here she is.

There are a few seconds of silence, unbearable for this woman
and welcome for us. People so often go on and on and on and have
nothing whatsoever to say.

"It depends on the kind of help you're talking about," Belladonna says eventually, just so the woman can breathe again. "And
something else."

"Yes?" she asks.

"It depends on the woman." She is looking right at this lady,
her eyes huge and green and glinting. "You must be willing to do
everything possible if you want my help," she says. "Failure is not
in my vocabulary. Shrewdness, frustration, and dexterity, yes. *Vengeance.* But failure? *Never.*"

Oh ho, the cunning Belladonna! She is a ferocious goddess,
presiding over the fire, a modern oracle, speaking in riddles to this
woman. Oracles can seem so obscure: They are meant to deceive

with their ambiguous words. Sometimes I wonder if Belladonna herself knows what game she's playing.

Belladonna gets up from behind her desk. I watch the woman flinch and steel herself. What can she possibly expect, poor thing, a spell cast over her on Gansevoort Street?

"Give me your hand," Belladonna demands.

She takes it, then turns the palm over. "Strong in love, I see," she says, tracing a line with her gloved finger. "Stronger than you think."

The lady looks at her hand in wonderment, a lingering whiff of Belladonna's perfume seeming to rise from it as Belladonna herself walks back to sit behind her desk once more.

"So," she says.

"My husband. Like the man at the Ball of the Elements. The one with the necklace."

This is what we expect to hear from our warm-up ladies. There are so many duplicitous men running around New York, it seems, that I'm amazed anyone manages to want to get married at all, much less remain faithful.

"An affair?"

"Yes." She nods as tears begin rolling in earnest. "With my best friend."

"Ex–best friend, you mean."

I hand the lady a lovely large handkerchief of the softest linen, trimmed in lace. There is a crimson *B* embroidered in one corner. She blows her nose and wipes her eyes.

"No man has the right to treat a woman like his own personal whore," Belladonna says, her voice harsh. She sighs, and I watch the lady begin to regain her composure. Belladonna isn't going to turn her into a toad. Perhaps she *is* on the lady's side after all.

"All women are vulnerable to deception," Belladonna goes on. "Deception makes you want to give up, because you think it's easier to lie down and die. Or so you wish."

The heat of her gaze could burn a hole through her fan. None of the ladies we see realizes that Belladonna is talking about herself. They can't imagine this indomitable creature in a vulnerable state, wanting to lie down and die.

"But that's only if you let a man kill your spirit. If he's so terribly cruel to you, then you must show him no mercy. He's got to be taught to crawl. Do you understand?"

The woman nods yes, fervently.

"Personally," Belladonna adds, "I never stick to a mistake." She slowly removes the rings from her gloved fingers, placing them in a midnight blue velvet box on her desk, and then opens another velvet box and carefully considers a different set from her large collection.

"What do you think?" she asks, pulling out a large sapphire, or perhaps a square-cut emerald, a topaz or a peridot laced with her infamous loops of dangling pearls, and trying them on. The lady looks at me, stupefied that Belladonna would be bothering to ask her advice.

"Once, there was a general from Thebes, who went to the oracle priestess at Delphi for advice," she says, still toying with her jewels. " 'Listen carefully,' the oracle said to him. 'Beware of the Sea.' Arrogant soldier, he thought he knew what she meant. He became wary. Not a sailing ship in his fleet escaped his concern. But he didn't die at sea. No, of course he didn't. He died because he didn't really *listen*. He died lost in a bewitched oak forest called the Sea."

After a few befuddled minutes, the woman says she thinks she understands what Belladonna means.

"Oracles never lie," Belladonna says, and I close my eyes to conjure a picture of Leandro sitting on his terrace as the heat shimmers golden around him. "It is all in the interpretation. To see the literal in the hidden, to be led to the edge of understanding. To hope that you can find the courage." She picks up her fan and waves it. "Are you ready?"

Again, the woman nods yes.

"Very well," she says. She shuts her blue velvet ring box with a loud click, stands up, and comes around to where the lady is sitting. Then she points her fan at me. The lady turns, sees my charming smile, and by the time she's turned back, Belladonna has disappeared.

"Before you leave, you'll give me the telephone numbers and addresses where we can contact you, and all relevant information about the people and particulars involved," I tell the woman brightly. "We'll be in touch about what methods might be most suitable for your case, and what you'll need to do. You, and only you. Don't worry." I wink disarmingly. "You'll do fine."

It is not Belladonna's fault if the woman falls into the abyss.

"Acting like an oracle is the exoneration of the ambiguous," Belladonna says to me one day, sitting lost in frustration, "and it's the only way I can remove myself from blame if something goes wrong." She sighs. "I'm trying to help them as best I can, so they can find some courage within themselves. Truly, Tomasino. I suppose I'm also trying to find some corner of my heart that automatically pities them because they, too, feel trapped." She picks up several pairs of gloves, trying to decide which pair to wear.

"I like the blue-green ones," I offer. "The color of Bryony's eyes." I don't know what else to say. She so rarely reveals any hint of weakness.

She pulls the blue-green gloves on without comment and riffles through a pile of papers on her desk before handing me a file.

"What's this?" I ask.

"Information on some properties. Next time we shut down for a few days, I want you to go to Virginia and look at them. The large one might be a good investment. And somewhere to escape to."

"You can always escape back to Italy," I say carefully.

"I can't escape back," she says. "I can't escape my life, period. But I want something new to think about. I can count on you to tell me if it's worth buying or not. If you like it, go ahead and make an offer. If it's the right place."

That's because I am such a devastatingly adroit judge of houses as well as character.

"I have to have some sense that what I am doing is worth something," Belladonna says, interrupting my smug reverie about a new house to decorate. "Not just entertaining people in the club while we wait. It is a supreme act of will and discipline not to give in. Otherwise, what have I been living for?"

"Remember what Leandro said," I tell her. "Train your thinking with concentration and discipline. Clear it of all thoughts but vengeance. There is no forgiveness."

"I remember," she says, her voice flat.

How could she ever forget?

*   *   *

*B*elladonna hands me a letter. "Read the beginning out loud," she commands.

" 'Dear Belladonna,' " I read, " 'Thank you for taking the time to read this letter, and I hope you can help us. I am writing on behalf of everyone in our office, and we are turning to you because we don't know where else to go.' " I frown. Nearly all the letters start like this. "What's so unusual?" I ask.

"Go on," she says impatiently.

" 'Someone we know told us what it's like to be in your club, although we've never tried to go. She said that it was the only place she'd ever been where the waiters asked her what she would like to drink. All of us here want to tell you that no other club or restaurant in New York or any other place we've been has waiters who speak to the ladies if they are at a table with a man. The men do the ordering and we are expected to sit in silence. That's why we hope you can help us. . . .' "

"Is that true?" Belladonna asks.

"I have no idea," I reply. "I don't go on dates. And I don't pay much attention to the waiters when—"

"Oh, Tomasino," she says. Her interrupting is her way of apologizing, and I feel my eyes fill with tears.

"What kind of world do we live in?" Belladonna says. "Do you think it will ever change, when a lady can go into a restaurant with a man and speak for herself, if only to ask for something as ridiculously simple as a cocktail?"

"Probably not," I say. "But I bet waiters ask Marilyn Monroe what she wants to drink."

"I'm not Marilyn Monroe."

"Thank goodness." I laugh. "Did you see her hair in *Niagara*? It's a mess."

Belladonna gives me a small smile, which means more to me than all the diamonds on Andromeda's collar. "Bring her in," she says.

"I will. How splendid. I've always wanted to invite Marilyn to one of our little parties," I say, knowing full well she means the letter writer, not the movie star.

The letter writer's name is Alison Jenkins. When she is sitting with me in Belladonna's office, waiting, she appears calm and collected, not frazzled with nerves as most of our ladies usually are. I decide I like her immediately, so I launch right into the Theodora test.

"I was just reading about dungeons," I say in a perfectly conversational tone of voice. Alison's face blanches. "They reminded me of the story of the empress Theodora, the much-maligned *bella donna* of the Bosphorus. It's a true story. Do you know it?"

Alison shakes her head no, puzzled.

"Theodora came from a poor family in Constantinople, with ambitious parents. They forced her to earn her keep onstage," I say, settling back and enjoying the sound of my own voice. "But she couldn't dance or sing, and she only became a hit once she started shedding her clothes. Eventually, she fell in love with a man who deserted her, leaving her with a baby son and no money. There was only one profession left for our poor talentless girl. I'm sure you can figure out what *that* was.

"Well, at the lowest point of those low days, Theodora took herself to a soothsayer, who had a vision. 'Get ready, my dear,' said the psychic, 'the tears and poverty and the horror of the disgusting, dirty slobs in your bed will soon disappear. You, yes you, my dear, are going to marry a monarch.'

"Nothing could have pleased Theodora more, so she farmed out her baby, packed her meager bags, and returned to Constantinople. She was still an actress, so she pretended to be a chaste born-again virgin, spinning wool in her little cottage. When who should pass by and see such charm but the senator Justinian, already reigning over the empire under the name of his aging uncle. He fell madly in love with Theodora. An award-winning performance, I admit, but she earnestly loved him back. Why wouldn't she, the power-mad little vixen?

"At this point, Justinian, who could have had any noble virgin in the land, was determined to make an honest woman of his whore, but those pesky Roman marriage laws forbade senators from ever marrying such 'ladies.' Not only that, but Justinian's aunt Lupicina, the empress, for some reason refused to accept a prostitute as her niece. Too bad, said our boy. He knew Lupicina was old enough to die soon—or at least have a nice timely mishap once she nibbled a sweetly poisoned fig—so he created a new law without much fuss.

"And so Theodora and Justinian were married. He seated her

on the throne as an equal and all the governors of the provinces had to swear allegiance to them both. Long may the harlot reign!"

Alison smiles a little. "Theodora reminds me of Eva Perón, that dictator's wife who just died," she says. My knee is humming pleasantly and I smile. Yes, I've definitely made the right decision about this one.

"For a while, though, Theodora disappeared. Personally, I like to think she was gloating in private while plotting how to consolidate her fortune," I go on. "How could she not worry about what might happen to her if Justinian popped off—she needed a ton of money to protect her family from ruin. She called in the astrologers and soothsayers and magicians, and deep in her secret apartments she was attended to by trusted favorites and eunuchs."

Alison is listening avidly. She doesn't know why, but she can't help herself. It is quite a saga, I'll admit, but I am such a talented storyteller. I managed to say the word *eunuch* without betraying the slightest twinge of recognition.

"And spies. Theodora's spies reported everything to her: words or deeds or a cross-eyed look. Whoever was accused of wishing her ill, fairly or not, was thrown in the royal dungeons, inaccessible to justice or hope, tortured until they begged for death. Abandoned forever.

"Not that Theodora was all bad," I continue. "Perhaps a little hasty, but she always kept a soft spot for her less fortunate sisters, forced into a life of prostitution. A palace on the Bosphorus was converted into a monastery, and five hundred women were collected from the streets and brothels to fill it. In this retreat, the lucky lassies became devoted to Theodora. It was touching, truly. There was no escape, you see—only a plunge feet-first into the sea.

"Yes, Theodora was an extraordinary empress. She was brave in the face of the continual duplicity of the courtiers, and a prudent counselor to her husband. She was chaste and faithful to Justinian—she wasn't going to blow it this time. But they had no son and heir. Only a baby daughter, who died soon after birth. All in all, I'd say they were pretty happy. They remained married for twenty-four years, until she died."

I sit back and smile. "Well," I ask Alison. "Isn't that a lovely story? What do you think? Anything in particular strike you?"

"What happened to the other baby she had?" Alison asks.

"Ah yes. The sweet little baby boy." I knew it. She's passed the Theodora test with flying colors, instinctively asking the right question. "He grew up in Arabia, where his father made the mistake of telling him he was the son of an empress. Naturally, he hastened to the palace at Constantinople, hoping for the best—a crown, a fortune, maybe even a harem of his own. His mother kindly received him, her very own son. But no one ever saw him again, not even after her death."

"No one knows what became of him?"

"And no one ever will," I say slowly. "Perhaps he died of a fever after so long a journey."

"Perhaps he was tied into a sack and weighted down with stones and thrown to a watery grave like so many before him," Belladonna says, making her usual silent entrance so that Alison nearly jumps out of her skin. "After all, he was the living embodiment of her youthful degradation."

She beckons to Alison to pull her gilt chair closer to the desk. "Change is rarely what one presupposes," she says. "How can I help you?"

"It's my boss," Alison says after taking a few calming breaths. "Our boss—there're nine of us all together. Mostly secretaries. It's an import-export company. Lots of paperwork."

"Are you here on behalf of the nine?" I ask.

"Yes," she says, biting her lips. "We drew straws, and I . . ."

"You got the lucky one," I say, and she stares at me, surprised by my encouragement. "What exactly does he do, this boss?"

"Our boss has already gotten one of us pregnant. Norma. He told her to get rid of it—the baby—and gave her a bit of money for an abortion, but she wouldn't do it. She had to make up a bunch of stories, then move to one of those homes for unwed mothers and give up her baby for adoption. It broke her heart. It broke *her*." She lifts her chin, anger fueling her determination to go on. "The thing is, he threatens to fire us and tell Norma's parents about her—they'd kill her, he figures. He's probably right. Plus he's a big guy, our boss, and intimidating. Mr. Baldwin, his name is. Paul Baldwin of Baldwin Import-Export. 'Call me Paulie,' he says," she mocks. "Now he's got his eye on the new girl, Joanie. She's panicking. She needs this job; we all need our jobs. It's his company. Well, his wife owns it."

"Tell me," I say, "how well does he pay you?"

"He does pay us well," Alison replies. "That's part of the problem; we can't afford to leave."

"Being beholden to men like Paulie is a form of slavery, no matter what he pays you," Belladonna says. Not a tremor in her voice. Oh ho, what sublime self-control!

"You mentioned his wife?" I say. "There's always a wife."

"Yes, her name is Suzie-Anne. She's as fat as he is, and just as awful. Worse in some ways, because it's her money. We are expected to pick up her dry cleaning, or run other errands, or walk her dogs. After work hours, so she can humiliate us." Alison's eyes are flashing. "Suzie-Anne comes into the office sometimes to check up on Paulie. Let him know who the *real* boss is. She's got to have figured out what he's like, but of course she treats us as if it's our doing." She shudders. "The sound of her bangle bracelets and her heels clacking on the floor makes us all crazy. Plus she wears this disgusting fox stole with the little heads dangling, and flips it around in our faces."

"Sounds like they should both be strangled with it," I say, picking up my notepad. "We need more specifics about Paulie, so we can fight fire with fire. Give him a taste of his own medicine."

"Well," she says, "when he's getting in one of his moods, he starts calling us 'honey-baby.' 'Honey-baby, come here. I need you,'" she mimics. "Then he says, 'Do you see what you do to me?' and points to his crotch," she goes on. "'I might have to show you what a real man is for.' When he can corner us in the hallway, he . . ." She sighs. "What he did to Norma is bad enough. It can't happen to Joanie, too. Some of the others are getting sick, they're so scared he might really attack them. I don't know what to do. I can't take the time off to look for another job, and my mother isn't well. She looks after my little boy, Toby. He's nine."

"We don't mean to pry, but is your husband . . ." I start to ask.

"He died at Guadalcanal," Alison says simply.

"I'm sorry," Belladonna says.

"Thank you," she says. Her office mates certainly picked the right representative; she's a trooper, this one. I like her more than ever. If Belladonna weren't such a solitary soul, I'd almost suggest they might be friends.

"Plus he has peepholes in the bathroom, I swear it," Alison

adds. "We aren't sure where, but we can feel it . . . a two-way mirror or something. Just the thought of it . . ." She shudders.

Belladonna and I exchange a swift glance. Better take extra precautions as long as Alison's in the club.

"We're not going to tell you what or how exactly we'll deal with him yet," I explain, having gotten the signal from Belladonna to proceed. "It's better if you don't know any of the details, because then he'll have fewer suspicions once his plans take some unexpected detours." I smile broadly. This one is really going to be a scream. "You'll know everything is in order when he receives an invitation to the Club Belladonna. He'll be gloating about that, no doubt. Try not to laugh, or let on that you know anything about it. Soon afterward, Paulie and Suzie-Anne won't be bothering you anymore. We promise you."

"I should like you and your colleagues to be my guests here the night that Paulie and Suzie-Anne are invited. To a costume ball," Belladonna says. It is a command rather than a question.

"We'll give you plenty of notice about the date," I add, immediately figuring out Belladonna's intentions. "And if you give us all of your measurements, shoe sizes, glove sizes, head sizes, et cetera, we'll have the costumes made and sent to you. That way, the Baldwins won't recognize you, even if you're sitting at the next table. And you'll hear everything. But no husbands or boyfriends allowed that night, just the nine ladies. Leave every detail to us. It'll be an evening you'll never forget, I promise you."

"You'd do all that for us?" Alison asks, her cheeks scarlet. "Why?"

"Because I can," Belladonna says sharply. She picks up one fan, spreads it open to see a scene of frolicking picnickers dressed as baroquely as she is, snaps it shut and chooses another. "So many women are dependent upon their circumstances and have few options to change them. I, on the other hand, am not. I create my own options, through whatever means are necessary."

Cunning, cleverness, Jack's devoted and well-trained staff, she is saying. Plotting and planning. Bribes, of course. Finding the best lawyers sympathetic to women, which is a Herculean feat in 1953. And determination never to fail.

"Who *are* you?" Alison asks.

Luckily, Belladonna does not panic, for she can sense that this is not a loaded question. Alison's face is merely shining with simple curiosity.

"I am Belladonna," she says. "But I was not always so. I shall tell you only that I have been acquainted with too many of the Paulie Baldwins of this world. That is all you need to know."

She is still toying with her fan. I am amazed. She's never revealed so much—even if it is, in fact, so little—to any of her ladies. Whenever the ladies are allowed into this office, they do most of the talking. Yet they leave with the impression that Belladonna has filled their heads with impossibly cunning ideas, even if she's said no more than *Why are you here?*

"We live in a time when, as you wrote me, a woman is not allowed her voice, even for something as simple as ordering a cocktail," Belladonna goes on. "Why, for example, should not a woman like you, with your brains and your courage, run an import-export company like Paulie's?"

"I'm not—" Alison interjects.

"Of course you are," Belladonna says. "You are brainy enough to have written a letter that caught my attention, and you are courageous enough to have ventured into my lair."

Alison smiles for real this time.

"Surely all of you know as much about the import-export business as Paulie does, if not more," Belladonna adds. "But do you think for an instant his colleagues would embrace you into their fraternity as long as he remained to undermine your confidence?"

Alison shakes her head.

"Of course not. But I don't let men like that stop me. I care not a whit for their approval."

"That reminds me of a woman who got back at a man like Paulie—her husband," Alison says.

"Tell us," I command.

"They had his and hers cars," she says, "and both had sets of keys for them. Well, she knew he was having an affair, even though he denied it and blamed her for all the usual, and she got so fed up she followed him after work. Sure enough, he was meeting his girlfriend in a motel near Idlewild. She waited awhile, then got out of her car, pulled *his* car out of the space and replaced it with hers, and drove home. Can you imagine his face when he came out of that motel room with his girlfriend and saw his wife's car?"

I burst out laughing, and I fancy even Belladonna might be smiling as she gets up to leave the room as silently as she entered it.

"Here are the checklists," I say to Alison, who is trying to digest all of Belladonna's comments, and doesn't seem put out that Belladonna didn't say good-bye, "which the nine of you need to fill out as soon as possible and send back to us. All the instructions are enclosed."

"Thank you," Alison says, taking the files and shaking her head. "I think I'm dreaming. Can I ask you something?"

"You can ask whatever you like," I reply, "but that doesn't mean you'll get the answer you're looking for."

"No, it doesn't," Alison says, "but I have to try."

"Of course." I get one of my altogether brilliant flashes. I'm going to have Jack handle Alison's case personally. I've just decided that she's the one for him. Oh, I tried fixing him up with Marisa, but she was more interested in painting her cavorting nymphs than in a brooding detective. He's not said anything to me or anyone else, but we know he's in love with Belladonna. We also know it's a futile proposition. He's such a good man, and works so hard for us. This club isn't going to last forever. He needs to think about his future.

"Does Belladonna know what she means to women like me?" Alison asks, interrupting my matchmaking thoughts.

"No," I say, "I really don't think she does."

"Will you tell her for me?"

"Of course. And now one of our drivers will take you home." I escort her outside, where Dickie G., one of our off-duty cops, is waiting in a Cadillac that seems to take up half the block.

"I'd like to give you a hug," Alison says. "Then I think I might believe this is really happening."

"We're not much on hugging in the Club Belladonna," I say, not wanting to hurt her feelings. I know I am eminently huggable, but I am a little self-conscious about my girth. "But I appreciate the sentiment."

She smiles, gets in the car, and waves good-bye. She will be even more astonished, I know, when Dickie hands her three packages. "The envelope's for you and the ladies you work with," he says, "to be divided evenly for preparation expenses or anything else. The larger package is for your mother, and the small one's just

for you. I've got something for your son in the trunk." Inside the
envelope are eighteen crisp hundred-dollar bills; inside the large
package is a pale blue cashmere shawl; and inside the smaller is a
pair of Belladonna's kidskin gloves in a shade of honey brown that
exactly matches Alison's hair. Her son will be amazed when he sees
the electric train set. There are so many boxes, Dickie has to make
three trips up Alison's stairs.

It's the little gestures that count.

*A*t the Countryside Ball a few weeks later, one of the banquette
tables is a vision, decked out with a dozen masked shepherdesses.
No, I haven't miscounted; we added three of our Washington
Street "hookers" to round out the number and not cause any suspicions. One of the waiters confidentially tells Paulie and Suzie-Anne
that the shepherdesses next to them are visiting from Iceland, so
they won't think the fetching creatures can speak English and recognize a telltale voice.

All we need are some sheep.

Paulie is dressed as a country auctioneer, while Suzie-Anne is
dolled up as the auctioneer's wife. Which means she is really not in
a costume at all. She is, in fact, still complaining that the bitch of a
coat-check lady made her check her beloved fox-head stole. "But
foxes come from the country!" Suzie-Anne protested, to no avail.

Belladonna herself looks like a pink Dresden shepherdess as
she climbs up onstage. Her bodice is pale pink satin, like her mask;
her skirt, different shades of rose pink over cerise-pink petticoats.
Her lipstick and gloves are a bright shocking pink, and her rings
are glistening pink tourmalines.

"Good evening, ladies and gentlemen," she announces to rapt
applause. "Thank you for joining me at my Countryside Ball." She
opens her fan, painted with what seems to be a bucolic scene of a
fresh-cheeked Jack clambering up the hill with a blushing Jill, and
begins waving it idly to and fro.

"The law of the countryside—of nature, I should say instead—is survival of the fittest, is it not?" she asks sweetly.

There is no immediate reply, because the guests in the Club
Belladonna are puzzled. Is this meant to be a special Belladonna
kind of rhetorical question? What if they give her the wrong an-

swer? Will she lift the lid off one of her rings and drop some bubbling poison into their drinks?

"Only the *fittest* are allowed inside the Club Belladonna, are
they not?" she goes on. "How many of you consider yourselves the
strongest and most powerful creatures in the country? You, sir?"
she asks, pointing her fan at one man, who turns as scarlet as Belladonna's shoes. "Or you?" She points to another. "Or you? Are you
the hunter, or the fox? The strong, or the weak?"

She takes a step closer to the edge of the stage. "If indeed the
law of the countryside is survival of the strongest, what happens to
the weakest? Where can they turn? Who will protect them? Must
the hunter always catch the fox?"

She steps off the stage, the spotlight following her as usual.
"Who looks after the weak?" she continues, the sweetness of her
voice instantly hardening into a cold tremor. "Who punishes those
who prey upon the weak? Who hunts the hunter who kills the fox?"

She walks slowly from table to table, pausing to ask each couple, "Who is strong, and who is weak?" Sometimes she stops before a group of terrified yet exhilarated guests, and they can sense
her frigid smile taunting them. "Who is the hunter?" she asks.
"And who is the fox?"

Who are you? Why are you here?

"She's the strong one," one man says, pointing to his wife with
such alacrity that Belladonna laughs, and the room breathes a collective sigh of relief at that delicious sound. How quickly they forget that only seconds before her voice had chilled the marrow of
their bones.

Belladonna moves on, trailing her fan over one milkmaid's wig
and pulling a piece of hay from her date's straw hat to chew on.
Everyone is laughing now, indulging Belladonna's little joke. She
stops before a group of farmers and their wives, dressed for a
square dance, their costumes clearly homemade. "They're the
hunters," one of the farmer's wives proudly announces, linking her
arm in her husband's.

"Hunting for his two left feet, you mean," another wife says,
and everybody giggles.

"Then you must dance for us," Belladonna tells them, and they
look at each other with happy amazement while she whispers instructions to one of the waiters.

She continues around the room, stopping to talk at every table, as all her guests volunteer to be either the fox or the hunter, amid much merriment. Just as the band is beginning to warm up for a toe-tapping reel, she pauses between two tables near her own. One is full of shepherdesses in brightly colored costumes, their blond braids tied with gingham ribbons; a rather portly and self-important couple is sitting at the other. "Country auctioneers, I see," Belladonna says to the couple. "Who, then, is the hunter, and who is the fox?"

Lucky for Suzie-Anne she isn't wearing her beloved fox stole right now. Still, she blushes deeply.

"Aha, the fox," Belladonna says to Suzie-Anne, her voice still low and mellifluous. Then she looks at Paulie. "You must be the hunter. How splendid. A rare sight in the countryside. A rare sight indeed: the fox and the hunter, peacefully side by side."

Paulie and Suzie-Anne have no idea what to do. No one's paying much attention to them, with the fiddle tuning up and the raucous conversation ringing in their ears, but Belladonna's strangely calm presence is making them nervous. They wish fervently that she'd go away, when only minutes before they'd been gloating about being seated so close to the goddess's banquette.

"Tell me, kind sir, what do you hunt?" Belladonna asks Paulie.

"I don't know—" he starts to say.

"Oh yes, you do," Belladonna replies, leaning over to him and placing her fan sharply under his chin. "You know very well indeed. You, the *strong*. You, the *hunter*." She moves her fan over to Suzie-Anne's many quivering chins. "And you, fine lady, you, too, know very well indeed. Does that make you, the fox, strong or weak?"

Then Belladonna quickly pulls her fan away and returns to the table of square dancers. "Where's my little haystack gone?" she calls out. "It's time for him to watch the dance." Everyone laughs once more. Everyone except Paulie and Suzie-Anne.

"I've had just about enough of this nonsense," Paulie is saying, his cheeks stained a deeper pink than Belladonna's kidskin gloves as he moves to get up. "Those bitches must have—" He freezes, though, startled by the sudden appearance of my darling big brother, who is blocking their intended exit. Matteo signals to them to stay put, and they have no choice but to obey the sinister doorman. All they can see are his eyes glowing behind his mask and the mocking downturn of his lips.

"Paulie and Suzie-Anne Baldwin, I presume, of Baldwin Import-Export?" Matteo asks. "Well, well, the fox and the hunter. Paulie, the hunter of *women*. Suzie-Anne, his little pet fox." Matteo's voice is pleasantly conversational, loud enough to be heard only at the next table. He is hardly lisping, so intent is he on making his point. "I have a few words of advice for you," he goes on. "If you *hunt* any woman in your employ, any woman whatsoever, I am personally going to *hunt* you down and chop your balls off."

This specific topic is my suggested addition for the evening's entertainment. Matteo didn't want to say anything like this any more than I wanted to think it up, but I knew it would add a special kind of resonance to his warning.

"Then I am going to take a butcher knife and cut your balls up into tiny pieces while you watch," Matteo continues. "And then I am going to pry open those lips that spill lies and cause pain, and I am going to shove them down your throat."

All the shepherdesses are listening intently, but Paulie doesn't notice them. His cheeks are now dead white.

Matteo turns to Suzie-Anne. "Shall I tell you what I'm going to do to the fox?" he asks. She shakes her head nervously, her lips beginning to blubber. "Very well. Have I made myself perfectly clear?" They both nod vigorously. "We're going to be watching you, the fox and the hunter, and I can assure you that it's not nice being the *hunted,* wondering when we're coming to get you. Rest assured, my dear Baldwins, we *will* get you."

Matteo straightens up, smiles, and ushers them out, giving them a complimentary bottle of perfume they don't know how to refuse. Josie gently drapes Suzie-Anne's beloved fox stole over her shoulders. For some reason, Josie neglects to tell her that she's been busy sewing frozen baby shrimp into the heads of the little foxes. As soon as they thaw and begin to decompose, Suzie-Anne's adored fur is going to stink with a most mysterious stench. One that makes the sulfurous waters of Saturnia seem like a summer bouquet of honeysuckle rose.

When I tell this to the table of shepherdesses, we laugh for a good long time. Even Norma is laughing.

Let me add only that, not long after the Countryside Ball, the nine female employees of Baldwin Import-Export walk out of the office one day and never come back. They've all gone to work for higher pay and better jobs at Paulie's most hated rival, taking his biggest client in the process. It wouldn't surprise me if Alison ends up running the company herself one day. She's always had the savvy. All she needed was a small steer in the right direction.

I'll ask Jack to keep an eye on her progress. Besides, it isn't too difficult to ask for a slight favor or two in the import-export business, you see. There are still a great many people who owe one to a certain shipping magnate named Leandro della Robbia.

Ah, Leandro, the very thought of you nearly breaks my heart. Can you see us? Can you send us a sign? What would you have said to us as the bewigged shepherdesses erupted in joyful celebration?

If only the Baldwins were people more important to Belladonna. Someone, anyone, just one member of the Club. It is so hard to be patient. She will get him. Of that, I have no doubts.

It's just taking a lot longer than any of us would like.

8

Voices That Could
Melt a Glacier

*M*atteo seems to have found his voice. It is all because of Annabeth, and I'm happy for him, truly I am. So is Belladonna. Don't doubt me on this one. We never dared dream that one of us might find some measure of normalcy, to be surrounded by comfort and love. Belladonna is not so cruel that she would deny it to my brother.

Except there is one minor problem.

It's not that Annabeth is pressuring him or, indeed, expecting Matteo to share her bed, but the issue is going to come up—or not, in this case—and there's no getting around it.

"What am I going to do?" he asks me one afternoon. "She deserves a whole man."

"She had a whole man, and look what he did to her," I retort. "Besides, she has children already, so that can't be too much of a worry."

"It's not having children. You know what I'm talking about."

"I have vague recollections that there are other ways of giving a woman pleasure, you know."

"Of course there are. I just don't know how to tell her. What if she doesn't want me?"

My heart flips over with tenderness for my darling big brother. "How could she not want you?" I say with some indignation. "She's madly in love with you. This is just a tiny little glitch."

"Don't be a fool, Tomasino. It's a lot more than a tiny little glitch."

"I'm not a fool. I'll be glad to tell her, if you want me to. It won't bother me at all," I say brashly, lying through my teeth. Anything for Matteo, anything to get this over with. The shame of our condition and the secrecy we impose upon ourselves are terrible burdens, especially when a person thrives on sympathy and concern the way I do. "And you know what, it's about time that Jack heard this story, so we'll ask him to join us. Let me do all the talking."

"What else is new?" Matteo asks, and I know his feeble comment is his way of trying to console me.

I'll need his consolation when I am through, looking at Annabeth's and Jack's stoic faces a few days later as we sit and have tea in Belladonna's banquette in the club a few hours before opening. They know something's up. I decided we should meet in neutral territory, as Belladonna is not yet ready to have a woman—even one so dear to Matteo—come to the house and blow our cover. This way, Annabeth can leave if she wants to, and Matteo can put his mask on and cover his misery at the front door. He's sitting now at the edge of the banquette, staring down at the highly polished dance floor. I try not to look at his face.

I pour a rather large shot of single malt into my tea, even though a nice bracing hot toddy is hardly enough to get me through what I'm about to say.

How many years has it been since that damp afternoon when my brother and I were tortured and cut? Ten? Yes, ten, that's right: It was 1943, and we were up in the mountains near the Italian/Swiss border. What month was it? I don't want to remember. It was cold, that's enough. I have blanked out the very worst, although I have always coped with our situation better than Matteo. Must be my naturally genial disposition, or maybe because my much-maligned powers of speech thankfully remain intact. Bored with all the screaming, they casually snipped the tip of Matteo's tongue when he still wouldn't talk. I've never seen so much blood. Or at least I hadn't until they cut us where it hurt the most, then threw our most cherished flesh to the dogs to stop their barking.

Then they left the room abruptly, and never returned. How His Lordship stumbled upon us—how an Englishman like him even got to the Germans in that part of Italy at that point in the war—remains a mystery, but I decided he was double-dealing with the Fascisti, or whoever was expedient, and they crossed him. Then he crossed them worse, killed them all, took their prisoners, their money, their guns, and disappeared.

When we heard the click of the lock on our cell we steeled ourselves for death, which considering what had befallen us might not have been such a horror for yours truly, as I had been a gloriously sex-obsessed young buck. Instead, we looked up from the blood-soaked floor to see the glossy polish of leather brogues and the hem of a loden cloak, wrapped around a bearded man wearing, surprisingly, sunglasses, the rest of his face shadowed by a wide-brimmed hat and a scarf. He beckoned to us with gloved fingers, and we crawled after him.

It was a terrible blur; I don't want to remember the journey, bouncing, bleeding still, and trying not to moan too loudly in the back of a convoy of long cars with fluttering flags. It was a marvel indeed that this man and his gang managed to drive through Switzerland and into occupied France; with what conniving connections, bribes, and thievery they arranged the gasoline and the route at the height of the fighting, I didn't want to know, for fear that the knowledge would be lethal. Why us? I wondered. Why bother? Perhaps it was our American accents, or just plain dumb luck. Perhaps he did it simply because he could, or to prove something to the double-crossers. Whatever it was, I figured, he needed loyal foot soldiers for some nefarious purpose, and assumed we'd be blindly devoted, forever indebted to the man who'd saved us from certain death. Who he was or what he really looked like—we never did see his face clearly—was of little consequence. "I've freed the slaves, so you can call me Mr. Lincoln," he said to us when the journey was over. We'd been deposited at a crumbling château hidden so deeply in the Belgian forest near the River Meuse that we never left the immediate perimeter. Not that we could have even if we'd wanted to, but had we tried I know we'd never have found our way back. When we could get up out of bed and started walking around the overgrown gardens, Mr. Lincoln showed us the barbed wire running the length of the stone fence that encircled the dozens of acres of the property. Then he introduced us to Markus, whose grimace meant to be a smile set me, weakened and no longer myself, to trembling. He was living with his equally hideous wife, Matilda, the housekeeper, in the stone house guarding the only gate out. Markus's cousin Moritz had a room upstairs and down the hall from us, and his disposition was even worse.

We didn't ask, and we didn't want to know.

Mr. Lincoln told us we were safe as long as we remained under his protection. He expected us to take all the time we needed to get our strength back, and then to start rebuilding and repainting the rooms damaged by departed soldiers. He told us Markus and Moritz would make sure we got whatever we needed, but they had very bad tempers, especially if they didn't know where we were at all times. So once we figured out what was most essential and gave Markus our shopping list, he and Matilda would disappear down the curving forest road to the nearest village on wobbly bicycles, returning silently with whatever they could scrounge from the black market.

Most important, Mr. Lincoln went on, was that we were forbidden to ask any questions of any houseguests there might be. He told us a man named Henry Hogarth would be his liaison. And he left us, for nearly three and a half years. The war ended and the world heaved a sigh of relief. Hogarth, a dapper small man with darting eyes, dropped in without warning from time to time. His nearly bald head was shaped like a hard-boiled egg, and he favored mahogany brown fedoras or jaunty red berets to cover it. But mostly I remember his skintight black leather gloves, his paisley silk handkerchiefs, and his brilliantly white silk scarf flamboyantly thrown over one shoulder. He'd watch us scrape plaster from the walls, then brush imaginary dust off the sleeves of his Kilgore French Stanley suit with a horrified flick, and leave again.

Once the war was over we no longer feared invasion, and Matilda's cooking gradually improved as more food became available. Slowly we healed, physically at least. I suppose you may well be asking yourself why we didn't try to leave, why we chose to remain hidden in the forest to lick our wounds. Look at it this way: The traumatic shame and humiliation and perplexity of our reality ran deeper than the cut itself. We decided to stay as servants, not yet ready to face the world, and servants we would remain. Until I would have one of my hunches and know that the time was ripe for change. I wondered from time to time if my hunches had disappeared with my manhood. The energy to fight had left us, you see. As well as the energy to dream.

And so we painted the walls and gilded the banisters, gardened, read. I devoured books from the immense library we found crated in the basement and moved, box by box, upstairs to the shelves we built. I filled my head with words and facts and experiences I'd never dreamed of in Bensonhurst, gulping down volume after volume in a vicarious stupor as each day and month melted into the next. We tried not to eat too much, and to stay fit, because we were starting to run to fat. We had wild mood swings. We moped; we raged. We got drunk on the bottles of Haut Brion we found moldering in the wine cellar. The bleeding had long stopped, but not the pain of loss, and the weirdness within that had changed us so. It's not that I don't think every man ought to have a bit of the feminine in him, to have the sensitivity of quick and delicate feelings, but no man ought to *be* effeminate if it is not his choice.

Matteo was no coward, but he had always been as desperately shy and unsure as I was full of the braggadocio of youth and virility. He'd taken life much more seriously than any of our gang. Already glutted with my share of women—in fact, I'd been as insatiable as a bull let loose in a field of heifers—I used to tease Matteo unmercifully that he was the only Guido in Italy who never got laid. Slow to conversation in any language, he'd been embarrassed by his broken Italian; I, on the other hand, had used it to my advantage to seduce the local maidens who thought we'd come from Hollywood, not Bensonhurst. How ironic that we were raised in Brooklyn, and were probably the only Americans dumb enough to go visiting cousins in the home country in late 1939. I'm not sorry my streetwise cockiness quickly got us hooked up with the partisans—until we were caught, that is. Sometimes, in my dreams, I have flashes of memory: of the feel of a woman's flesh as she squirmed and moaned in pleasure beneath me, the ravenous gluttony of physical satiation. Matteo has nothing but pain and silence, and for that, I blame myself.

That was when we met Belladonna.

There's nothing to add about *that* encounter. I told you about it already, so don't ask me to elaborate now. No no no, you're going to have to wait for more.

There is a very long silence when I finish my tale. Matteo barely seems to breathe, he is sitting so still and looking so forlorn. Annabeth has been in tears since I first mentioned Mr. Lincoln, and even the imperturbable Jack looks stunned.

Annabeth wipes her tears away and gets up to go over to Matteo. She kneels down next to him and tries to take his hand, but he pulls it back. "Don't push me away, Matteo, please," she begs. "I don't care what happened to you. It doesn't matter, truly. You're the bravest, the sweetest, the most wonderful man, and I love you the way you are. So do Marshall and Charlotte. You've become part of our family, and we need you."

Two tears trickle in a slow straight path down Matteo's cheeks as he stares down at his shoes. I feel her presence and look up to see Belladonna watching us from the shadows. She shakes her head ever so slightly, so I look away, back at my brother.

Annabeth leans over and cups Matteo's face with her hands, tracing his tears with her thumb before wiping them away. "Come home with me now," she says gently. "Please. Can you take the night off? Darling, please. I need to be with you tonight."

"Go," I say, "Geoffrey will be thrilled to be in charge."

Annabeth stands up and holds out her hands. Matteo looks at her eyes shining with love and tenderness, and two more tears spill out of his own. It is all I can do not to burst out sobbing, sentimental softy that I am. I glance over to the shadows and see that Belladonna has disappeared.

Matteo looks at me and I try to smile at him, and he leaves with Annabeth.

"I'm sorry, Tomasino," Jack says eventually.

"Thank you, but you don't need to say anything," I tell him.

"May I ask you one thing?" he asks, and I nod. "What about your family? Do they know you're here? Do you want me to check for you?"

"That's very kind," I reply, trying to blow my nose with some dignity, "but they were told we're dead. Besides, our father died in 1944, and our mother died two years ago. We had someone ask, just to be sure. I don't think we could face the rest of them. Not after all this time. It's easier for them, this way."

"Would you like photographs, just to see them?"

Yes, I want to scream, but I don't. I can't think about them. Nor can Matteo. We've blocked it all out: our past, our childhood and home, our other brothers and sisters and cousins and the whole noisy lot. About what we used to be.

"Belladonna is our family now," I say.

"I understand," Jack says, and leaves me to sit in the empty room with the ghosts of what made me.

*A*nother steamy night in the club, and we are rather desultorily spooning our gin and tonic sorbets, the summertime special, out of silver bowls. No one around us is remotely interesting, and Belladonna is in a foul mood.

I can hardly blame her. The waiting game is not fun anymore. Not even for me, with my boundless capacity to enjoy the silliness and stupidity of the thousands who've stepped through the mirrored gateway into the Club Belladonna.

"I woke up and couldn't remember what happened yesterday, not even anything Bryony said," Belladonna frets. "What does that say about me?"

"All it says is that you didn't do anything particularly worth remembering."

A new group of guests arrives, and after avid, pointed nods in our direction, start loudly gossiping, trying and failing to prove to us that they are worldly sophisticates.

"Married men are always safe to chase," says a woman, "but it so annoys their wives."

"Safe only because they're *already* married, you mean," a man retorts, "and you're spared the horror of having to live with them."

How true, I think, looking at the man, whose shoulders slope so steeply his shape resembles a wine bottle. His cheeks are as florid as a glass of cabernet, and his date's face is powdered as white as a stalk of asparagus grown in a cellar. They look like a nightmare version of Snow White and Rose Red.

"What a shock to contemplate—sober sex," he goes on. "Why, I'd completely forgotten that all my nerve endings could work. What terror! Frankly, I don't know if I could cope with it more than once every five years or so. Why, people say the *most* extraordinary things when they don't have any clothes on. Plus you can see *everything* so clearly. Honestly, you don't mind so much about the face if the rest is all right. Or is it the other way around?"

Snow White yawns widely.

"Am I boring you?" he asks.

"Not yet, Ronald darling, but I'm sure it won't be long now. You are *horribly* rude," Snow White retorts, patting his cheek a little too hard, "but I like that in a man. It's *so* endearing. Be sure to tell everyone about your new lover." She eyes the table. "She's half his age, double his height, with twice his stamina. Isn't that sweet?" Then she excuses herself to sashay off to the ladies' room.

Ronald watches her leave, then shrugs. "Isn't her hair lovely? Such a marvelous color, and it takes only a tiny bit of dye to get it that way."

"She was an amazing child prodigy," someone else says.

"My dear Dorothy, child prodigies stay seventeen until they're at least twenty-five," Ronald says.

"Like Dulcie," Dorothy says. "Did you hear what the oil tycoon did to her?"

"No," everyone at the table coos. "Do tell."

"Well," Dorothy says, batting her alarmingly fake eyelashes to see if I'm listening, "the tycoon invited her to dinner, and his butler let her in and took her to the dining room, telling her the tycoon would be right there. He poured her a drink and left, so she started gulping down the caviar. All of a sudden, she heard a dog barking from under the table—and there was her tycoon, his face made up like a dog, a dog collar around his neck, with a leash attached to the table leg. He barked again, then started whining that he was hungry and he wanted her to throw him some food."

"What did she do?" Ronald asks.

"She didn't know what to do, so she left!" says Dorothy. "What a fool! If she'd played her cards right, she could have gotten much more out of the evening than a few spoonfuls of caviar."

Dorothy's right. She should have taken the tycoon out for a walk. And then she should have tied him to a tree and left him there to bark for all the neighbors to see.

"Men like that don't pay for sex. They pay women to leave," Ronald says. "They have a lot more respect for the women they *do* pay."

"What about women who pay men?" asked Dorothy. "Gina de Lorenzo is seventy-eight, and her new boyfriend is forty-one. His mother said Gina should adopt him."

"Gina is a nymphomaniac," Ronald states.

"Every woman who likes sex is a nympho to you, dearest," croons Snow White as she returns to the table. "It's all about conquest, dearest Ronnie. But I've found that the great conquerors usually can't get it up." She smiles broadly. "I think all impotent men should be thrown off a cliff. If they *were,* the world would be a much nicer place for us. *I'd* never go to bed with a man who couldn't get it up. It's immoral *not* having sex if you're sharing the same bed."

"Julius says he can have sex only once a month," says one of the women, "when there's a full moon."

All this talk of sex is beginning to annoy me. Frankly, I'm sure most of these alleged sexual sophisticates go home and either read the Kinsey Report for kicks or tie on one of Mamie Eisenhower's little aprons before putting hubby's dinner in the oven.

"I want my cousin June here," Belladonna says to me suddenly. "As soon as possible. I've got to do *something;* I've got to feel that something is going to happen."

Naturally, just as she says that, Jack joins us. "There's a bit of a situation outside," he says, and he tells us what's happening.

A long black Cadillac had pulled up near the door, scattering the waiting crowd in the street, and two goons stepped out, straightening their fedoras and their ties in exaggerated gestures. They could have been sent from mobster central for the roles of swaggering hoodlums. Matteo stood guard, Andromeda growling softly, before nodding nearly imperceptibly to Geoffrey, who switched on the microphone. Our shadow bouncers had approached in an ever-narrowing ring, while the crowd remained frozen and silenced. The mobsters went up to the door, Andromeda barking fiercely.

"Shut the damn dog up," one of them said.

"I beg your pardon?" asked Geoffrey.

"Shut the damn dog up, I said. Mr. Bonaventura is coming in."

"Do I take it," Geoffrey replied with icy calm, "that neither of you is Mr. Bonaventura?"

"Get off it," said the other, pushing back his jacket to reveal his shoulder holster. "Mr. Bonaventura wants to come in, and Mr. Bonaventura gets what he wants."

"Is that so?"

"Yeah, it's so."

They hadn't realized yet that the entire conversation in all its eloquence was being broadcast to the crowd on the street, including the police, who were eating their sandwiches in their cars on each corner.

"Why, sir," Geoffrey drawled, "I do believe that's a gun you're flashing at me. Do you have a permit to carry such a formidable weapon, or am I just a lucky boy tonight?"

There was a nervous ripple of laughter.

"Quit stalling," the first goon said.

"But Andromeda is afraid of guns," Geoffrey replied. Before they knew what hit them, both goons were flat on their backs, their own guns pointed at their heads by the nimble fingers and superior skills of Matteo and Geoffrey. The crowd applauded as the police snapped cuffs on the cursing goons and hauled them away.

You could hardly imagine that Mr. Bonaventura himself was, at this point, a very happy bunny. But to everyone's surprise, he got out of his shiny black car, said a few words to his driver, who seemed to be arguing with him, and slowly approached the door. He was walking with a cane, just as Leandro had done, although there was no nobility in this Italian's face.

Jack had come out to join his trusted sentinels at the door, and there was a brief consultation. "It may be useful," Matteo said. "He may be Bonifacio Bonaventura, but he's not gotten this powerful by being as foolish as his bodyguards."

By the time Mr. Bonaventura reached the door, you could have heard a pin drop on the street. Even the cops preparing to haul the goons away were watching in surprise.

"Good evening," he said.

"Good evening, sir, and welcome to the Club Belladonna," Geoffrey replied. Andromeda, our obedient darling, remained silent as she had been instructed, her tail wagging. "Please, do come in."

Mr. B. nodded and strolled in. Jack hurried down the passageway to Belladonna and me while Mr. B., like everyone else, paid the entrance fee and checked his coat and hat. Josie looked questioningly at Matteo, but when he nodded, Mr. B. was allowed to keep his cane.

Jack meets Mr. B. at the end of the mirrored hallway and bows slightly. "Belladonna would be most honored if you would join her," he says.

Mr. B. is small and as dark as a Havana cigar butt, with the eyes of a sturgeon, I decide as he sits down at our table. Jack slides in next to him. Not what I'd call an attractive package, but I am not the one to judge any man's appearance, am I? Of course I am.

"I am ravished with delight that you could join us tonight," Belladonna says coolly to Mr. B., waving her fan at one of the waiters. "How might I make your visit as enjoyable as possible?"

The clubgoers are rapt and hushed, watching them. Everyone knows who Mr. B. is. Everyone's scared to death he's going to whack them right here in the Club Belladonna. They're forgetting whom he's talking to.

"I think you know what I want," he says.

"No, I don't believe I do," Belladonna replies, her face stony under the mask.

"I prefer to speak to you in private," he says.

"This is my private table. Consider yourself cut off from the rest of the world." And then, slipping into Italian, she adds, "We may speak in this language if you prefer."

She points her fan in my direction. "This is Tomasino, my personal manager, and Jack, who is in charge of security. Jack is not very fluent in Italian, so he won't be able to understand exactly what we're saying." No matter, he's savvy enough to figure it out himself.

That's what happens when you hire the best.

Mr. B.'s sturgeon eyes narrow a little bit more. He is not amused.

"So, *caro mio,*" Belladonna says brightly, "after that spectacular display outside, I am assuming your proposition is one of the utmost urgency."

Mr. B. frowns. This is not going according to plan. Belladonna does not fit the mold of the kind of women in Mr. B.'s rather particular, limited orbit.

A waiter comes by with a bottle of Dom Pérignon. "Thank you, Charles," she says after he pours Mr. B. a glass, and she beckons him closer. "Charles, Mr. Bonaventura has been discussing the quality of our staff with me. I believe he would like to see your papers."

Mr. B. looks perplexed. No no no, I am not impressed with him at all. This is the difference between Jack and men like Mr. B. Jack possesses that rare quality of stillness, of trained instincts and quick intelligence, of visual perspicacity. Of eyes in the back of his head, and a nose to ferret out danger. Of a willingness to wait, and plot with careful deliberation. Mr. B. wants what he wants when he wants it, and he wants it now.

Instant gratification is such a bore!

Charles flashes his FBI badge, and Mr. B. looks from him to me and Jack, and then to Belladonna. Then he surprises us all by bursting out laughing.

"You have my sympathy, signora," he says, toasting her with his glass. "They have beaten me to it. Although you will perhaps have need of my protection to keep you safe from these brutes."

"If I do," she says with a wink, "you shall be the first person I call." She waves Charles away and the crowd heaves a mass sigh of relief. "So, tell me about your family. And Italia. Where were you born?"

Jack slips away as they chat, and I pour myself another drink. Mr. B. is talking about the town of Sorrento.

"I've never been there, but whenever I hear 'Torno a Sorrento' I wish I were on the first boat over," Belladonna says.

"I sing it often," Mr. B. says, looking surprisingly wistful.

"Do you like to sing?"

"Only in my house. I always wanted to be an opera singer."

Of course he did. I smelled that one coming, but Belladonna doesn't miss a beat.

"Well," she says to him, fanning herself slowly, "perhaps you would like to sing it here."

"Here? What do you mean?"

"We're planning a masked ball in a few weeks, a forest fantasy. We shall make it an Italian forest, and you might please us by singing that aria, or any other aria of your choice. As you see, we have a wonderful band. I shall speak to our bandleader, so that you may come in that afternoon for a brief rehearsal, and sing to us that night. If you wish, you may wear a mask." She is nearly smiling behind her own mask. Nearly, but not quite.

Mr. B. is scrutinizing her carefully, finally. "You would do that for me?" he asks.

She shrugs. "It would be a pleasure."

*I*t is just like Belladonna that the only male recipient of her favor in the Club Belladonna is a thug, a boor, and a mobster. She hadn't asked him to sing because he intimidated her, or expected a favor in return, although Mr. B. assures her after his appearance the night of the forest fantasy—incognito, of course—that he would happily pull any strings or knit a pair of cement booties should she wish it. It's not such a bad thing to have a mobster owe you one.

She does it because she feels like doing it. Besides, Mr. B. has a surprisingly nice baritone.

But his voice pales and disappears into insignificance when Matteo comes to Belladonna just as Mr. B. finishes his second set. Even under his mask I can tell there's a look on Matteo's face I've been waiting to see for a long time. One of heightened expectation.

"It's Laura," he says. "Laura Garnett. She's here with a group."

Laura Garnett, well, well. An uninvited jolt from the past. This is a sign. I feel it careening down the veins from my knee to twinkle between my toes. First Laura, then June will come. She won't be able to resist the invitation we sent her for our Night in the Casbah Ball.

And then one of them. The members of the Club. One of them has to come now.

The sound of Laura's name transports me instantly back to Merano, to bitter water and a man with piercing hazel eyes, a cane topped with a golden lion, and a heavy burden. Leandro told us Laura had a voice that could melt a glacier. How appropriate that she's come here tonight. Maybe we could ask her to sing an encore with Mr. B.

Belladonna and I look at each other. "Did she recognize you?" I ask.

Matteo shakes his head no.

Belladonna smiles. She actually smiles broadly under the mask.

"How splendid," says my darling Belladonna. "Show her in. Show them all in."

9

A Whiff of the Waters

"Guy, you are such a *roué,*" says Laura with a fond smile. She is sitting with her friends at the next table, and we are listening carefully as they direct their comments our way. Two of them look vaguely familiar: the man named Guy, and the other Englishman. I know I've seen them in here before; I can't remember yet when.

Laura is as beautiful as ever, her skin flawless cream, her blond hair twisted into a tight chignon, her lips full and pink, her cheeks flushed with excitement. In the dim light of the club it seems she's aged only so slightly, but I'll bet that in the light of day the undeniable marks of her misery have left deeper tracings etched into her face.

"Naturally," says Guy, "like Peregrine, I have my reputation to uphold. But that's no reason for me to have patience with a man who is both a fool and a rogue, and willing to serve any master. Especially if that master is a woman." He winks broadly at Laura. "It is quite impossible to be 'in love' with a woman without experiencing on occasion an irresistible desire to strangle her." He pulls out a silver cigarette holder. "If you treat your lovers like dogs, you'll be much happier. What do our dogs want from us? Affection, firm discipline, and food. Give them that and they love and worship you."

"It reminds me of the lady who complained about her lover, who kept calling her a randy bitch in bed," Peregrine says. "He said, 'But darling, it's a compliment. I'm an Englishman, and you know how much we love our dogs.'"

General hilarity all around. Except from Belladonna, who is idly waving her fan back and forth. I can imagine the look on her face.

"Well, you've called your wife a bitch often enough, haven't you, Peregrine?" someone says.

"Quite right," he replies, "because she is. *Pauvre moi.*"

"*Pauvre toi,* bollocks," Guy says. "We all know she's"—he pauses for dramatic effect, then says in a stage whisper so loud we can hear it—"a lesbian."

Peregrine shrugs. "One can't have everything. Do you know what she said the other night? We were at a lovely dinner, and just before I was about to tuck into the most delectable roast quail she announced, 'Darlings, I have a terrible confession to make.' Naturally, I assumed she'd totaled the car or broken the Ming vase or contracted leprosy. But no. 'Twice,' she said, 'twice in my life I've slept with men.'"

More laughter.

Now I remember. Guy and Peregrine were here the night of the Ball of the Elements, sitting at the next table with a bunch of haughty fashion people. Guy is still tan and trim, his deep-set dark blue eyes flashing with wit and good spirits. Or is it malice? Botheration. I'd completely forgotten about them after the excitement with Annabeth. Now I am wondering who they are and how they know Laura.

"What a honeymoon you must have had! But can you blame her?" says one of the women at the table. "It is an indisputable fact that nearly all Englishmen—present company excluded, of course—are pathetic in the boudoir. If a man has gone to public schools, he's ruined for life. And I should know: I sampled the entire sixth form at Eton. Or should I say it certainly felt as if I had." She smiles. She has a lot of teeth. "The courtship la-di-da is quite fine and dandy, but when push comes to shove, well, they simply can't manage."

"But it is nice being courted," Laura says. "Nice does start to work on you."

Not in my Belladonna's book. Nice gets you nowhere.

"I suppose you heard what happened to Dragonier's *nice* sister," Guy says. His friends shake their heads no as he inhales deeply and blows perfect smoke rings into the haze of the club. "She fell in love with a wonderful man she met in Paris, married him rather spur of the moment, in the heat of passion, that sort of thing. He reminded her so much of someone she knew, you see. They both have eyes the same beautiful shade of blue, and they laughed about it, deciding that they were soul mates indeed. What luck to have found each other. They had an ecstatically passionate honeymoon and settled in for a long life of domestic bliss, although personally you are quite aware that I see no point whatsoever in entering the marital state. Are wedding bands and a mortgage in some mysterious way recompense for a lifetime of incompatibility and boredom?" He shudders. "We so often mistake chaos for passion and obsession for love."

"Oh do go on with it," Peregrine says, pouting. "One needn't pontificate in the midst of such splendid gossip."

Guy blows more smoke rings and waits a minute before continuing. He's a genuine piece of work, this one. A seductive, master manipulator, the type who's always going to be the one walking out the door, with his latest lady love begging him to stay.

"After a few months, Dragonier's sister—her name is Clementine, I believe—decided to go home with her lovely husband to introduce him to dear old mum and dad. As I recall, she was with child at this point. Yes, pregnant and beginning to show. Very sweet." He downs his drink and signals the waiter for another bottle of champagne. "There was only one slight hitch. Which, had Clemmie been a bit more observant, might have brought this sorry saga to a rather more abrupt ending before it was given a chance to begin."

The champagne arrives and Guy waits for his glass to be refilled. He certainly knows how to stretch out a story. I notice that Belladonna is paying very close attention. My toes start to tingle, and I feel a twinge of weirdness travel up my leg to lodge behind my kneecap in my premonition place.

"When Clementine arrived with her husband for the happy homecoming, her father took one look at the charming young chap and his face turned a rather interesting shade of puce," Guy continues. "It seems that daddy's dearest darling, in fact, had married the son of daddy's dearest mistress. She didn't know it, of course. Nor did her mummy. Only dear old darling daddy, who naturally felt his eyes drawn to Clemmie's lovely swollen belly."

"Is this true?" Laura asks. "How do you know?"

Guy smiles. "Would I make up such a wicked story merely to amuse you?"

"Well, what happened?" Peregrine presses eagerly. "I'm quite put out that I never ever heard one iota about this."

"She had the baby, of course," Guy says. "Dear old daddy was not about to confess to the monstrous consequences of his infidelity at this late stage, was he? It was rather divine retribution, though, don't you think?"

"Was the baby all right?" Laura asks.

"You could say she resembled both her parents quite strongly."

"You ought to be ashamed, Guy," Laura says, all humor wiped off her features. "Joking about an innocent baby isn't funny."

"You're quite right," he replies. "I do most humbly beg your forgiveness, darling Laura." Then he picks up her hand and kisses it. She smiles slightly, but I can tell she's still upset. Guy starts to pour her a drink but she waves his hand away.

"What do you think?" I ask Belladonna.

"I think she's still a mess," she tells me. "I want her in my office. And soon. I want to talk to her."

I show Laura in to Belladonna's secret lair a few days later. It was easy enough to have her tailed, and send her a note asking her to come to tea. We'd never been quite so brazen, but I figured Laura would be curious enough to show up. Surely she's heard that Belladonna has a way with women in need. Everyone in the world seems to know it, from the letters we get by the sackful.

Nor would she dare turn down an invitation from Belladonna herself.

Belladonna is already masked and costumed, sitting behind her desk, toying with her jewelry boxes, when Laura walks in, nervously clasping a camel-colored Kelly bag. I offer her a cup of Belladonna's favorite Lapsang souchong, and she takes it with a polite smile.

"Here at the Club Belladonna we have costume balls with different themes, as you may already know," I say conversationally.

"Yes, I'd heard that."

"Our Countryside Ball was a big hit," I go on. "Likewise the Carnival Ball, the Zodiac Ball, the Garden Ball, among others. We always welcome new ideas, especially from those who come from abroad. Americans can be so, well, *limited* in the scope of their imagination."

Laura looks a bit astonished that I seem to be soliciting her advice. "We were thinking of having an English Hunt Ball," I say, lying sweetly. "Perhaps you could advise us."

"I've never been much of a hunter," Laura says, "but I do have friends who would be pleased to talk to you, if you like."

"That's very kind," I say. "Do you happen to know if there are English-type hunts in countries like France or Italy?"

"France, I wouldn't know about, but in Italy . . . let me think," she replies.

"Ah, so you have been to Italy?" I ask. "I'm of Italian ancestry, so I'm partial to all things from that country, *senza dubbio.*"

"Yes, I used to go there quite often," Laura tells me. "I had a friend from school who lived there with her father. I'd visit her on school hols and wish her father were mine."

"What was her name?"

"Beatrice." She says it the lovely Italian way, *Bay-a-tree-chay,* and it instantly conjures a scent of basil wafting over us as we lounge on the terrace outside Leandro's bedroom.

"What happened to her?" Belladonna asks. It's the first time she's spoken.

"She died during the war," she says, venturing a glance at Belladonna. "In childbirth."

"And her father?"

"He died, too."

"Died when she did?"

"No, several years later. It was about six years afterward."

"What was his name?"

"His name?" Laura is perplexed by these personal questions. "His name was Leandro. Leandro della Robbia. He was a count, and in the shipping business."

I can't describe the effect of her innocently saying Leandro's name in this room, the blessed sound of it like a whiff of rosemary and lavender from Caterina's gardens. We so rarely speak of Italy, or Leandro. How I wish for Belladonna to bring him up so I can talk about how much I miss him, the conversations we had, everything he taught me. How he would have been pleased by our meticulous plotting and planning, by the ever-vigilant diligence of Jack and the Pritch and our spying waiters. How he would have smiled at the sight of Andromeda and her red toenails, guarding the door with her bark, and the sinuous curves of mirrored hallway leading our visitors into paradise. How he would have loved to have been seated with us at the center banquette, his golden-headed cane by his side as he watched and listened and laughed at the happy and ridiculous throng in the Club Belladonna.

"You miss them."

Laura nods. "Leandro helped me when things became difficult with Andrew."

"Andrew is your husband," I say. Belladonna had given me a signal, so I could take over the questioning once again. "What happened to Leandro?"

"He met this woman at a spa, in Merano. In Italy. It's where one goes to take the waters. This woman had a little baby, and she needed help. Leandro never told me what had happened to her, but it must have been something awful. She had two strange big men with her, bodyguards, I suppose. I really don't know anything about her. But I didn't like her. He took them in, you see, the woman and her baby and those two men. They went to live at his palazzo in Tuscany."

Funny to hear yourself described, especially as a strange big man. I'm glad Matteo is off this evening, home with Annabeth, and the slightly built Geoffrey is preparing to man the door proudly on his own. I don't want her to suspect that Belladonna is the woman with the baby, even though there's no reason she should. Laura rarely saw Belladonna when we were in Merano. Only me, really. Not that I am any less devastatingly attractive now, but my mask and costume are slightly more flashy than the casual wear I used to throw on in Italy.

And I'm not *that* big.

"Were you jealous?" I ask, trying to keep my voice kind. "I'd be."

Laura looks at me, and her eyes narrow slightly. I see her stiffen, realizing what she's confessing, but she's still too intimidated by Belladonna and flummoxed by our conversational twists not to reply.

"Did that woman live with him?" I press on.

"Not exactly together. Leandro had several houses on his estate. She kept to herself, getting over whatever it was that had happened to her, I suppose, but eventually they became quite close. Leandro wrote to tell me this."

"So what happened?" I ask.

"Leandro died." Laura shrugs, trying to pretend she doesn't care. "And the worst was that he married her."

"Who? The woman?"

"Yes. I was shocked. He'd married her secretly in Florence and they never told anyone."

"Did she want his money, do you think?"

It's strange. Laura never calls the woman she's talking about by the name she knew she had—the long-lost Ariel—and we are certainly never going to mention it.

"I don't think so," Laura says. "Obviously, he left her most of his fortune, but he also left me a tremendous sum. He was always generous." She is growing more confident. Must be Leandro's influence. "I think she had money, but I'm not sure. Leandro mentioned that she was not in need of anything but a man who asked nothing of her."

Belladonna is waving her fan back and forth like an automaton.

"What do you think he meant?" I ask after a long pause.

"I've no idea." Laura shrugs again, and frowns. "I find it quite difficult to believe I'm telling you any of this."

"It's always easier to talk to strangers," I reply. "Particularly when they are masked. It happens to us all the time, in the club. You've nothing to risk and much to gain."

"Gain? What do you mean?"

"You are in need of help, are you not?"

"How did you know?" Laura asks, her eyes narrowing again as she flushes a deep pink, like her lipstick. Lilac Champagne, I think the shade is. It suits her.

Blondes always do have a problem hiding their blushes, don't they? Natural blondes, I mean.

"A feeling," I reply calmly. "We were sitting at the table next to yours the other night when your friend began talking about a woman named Clementine and her baby, and it became obvious to us that you were upset."

"Wouldn't you be?"

"Of course. That's why we asked you here. To see if we could be of any assistance."

"That is terribly thoughtful." Laura bites her lip. I think she is wavering between misery and hauteur, just as I'd first seen her in Merano. "I don't know what to say; I don't really know Clemmie. Or her brother. I think they're all right. I'm quite . . ."

"Yes, it is a bit of a dilemma," I say to help her out. "I doubt Clemmie knows of her husband's quarterings. Alluding to such may create more problems than it would solve. But do you think your friend was telling the truth?"

"I honestly don't know," Laura tells me. "Guy can appear to be perfectly horrid, but he's a terribly good egg. He is not the type of man capable of inventing such a dreadful story."

"How do you know him?" I slip the question in so smoothly, Laura doesn't pick up on it. That's because she is blushing an even darker pink.

"He's a friend of my friend Hugh," she says.

I know what that means. Guy's the liaison between Laura and her *friend,* Hugh. How sweet. How convenient for us, once we get the Pritch on the case, I mean. Let's hope her taste has improved and this man is nothing like Mr. Nutley.

"Well then," I say. "Let us know if you need us for anything whatsoever. We can be very thorough."

"You're very kind."

"Kindness has nothing to do with it."

Laura pats her hair, that nervous gesture I remember, and wavers further. "Is it that obvious?" she asks eventually, bitterness tinging her voice.

"Of course not," I reply. "I have only assumed the problem to be your husband because that is so often the problem we find ourselves handling with the women who come to this office."

"My husband is an expert at *handling,*" Laura says.

"Then you must be more expert. We have a man in London who is a marvel at procuring the necessary evidence. If you write down the particulars, we shall be only too happy to pass along the information. With the utmost discretion, I assure you."

"I believe you would," she says.

Belladonna shuts her fan with a smooth click and Laura jumps.

"You have one thing working in your favor," Belladonna tells Laura, her voice flat.

"I'm sorry," Laura says, "I don't quite understand."

"He doesn't expect you to fight back."

Laura gives a ghost of a smile. "No . . . no, he doesn't."

"In the meantime, how long are you staying in New York?" I ask.

"Another week or so."

"And what are your plans? If you could do anything while you're here, what would you really want to do?"

"What I really want to do? More than anything?" Laura is still befuddled by the strange twists of my questioning—I'd certainly be—but too well-bred not to reply truthfully. "I suppose I'd like to sing before a crowd of people who are all deliriously pleased to hear me." She smiles coyly. "Isn't that ridiculous? Leandro used to compliment me on my voice, and encouraged me to take voice lessons, so I did. I still do, actually."

Her eyes nearly well up again, but a touch of weakness suits her. Under her brittle exterior she seems much nicer now than she was in Italy. That was years ago, after all. We're hardly the same; we can't expect her to be as she once was, either.

Yes, we have all changed. I am certainly more wonderful; my brother has found love. And Belladonna is her own creation. Sharper, harder, colder. *La fata,* the fairy princess locked in her tower. No longer is she a terrified woman with a little baby and two strange men, soaking up the bright sunshine by the fountain in Merano in a vain attempt to erase the memory of dark years. No longer is she a woman who could do no more than shut herself off in a tiled room in a Tuscan palazzo, pacing away her demons. Now she is mistress of the most famous club in the world. There is no similarity whatsoever between the masked marvel and the person Laura once glimpsed six years before.

I look at Belladonna and know her thoughts are exactly the same as mine. First Mr. B., and now this. It would almost be too much if it weren't so sad.

"Would you like to sing here?" I ask. "As a matter of fact, we just had a guest soloist for our Italian forest fantasy, a lovely baritone, who'd also told us he dreamed of singing before an audience. He came one afternoon before we opened and rehearsed with the band. I can assure you that he was thrilled with his performance. We would be pleased to do the same for you."

"You would do that for me?" Laura asks Belladonna, although I have been the one doing all the talking. "But why? You don't know anything about me."

Just like Mr. B.

"Because I can," Belladonna says. It is what she usually says. Laura feels Belladonna's bright green eyes boring into her, and her flush deepens. I would not like anyone to look at *me* like that.

Laura thanks us, and I show her out. She is still reeling; in fact, she hasn't got a clue about why the conversation veered the way it did during this extraordinarily odd encounter with the mysterious masked creature.

Belladonna is taking off her mask and wig when I come back into the office. She looks very tired. Bereft, even. Depleted. If hearing Leandro's name had that effect on me, how must it have been for her?

She disappears into her room at home, telling Bryony she has the flu so she will be disturbed as little as possible, and doesn't come out until the afternoon of Laura's rehearsal with the band. If Richard is surprised to see Belladonna hours earlier than usual, sitting in a dark corner, out of Laura's sight line, already costumed and wearing my favorite wig of honey-colored ringlets, he doesn't let on. Nor does anyone else. They're professionals who maintain their silence. If Belladonna is there, they figure, there must be a reason, so the musicians keep playing and the waiters bustle around, whistling as they check their tables.

After Laura finishes singing "You're Nobody Till Somebody Loves You," the band surprises her with a loud round of applause. She curtsies to them, and now I know what Leandro meant. Rich and surprisingly husky coming from such a fragile-looking blonde, her voice *could* melt a glacier.

She thanks the band and comes off the stage for a cup of chamomile tea that I have waiting for her.

"Thank you," Laura says to me, her cheeks flushed with excitement. "You have no idea what this means to me."

"You have a wonderful voice," I tell her. "You're going to be a big hit tonight."

"I hope so," Laura says, "and I needn't worry about the dog barking."

"You seemed to have no problem when you came here last week."

"That's true. I guess your dog likes me." She laughs in pure happiness. "I can't believe I actually sang with a professional band. And I didn't make a fool of myself!"

"I can't imagine you ever making a fool of yourself," I venture to say.

"Oh, I have done," Laura says. Still exhilarated, she's let her guard down. "I have done indeed. And you know, talking about Italy the other day made me remember something. Or rather, someone. It was years ago, at Merano, that spa I mentioned. I met this ridiculous man there who paid me all sorts of flattery, and I was too dreadfully muddled to see what a buffoon he was. Leandro wrote me afterward that some of the guests had nicknamed him Mr. Nutley."

Belladonna laughs, and Laura positively starts. She hadn't noticed Belladonna sitting in the shadows. But as Belladonna continues to laugh—the divinely intoxicating sound that could enchant the deaf—I see much of the fear in Laura's face melt away. The intense effect Belladonna has on people never ceases to amaze me. Perhaps they sense they can never have any approbation from this strange woman. Just who, exactly, is she?

A whiff of Belladonna is never enough.

10

The Steeling of
the Nerves

"Mommy, what's a spy?"

Bryony, perfectly nonchalant as she picks up her fork to make
a crater for gravy in her mashed potatoes, poses this question at
dinner.

I try not to choke as Belladonna calmly says, "What do you
mean, sweetie?"

"Jack and Tomasino were talking about spies. I heard them
when I came back from school."

"Where were they talking?"

"Here."

"Here in the dining room?"

"Mmm-hmm."

"Where was Rosalinda?"

Yes, where was her nanny at a crucial moment like that? And
where was my brother? Busy at Annabeth's apartment, I expect.
Frankly, I can't for the life of me remember talking to Jack about
spies, not here in the house. Just because I'm naturally gifted with
a prying disposition doesn't mean I'm indiscreet, and certainly not
around Bryony. Botheration. Perhaps we were talking about something else and she misheard us. That must be it, I tell myself.

"I wanted a cookie, and she was getting it from the kitchen, so
I came in here to look for Sam."

Double botheration. That transvestite doll is about to have Dr.
Tomasino perform a Christine Jorgensen kind of sex-change operation on it. This must also mean that my ineluctable penchant for

overhearing tasty tidbits is running in the family, if Bryony is already tiptoeing around grown-ups who are having conversations about boring grown-up topics. She doesn't need to know what a spy is—she *is* one already. Just like Belladonna, Bryony seems to have an uncanny knack for sudden appearances. We are going to have to be much more careful as she gets older. Very careful indeed. My knee is starting to twitch. This is a bad sign—I can feel it, like the wind changing course over the river sparkling at the end of our street.

"A spy," Belladonna says carefully, "is a person who watches people or places in secret, so no one knows he's there watching."

"Oh," she says, making gridded patterns in her potatoes with the tines of her fork. "Are they good or bad?"

"Well, some spies are good, if they're trying to catch bad people and that's the only way they can do it. When people are very angry and go to war, they use spies. And some spies are bad, because they watch people so they can steal things away from them."

"Were you a spy in the war, Mommy?"

"No, sweetie, I wasn't."

"Was Papa?"

"I don't know," Belladonna replies. "The war made a lot of people sad and hurt, and we didn't like to talk about it. Besides, I didn't know your Papa then. I met him after the war, when I was very sick, and he took care of me and made me all better, and then we had you."

Well, that's stretching the truth, but it's close enough.

"Can I be a spy? A good spy?"

Belladonna smiles. "Why would you want to do that?"

"So I can be like Jack and Tomasino."

I'm about to sputter that I'm not a spy, when Belladonna shakes her head almost imperceptibly.

"Stop playing with your mashed potatoes, and eat them up," Belladonna says. "What do you think Jack and Tomasino do? Why do you think they're spies?"

Bryony takes a bite and then says, "Jack works in a big office with the other spies."

"Did he tell you that?"

Bryony shakes her head no.

"Did Tomasino ever tell you he's a spy?"

Bryony shakes her head again, then looks at me carefully. "I changed my mind. Tomasino's not a spy," she declares. "He's too fat to hide."

Children can be such a nuisance sometimes. I stick my tongue out at Bryony and then pretend to start crying, until she laughs.

"You know it's not polite to tell anyone they're fat," Belladonna tells her daughter. "So what do you owe Tomasino?"

"A 'pology," Bryony says, pouting. "Sorry sorry sorry, la de da de da de."

"I was very sad when you said that," I joke, "but now I'm not anymore."

"Does Tomasino make you laugh so you won't be sad?" Bryony asks her mother.

"I'm not sad, sweetie," Belladonna says, leaning over to give Bryony a faceful of kisses, tickling her with her hair until she dissolves in laughter. "How can I be sad when I have such a delicious little girl?"

"Betsy's mommy said you're sad," Bryony states. At least she's moved off the spy kick for the moment. "Betsy said her mommy sees you pick me up from school, and she wants to know why you're so sad. Is it cuz Papa's dead?"

Not only are children a nuisance but they can be so damn honest you want to scream. No, this kid isn't going to need any spy training at all, she's so perceptive.

"Yes," Belladonna says, "sometimes I do miss Papa a lot and it makes me sad. But then I see you and I'm happy again."

"I know a song about spies," I tell Bryony. "Do you want to hear it?" She nods yes, so I start singing:

"Spies and spies and spies and spies and spies and spies and
    spies
Miles and miles and miles and miles and miles of spies.
You can't buy anything
You can't do anything
Because there's
Miles and miles and miles of spies and spies
Miles and miles of spies."

"That's a good song," Bryony says. "Do it again."

"But this isn't just a song about spies. It's about lots of things," I say, and start singing:

"Flies and flies and flies and flies and flies and flies and flies
Miles and miles and miles and miles and miles of flies—"

"I like spies better than flies," Bryony says, giggling.

"How about pies? Blueberry pies and strawberry pies and apple
pies. Let's sing about pies instead of flies."

"Okay," Bryony says happily. "I want pie for dessert."

"We're having applesauce for dessert tonight," Belladonna says,
"but tomorrow you can have any kind of pie you want."

Later that night, Belladonna sits down with me in her office
before the club opens. "When is June arriving?" she asks.

"About ten days, I believe," I tell her. "They're coming for the
Night in the Casbah Ball."

"Fine," she says. "Then you and I are going to Virginia tomorrow for a few days. I need a change of scenery, and I want to see
the house. Tell Jack and Matteo."

I try not to look surprised. We'd closed on the large plantation
house about six weeks ago, but Belladonna hadn't said a word
about it since then.

"I need to know we can move down there quickly if necessary,"
she adds, her voice flat. "I can't risk Bryony finding out anything.
This spying thing is too much. I know it's not your fault, but what if
she wakes up and catches us coming in from the club, or overhears
something else that's perfectly innocuous and asks more questions?
What if someone finally gets clever enough to figure out what's
going on? What are we going to say to her then? I couldn't bear it.
Truly, Tomasino, I couldn't. It's getting too risky."

"It's more than that," I say simply. Although she ignores me as
she adjusts her wig, she knows I'm right. Besides, I've got to divert
her from thinking we can pack up and move away, mainly because
we can't admit defeat. Not when we're so close. Not when I'm still
having such a good time lording over the Club Belladonna.

"I can't make it so easy that women begin to rely on someone
like me to solve all their problems," she'd told me the day before,
after her latest damsel in distress had left, glowing with happiness
that she'd met the infamous masked woman. Did this lady give a
thought to the scope of Belladonna's generosity, or the price she
herself paid for it? There sat Belladonna in her office afterward,
sad and dispirited. "After each blow *their* hope manages to revive,"
she added. "But where is my hope?"

"It's coming," I told her. "You have to believe it's coming. Leandro once told me that creating something is the only truly godlike thing we can do, whether it's creating a child or a sculpture or a loaf of bread for your dinner. Or creating a solution to a dilemma. And that it's a compensation of sorts."

"Compensation for what?" she asked. "Is my only calling to have created this creature, and be doomed to do nothing more than re-create it every night for the benefit of fools and desperate women? How many more nights can I endure, presiding over my table or walking around the room, anointing my guests as if I were la Santa Belladonna? How many more women can I face? How many more foundations can we set up? How much more money can I give away? The Lady Bountiful act is a farce, Tomasino, truly it is. Do you know, I take a wad of twenties with me whenever I go out for a walk, and some of the local bums are too embarrassed to take any more money from me. Can you believe that? Even they think I'm crazy."

"No they don't."

"How do you know? Do you have any idea what I did the other day?"

I shook my head no. My knee was now throbbing with anxiety. Where is Matteo? I thought. Why isn't he here? I can't do this all on my own. I need my big brother to come in and do something. He can soothe Belladonna when I can't. Anything to make her stop talking like this.

"I was out shopping for Christmas presents, and I saw a little boy ogling a train set in Macy's, like the one we'd given to Alison Jenkins for her son. Well, this mother said maybe Santa Claus would bring it, but from the look on her face I knew she couldn't afford it. I couldn't stand it, so I started talking to her, and I told her I'd overheard her son. I asked if she would please let me buy the train for him. Naturally, she was shocked and offended, but then I told her I wasn't meaning to insult her, but that I'd had a little boy once, and that she'd be doing me a great kindness if she let me help her. She gave me her address just to shut me up and get away."

"So you sent it to her house?" No one can refuse Belladonna, even when she is being least like her self-imposed persona.

"Of course I did," she said. "But that's not the point. I'm losing, Tomasino. Who can console me? Where am I to go?" She picked up a fan and left her office, slamming the door so hard my teeth rattled.

When Jack asks to speak to Belladonna a few days later, I assume it's about final preparations for June and George's visit. Yet I am only mildly surprised when he tells me he'd like to speak to her in private. No problem, I tell him, and promptly install myself in a hidden nook where I can snoop on the entire conversation.

"I need to ask you something, Jack, so I'm glad you wanted to see me," she says when Jack sits down. "Were you and Tomasino talking about spies the other day, when Bryony came home from school and found you in the dining room?"

"Spies?" he asks, bewildered. "I can't imagine we were. Certainly not in the house." He frowns, thinking. "The last time I talked to Tomasino in the dining room, I think we were discussing applesauce, because Bianca was making some and the house smelled of it. Maybe we mentioned Northern Spies or some such."

Yes, he's right. Now I remember. Silly of me to have forgotten such an important conversation.

"I see," she says, not mollified.

"Is something wrong?"

"No," she replies, but from her mood he can tell that something obviously is wrong.

"Belladonna," he says, "can I ask you a personal question?"

Jack is nervous. I've never seen him like this before, and he's much too much the pro to show it, but I can tell. Even though there's not a hair out of place and his shirt is as crisp as ever, the agitation is rising off him in slow, circling waves. My heart does a flip-flop for the poor guy, churning with lovesickness. He's savvy enough to know that his love is doomed to failure, but he's desperate enough to need to try.

I simply must find him a woman of his own. Encourage him to flirt with Alison or someone else, and soon. Jack is altogether an admirable man. I realize that it is hard for me—as well as Belladonna—to admit how true it is, considering that we view as loathsome nearly all male types overloaded with the testosterone I lack.

"That depends," she snaps.

"Forgive me if I am intruding on your privacy," Jack plows on gamely, "but I was wondering if I could do anything to make you feel better."

"You can find them and bring me their heads on a platter," she says. "I hardly consider that a personal question. You know what I want."

"I'm trying. We're all trying. You know I would if I could."

"I know." Her face softens, just a little.

"Belladonna—"

"Don't, Jack. Please don't," she says. "Not now. Not ever."

"You don't know what I want to say to you."

"I think I do. You're the last person I want to hurt. Please, don't make me say anything to cause you pain. You're very dear to me, you know, whether you believe it or not. But that's all you can be. You've become part of my family, ragtag misfits that we are. We couldn't do it here without you. Truly." She tries to smile, but she can't. "There would be no Club Belladonna without you, Jack Winslow, at least not a successful one. I'll never forget what we owe you. What *I* owe you. But I can't give you more than my regard for you as part of my family, and my respect and devotion. I can't love, Jack. It's as simple as that. I've no heart."

"I don't believe you. You love your daughter. You loved your husband."

"How do you know I loved my husband?" she asks, staring out to some unnameable place. "He saved me, he took care of me, he kept me safe. But love, as a husband and wife should love?" Her face is a blank. "And yes, I can say that I love my daughter, in my way. Tomasino and Matteo, too. But Bryony's all that keeps me going. Without her, I'd be mad, I'm sure of it. If I let myself think about how she came into this world, who her father—"

"You don't have to say anything more," Jack interrupts.

"You've never asked me for the details," she says, her face still that awful blank, "even though I think you have a right to have asked, considering how faithfully you work for me. You don't know how grateful I am that you haven't pressed me; it makes me trust you even more. I should have told you, but I can't, at least not yet. All I know is that I'm almost ready to leave. I'm not yet ready to give up entirely, but knowing I have a place to escape to will help me cope. I can't take much more."

Jack is terribly startled, but he tries to hide it. "Where are you going?" he finally manages to ask.

"Virginia, of all places. Tomasino chose a plantation there. It's perfect for my needs: a huge property, extremely private." She sighs. "The houses on the property are in remarkably good shape, so the necessary renovations are minimal. I've found a good school for Bryony, and we're moving after the holidays."

"What about the club?"

"Close it, of course. Leave it empty and mysterious. Just like me." She gives a bitter laugh. "I don't think we can give notice to any of the staff, in case word leaks out, so we'll continue to pay their salaries for a few months and hope that as many as possible will come back if we ever reopen. I simply don't know yet. I can no longer face the thought of this going on and on and on. I haven't the strength to do it."

"You can't give up now," Jack says, even though he knows nothing he can say will make her change her mind once it's made up.

"I'm *not* giving up," she says fiercely. "I prefer to think of it as a retrenchment. The women who come to me have become more of a faceless blur than they were at the beginning. There's no satisfaction in helping them, watching them find their way back to a measure of hopefulness. I can't do it anymore."

"You don't need me anymore," he says, staring down at the hands he's clasped so tightly in his lap that even from my hiding place I can see that his knuckles are white.

"I didn't say that," she replies. "I need you more than ever, but you know I can't ask you to move to Virginia. I don't think it would suit you; you'd be bored silly in the country with nothing to look at but trees and horses. But I'd like it very much if you moved in here, to watch over my house. There's always an endless pile of paperwork to keep the machine greased. And I'd also like you to set up an office somewhere else, for the foundation that will keep helping the women who write me. I think I know just the person to administer it. You'll like her."

Oh ho, my darling Belladonna, you are a bigger matchmaker than I am. I'm glad I'm not the only one who thought Alison and Jack would be a perfect couple.

"Don't patronize me," he says.

"I hope you'll never think that of me," she says. "I wouldn't fob just any woman off on you to assuage my conscience. If I had a conscience."

They sit in silence for a few minutes.

"What about Matteo and Tomasino?" Jack asks finally.

"I think Matteo's going to get married to Annabeth, and if he does he'll have my blessing. Much as I'd want him with me, I can't be so selfish that I'd deny him a chance for the happiness I'll never find." She sighs. "If they decide to stay in New York I'm going to have to learn to get along without him. But then you can continue to work together. Tomasino is coming with me."

That's because I am ever so indispensable.

"You love Tomasino," Jack says.

"Not the way you want to be loved," she says, "or the way you deserve to be loved. He's become a brother to me, and he's been damaged, too. It's as if he's my masterpiece of ruined civilization. A constant reminder of what brought me here. Do you understand?"

"No," he replies. "I'll never understand you."

"That's as it should be, Jack. I'm beyond understanding. I am a creature of the imagination, nothing more. *He* molded me. *They* warped me. I am hanging by a thread, and there's nothing I can do now to undo it but find them and make them suffer," she says, her voice low and harsh. "To torture them the way they tortured me."

Jack looks her full in the face. "I don't care about what you're saying to me now. I still feel the way I do. I still love you, whoever you are. Whatever happened to you."

"Don't ever say that to me again," she says after a few agonizing moments of silence, her face as hard as the masks she wears in the club. "You must promise me never to say that again, or I shall go mad."

Jack shakes his head no.

"Swear it," Belladonna says, her voice a hoarse whisper. *"Swear it."*

"I swear," Jack whispers back, tears in his eyes as he watches her get up and leave the room without a backward glance.

*A*fterward, it is as if that conversation had never taken place. Belladonna takes to her room with a stomach ailment, she tells us, and stays out of the club for nearly a week. When she does return, it is for our Night in the Casbah costume ball, one we had long prepared for. We pour hundreds of thousands of rose petals, both silk and real, on the floor, so guests will sink ankle-deep in them. Yards and yards of parachute silk are draped from the ceiling to give the illusion of a grand pasha's tent; the air is scented with frankincense and myrrh; and all our staff are wearing glistening turbans in addition to their usual masks. There are a lot of turbans tonight, actually, along with veils and swirling robes and extra bolts of chiffon, seen on guests too lame to think of anything but costumes copied from Rudolph Valentino films.

Belladonna is clad in an unusually sober costume, a chador, worn by devout Muslim women. Except theirs aren't dyed a deep crimson, or accessorized with endless loops of pearls. It hides the shapeliness of Belladonna's body and nearly all of her face. Only the faintest glint of her eyes can be seen burning intensely in the dusky light of the club.

Tonight, this glimmer is dark and disturbing. Belladonna had been fitted with brown contact lenses to mask the unforgettable color of her eyes. The lenses are thick and uncomfortable and hurt after being worn for more than fifteen minutes, but she doesn't mind. The discomfort keeps her focused, and we can't risk anything that might give her away, not one hint of who she had been. Not now, not after all our waiting and planning and plotting.

Pretty teardrops in her eye.

Tonight, Belladonna is unfathomable. That's because her faithless cousin June is sitting at the next table, gobbling down drinks with her husband. June has curled her hair into blond wisps, rouged her apple-dumpling cheeks and nails, and squeezed herself into what she must think is a flattering embroidered and gold-tasseled number, her bosom swelling like the storm surge during a hurricane.

Jack has joined the gleeful couple for their wonderful evening, and all the staff have been alerted that under no circumstances should he be recognized or acknowledged by any of them. He's just the nice Jack who met and befriended the Hauxtons in Kansas City several years ago, who's been kindly showing them the sights of Manhattan on their whirlwind visit.

The nice Jack who's an expert in cattle futures. The nice Jack who's about to devour George's company and leave him bankrupt. The nice Jack whose accomplices have begun to whisper appalling allegations about George's financial shenanigans and June's shameful betrayal to the pious members of her beloved Groveside Country Club. The nice Jack who will not sleep until the Hauxtons are reduced to social pariahs in their insufferable little world.

Let them find out what it's like to be cast adrift, to have no one to save you, to not understand why the world has betrayed you.

Let them find out what it's really like to suffer.

Seeing June and George makes me remember the afternoon when we sat on Leandro's terrace with the Pritch, as he downed one grappa after another and told us of Mr. Winslow and Kansas City and Camp Minnetonka and two young women who went off to London.

Another world away, a lifetime ago.

Belladonna says nothing when they come in. Clad in her chador and her veils, she resembles a cloaked statue, and the aura around her is so fraught with weirdness that no one dares approach her, even to thank her for such a splendid party.

"You wouldn't believe the problem we have with our cats," June, the brilliant conversationalist, is telling Jack with a giggle. "Sandy is the worst—she's so spoiled. Why, she won't come down to meals unless we're all ready for her in the dining room, and George rings our dinner bell. It simply must be the Lalique. Then she sashays in with her tail up and deigns to eat. It's *too* precious."

People are so utterly banal sometimes I despair of them entirely.

"That reminds me of a cat story. I had a friend during the war who was recuperating from surgery to amputate his little toe," Jack says. "From frostbite, I think. He was a bit of a showoff, so after his operation he took to reclining on a pile of cushions and receiving visitors who'd be dripping with sympathy and black-market goodies. He forgot to warn his visitors that his little toe would be reclining on a Limoges plate at his side, surrounded by flowers. A sort of makeshift shrine to his brave stoicism in the face of adversity."

June's smile fades and George's fingers tighten on the stem of his glass.

"Well, just as we're about to toast to my friend's health, his cat comes bounding in, pounces on the lovely Limoges plate, and runs off with his toe."

Now June looks positively green. George puts down his drink.

"Not every pet finds its master good enough to eat," Jack adds, ignoring their discomfort.

Belladonna bursts out laughing, so loudly and so very near to hysteria that the guests around us stop talking all at once, speculating about what's going on and what prime piece of gossip they might have missed.

"You sir," she says, pointing her fan at Jack. "Do join me. And your friends, too."

This is the cue. This is it.

Face-to-face after eighteen years.

They will come to you if they don't know who you are.

I study June's eagerly flushed face as I stand up and move aside to let her sit next to Belladonna. I can easily imagine what she looked like that London spring in 1935, her hair waved like Jean Harlow's, wearing bias-cut chiffon dresses that did not suit the round, flabby slope of her belly and bosom, her features soft and girlish. So eager to find herself a husband and a tiara that she'd do just about anything to get rid of her pesky, smarter, more beautiful cousin with the immense green eyes and alluring manner. Now, June is just a corner shy of blowsy, while Belladonna is ageless. There is nothing soft about *her*.

"I'm very pleased to meet you, madame," Jack is saying.

"Please, call me Belladonna," she says. Jack can't help a small smile. That's what she said to him the first time they met.

"And these are my friends, June and George Hauxton."

"Oh, I'm so excited to meet you," June gushes, "we've—"

Belladonna cuts her off with a pert snap of her fan, and June shuts her mouth. I wave one of the waiters over and he brings us a bottle of champagne.

"Here's to a night in the Casbah," I toast the table. We clink glasses, and I see Belladonna studying June intently as her cousin sips and tries not to hiccup with the bubbles.

"Tell us where you're from," I say.

"Kansas City," George says, puffing up with pride.

"All three of you?"

"Not I," says Jack. "I'm based in New York, but it seems I'm always on the road."

"And your line of business?"

"Hauxton Enterprises," George says, still beaming. "I specialize in investments, cattle, this and that."

"Is it risky?"

"Not if you know what you're doing."

"I take it you know what you're doing," I say doubtfully. My tone of voice zings right over his head.

"I sure hope so," he says with a raucous, self-satisfied laugh.

Oh ho, you fine upstanding Presbyterian, you're just about to find out all about the meaning of *risk*.

"Do you have children?" I continue.

"Yes, two daughters," June says. "Helen, she's sixteen. And our little Caroline is fifteen. They're both in high school."

"Not so little," George says, emptying his glass. "Why, Caroline eats like a horse! They're eating me out of house and home!"

"George," June chides him.

"They're both charming girls," Jack says.

"Why, thank you, Mr. Winslow," June says, trying to play coy as she studies the ruby and pearl rings dangling from Belladonna's gloved fingers. Dramatically effective, June decides, just the trend to start with her bridge club. They're going to be positively sputtering with jealousy! Why, June is flattered beyond all reckoning that the magnificent Belladonna has allowed her, June Hauxton from Kansas City, Missouri, to sit at her very own table.

"Do you have any other family?" I ask June.

"Just my parents," June replies. "They live in Minneapolis."

"Are they hale and hearty?"

If June is surprised to have been asked such a peculiar question in a nightclub, she doesn't show it. Obviously, we're talking about her favorite topic—anything related to herself.

"Oh, that's so kind of you to ask," she says. "Unfortunately, they're both not well. My mother has, well, female problems. And my father has heart trouble. We're so worried about them."

Yes, we know all about troubles of the heart.

"I'm ever so sorry," I say. I'm sure you're ever so worried about what they're going to leave you in their will.

"You approve of my rings?" Belladonna asks June suddenly, her voice cold.

"Oh, yes," June gushes ecstatically. Belladonna is actually talking to her! Just *wait* until she gets home to tell everyone in the

Groveside Country Club about her magical evening and the won-drous Belladonna talking to her! "They're marvelous."

"This one opens," Belladonna says, extending her hand as she lifts the hinge of one of her rubies. "You see? Most convenient cache for *essentials*." She dips her scarlet-clad pinkie in what ap-pears to be powder, then licks it. "If you ingest an infinitesimal amount of poison every day, eventually you develop an immunity to it. Even if there is no antidote."

She snaps the hinge shut, stands up, and strolls away without another word.

"Well, whaddaya know," George says. "That dame's one egg short of a dozen."

"George," June admonishes.

I am trying not to laugh. June and George are completely oblivi-ous to Belladonna's hostility. They're too busy gloating about their night as members of Belladonna's harem.

More like the Empress Theodora's harem on the Bosphorus, I want to tell them. The harem with only one exit: in a weighted sack, hurled into the sea to sink without a trace.

An hour or so later, George doesn't feel so hot. His face is flushed and his pulse is racing. "I need to get outta here," he moans to his wife. "What did that dame do to me?"

"Oh, George, don't be ridiculous," she says, annoyed. "Why would Belladonna want to poison you?"

"Why indeed?" Jack says blandly. "But do allow me to drive you home."

June trills her thanks, thrilling to the feel of Jack's steady arm as he leads her out to Josie, then into the crowd on the street. George is straggling on uneven feet behind them. Jack murmurs to one of the doormen, and his car quickly materializes. Had June been paying attention, she might have thought that a tad unusual. But June is not what I'd call a particularly observant type.

George slumps on the front seat, while June sits in the back and prattles on to Jack about her fabulous night. The car turns a dark corner and stops for a red light. Without warning, the doors open. "Hello, George," someone says before decking him with a swift chop in the jaw.

"What—" is all June has time to say before a heavy hood is

placed over her head and she is rudely shoved down on her side, powerful hands pressing her so she can't move.

The doors slam shut and the car moves again. It is a fairly short drive, just around the block a few times to the abandoned loading dock of the Kiss-Kiss Kandy factory, but to June it is long enough to be certain these men are going to rape her and then kill her.

Please oh please oh please stop—

The car stops and the doors open. Someone pulls the squirming June out of the car and throws her over his shoulder, so her head is upside down and she is sick with dizziness. Someone else is tying her wrists together, while she is bleating in fear under the heavy hood. She can't breathe; she can't see; someone help her, *please.* She is being carried down a stairwell to die.

They stop moving and June is placed none too gently in a chair, facing a wall, and her ankles are tied to the legs. The hood is pulled off and each cheek slapped. The room is dimly lit, and she can barely see a thing. She is too terrified, a second away from fainting, to call out for her useless husband to come and save her.

Sit there and think you're going to die, June Nickerson. Now you know what it feels like to be alone in the dark.

June can't tell that Belladonna is sitting close by, behind her. She can only feel the presence of something bad, someone bad, someone who wishes her nothing but pain and degradation and oblivion. This can't be happening, June thinks. What have I done to deserve this? I must have been poisoned in the Club Belladonna and I'm having a nightmare and I'm going to wake up by the pool at the Groveside Country Club and realize it was all a bad dream.

"June Nickerson? June Elizabeth Nickerson?" she hears a voice saying. The voice is behind her. It is mine, of course, deepened and with a slight accent added so she won't recognize it as belonging to the man who'd been sitting with Belladonna not so very long ago. I volunteered to conduct this little conversation, and I think Jack was relieved that I was so eager.

"Yes," June says, so astonished that the voice knows her maiden name, she talks back to it. "Who are you? How on earth did you know that?"

"June Elizabeth Nickerson, who grew up in Minneapolis, with her parents, Paul and Blair Nickerson?"

"Yes," she says, her voice quavering.

"Well then," the voice goes on, "you must indeed be the June Elizabeth Nickerson who went to London, England, in February of 1935."

June says nothing, until she feels a hand on her throat. She screams. "Answer the questions," I say in sugared tones, standing behind her so she can't get a look at me, "and I won't hurt you. Do you understand?"

She is sobbing too hard to reply.

"Do you understand?"

"Yes," she says eventually.

"If you don't answer my questions, I'll be forced to hurt you. You don't want me to hurt you, do you?"

June shakes her head so violently that one of her false eyelashes flies off.

"Good girl," I say. "Are you indeed that June Elizabeth Nickerson?"

"Yes," she says, sobbing.

"June Elizabeth Nickerson who went to London, England, in February of 1935, and whose cousin arrived to stay with her in March of 1935, and who left London, England, in May of 1935, without her cousin?"

"Yes," she says, "yes."

"What was the name of your cousin?"

"Isa . . . Isabella." She says it so faintly, it sounds like *Bella*. Her skin is now a paler shade of green than it was when Jack told her about the cat who ran off with a toe.

"How old were you then?"

"Nineteen."

"How old was your cousin?"

"Eighteen."

"Why were you in London?"

"I want to go home," June sobs. "Please let me go."

Hogarth was right. June is dreary. "I'll let you go home if and when you answer my questions," I tell her, sighing melodramatically. "I promise." Of course I conveniently forget to tell her *when* I'll let her go. In this case, ignorance is bliss.

"Why were you in London?" I repeat.

"To meet people," she says, hiccuping. To meet a nice rich husband, she means, although how this spoiled, deeply bourgeois debutante from Minneapolis might have attracted some eligible gentleman of consequence in London is beyond me.

"Did you like your cousin?"

"What do you mean? She was my cousin."

"Was she like a sister to you? Or was she smarter and nicer and prettier?"

"She wasn't prettier," June protests. "Everyone said I was prettier. But she had big green eyes and the boys were always going batty about them."

Even here, even now, June is still jealous. I'm bracing myself for talk of a tiara.

"Where is your cousin now?" I ask.

"I don't know," June says, sobbing again. "I don't know. Please, who are you? What do you want? Why am I here?"

Who are you? Why are you here?

"I want to know what happened to your cousin."

"She got married," June whispers. "She went to a costume ball without me and met a man and ran off and got married and left me all by myself." She starts to scream in earnest, a high-pitched wail. The sound of it is so annoying that I tie a gag around her mouth and go pour myself a drink. Jack is sitting in the next room, and he shakes his head. After a few sips, I go back in. Belladonna is sitting on the floor, wrapped in her chador, motionless.

I lean over June's shoulder. "Do you want me to take the gag off?" I ask, and she nods. "Are you going to be a good girl?" She nods again. Just to be nice, I go back to finish my drink and let her stew while I read a chapter of *The Last of the Mohicans* to juice myself up. Then I go back to her and remove the gag.

"Did that not strike you as peculiar?" I ask June, who is trembling uncontrollably. "That your cousin ran off, at the age of eighteen, with a man she barely knew, and you never heard from her again?"

"She called our flat and left a message," June manages to say. "Then she wrote me a letter."

"I see. But you didn't want to stay in London by yourself once your cousin ran off to get married?" I ask, and June nods yes. "So you went home to mommy and daddy, all by yourself. Did you hear from your cousin again?"

"Yes," June says, "she wrote me and my parents. She wrote that she was happy and wanted to start a new life."

"You believed her?"

June nods again.

"But you never spoke to her directly?"

"She left me a message!" June protests. "She left me all alone in London. She was gone. Hogarth was gone." She is sobbing again.

"You were jealous of her, weren't you?"

"No."

"Yes, you were," I insinuate. "You must have been. Your younger cousin with the nice green eyes went to a costume ball full of rich, eligible bachelors, and you couldn't go. Rather unforgivable of her, wasn't it?" My voice becomes a tad more threatening than its usual sweet benevolence. "Wasn't it?"

"Please let me go," June says.

"Who was Hogarth?"

"Hogarth was *my* friend," she says.

"How did you meet this Hogarth?"

"At the Ivy. At dinner."

"Was he nice? Did he take you places?"

"Yes," June replies, "and he bought me presents."

"Did you go with your cousin, when you stepped out with Hogarth?"

"Sometimes."

"Did Hogarth introduce you to people? Interesting people?"

"Yes."

"Were they nice?" Nice suitors for yourself, you silly girl. Botheration. I really am starting to sound like Hogarth. "Were you more upset about Hogarth disappearing than you were about your cousin?" I ask sternly. "Tell me the truth."

"Yes." June has two bright circles in the middle of her cheeks, redder than the rouge she'd applied with such a heavy hand. "Please don't kill me," she says. "Please let me go."

Pretty poison is her cry.

What a blithering baby, I think. No character. After all this time and wondering, she is hardly worth the energy it's taken to have to deal with her. Of course, I'm not the cousin she abandoned without another thought.

"Stop blubbering. I have no intention of killing you. That would make far too much of a mess," I go on. "But what about your parents? Didn't they wonder about the child entrusted to their care?"

"They were glad she was being taken care of. It wasn't their fault that she had to come live with us because her parents got killed when they were drunk." June realizes what she's said, then starts to wail. I can only imagine what the conversations must have been like for the teenaged orphan in that house, and how warm her welcome.

"Shut up," I say, and there is soon only a painful silence, broken by an occasional sobbing hiccup from June. "Your eldest daughter is now only two years younger than your cousin was when she disappeared. What would you do if the same thing happened to your sweet little Helen?"

June's eyes widen in shock. "You wouldn't. You couldn't—"

"You insult me," I say harshly. "I could care less about your precious Helen and your precious Caroline and your precious husband, George. What I am finding so alarming is that not once have you inquired as to the health and well-being of the cousin who disappeared so many years ago. If indeed she is alive. Have you any explanation for this oversight?"

June resumes crying. "Don't hurt me," she says again.

"Why did you do it?" I ask, leaning down to whisper these words in June's ear. I think she is going to faint. "Why? Answer me. I want to know why you did it. Did you hate your cousin so much? Did she deserve what you did to her? Did she?"

"I, I . . ." June is like a quivering puddle of blancmange.

"Did she?"

June's mouth opens, but no sound comes out.

Just then, there is an urgent knock on the door, so loud that June gives a yelp of abject terror. The sound of it breaks my concentration, and I quickly answer the knock, wondering what could be wrong. It is Matteo standing there, breathless. Jack is pacing behind him. Matteo hurries over to where Belladonna is crouching, to whisper in her ear.

It is so dark I can barely see her, yet I know. *Finally.* One of them has appeared, like an ant at a picnic. One of the members of the Club.

One of them is here, now. Tonight of all nights, when we are most distracted. Well, aren't I the clever one. Always trust a twinge, if I do say so, patting my knee. Hadn't I told Belladonna that maybe in some awful weird way June would bring her luck?

I walk over to Matteo and Belladonna. "Get rid of her," Belladonna whispers. "I need Jack." I can tell that under her veil her skin has gone dead white, but her dark eyes are glistening with such deadly intent I almost expect them to start shooting sparks. June has dwindled into pale insignificance.

Small punishment is all a small mind can handle.

The silly cow has had a good scare, her magical evening ruined and her gloating, gleeful plans to lord everything over her equally silly friends dashed and gone forever.

But we're not through with June and George and Mom and Dad quite yet. Soon, very soon, their company will be sold out from under them, their money gone, their reputations ruined. Nothing less than the best for the Nickerson family.

I walk back to June, who is whimpering. She knows something bad is coming. "Bye-bye, little June bug," I whisper in her ear, then tie the gag back around her quivering lips before I have to listen to another one of her screams. Then I tie a narrow blindfold around her eyes. I almost want to thank her. She's given us a chance to perfect our technique for what we plan to do to one of *them*. The one of them who's upstairs in the Club Belladonna while we're down here wasting valuable time on a sniveling fool.

Belladonna stands up and comes closer, scrutinizing her immobilized cousin in silence. She takes off the glove of her right hand and traces the line of June's jaw with one finger, feeling her tremble in shock and terror.

"Who are you?" Belladonna asks her in a strangled whisper. "Why are you here?"

She turns and walks away, back up the stairs with Matteo. After letting June sit and stew for a few more minutes, I come back, remove her gag, and hold an icy glass up against her lips. "Drink this," I command, "and when you wake up you'll realize that all of this has been nothing more than the worst nightmare of your life."

"Please don't poison me," June whispers, "please."

"You are much too boring to bother with poisoning, little June bug," I tell her in no small exasperation. "And you're too fat to have to lug around. Okay? So stop your blubbering and *drink.*"

I shouldn't have made that last crack about her weight, considering. But June has for some reason brought out the very worst in me. I expect you've figured out why already.

When June and George wake up, they're back in their hotel room. Both have vicious headaches and a queasy feeling in their stomachs. Something sickeningly awful has happened to them, something larger and more terrible than anything they've ever experienced.

George manages to get up first. His jaw is throbbing and he can't remember a thing past sitting in the Club Belladonna with a bellyache. Then he spies a package on the coffee table. He takes it over to June, who sits up in bed and opens it with trembling fingers. It is a bottle of Belladonna perfume, of course. Inside the box is a tiny envelope sealed with thick crimson wax. Slowly, June tears it open to read what's written on the card: "How could you leave her?"

*B*ack inside the club, we're on code red. This is what we've been trained for, so the air of heightened expectancy and alertness is noticeable to none but our staff. It is no drill, though. Josie first saw his ring and heard his accent and figured out his approximate age when she was checking his coat. One of the waiters is in the darkroom processing the film. Another waiter posing as a guest in a djellaba is sitting at the next table, listening to his conversation. Our guest's pockets have already been picked, and one nimble-fingered waiter is huddled at a counter in the kitchen, photographing every card and bit of identification with his Minox before handing them to another spy to write down the essential particulars for use right now. The wallet will be returned to the man's pocket before he notices that it's missing. No mistakes are permissible. Matteo has gone back to the door to assemble the outside team. The minute this man sets foot outside the club, he must be tailed every minute, his plans uncovered—where he's staying, where he's going. Every minute. I don't want him to blow his nose without our knowing what's in his handkerchief.

Jack rushes into Belladonna's office. "His name is Sir Patterson

Cresswell," he says. "We're already on the phone to Pritchard. Does that ring a bell?"

Belladonna shakes her head no. Her skin has taken on the same greenish pallor as June's, and her eyes are wide and staring at nothing.

"Are you okay?" Jack asks, then looks at me. I go around to Belladonna and kneel before her, taking her hands in mine. She is trembling, so I hold them tightly.

"Who are you?" I ask her sternly.

"What?" she says, shocked. Only that question could have roused her.

"Who are you *now*?" I ask her again.

"Belladonna," she whispers.

"Why are you here?"

"To find them," she replies, her voice getting stronger. "To find them all and watch them suffer."

"You're not *her* anymore," I go on. "He has no idea who you are. You're Belladonna. This is your club, and you're safe from all of them. We're here with you. Concentrate, and think. Take a deep breath. Shoot steady. Aim for his heart."

She looks at me, her eyes fathomless.

"Aren't you lucky you're still wearing the contacts?" I ask, trying to make a joke.

"Luck has nothing to do with it," she says, and goes out to greet him.

11

The Roof of
the Schoolhouse

*H*e looks like you'd think a Patterson Cresswell would look: running to fat, with pink mottled cheeks and jowls this side of a rooster's and teeth that badly need a cleaning. The ring he's not supposed to be wearing in public is nearly buried by a chubby knuckle. What irks me most is his air of supreme self-assurance. Yes, I'd like to see his arrogance evaporate after one long night in the dungeons.

Cowards need only one night before they break.

The only thing is, we don't have dungeons here. We didn't need one for June; we'd planned everything for the basement under the Club Belladonna. Our own dungeons have already been built in the house in Virginia. Or rather, we've remodeled the wine cellar. That's what we told the contractor, who hardly suspected ulterior motives. Belladonna told me in meticulous detail what she wanted done there. I know she'll refuse to set foot in it, or any other place that's dark and damp, until it's absolutely necessary. I suppose it'll be left up to yours truly to put in the final touches once we get down there. Don't think I'll mind. It'll be a pleasure.

Well, I suppose we *could* borrow a meat freezer from one of the butchers around the corner and lock Sir Patty in that. That's what I'm thinking as we snoop on his conversation at the next table. He's sitting with two other couples.

"Some of them are young, some of them are old tarts, some will oblige you for a pittance, some will do it for not a shilling, some need to be fed dinner, some need to get drunk, some are clever, some are stupid, some are nice girls, and some are simply mad. She's one of the mad ones. A quite mad bitch in heat." Sir Patterson is talking about women. How charming.

"Speaking of dogs, I heard the most amusing story about Felicity Everdane," the lady says, ignoring him. "Her daughter's little King Charles spaniel—Paddy, can you believe she gave it such an appalling name?—was run over by a car, and Felicity despaired of what she was going to tell her daughter. She waited until dinner, until pudding, actually. Well, much to her relief, after a second's pause, her daughter seemed to take the bad news quite admirably. But when Felicity went upstairs to kiss the child good night, she found the young thing convulsed with sobs. 'Why are you crying, darling?' Felicity asked. 'Because Paddy's been killed,' the little girl said. 'Yes, my angel, he's been killed, but I told you that when you were eating your puds.'

" 'Oh,' her daughter sobbed, 'I thought you said *Daddy*.' "

Amid the laughter, I take the opportunity to ask the group to join us. They act as if they'd been expecting my invitation, as though their studied, world-weary insouciance makes them automatically covetable guests. Belladonna, wrapped in her scarlet chador, is waving her fan casually back and forth to hide her tension. The entire incident with June has taken less than an hour and a half.

"You sir," she says, pointing her fan at our intended, "you look like you've been licked by a cat."

"Sir Patterson Cresswell, at your service, ma'am," he says.

"And you reside where, Sir Patterson Cresswell?" she says. You'd have no idea looking at her that she is desperately trying to place his voice.

"London, England, of course," he replies.

Her fan stops. "Why do you say, 'of course'? Might you not have a home elsewhere? In the countryside, perhaps?"

"Oh yes, oh yes indeed. In Gloucestershire. Charlton Woods Manor. Do stop by should you be in the vicinity. We'd love to have you."

"You're too kind," she says, her voice as soft as frayed rope. "And how long will you be gracing our city with your presence?"

"Only a short while, I'm afraid," he says, her sarcasm completely eluding him. "I'm sailing on the *Royal Splendour* in two days' time."

"Well, then, you must return to my club," she tells him, standing up. "I fear I have other obligations at the moment, and I should dearly love to continue this fascinating conversation. All of you, should you wish it, tomorrow night, eleven o'clock sharp. I insist."

They nod assuringly as she passes them by, a whiff of her yellow jasmine and lily of the valley wafting in her wake. What splendid luck! To be singled out and asked to return by Belladonna herself. Why, whatever else could she do with the wondrous likes of *them.*

It's only because we need a day to prepare.

We've waited all this time. We can wait a few more hours.

"Listen to me: Few people can cope with the guts of life; you know that. Certainly not the likes of Sir Patterson Cresswell, the useless bastard. And if these guts were coiled in a bloody heap in a bloody bucket—as Sir Patterson might say—most people in this world would close their eyes tightly at the sight of them. Not you. You've been waiting all this time."

I'm talking to Belladonna, who is pacing up and down the living room. It's 4:30 in the morning, but we are all wide-awake. We've been on the phone to the Pritch. Jack's team is going to book several first-class staterooms on the SS *Royal Splendour,* and the Pritch will be waiting to meet the ship with his team once it arrives in Maidstone. We will go over our plans once more. We will go slowly. We will be methodical. We will tease out as much information as we can from him tomorrow, before giving Sir Patty a nice surprise.

We can afford to make no mistakes.

"You have to keep busy tomorrow," Matteo tells Belladonna. "Do something unusual to distract yourself."

"Such as?" she snaps.

"Such as going to Bryony's school," I offer. "You've been planning to do this for months. The time is right, don't you think?"

"Yes, the time is right." She sighs. "You know what this means."

Yes, I know very well what this means.

Several hours later, she surprises Bryony by walking with her and Matteo to the Little Brick Schoolhouse. I follow a few blocks behind. Belladonna's face is pale but calm. I can't imagine what she's thinking, what torments the sound of that man's voice must have kindled.

Once Bryony is in her classroom and Matteo returns home, Belladonna asks for an urgent meeting with the school's principals, Hyacinth and Daisy Hamilton. I wait with her in the hall, feeling like the truant I once was. They run a wonderful school, and I've always liked them for the simple reason that they have flower names, like Bryony.

"Is everything all right with Bryony, Mrs. Robbia?" Hyacinth, looking anxious, asks once we're settled in the office.

"Yes," Belladonna replies, reaching in her bag for a large manila file, which she hands to me. "My business manager would like a word with you. Good day to you, ladies." She nods, then walks out, leaving Hyacinth and Daisy in a state of rather perplexed anxiety.

"I'm afraid that Bryony will not be back after Christmas vacation," I say.

The sisters exchange concerned glances, steeling themselves for the worst. "Is there some problem with the school?" Daisy asks.

"Of course not," I reply. "Mrs. Robbia has asked me to express her gratitude for all you've done for her daughter. Bryony has been very happy here, but we're going to be moving out of state; we are truly sorry that business commitments are taking us away. Mrs. Robbia also wishes me to tell you that she regrets not having been more of a participating parent in school activities. As you have just witnessed, she still finds it most difficult to be sociable, to mingle with the other mothers."

"We understand," Hyacinth says slowly, although she doesn't. Not really. Not yet.

"Mrs. Robbia wishes to give you something in return for all you've given to Bryony. Forgive me if I sound blunt, but I was wondering if you had a building fund for expansion."

Now the sisters' glances at each other are slightly flummoxed. "Yes, we were hoping that someday we could expand, and we do have a fund," Hyacinth says carefully. "A very small fund, unfortunately. We've had one since we started the school; we use it for emergencies, repairs, whatever. It seems that there's always some emergency." She laughs ruefully.

"We were hoping someday—this was our dream—to buy the building next door," Daisy adds. "It would have been ideal space for expansion, to add more teachers, a larger gym, music rooms, but unfortunately, someone bought the building. A corporation. We've no idea who."

"Yes, I know that the building was sold," I say. "That's because we bought it."

"I'm sorry, I don't understand," Hyacinth says. "Are you in the property business?"

"Not exactly, no. Please read this carefully." I hand the file over. They open it, look at the top document, at each other, and then at me in total astonishment. Daisy's cheeks become as red as an apple polished for one of their teachers.

"But this is the deed to the building next door," Hyacinth says. "With our names on it."

"Yes," I reply. "We bought it with the explicit intent that it should be given to the school, for expansion. You'll also find information about the account set up to pay for all the necessary renovation, your new architect, builders who are actually trustworthy, believe it or not, suppliers, that sort of thing. All your projected expenditures will be vetted by our accountants and quickly approved, I am sure. Once the building is finished, you'll find there is also a fund to hire more teachers of the caliber you require and to purchase all necessary school supplies. Et cetera, et cetera. Should you need more money or assistance, arrangements can be made. There is also a discretionary fund to be used for whatever you desire. This includes a long-overdue vacation. You've certainly earned it."

They are stunned into speechlessness. They look at each other again, and then back at me. Tears have started in their eyes.

"You want to do all of this for us?" Daisy asks, still incredulous.

"You deserve it. No price tag can be put on a superior education."

"But it's so much money—"

"As I said, you more than deserve it. There is only one condition."

"Yes?" A flicker of panic crosses both their faces. Surely they must be dreaming. This can't be happening; impossible dreams do not come true. Not like this. I'm going to say it's a cruel joke, and depart as mysteriously as Mrs. Robbia did.

"This must remain an anonymous contribution," I tell them.

"Mrs. Robbia does not wish to be acknowledged in any manner whatsoever. Should we find any breach of this condition, I'm afraid all funding will cease."

Their faces relax into relief. "Are you sure?" Hyacinth asks quietly.

"Absolutely," I reply. "It's to protect Bryony. It is not generally known that her mother is—how shall I say it?—more than comfortably well-off. She prefers that her financial status remain as private as possible. I'm sure you can understand her fears on this topic."

"Of course," Hyacinth murmurs.

"The contracts are quite explicit. Several gentlemen in our employ will be contacting you imminently to see to all the paperwork. Have your lawyers review everything, and please feel free to contact us should you have any questions. The numbers you'll need are in the file." I smile. "Perhaps we shall be back someday, and if we are, we hope Bryony can re-enroll. We expect your standards of excellence will remain as exacting as they ever were."

"We'll miss Bryony," Daisy says.

"And she'll miss you," I say, standing up. "We are hoping the adjustment won't be too difficult for her. But we must go."

I extend my hand, and both of them shake it.

"Bless you," Hyacinth says, tears now running freely down her cheeks. "We'll never forget what you've done for the school."

"If only everyone were as worthy," I say, and bid them farewell.

"All done?" Belladonna asks when I come home.

"Yes, it's all done."

Yes, she's done with it. Done with kindness.

*B*otheration. I suppose you want exact details of everything that happened in the Club Belladonna that night. Forgive me; this is one of the few times my memory fails me. I can remember little of what happened before Sir Patty's arrival at our table. All I know is that he's suddenly sitting there, beaming and proud. His friends, unfortunately, are delayed. What a surprise. He wants an evening with Belladonna all to himself, and he's going to get one.

Only not in the way he has imagined.

"That is a very unusual ring," she is saying. "Is it a family heirloom?"

"Yes," he says, beaming. I'd like to pour a healthy dose of belladonna in his drink and see how colorful his chubby cheeks are *then*. How Belladonna herself must be struggling to maintain her composure. The ring's the kicker, you see. The ring is what gives him away. "My father gave it to me, and his father to him."

That makes sense. Membership in this club is passed down from one perverted generation to another. No new blood need apply, thank you very much. We prefer to keep our depravities in the family.

"Might I see it a bit more closely?" she asks, all sweetness as she waggles her pearl-dripping fingers. "Being such a ring aficionado myself."

"Of course," he says, holding out his hand. He's a smoothy, this one, knowing full well he's not supposed to wear his ring in public. He doesn't recognize her voice. He has no idea she's seen the ring before, that the very thought of it—

No no no. Enough of this. Focus, Tomasino. Breathe deeply. Remain calm. Aim for his heart.

The ring is an exceptional piece of carving. A heavy signet that would normally display a family coat of arms, it is instead a meticulously sculpted snake, engorged on an apple, twisting around what seems to be a tree but is in actuality a very tiny, perfectly naked body of a woman.

Belladonna won't touch it, but she leans over, close, and smiles up at him. "Thank you," she says, "it is quite extraordinary. Is it one of a kind?"

His smile barely falters. "I believe so," he says, lying through his teeth. "Or so I've been told. I should *hope* so."

Indeed he should. How many more are there? One for each member of the Club? Is that the exclusive password they wear brazenly on their fingers, allowing them into places no normal man would dare to go?

"Tell me, Sir Patterson," Belladonna says, abruptly changing the subject, "about clubs in London. Are there any comparable to mine? Do you think I should open one there?"

"There are many nightclubs, but none quite so charming as yours," he replies. "The Club Belladonna in London would be smashing, simply smashing."

If she weren't wearing a silver lace mask encrusted with tiny sparkling diamonds, Sir Patty would have seen her blush coquettishly. But he can see her ruby-stained lips curve into a smile, and her dark-brown eyes glowing, contact lenses be damned. Her wig is platinum blond, cascading in ringlets down her back, glowing against the golden brocade of her embroidered bustier as if they were spun silver. In fact, she is a veritable vision of silver and gold. Her gloves are of the same lace as her mask, and her fan is a shimmering kind of golden foil. There is such a radiance surrounding her that no patrons in the club can tear their eyes away.

"That is very kind. What I know little about, though, are private clubs," she presses. "Surely a man of your stature is a member of one, if not several. I'm very curious, as we have so few here. And those that are successful are not frequented by women, I believe. It is quite unfair, don't you agree?"

"Quite unfair indeed. Although I am thankful my wife is barred from entry." He laughs so loudly I think his collar is going to burst.

"How does one become a member?" I ask.

"One is born to it, perhaps, or recommended by one's peers," he replies.

"I see," Belladonna says. "And what about clubs that are—how shall I put it—slightly more exclusive? Clubs that one may not know about unless one is rather well connected."

"Ah," he says, clipping off the end of his cigar, "that is not a suitable topic for a lady."

"What makes you think I'm a lady?" she retorts, snapping shut her fan.

"My dear Belladonna," he says. "I should never presume—"

"No, you never should," she says sternly.

We sit in an uncomfortable silence for a few minutes. No, Sir Patty is not as dumb as he looks, nor as drunk as I'd wish. Double botheration. I almost wish his friends were here to lubricate the situation. But they're not, so I start blabbing, about nothing in particular. I can't remember exactly. Anything to keep him here a little bit longer. It's too early for Belladonna to make her exit, for him to leave.

So we sit and talk, and drink. Belladonna gets up after a while and walks around the club, greeting her guests with kind smiles. She is much more friendly than usual, sparkling and flirting and laughing. Her gay mood infects the club as if she had waved a fairy wand of enchantment. Nothing can go wrong tonight, think our delighted revelers. The band's music is lilting and the Belladonna cocktails are flowing and the lights are twinkling and we are here, we the chosen few, we are part of the magic. If only this night could go on forever.

Yes, for hours Belladonna is as charming as Sir Patty is an insufferable bore, but a bore we desperately need to stay where we can keep an eye on him.

Eventually, Belladonna gets up and says her good-byes, thanking Sir Patty for such a wonderful evening and wishing him well on his transatlantic crossing. "Do allow my chauffeur to take you to your hotel," she says as he rises. "I must insist."

"You are too kind," he says. Naturally, he thinks he deserves no less an honor. Why not? Isn't he the great Sir Cresswell? Doesn't the world revolve to do his bidding?

Matteo, our chauffeur *del giorno,* politely holds open the door of one of our Cadillacs for Sir Patty, who pours himself into the backseat with a satisfied *humph.* The car drives away, but not in the direction of the St. Regis Hotel. It has turned around one dark corner, then another, and while waiting for a red light to change, the back doors are suddenly flung open. Jack coldcocks Sir Patty with such precision that he doesn't have time to blink. He'll have a sore jaw with a little swelling, nothing too noticeable for someone with such droopy jowls. Nothing too obvious to remind him of what is about to happen.

We've got about twenty minutes before he comes to. And when he does, he'll be sorry he ever woke up.

Sir Patty moans, shakes his head slightly, and opens his eyes. The room he's in is barely lit, and damp. He is, in fact, in the sub-basement of our house, the level below the basement room where we'd taken June. He is down so deep he could yell and scream and no one could hear him. Certainly not Bryony, peacefully sleeping several stories above us. We loaded him in through the old Kiss-Kiss warehouse entrance, but for all he knows, he could be in hell. He is certainly as far, far away from the Club Belladonna as imaginable.

He tries to move and realizes he's tied to a chair, and he starts thrashing about in a panic. It is then that he sees Matteo, Jack, and myself standing before him, clad in monk's robes, our faces concealed behind masks. Belladonna is dressed as we are, but she doesn't want to look at us, at least not at our faces. She is sitting behind us, facing our backs, hidden in the shadows next to a small wooden table where a large reel-to-reel tape recorder is slowly whirling. Sir Patty can't see her there. She doesn't want to be seen.

We are dressed as exact replicas of the members of the Club, and when Sir Patty realizes this his eyes widen in even greater terror and he blanches.

"I said nothing," he says, his voice trembling. "I swear it. Not a word."

"Didn't say what?" Jack replies. His voice is perfectly clipped, pukka English, as if he were precisely to the manor born. No wonder the Pritch had recommended him so highly.

Belladonna has asked him to moderate this interrogation. Although I'd conducted such a charming conversation with June, Matteo and I are not experienced enough for something this important. And much as we'd like to see Sir Patty lying in a pool of his own blood, tortured and cut as we had been, my brother and I could never do to another man what had been done to us. No matter how deserving, and despite what Matteo had said to that repulsive Paulie Baldwin.

Yes, they all deserve it, and worse. All the members of the Club. We've finally got one of them here, and he is going to tell us what we want to know in the twelve hours we have before his ship sails. Several of our waiters have already gone to his hotel room with the key we filched out of his pocket, packed his bags, checked him out, and are in the process of bringing us his belongings to riffle through. Perhaps there is another name in an address book, a hint, a clue. Something. Anything to help us.

Sir Patty doesn't answer.

"Said nothing about what?" Jack repeats. His voice is calm, not overtly menacing, but if I were in Sir Patty's shoes I'd certainly want him to shut up and go away.

"Who are you?" Sir Patty asks feebly. "You sound like Norris. Is that you, Norris? How dare you, you miserable coward. Untie me at once."

Norris? Who is Norris?

"It's not Norris," Jack says. "Guess again."

"Who are you?" he cries. "Why am I here? What do you want?"

Who are you? Why are you here?

"Who do you think we are?"

"I don't know. I don't know why you've singled me out, or why you're in New York. Have you followed me here? You've no right to follow me. We aren't scheduled to meet till next year. I've done nothing wrong, nothing at all. The books are in perfect order. I've not said a word. Upon my honor, I've not said a word, not now, not ever."

Yes, she knows that they meet every three years.

"A man such as yourself may not use the word *honor* in my presence," Jack replies. "You are not honorable, and you are no gentleman. Besides," he adds, "if you've not done anything wrong, why have we singled you out? Could there be a discrepancy you might have missed?"

"Discrepancy? Never! I don't know what you're going on about!" he cries. "I demand that you let me go. There'll be hell to pay when I find out who you are. This is an utmost transgression of the rules, and you know it."

Matteo and I exchange glances and we nearly smile. Utmost transgression, I like that. That's rich, coming from him.

"Someone has been talking," Jack goes on. He's the smoothest bluffer I've ever heard. "One of us has been talking. Who do you think it could be?"

Sir Patty visibly relaxes, thinking he's out of danger. I find it absolutely amazing that he's not more panic-stricken, tied up in a strange dark room with strange dark men. They must be used to the dark, all of the members. It must be what spawned them.

"I can't imagine," he says. "Such a thing has never happened before, certainly not since I've been a member. Or my father. We haven't had a problem since that Duffield in 1887. And the king, of course. Bloody fool, Edward, and that dreadful Simpson person. You know that. But never a discrepancy, not since my family has been keeping the books. Never."

Duffield? Who is Duffield?

"Yes," Jack says, "but it must be someone. If it's not you. I personally happen to believe it *is* you. Cavorting in a public space, flaunting your ring to all and sundry. To the woman who runs a *nightclub*. Whatever possessed you to do such a thing?"

"She's just a silly woman who likes rings," he says, pouting and defensive. "It doesn't mean anything. I concede that I should not have worn it, yet drawing attention to the ring should I be asked about it is the best method of deflecting interest. You know that. We all know that. It's what we've always been told. I did nothing wrong."

"Then you must tell me who it can be," Jack says, pulling out a notepad. He ignores the crack about Belladonna being silly. The time to pay for that one will come later. "Either you tell me now or we shall leave you here to rot. No one knows you're here. No one will ever find you if we bury you alive. I'd think about it, if I were you, and tell me quickly. We have no time to waste."

Sir Patty frowns, but says nothing. We stand there for what seems like an eternity. I am willing myself not to turn around and look at Belladonna.

"Very well," Jack says, and turns off the lights. "Stay here until you change your mind."

We walk away and leave him there. I walk over to Belladonna, and she shakes her head in the gloom. She's not leaving. She's going to sit there, in the dark, until he talks. I try to sit down beside her, but she waves me away impatiently.

I can't help her. No one can. Matteo tugs me away and I leave her to sit with her demons.

We sit down in the next room and wait, listening to Sir Patty hollering and blustering. Jack's spies return from the hotel with the suitcases, and we quickly pore through them, photographing every page of his slim leather address book before copying down as much as we can. Names are what we need. Names, addresses, phone numbers, even if they're in code. The Pritch and his team will be working their magic on every name we give them.

We're going to find them, every last one.

Eventually, after what feels like a lifetime but is only about an hour, Sir Patty stops hollering and starts blubbering. What a baby. How time flies when you're a captive in the dark. How every second counts, and every noise is magnified into something terrifyingly unbearable, and every footstep means only panic and pain.

"Are you ready?" Jack says, seeming to appear out of thin air in front of him.

Sir Patty shakes his head no in a vain attempt at bravado. Does he betray the membership vows of his club and become a traitor? Or does he give them away to save his own precious skin? Such a dilemma. Upon his honor indeed.

"It is forbidden to divulge any information whatsoever about the members to an outsider," Sir Patty says. "You know that."

"You don't know I'm an outsider."

"You are, you are," he mutters. "You're not Norris. I've said enough, mentioning his name. I don't know who you are. Only that you're a nameless bastard. Unmask yourself, sir. I demand that you unmask yourself!"

Jack's laugh is harsh. "Why should I? Have you unmasked yourself? Have you?"

Sir Patty says nothing. There is nothing for him to say.

"The punishment for unmasking is excommunication forever," Jack bluffs. "A fate worse than death."

"Yes," he whispers. "How did you know that? Who are you?"

"Are you prepared to die?"

Silence.

"Are you?" Jack asks again, and motions to Matteo. We huddle around Sir Patty so Belladonna can't see what we're about to do, and he screams in sudden, excruciating pain. I'm not going to tell you what made him scream so. It doesn't matter; it didn't leave a permanent scar on his flabby white flesh. Not like our torture did to us.

I tell myself he is payback for what happened to Belladonna, to us, he and all the men in the world like him, arrogant and selfish and power-mad bastards, one and all.

I didn't say we were nice, did I?

"The list," Jack says.

"No," he repeats, and then screams again, and again.

We walk away and sit in the other room for about forty minutes. I need a drink; we all do. Belladonna is huddled in the corner, lost in her cloak and mask. Small and lost. I don't think she's moved a muscle since this started.

We go back in to do it again.

"The list," Jack says. "The list, or you die. Don't be a martyr, and don't be silly."

Sir Patty is about to pass out, so we throw a bucket of water on his head.

"The list," Jack says again, relentless and implacable. "What do a few names matter? They'll never know. No one need ever know; it'll be our little secret, and I can promise you that I'll never tell. You're going to have to trust me if you want to live. And you don't want to die, do you, Patterson Cresswell? Do you?" He tilts Sir Patty's head up toward the feeble light. "You don't want to die, do you?" he asks again, almost crooning. "No . . . no, you don't want to die, not here, not now, not like this, cold and forgotten. Not like the women you use. Not like this."

"We never killed anyone," he says, his voice a croaking whisper. Defensive to the end, even with his hair dankly plastered to his head and pain searing the very tips of his nerves. This is not a time to get sanctimonious. "Not anyone, ever."

"You killed their spirit," Jack says fiercely. "So tell me. My patience is wearing thin indeed. The list, or you die."

"Why me?" he asks, moaning. "Why me?"

Belladonna watch you die.

"Because it's your lucky day," Jack says. "Because it had to be someone. And it's not just you. It's all the members of the Club, all of you. Do you hear me? All of you. And if we don't kill you now, believe me, it's going to get worse. We're very good at what we do, and we'll be following you every day for the rest of your unnatural life. You won't be able to escape us. Turn around and we'll be there, following you, your wife, your children, your friends. Put a cigarette in your mouth and we'll light it. Order a meal and we'll serve it. You'll never know when we'll strike, and you'll never feel safe again. Not now, not ever. And trust me when I tell you that the threat is always worse than the deed itself."

Jack steps back and risks a glance at Belladonna. Only his love for her could propel him forward now.

She is no more tangible than a shadow.

"The list," he says, his voice wearier than death. "Give me the list, and we'll disappear. Only a few names. We know they're in code."

We don't, actually. He's bluffing again. I remind myself never to get Jack angry. He is beginning to scare even me.

"Norris. Duffield," Jack says, almost crooning. "Norris and Duffield. Norris and Duffield. These we know already. So what do a few more matter? You've already given them away. Don't worry. Trust me." His voice is so soothing, so calm, so entreating. "Be a good boy, yes, I know you can do it. Norris and Duffield. Who else? That's a good boy, you can do it. Only you are brave enough to do it. Only you, that's right. You're the chosen one. We chose you because you're the bravest. No one else could have survived this, only you. Tell me—you're a good boy."

Sir Patty looks at him, his eyes pleading. His mouth works. He can see only Jack's eyes burning back at him. The pitiful act will get him nowhere, and he knows it.

"I'll never tell," Jack says. "You have my word. They'll never know. No one will know but you and me. Tell me, and you can go."

Sir Patty's mouth works again. "Bates," he says, so low Jack has to kneel down beside him to hear him clearly. "Dashwood, Duffield, Francis, Henley, Lloyd, Morton, Norris, Stapleton, Thompson, Tucker, Whitehead, Wilkes."

"Which one are you?" Jack asks. "Tell me that, and you can go. Go free forever."

"Wilkes," he says. "I'm Wilkes."

The light goes out. Sir Patty feels a sharp pinch in his arm, then oblivion.

No no no, we didn't kill him. How could you think such a thing?

We clean him up and change his clothes, and when he first stirs a few hours later, he is slumped in the backseat of a car driven by Matteo, waiting outside the pier where the *Royal Splendour* is embarking. We tell the first-class stewards that poor Sir Patterson had, well, just a *tiny* bit too much to drink the night before, and ask if they could help us load him into his cabin, along with all his luggage. We tip them magnanimously and speed away. When Sir Patty finally awakens from his stupor, he is already far out to sea. Adrift, you might say.

It's not our fault he has a stroke not long after arriving home, rendering him speechless and partially paralyzed. In fact, it is quite annoying, because now he can say nothing to any of *them* that might be of use to us. The Pritch quickly rallies, though, and sends trained nurses he just happens to know from the poshest agency in London to watch over Sir Patty's drooling.

Not the kind of drooling he did as a member of the Club.

Or, perhaps, just a tiny bit of poison found its mark.

Just perhaps. Think about it. How easy it would have been to slip a wee dram of a very toxic substance into his nightly scotch.

Pretty poison is her cry.

Poison is the weapon of a woman. The venom of her rage is often the only thing she has left.

$\mathcal{N}$o one knows it yet, but that was the last night of the Club Belladonna.

At first, they think it is as it has always been, the club shutting down for no reason at the capricious request of its owner who, had they known it, retreats to her bedroom just around the corner and refuses to come out for over a week. Surely it will just as suddenly open up again. It is so irritating to find the club locked and silent just before Christmas and all the seasonal celebrations. It is even more annoying to be deprived of the Club Belladonna on New Year's Eve. Oh well, the revelers tell themselves with a sigh, Belladonna is one smart cookie to be able to get out of town for the holidays.

But as the weeks turn into months and the crimson door remains shut, the rumors multiply and panic sets in. Gansevoort Street is deserted and cold, a marrow-freezing wind howling in from the river like a wailing, wandering spirit. It taunts the desperate social climbers milling about aimlessly, even in such bitter weather, hoping against hope that if they stay out there long enough somehow they can will the door to open and allow them into paradise.

"Wait. I hear a dog barking," one of them shouts. "It must be Andromeda."

Dream on. It's not Andromeda. It's just a stray dog barking because it's hungry and bored. Andromeda has disappeared, and no one knows why.

Around the corner, Jack moves quietly into the house—our combined houses, that is. Richard and Vivienne are staying down at the other end for the time being, working for Jack, following up on whatever leads he needs them to. The band is busy playing gigs, because everyone wants the musicians from the infamous Club Belladonna to enliven their parties, hoping against hope that one of them might divulge something, *anything*. No chance, of course; the band members are as astonished as everyone else at the club's sudden closure. The six months' salary they've been paid is more than enough, of course, to keep their lips sealed. None of them dares risk the wrath of Belladonna. Not if she might be coming back someday.

She *must* come back.

Jack is keeping his keenly practiced eye on the abandoned club and his keenly practiced mind on detecting; we need him more than ever. He does whatever the Pritch asks, and he is overseeing the team helping the women who continue to write dozens of letters to the club's address every day. Many of the waiters and other staff who worked in the Club Belladonna will now be spying on philandering husbands and self-absorbed businessmen. It's easier work for them, with better hours. Plus it's much less stressful on the feet. Belladonna insists that Jack contact Alison Jenkins and lure her away from the import-export business so that she can help him run the foundation from an office we set up on Park Avenue.

I won't give up hope that Alison and Jack will fall head over heels. They'd be good for each other. Besides, it would take Jack's mind off Belladonna, and it would be a relief for her to know that a man who so willingly helped her might find the love he deserves.

Furthermore, love is in the air: Matteo and Annabeth marry one afternoon in a quickie ceremony at City Hall, attended by her delighted children. For now, they'll live in Annabeth's apartment, while they decide if they want to move down to Virginia, as we hope they will. Belladonna is struggling to keep her need for my brother in check, but she tells herself she doesn't want to deal with the complication of divulging anything to Annabeth. I'll just have to do for the both of us, not that I'm *not* up to the task, of course. Annabeth told Matteo that she already has the children she wants, and frankly never was that enthralled by sex anyway. My heart turned over when a disbelieving Matteo told me that, and it took weeks for me to convince him that she really might love him so much that she meant it.

Or rather, I should say that love is in the air for some of us. For others, hearts are swollen not with tenderness but with a passionate need for vengeance.

*T*he rumors are still flying like a bomber on endless secret missions. Loose Lips is at a loss. He's reported every single statement he's heard, no matter how ridiculous. Belladonna killed someone, and had to disappear. Someone wants to kill her. She's gone back to Europe. She bought a château in France. No, England. She's on a retreat in Tibet. She lost all her money. She fell in love and ran away with the lucky bastard, whoever he is.

No, that's not true—she drank a bottle of her own perfume, and it killed her.

Who are we to dissuade him from printing such lovely gossip?

All they know is that she's gone. Will she ever come back? Why did she go away? Where has she gone? How could she do this to them?

Everyone who is anyone boasts that they've been in the club, of course, invited by the crook of a gloved finger to sit at Belladonna's exclusive table. That, of course, they've seen a hint of her smile curving under her mask as she toyed with a cerise-colored ringlet, her dangling pearl rings swaying hypnotically.

Belladonna leaves them with nothing. Her club closes as mysteriously as it opened. She is depriving everyone of the gift of her presence, and, in doing so, is spared the cruelty of dwindling interest.

This way the Club Belladonna will be alive forever.

"And you know what?" Loose Lips asked in his column one day, months after giving up hope of seeing the mysterious Belladonna once again. "No one managed to take a photograph of her. No one recorded her voice, or sketched her face."

No one ever found out who she was.

After a while, the Club Belladonna becomes a living legend, there and yet not, an empty shell of a building that once was the Kiss-Kiss Kandy factory, silent and deserted. It was all a dream; it wasn't real.

She wasn't real.

No one would believe the truth.

The Diary

(1935)

—*How are you feeling, my sweet? Hogarth asked. Better?*

The room was very dark. She was lying under something heavy and she couldn't see anything, not Hogarth's face, not her own hands. She couldn't move. What—

—*What happened? she managed to say. I was so dizzy. Did I faint?*

—*Yes, in a manner of speaking, Hogarth said. His voice sounded different. Husky and impatient. Excited in a way she'd never heard before. There was something in his voice. Something that scared her.*

—*Listen to me very carefully, Hogarth said, taking her hands in his. I have something to say to you. He cleared his throat. I have been looking for you for a long time, he went on. We all have. You have been chosen. Out of all the beautiful and clever girls in the world whom we have seen, you are the chosen one. You alone.*

—*What? What are you talking about? Her voice sounded odd, as if it were coming from a great distance away. She could barely open her mouth.*

—*I'm afraid I haven't been quite honest with you, my dear child.*

Her heart started to thump. She couldn't breathe; the corset was laced too tightly.

—*I have brought you to a costume party, yes, but of a most particular kind, Hogarth was saying. A most particular private kind. A sort of Club, if you will. It is an ancient order of gentlemen who meet every so often for their own amusement.*

His voice was getting more excited. Amusement, yes, he said again. And you, my darling, are our chosen amusement for the evening. You have been chosen.

—*No, she said, struggling to get up. It was futile. She couldn't move. She was trapped.*

—*Be still, he said. Don't try to move. Don't say a word. If you cause a fuss or start to scream I'm afraid I shall have to gag you. Besides, there's no one here who could help you even if he heard you scream. Lie still, and be a good girl.*

She didn't understand, in her growing panic. What could he be talking about? Hogarth, gag her? He was joking; he must be. This was a sick joke. She had been dancing with Hogarth and she got dizzy, and now she must be dreaming.

—Do you remember what I said to you at June's flat, about taking a chance to do something remarkable and splendid, to change your life utterly? he asked her. To take a step into the shadows.

His voice wasn't the same. This wasn't Hogarth, the silly, fussy Hogarth who took them for tea at the Café Royal.

—You, my darling, have taken that step. You are in the shadows here. And when you leave, nothing will be the same again. Yes, you have been chosen.

He wouldn't stop talking, his hands still holding hers tightly.

—We have created our own rules, and they cannot be broken, he was saying. We are responsible to no one but ourselves. And you, our chosen guest, of course. It is a great honor, passed down from father to son, and so on and so on. To be a member of this Club. The most exclusive and splendid Club in the world, if I may be ever so slightly boastful. We meet every few years and share our secrets. Yes, we are bound by our oaths and our rules, and we will never betray them.

He let go of her hands, then propped some pillows under her head. She couldn't move, not really; there was still something heavy on top of her. Hogarth held a glass of ice water to her lips, and she drank. She was so thirsty.

—You drugged me, she said. You drugged me and you tricked me.

—Yes, I'm terribly sorry. Please do forgive me. It was most unseemly.

—Unseemly? she said, her voice barely audible though she felt she was screaming. Are you mad? Let me go. You can't do this, you must—

—I can do whatever I please, he said. We all can, and we all do. This Club has existed for hundreds of years, doing as it pleases. I am happy to say that you are one of the most magnificent of all the guests we have brought here. And I am responsible for finding you.

If she could see him clearly, she thought wildly, he would have his fussy little Hogarth smile on his face. She lashed out and tried to scratch his face, but he grabbed her hands again. He was surprisingly strong for such a small man.

—Listen carefully, he said. I very nearly had a fit of conscience on our drive in the country, which is most unlike me. Therefore, I have decided to tell you this, although I shouldn't, because I have grown

fond of you, truly. I don't wish you any harm. Indeed I do not. It is my fondness for you and your splendid youth—your innocence and your curiosity and your lovely American energy—that has led me to choose you. Plus the absolutely perfect circumstances of your visit to our fair land. No family to speak of, no, and your ridiculous cousin June will not miss you, not at all.

—What? she said. She was starting to get hysterical. What are you going to do to me?

—A touch of the forbidden sharpens one's focus, he said. That is why you are here. Here for the members of the Club. They all want you, you see, but only one can have you. Be the sensible girl I know you are and do as he says, and your stay here will be as painless as possible.

—No, she said, no no—

—We have rules, you see, he said. Rules of a most particular sort. The rules must not be broken, or the member is blackballed forever. No one risks that, I assure you. We look after our guests. All the money, therefore, will be yours to keep.

—What? Money? What money?

—The money from this evening, that you are about to earn, of course. You will be able to retrieve that money from the Swiss Consolidated Bank Limited. Account number one one six dash six one four. Remember that number carefully. One one six dash six one four. It will be waiting for you along with whatever else you . . . well, you will find out soon enough. As well as jewelry, and whatever other favors he chooses to bestow upon you. All our members have been of a most generous nature in the past. I suspect you are about to inspire a generosity of the most munificent sort. I am very pleased indeed.

No, she must be dreaming. The sound of Hogarth's voice was coming from the depths of a nightmare. She would wake up and be back in London, in their little flat, June snoring in the other bed.

—We have rules about the length of your stay, my dear, he said. So you needn't worry. The more you are worth, the longer you stay. But the more you are worth, the more you will have earned. It's quite simple, really. Quite simple. You needn't fret. I'll be looking in on you as often as I can.

She heard a noise from somewhere. Hogarth kissed her clenched fists and let them go, and before she could scream a hood was placed over her head and something tied tightly around the bottom of it so *she couldn't make a sound. Then the heavy cover atop her was folded more tightly, and she felt herself being picked up and slung over someone's shoulder.*

Where were they taking her? She was too terrified to think.

This must be a nightmare. People don't do things like this to each other. People don't—

She was being carried in a cold hallway, up some stairs, down again, through different rooms. She heard doors opening and closing. She thought she heard voices, a man laughing. She couldn't breathe. They're going to kill me, she thought. Please don't kill me, I don't want to die.

They stopped abruptly, and she was eased to her feet, the heavy thing covering her pulled away. A cold bracelet, thick like a cuff, was snapped on each wrist and her arms were pulled out slightly away from her body and attached to hooks on pillars on either side of her. She tried to move, but someone tied something thick and stiff around her middle, under her green satin bodice and around her corset, then pushed her up against a sort of pole.

Help me, someone, please help me. Don't kill me, not here. I'm only eighteen, I haven't lived—

—If I hear you make a sound, a low voice she'd never heard before whispered in her ear, I'll slit your throat. Understand?

She nodded yes, trying not to whimper. Help me someone, please, what are they going to do to me, help me—

—Gentlemen, your attention please. It was Hogarth's voice. The moment you've been waiting for has arrived.

The room instantly became silent.

—You are going to be very pleased, he said, very pleased indeed. We have here tonight an American, an orphan, poor darling, only eighteen years of age. Not only is she beautiful, charming, energetic, intelligent, but totally unspoiled. Exceptionally lovely. Eminently suitable for training. An absolutely enchanting creature. An absolutely enchanting virgin.

Not a word was spoken, but the room filled with applause.

—Gentlemen, here she is.

Her hood was unfastened and taken off, and she heard that sickening voice whisper again. Not a word, he said, I'll be standing right behind you.

No no no—

She was standing behind a large painted screen, up on a sort of podium. The screen was taken away. The room was dark, except for a spotlight being shined on her face, and one smaller light near Hogarth, who was standing a few feet away from her at a lectern. His white satin suit was glistening in the light, and he held a gavel in one hand.

The bright light hurt her eyes and she squeezed them shut.

—I shall start the bidding at one thousand pounds, said Hogarth.

She squeezed her eyes tighter in horrified astonishment. He had tricked her here and drugged her, and now she was being offered for sale to the members of the Club.

Hogarth was the auctioneer.

No no no—

She couldn't help herself. She opened her eyes, and gradually they adjusted to the bright light still shining on her face. There was no sound at all from the men seated below. They were dressed as monks, in dark robes with their hoods pulled over their faces. She couldn't see their faces; they had black masks on as well.

—Fifteen thousand, Hogarth was saying, twenty thousand.

Shiny black leather gloves covered their hands. She saw this every time they raised their paddles.

They all looked horrifyingly identical, indistinguishably faceless men who sat devouring her, silently bidding.

She was too terrified to move, even if she could. Too terrified to scream.

—Twenty-five thousand, Hogarth said. Splendid. He nodded at the man standing behind her, and before she realized what he'd done, he unfastened her bodice and took it off, leaving her breasts exposed.

The men moved restlessly in their seats. They all wanted her, every one. She could feel their desire rising toward her, choking her.

No no no—

—Forty thousand. Forty-five thousand. Fifty thousand. Excellent, Hogarth said.

The horrible man behind her stepped forward again and unfastened her skirt and all her petticoats. She was standing there with nothing on but her knickers, her shoes and stockings and golden garters, her corset, and the emerald and diamond choker shimmering like green fire on her neck.

—*The highest bid on record, as you know, is eighty-five thousand,* Hogarth announced. *Gentlemen, shall we continue?*

The paddles went up again.

—*Seventy-five thousand. Eighty thousand. Eighty-five thousand.*

Another round of applause.

Ninety thousand. One hundred thousand pounds. Hogarth wiped his brow with his spotless white handkerchief.

—*A toast, gentlemen, he said, raising a glass. A toast to the splendid generosity of the members of the Club. Polite applause once more.*

—*Shall we continue? Hogarth said, pointing at a paddle. One hundred ten thousand. One hundred fifteen thousand. One hundred twenty thousand. No more paddles went up. One hundred twenty thousand pounds, gentlemen. Most satisfactory. Most satisfactory indeed. One hundred twenty thousand pounds, going. One hundred twenty—*

—*One million pounds, a voice rang out.*

There was a hushed intake of breath. Not only that someone had spoken, a flagrant flouting of the rules. That he had spoken those three words. Such a stupendous sum.

—*Sir, Hogarth said, frowning, this is most unseemly.*

Unseemly, she thought wildly, unseemly?

—*Kindly step forward, Hogarth ordered. The man behind her joined Hogarth as the bidder approached them. There was a short conversation; then Hogarth returned to the lectern, beaming.*

—*Well, gentlemen, forgive my haste. Every detail appears to be in order. The funding is secure, and, as we all know, there have been exceptions before in especially unusual circumstances. This appears to be one of them. A most historic occasion, I say. Yes indeed. Most historic. Therefore, I throw the vote to you. Shall we honor his bid? Your paddles, gentlemen, for aye.*

The paddles were slowly raised, all save one. The second-to-last bidder.

—*The vote must be unanimous, Hogarth said, frowning again.*

All eyes turned to the holdout. After a moment, he grudgingly raised his paddle.

—*One million pounds! Hogarth cried, banging down his gavel. A new record! One million pounds, he was thinking, unbelievable! All because he'd discovered her, thanks to a revolting American, that* dreadful June Nickerson, trying to flirt with him in the Ivy one evening he'd thought was going to be an interminable waste of his time.

—Gentlemen, he said, dinner will be served in twenty minutes.

She saw them put their paddles down and stand up, all except one. And she started to laugh. A wild, hysterical laugh. Sold for a million pounds to a masked monk! A masked madman! She couldn't help herself. She didn't care if that man was going to slit her throat— she couldn't stop.

They were all looking at her, she knew. Then they all started laughing as well.

The screen was replaced so the men could no longer see her. That was the signal for the room to be emptied, and she heard a collective groan. The hood was pushed over her head and tied tightly, and her laughter died away as she panicked. The moment she was released from the pillars the heavy thing was wrapped around her again so she couldn't move. Then she was picked up and slung over someone's shoulder and taken down the steps, through hallways, up and down. They were moving very fast. She was dizzy and thought she'd be sick.

A door opened and shut, and they stopped. Her head was still upside down. The hood was removed, and her wig and the cap covering her hair, but it was pitch-black and she couldn't see. Someone was gathering the mass of her hair.

Don't cut off my hair. Don't cut off my head.

With her hair held tightly, someone else was wrapping something around her eyes. A blindfold of so many layers she couldn't possibly see through it or unbind it herself, even if her hands were free.

They were moving again. Into another room, the door opening and shutting. Then she was eased down onto a bed, facedown. Her shoes were removed and something cold was attached to one of her ankles. They unfastened her wrists and turned her over, taking off the heavy thing around her. Her arms were pulled away from her sides and she felt them hooking something into the cuffs still on her wrists. They unfastened the necklace. Then they were gone.

She was lying in utter darkness. She tried to pull against what they'd attached her to, but she could barely move. The corset was so tight. She couldn't breathe.

This couldn't be happening. It wasn't possible.

She was trapped inside a nightmare. There was no escape.

Back in the other room, the members of the Club were milling *about, talking eagerly. Who could it possibly have been among them to have bid that stupendous sum? Ah, she was luscious indeed. A fine figure of a girl. So young, so fresh. So easy to train. They all sighed at the unfairness of it.*

—Could any woman be worth it?

—How long will it take him, do you think? How long can he have her?

—I say, good question. A thousand per week, that's the rule, he said. One million pounds equals one thousand weeks. Fifty-two weeks per year. That's, let's see, nineteen and nearly one-quarter years. So he will have to keep her until 1954.

They laughed.

—Not worth the time, someone said. Worse than a bloody wife. Cost a bloody fortune.

—Plus the secrecy. And the maintenance. Bugger of a headache.

—She's going to be a handful. Did you hear that laugh! He'll have his hands full, I warrant.

They laughed again.

But they all still wanted her. Wanted her more than ever.

PART III

The Phoenix
of the Hills

(1954–1956)

Belladonna passing by
Do not let her see you cry
Hurry, darling, better fly
I don't need to tell you why
Belladonna watch you die

12

The Banisters of
the Plantation

Stand on the veranda outside the big house and twirl around. Everywhere you look, everything you see: All belongs to Belladonna. The grounds and the rolling hills, the streams and ponds, the paddocks and fields, the huge oval of our own racetrack and the long stretch of private runway, the forests and the fencing, the vegetable and rose and flower gardens, the hedged maze and the gravel walkways, the sculpted fountain spewing cascades of scented water and the smaller fountains misting around it, the azure pool and the fish pond full of koi and the mysterious grotto and its fanciful caves. The stables and the garages and the shooting range and the carpentry shop and the dozens of outlying cottages and houses for all the employees of the estate. All 247,623 acres belonging to La Casa della Fenice.

The House of the Phoenix.

Nothing like a gentle whiff of fresh country air in our faces!

While our connected town houses in New York belong to a city, cool and sophisticated, La Fenice is a quite different place. The big plantation house radiates cheerfulness and comfort as the curtains stir with the windows open wide on the surrounding vistas. Belladonna knew exactly why I picked this house: It reminds us of Italy.

If only we were still there, at Ca' d'Oro. If only Leandro were here. How much we miss him; how much I wish I could talk to him, to be given a few words of guidance. How proud I think he'd be of what we created in the Club Belladonna. Of how we taught June a lesson she'll never forget, and what we did to Sir Patty. Of how Belladonna could have cracked at the sight of him, at the sound of his voice and the sheen of his ring.

But she didn't.

We've left the reality of all that behind, at least for now. The expanse of our vast properties is consuming us—trying to sort out how best to have it run smoothly, that is. We can take nothing for granted.

The big plantation house was already structurally sound and we had started renovations months before, remember. We assembled as much of our New York architectural team as possible, set up camp, and had crews working around the clock; we wanted them finished and gone. Who knew when we might need to move in, if indeed we ever did?

Luckily for us, Sir Patty showed up when he did.

Unluckily for *him*.

The Pritch knew what those names meant as soon as he heard them. They were the members of the Hellfire Club. It had really existed, he explained, a small ensemble of degenerates in the mid-eighteenth century, and any schoolboy knew of their exploits and debauched revelries, led by one Sir Francis Dashwood. That would be the code name of their leader, we assume.

The Knights of St. Francis of Wycombe, the members of the Hellfire Club fancied themselves, and they met in caves under the ruins of Medmenham Abbey, not all that far from London. It didn't surprise Pritch that the members of *this* Club would take their names from the original Hellfire members, protecting their anonymity; their own perverse little joke, I suppose. Nowadays, some people claim the original Hellfires weren't so bad, but Pritch, who always assumes the worst about human behavior, never believed it. Why, even Churchill himself had written a little ditty about them:

> Whilst Womanhood, in the habit of a Nun,
> At Med'nam lies, by backward Monks undone.

They'd had a motto, too, Pritch added: *Fay ce que voudras*— "Do as you wish."

It figures. But how are we to find out the real names behind the code names? Simple, Pritch told us. He'd start his discreet investigations in London, now that he had Sir Patty's name. Round up the usual suspects who've been known to associate with the Cresswell family. Monitor Sir Patty's phone calls. Of course, he personally wouldn't be doing a whole lot of talking since his stroke. No matter—he'd be sure to have lots of visitors, and the ever-so-competent nurses whom Pritch had sent over from the posh agency would be supervising all visits when they weren't rummaging through the mail and sucking up to the family. "They're already absolutely indispensable," the Pritch told us, gloating.

"He's sure to pop off any day now," the Pritch added, sounding positively cheery during our last phone call. "Just you wait till the funeral. That's when we'll move in for the final push." He cackled. "Someone important is bound either to go to the service or to pay a condolence call. Just you wait."

And so we wait. In the meantime, I survey with justifiable pride our newest acquisition, which sprawls out over the verdant rolling countryside of eastern Virginia. La Fenice is a working farm—even if it has been sorely neglected for the last decade—with hundreds of cows, horses, oxen, bulls, pigs, sheep, chickens, ducks, and geese, and endless fields of hay, oats, and alfalfa. We quickly fix up the old overseer's house about a quarter-mile down the hill from the big house; it's where our assorted collection of spies—we prefer to call them "security"—live. Two are waiters from the club; two others arrive, only slightly shopworn, after years in Washington, D.C. All are confirmed bachelors of a certain age and irreproachably trustworthy. So says Jack. So we hope. They have the savvy to laugh at the plaque Belladonna chose to hang over their front door, the one that reads TANTALUS HOUSE. They know that Tantalus was the son of Zeus, condemned by his arrogance and transgressions to stand in Hades, where water would recede when he attempted to quench his thirst and food disappear when he tried to fill his gnawing belly.

Tantalized forevermore. No wonder Belladonna thought of that myth.

I like this quartet a lot. They're pleased with the work and the landscape unfolding around them. Their house is cleaned and their cooking provided by some of the wives of our gardeners. We give them the funds they've requested and leave them to their own devices. Orlando checks in to make sure everything is copacetic. Besides, it's hard not to like men who have given themselves code names pinched from nursery rhymes: Winken, Blinken, and Nod, and Hubbard. "I'm the Old Mother," Hubbard tells me, and I leave it at that.

Their first job is to oversee the building of a series of gates, in addition to reinforcing the huge wrought-iron gate at the main entrance and the dilapidated house guarding it. After the renovations are finished, another one of Jack's semiretired spies, a man with the delectable name of Thibaud Winfrey, moves into it with his wife, Anita. The Winfreys are quiet and unassuming and keep their eyes on everything, eager to have useful work to do, logging in all our callers. As soon as any car or truck arrives at the gate, identification is checked and a call made up to the house for verification. Just to be sure, there are cameras hidden in the eaves of the gatehouse to take photographs of every vehicle entering and exiting the driveway; cameras hidden in the lovely sculpted light fixtures lining that driveway to the house; cameras by the pool and the maze and the gardens.

Old habits, you know. We don't appreciate surprises.

Thibaud loves to cook gumbo, and Anita is rarely seen without her knitting. They are as unlike the dreaded Markus and Matilda as—

No no no, I don't want to talk about *them*. I don't want to think about the last time we lived in an immense, isolated house. Not Leandro's house. The other one.

Unlike the house in Belgium, though, it would be impossible to put fencing around our vast amount of acreage, so we're thrilled when we meet Stan Penrose, the head groundskeeper. He has a kennel full of bloodhounds to keep him company when he and his guys tramp all over on their daily rounds, keeping the lawns in order, clearing the forests and underbrush, and checking on the indigenous plants and animals. Orlando is very pleased with this concept; it's a built-in security patrol. When Orlando says that we want to expand the kennels and start breeding the bloodhounds, Stan's face lights up with pleasure. Stan is the spitting image of Calvin Coolidge, a man of few words and simple tastes, but he knows the land, and we feel that we can trust him, too, without having to divulge our reasons for constant patrolling. In fact, I have a feeling he will be as good a friend to Orlando as Matteo had been, so that is one less worry for me.

We also put a series of gates and hidden cameras on the service road that the tenants are accustomed to using. So sorry for the inconvenience, we explained, handing out keys. It's for everyone's protection. We don't like trespassers, and there are too many people who are too curious about the Contessa. They've no choice but to agree. There are more than a dozen farm families who live in cottages about a mile away from our house, nearer the fields, as well as groundskeepers, shepherds, gardeners, horsemen who live near the stables, and our chauffeur, Templeton. Another Jack discovery, he's moved above the garage and loves cars almost as much as the conversations he overhears in them.

We can't tell them that all this security is not so much to keep people *out,* but to keep several unlucky few *in.* Locked away. Left to rot.

But before we can deal with the property itself we must make our house livable. We have our team install tiny security buttons, hidden in all the rooms. Hit one, and it automatically triggers a ringer specifying the room; the ringers sound in Tantalus House, in Orlando's room and my room, of course, in the kitchen and in the guardhouse. That way, someone who knows the code will quickly be able to summon help.

A little bit of leftover paranoia goes a very long way.

Belladonna and I decide to have lots of theme rooms, to play in and relax in. One is lined entirely with mirrors, so naturally we name it the Narcissus Room; another has piles of vibrantly colored velvet cushions and a votive-lined shrine, with statues of Buddha, Ganesh, Thor, and Apollo to appease all the gods, for meditation. There is a billiard room, and a miniature electric-train room with dozens of tracks set up for Bryony and her Sam doll to play with. There is a music room, lit by lamps whose shades are made of parchment discards from one of Mozart's early symphonies, with a grand piano and a harpsichord and an entire setup for a string quartet. Cork lines the walls of the green room, filled with blooms rotated from our hothouses: camellias and lilacs and orchids, a riotous display of ferns and fronds below them. The ballroom has walls and a ceiling of the thinnest hammered copper, which will reflect and slightly distort all the shapes and colors of the clothing dancers will wear in it, spinning them together like a crazy patchwork.

Belladonna hates the ballroom. She takes one look at it, says it's beautiful, and refuses to set foot in it.

We buy, at auction, the entire fifteen-thousand-volume library that had once belonged to the estate of Madame de Pompadour—all bound in colored morocco leather, emblazoned with her crest, the pages gilded—to line the shelves of our own library. Then I disembowel the insides of books that were damaged by years of neglect, to hide cigarette boxes and little objects.

One of my favorite tricks.

In the grand salon, gigantic marble tables, groupings of over-stuffed sofas, leather club chairs, and several chaise longues carved to resemble gondolas, upholstered in vibrant crimson silk the color of a Belladonna cocktail, are strewn about. The walls are decorated with Marisa's lovely painted friezes of nymphs and goddesses. A huge Valadier candelabra presides over the salon, with female nudes gracing each stem, dancing with their arms raised as they support the curving gold-leaf candle holders. The formal dining room is equally glorious: The immense glass table, which can seat forty at an intimate dinner party, had been engraved by Lalique and is lit from below, so it seems to glow with inner light. Glass shelves at varying heights hold Minton porcelain, Wedgwood fish plates, Spode game plates, Staffordshire oyster plates, and Bryony's clay carvings from school. Enormous arched windows overlook the rose and flower gardens, reflecting them in a pale green and silvery light. The smaller family dining room off the kitchen will soon become the choice destination for all the children on the estate: The floor is made from a thick slab of movable marble glass, covering a trout pool. This way, we can tell our guests to fish for their own dinner.

Upstairs, there are eight guest bedrooms, each a different color. Bryony's pale pink bedroom has a midnight blue ceiling painted with the constellations, just as she had in New York. Rosalinda's bedroom connects to hers, and mine is down the hall, near Orlando's. Belladonna's bathroom is divine. Even larger than her bedroom, it seems, it has a luxurious chaise covered in zebra-printed velvet and a plush pile carpet to match, and two small sofas strewn with velvet pillows in different animal prints. The freestanding bathtub, on a dais in the corner, is almost deep enough and long enough to swim in, and the piles of towels stashed on shelves above it are of the softest Egyptian cotton. The door handles are made from molds of Bryony's hands, and the walls are covered with some of Belladonna's favorite photographs of the Italian countryside.

Smaller, silver-framed family photos sit atop Belladonna's dressing table. Bryony's favorite coloring place will soon be sprawled on the floor under this pink marble table, as Belladonna reclines in the chaise and reads aloud one of Madame de Pompadour's fifty-two books of fairy stories.

Belladonna's bedroom is equally wonderful, though, all white and silver, with shimmering silver curtains in front of white linen blinds embroidered in silver thread with several of Voltaire's pithy maxims. Her vast bed is topped with a white fur spread and heaped with dozens of pillows, each a different shade of white and the palest cream. The light fixtures are made of mother-of-pearl and hollowed-out sea urchins' shells. They glow, soft and delicate.

Unlike Belladonna as she is right now, hard and unapproachable.

The gardens, on the other hand, are expansive and welcoming. The rose garden is delicious, beds of different-colored blooms edged with nasturtiums and parsley to keep the aphids away. I love to sit for hours in the scented flower and herb garden: the freesias smell like plums and the iris smell like apricots; the honeysuckle and clematis crawl up over lattices; the lavender, rosemary, sweet woodruff, and lemon verbena compete crazily with one another. There are mint and myrtle plants, yellow jasmine and violets. Marjoram and oregano and basil spill over clay pots. And everyone is instructed to stay away from the oleander.

Oh ho, the whiff of a killer!

Belladonna sounds so sweet.

Belladonna spends days reading Pompadour's medieval gardening books so she can create one special garden plot. In it, all the flowers have a special significance: a fig tree for "I keep my secret"; lemon geranium for "unexpected meetings"; morning-bride for "I have lost all." Rhododendron spells "Beware—I am dangerous." A Judas tree for betrayal, dozens of peonies for anger. Laurel for treachery.

We dub it the Hellfire Garden. The gardeners wonder to themselves, I know, when Belladonna gives them detailed instructions about precisely what she wants, but they are good at their jobs and they know enough to keep their mouths shut and do her bidding. Even they, though, are forbidden to touch one corner of the Hellfire Garden. That's where she keeps the mandrake.

Mandragora officinarum, the preferred talisman of spell-casters, wrapped in a shroud like a mummified corpse, is almost as much fun as the *Atropa belladonna.* A nice long root can grow to be almost five feet long and look like a man. Well, nearly. It's practically impossible to cultivate it in this climate, but Belladonna's going to try, soaking the ground around it with honey water, as Caterina told her to. Caterina had explained everything when the two of them used to sit in the kitchen in Italy, chopping basil for pesto sauce. She said that the mandrake has magical powers, that on the surface it grows like a big rosette almost flat on the ground, with long leaves and short-stemmed bluish purple flowers and fruits that nestle in the heart of the rosette like tiny little tomatoes. But it's what's under the ground that counts, the twisted root itself.

"Dig it up only at sunset," Caterina said. "Do not tug violently on it or it will scream. Wrap it in a shroud and keep it in the dark."

I stay away from the Hellfire Garden. Everyone does. We prefer the other gardens or the lawn itself, with hammocks and comfortable chairs strategically placed at beautiful vista points, and where Rodin statues stand silent sentinel as Andromeda had in front of the Club Belladonna. A curving gravel path leads to the pool, its azure tiles like those at Ca' d'Oro, with a pair of gigantic cherubs presiding at the deep end, water pouring from their upturned urns into the pool itself. The pool house has a small padded room for judo practice, changing rooms, a sauna, and a steam room scented with eucalyptus. Still farther down another path is a wide staircase of carved limestone, pots of giant hydrangea arranged every few steps. It is flanked by two narrower stone staircases with an endless trickle of water carving a fluid trail down into the fish ponds below, down to the grotto and its folly. Resembling a dollhouse for grown-ups, the folly is a cozy little cottage with a thatched roof; inside, a terra-cotta tiled floor is scattered with several small Moroccan prayer rugs. A huge fireplace and its celadon-veined marble mantel dominate one wall. Rocking chairs and a large daybed, strewn with one of Belladonna's favorite piles of embroidered cushions in a jumble of brilliantly colored velvets and silks, fill the room. It is where she goes to hide when she wants to lock the door and be left alone to plot. She is the only person here whose moods are not soothed by the water cascading in gentle streams just outside the windows.

She cannot be soothed by the sound of water. Only by the

sound of *him*, screaming in the blackness as we leave him to rot in the dungeon where he belongs.

The original members of the Hellfire Club had their caves dug out of limestone by slave laborers, who then used the stone to pave the local roads, the Pritch told us. In the caves, their own private dungeon, the walls would perpetually ooze moisture, and footsteps crunching on curving gravel paths in the darkness, winding around in the cool dark air lit only by a few dim torches flickering eerily in unseen air currents, sounded loud and menacing.

It's the crunching sound that is the terror, worse than the sudden chill like the fingers of a ghost. The crunching sound and the dull thud of the thick wooden door clanking shut, and the echo of footsteps dying away until there is nothing left but the ravenous darkness. Maybe in the cell there is a small covered pot with a lid, to piss in. Maybe there is a stale hunk of bread. Maybe not.

Sleep tight, sweetheart. Who knows when we shall come to check on you again?

It is then that the screaming always starts.

No, the most important rooms in La Fenice are not gorgeously decorated and filled with marvelous things. They are unknown to all but a few, hidden behind a secret panel in what used to be the wine cellar. Actually, the wine cellar is still there, keeping our thousands of cataloged and dusty bottles in mint condition. Anyone who comes down for a bottle of d'Yquem to drink with dessert would not suspect that nascent terrors are lurking behind the claret.

In the dungeons, we've carved out our own simple structure. There are no windows opening onto lush countryside; there are only small pitch-black rooms with rough brick walls and low ceilings, smelling of damp and desperation even before anyone is left inside them. There are thick wooden doors with metal bars across a tiny square opening. There are hooks in the walls so *he* won't be able to escape.

We don't speak of the dungeons. It is enough to know they exist.

I'm sure you've realized that I'm leaving out a lot of the picky, aggravating details about our move. Suffice to say the trip down to Virginia, right after Christmas, was not pleasant: Belladonna taciturn and morose, as she had been for weeks; Bryony fretting in response to her mother's state of mind, dressing and undressing Sam until I thought the poor doll would fall to pieces. Although Bryony's not quite seven, she's both precocious and prescient. In fact, she is often better at managing her mother's moodiness than any of the rest of us, including Matteo. It worries me that this lovely little girl willingly tries to share the burden of her mother's struggles. Children are often so generous by nature. Still, I watch Bryony carefully to see any signs of her father's character emerging by default.

We all do. We don't talk about that, either.

Bryony is going to be very unhappy when she realizes that we're not going back to New York, that we have taken her away from her routine and her beloved school. I think we should have prepared her before we left so she could say good-bye to her friends, but Belladonna didn't want to deal with it. Or anything else. She gave Jack a ring made of thick bright gold, a beautifully curved *B* carved into it, but could say little to him, not after what we'd done together in the dark. He and I had a long, terribly poignant conversation, and he's promised to be in regular contact with us. I know his heart is breaking, but he is as stoic as Belladonna is adamant.

I miss Jack already, but I am wishing even more that Matteo were with us. It's too much to hope for, selfishly unfair to wish they'd move down tomorrow. We must give Matteo and Annabeth time to be together, away from all our weirdness. I can't blame my darling big brother for wanting to stay away. Not that we aren't fabulous, of course. It's just that—

Botheration. At least someone I know is having a good time.

One day not long after our arrival, I find Bryony crying her heart out under one of the giant marble tables in the salon. Sam, dressed in a hot-pink bathing suit, is in her lap. "Whatever is the matter?" I say gently, trying to take her in my arms. She pushes me away, and I hurry off to summon her mother. This conversation is long overdue.

Belladonna comes over and sits down next to her daughter, under the table, holding her until her sobs dissolve into hiccups. "I want Froggy," Bryony says, tears still running down her cheeks. "I want Dromedee. I want Tinkletime. I want my doggies. I want to go home."

"The doggies need to stay in New York," Belladonna says softly.

"Why?" Bryony asks. "Why can't they be here with us? There's lots of room for them to play."

"I know that, sweetie," she replies, "but there are several reasons why we didn't bring them down here. First of all, Jack is up there all by himself, without us, and we don't want him to get lonely, do we?" Bryony pouts, then shakes her head no. "And we need the dogs to guard the house in New York. They're house dogs, and they belong to our house there, and they need to stay in the same place. You wouldn't want them to be crying every night because they miss their house, would you? Dogs can't tell you that they feel bad, but people can." She sighs deeply.

Bryony looks at her mother, not knowing what to say.

"It's the only house they know," Belladonna goes on. "I'm afraid that if they came here, they might run around too much and get lost and we'd never find them again." She can't tell her daughter that her Irish wolfhounds are too famous to risk detection. Even at an isolated location in Virginia, someone is bound to have heard of the Club Belladonna and its barking sentinels.

"I want to go home," Bryony says, starting to cry again.

"I want to go home, too, but we need to stay here for a while," Belladonna says. "We're going to make lots of new friends, and you're going to a new school, and—"

Bryony starts wailing in earnest. I can't say I blame her.

"I don't want new friends and I don't want a new school. I want to go home," she screams. "I hate you." She heaves Sam at Belladonna and runs up to her room, throwing herself down on her bed and sobbing with heartrending passion.

Belladonna looks at me, her eyes scarily opaque. No, she hasn't been herself since that scene in the basement. Or perhaps she is more like herself than I care to admit. She's as brittle as an icicle dripping off the side of a roof, and I keep waiting for her to shatter.

"Shall I go get him?" I ask. She picks up Sam and nods, and I hurry into the pantry where Bianca has been hiding a surprise for Bryony.

Belladonna and I go upstairs together and into Bryony's bedroom. She is still sobbing. Belladonna lies down next to her on the bed, and Bryony tries to push her away.

"Listen, darling, I was very wrong not to tell you sooner that we were planning to move and stay down here," Belladonna says. "I didn't want you to be upset at Christmas. But we'll all get used to it soon, I hope. There are lots of other children here for you to play with, and it's much nicer and cleaner than it is in New York. Can you forgive me?"

"No," Bryony says, her face buried in pillows. "I like New York. I hate Virginia."

"I don't blame you for liking New York," Belladonna says after a few minutes. "I like it, too, as much as you. But we can always go back there and visit, you know. Maybe in a few years, we can go back there to live. We have to see. In the meantime, I have something for you that I hope will make you feel a little better. Don't you want to see what it is?"

"No. I don't care," Bryony replies, her face buried in her bed-spread. "Go away."

"But he needs you," Belladonna says.

After a few minutes, Bryony sits up, her curiosity winning out over her distress. "Here," Belladonna says, "he's all yours. His name is Basilico."

It's a miniature longhaired dachshund puppy we've named after the Italian word for basil. He is altogether ridiculous, like a tiny hairy sausage with legs. I can't wait to see what the bloodhounds do when they meet this one.

"His mommy got sick and she couldn't take care of him," Bella-donna says, "and he really needs you. We have a nice little bed for him, and he can sleep here with you so he won't be too lonely. Do you want to take care of him?"

Bryony takes the squirming little bundle in her arms, and he immediately licks the tears on her face. "Is he all mine?" she asks.

"Yes, he is. And next week, we're going to get some more dogs, for our house here." Belladonna wipes Bryony's eyes and has her blow her nose. "Getting new dogs doesn't mean you still don't love Dromedee and Froggy and Tinkletime, you know," she adds. "You can have lots of love for lots of different dogs."

"Are they going to be Irish wolfhounds?" Bryony asks.

"No, they're going to be another breed, called Neopolitan mas-tiffs, and you can pick three of them from a litter that was born a couple of weeks ago. These are really sweet puppies, and they're going to grow to be very big and very slobbery." And very trainable. "Now I think we should find some really wonderful names for the new puppies, don't you? Tomasino's going to go get your book of the constellations, and we'll see if we can find something you like, okay?"

Bryony nods and snuggles close to Basilico. Our Neopolitan mastiffs are going to grow to be startling, scary-looking dogs, squat and huge, with dripping, drooping jowls. They are much sweeter than they look, especially once you've been approved by their doggy sensibility, but they're going to be perfectly trained for our needs. All the staff will know the commands to keep them in line, just in case.

You never can be too careful.

Bryony decides to call them Casseopeia, Hector, and Drizzle-puss. "Why can't we call them Froggy and Dromedee and Tinkle-time?" she asked at first.

"What if Dromedee and Froggy and Tinkletime come down to visit us?" Belladonna replies. "Wouldn't they get confused with the other doggies? Besides, every person and every animal has a right to have their very own name, something special. Don't you think?"

Every person except Belladonna.

When I introduce myself to the tenant farmers and other workers on the estate, I tell them to call her the Contessa, when and if they meet her. Simple enough, don't you agree, and perfectly evocative. She never wanted to be called Ariel again; she couldn't bear it. Nor could we call her Belladonna in earshot of anyone who didn't really know who she was. She told us to call her Bella, even though she loathes that name, too. But that's what we used to call her in the house in New York, in case Bryony overheard. She thinks her mother's name is Bella. Bella della Robbia, the Contessa.

It does have a nice ring to it.

*A*ll the neighbors think so, too. They're practically falling over themselves to be invited to the house newly renovated with such fantastic care by the bereaved Italian widow, even though none of them has been so much as let near the long driveway curving up to the big house. She must be loaded beyond belief. What a thrill to have real live royalty in down-home King Henry, Virginia!

It doesn't take much to have a few rumors spread, even without the help of a local version of Loose Lips. Several extremely sizable contributions have already been allocated to the local Police Be-nevolent Association, the sheriff's office, the parks beautification project, the volunteer fire department, the school library, the marching band, and the courthouse fund. The local politicians as well as the trustees of Jefferson Davis Hospital are beside themselves with gratitude for the Contessa's stupendous generosity. If there's anything they can do, please, all you need do is ask.

Yes, the Contessa must be a real marvel! So generous, so mysterious!

At the moment, though, we're more interested in getting to know the rest of the employees we've inherited with the property, and continuing to secure the grounds. We quickly learned that the tenants had been barely paid, lied to, and abandoned, and many were ready to move away in despair from land they thought was theirs. Except that they had nowhere to go. We paid their back wages, tripled their salaries, fixed up their tumbledown houses, put in electricity and proper plumbing and telephones. We told them we wanted La Fenice to become the most profitable farm in all of Virginia, and that they should come to me whenever they needed to, with suggestions or questions. We asked them who would be the best manager, and we appointed their choice, a man named Gilbert Scott. In short order, the farm that had once been the laughingstock of the county is on its way to becoming its most successful and most beautiful.

Oh ho, how a little faith and a lot of money bring their rewards!

There is one family, though, that soon becomes a more important addition to our motley group. Belladonna has taken to exploring the property, often with Orlando, and none of the tenants know yet who she is. They think she's Bryony's governess, or Orlando's wife, perhaps, and they call her "the nanny." One afternoon, she sees a farmer sitting on the steps of his house, his hugely pregnant wife by his side, whittling a long piece of wood into what seems to be a walking stick.

I summon this farmer to Gilbert's estate office, housed in a small building near Tantalus House, a few days later, telling him to bring whatever it was he'd been carving as well as any other pieces he'd whittled of late. When he arrives, placing the walking stick and a bulging bag near the door, he is so nervous he doesn't realize he's taken his cap off and is turning it in an endless circle in his hands. No other tenant has been singled out for such a meeting.

"Baines, is it?" I ask. Belladonna is sitting just outside, so she can hear our conversation. She's still in no mood to be talking to any of our tenants. "Jebediah Baines?"

"Yes, sir," he says.

"How long have you been living here, Jebediah? May I call you Jebediah?"

He nods, surprised by the courtesy of my question. "All my life, sir. My daddy was a farmer, and my granddaddy and his daddy."

"Are you descended from slaves who worked this plantation?"

"Yes, sir, I believe so."

"Please, sit down." I point to a chair and he sits on the edge of his chair, still twisting his cap around, as if preparing to bolt any minute. I bring over his bag, pour the pieces out onto the table, and examine them in silence for a few minutes.

"Where did you get the wood, may I ask?" I say.

The cap is still twisting around, like the wheel of a truck stalled in mud. "From the forest," Baines says, his anxiety so palpable I could pickle it. "Not from trees. Only pieces we found, me and my daughter. We go walkin' to look for wood. We never cut a tree, never."

I pick up one small figure, the head of a little girl, her hair carved with such exquisite finesse it almost seems to be real.

"Is this your daughter?" I ask.

"Yes, sir," he replies. "My daughter Susannah. She's near to seven."

"And your wife is pregnant."

"Yes, sir, Dionne, her name is. The midwife says she's havin' twins, and she's been feelin' poorly, so I was whittlin' her a walking stick so's it's easier for her to get round."

"Let me see it." I finger it carefully. "Do you know what you've done here?"

"No, sir," he says. "I hope I haven't done wrong."

"No, Jebediah, you haven't done wrong." I say soberly. "You've done some of the most beautiful carving I've ever seen, that's what you've done."

He is so astonished by my comments that his cap stops turning. He'd been certain I was about to kick him and his family out into the cold cruel world.

"In fact," I go on, "I want to hire you to carve the banisters of the grand staircase in the big house. They're either cherry or walnut, I believe. Are you interested?"

He's still so shocked he can only nod.

"Very well. Come with me." He looks at me, still disbelieving.

We gather up his little pieces, put them back in his bag, and walk briskly up to the house. When he sees the immense staircase, which winds up in a graceful curve to a landing and then to the second floor, his jaw drops. Then he runs his fingers over the wood, thumping it to see how sound it is. The color is lovely, but the banisters themselves are thick and shapeless.

"What do you think?" I ask.

"The wood is good," he says. "Walnut."

"We've already cut some pieces that are roughly the same size, so you can experiment with a design," I say. "Do a few samples and we'll go from there. We want each one to be slightly different, an ever-changing design. How does that sound?"

Poor Baines, his heart thumping in shock. He'll be practically comatose when I tell him how much we're prepared to pay him. "Listen," I go on, "we were going to have to bring over a sculptor from Italy to do this. We'd much rather have you. We'll pay the other farmers for your share of the work in the fields, so don't you worry."

"Yes, sir," he says. His eyes are starting to shine. I'm not teasing him; I'm not going to fire him. He's about to start living a dream.

How I love discovering true talent and allowing it to thrive!

"There's one thing I want you to do before you start," I say.

"Yes, sir." He instantly looks anxious again.

"I want you to do a carving of the Contessa's little girl. Her name is Bryony. She's about the same age as your Susannah. We would be most grateful if you could arrange your time so that she can sit for you. Perhaps she can meet Susannah then. It would be nice for her to have a playmate here."

I think this astonishes him most of all. The children of the owners do not play with the children of the tenants. It simply isn't done in 1954. Not here in King Henry, Virginia.

He will learn soon enough that Belladonna does what she wants.

*T*his is how Bryony became best friends with Susannah Baines, and our banisters become the talk of the estates for miles around. Not only because the carving is so striking, garlands of interwoven fruits and flowers and branches arching up in intricate patterns, but because Baines has been allowed into the house to carve them.

Of course, no neighbors have yet been invited to see the famous banisters, though they've tried, sending us weekly invitations to balls and dinners and cocktail parties and hunts. We politely decline. Their children go to school with Bryony and try to invite themselves over, but we outfox them. They think they're in luck when Bryony announces that her seventh birthday party in February is open to all her second-grade classmates, but hopes are dashed when the party is held at the soda shop on Main Street in King Henry, and the Contessa is nowhere to be found.

The neighbors have yet to see the rumored marvels of our house, as well as its mistress. Belladonna wants to be left alone, so she has not yet ventured off the property. She has no need to, it's so immense. She often goes riding with Orlando, on a mare she names Artemis, after the horse she loved at Ca' d'Oro. She speaks to Jack nearly every day, and often takes target practice with the Tantalus spies on the shooting range tucked in a small corner of woods near the Hellfire Garden. Templeton drives Bianca to do the food shopping; he drives Rosalinda and Bryony to school in the morning and then picks her up in the afternoon. That Bryony is adjusting and content is what we really care about.

And I, being my naturally indefatigable self, am finishing the final flourishes of decorating nirvana. It is small recompense for my indispensable role in the Club Belladonna, which I miss more than I can say. How many castrati get to lord it over highly select riffraff in the most fantastic and desirable nightclub in the world? But I suppose I can live without it for a while. I have to admit I'm still exhausted. From everything.

From waiting.

We're still waiting for Sir Patty to keel over, but he's hanging on, dribbling into his diapers. I hope he's suffering unspeakable indignities; that's the least he deserves.

So when I wake up one raw morning in early March with my knee throbbing, I wonder what it could mean. As the day goes by and Bryony returns from school, nothing seems out of the ordinary. Until she comes running up from Susannah's house, her cheeks flushed. "She's having the babies!" Bryony calls out as she dashes into the house. "Call Auntie Ruby!"

Except the midwife doesn't have a phone. Poor people in this county don't have phones; they don't have running water. I wondered how doctors had been summoned before when the tenants got sick, until Stan told me that they either used a weatherbeaten pickup, or a horse and buggy. The previous owners hadn't cared.

Well, we do. Dionne and Jebediah have insisted that Auntie Ruby, the midwife, take care of the birth. She's a local legend, nearly seventy and a little deaf, but she's never lost a baby yet, they tell me. I make them swear to let us take them to a hospital should anything go wrong, and they reluctantly promise.

Nothing is going to go wrong, not with these twins. That's why Belladonna is so anxious about this birth, and is pacing near the Baineses' house, where the other tenants can't see her. They wouldn't be able to understand why she's so caught up in this birth, and I'm certainly not going to start explaining.

Templeton arrives with Auntie Ruby, who calmly clucks and fusses. Belladonna paces amid the trees while Bryony and Susannah sit quietly near the house, playing with their dolls. When the babies are born after only a few hours of labor, Bryony comes to find me, beaming. "Twin boys," she announces. "Ezra and Ezekiel. Susannah named them. They're perfect."

"Let's go and see them. Twin boys, like me and my brother," I say, and she slips her hand into mine, singing a nonsense song as we walk down the path.

At the sight of Dionne lying in bed with a sleepy smile and the perfect swaddled little boys at her side, I get all choked up. "Lovely names," I say. "Very biblical." I smile and try to compose myself. "The Contessa is very happy for you and your entire family." Sometimes I am such a trooper I deserve a medal for valor. "And she's decided we should have a christening party." It is a command, not a question. "A nice private party for everyone here, to welcome the first babies born since the Contessa's arrival. Then we'll have an awful, overcrowded party for all the nosy neighbors, to shut them up for a while."

Jebediah and Dionne laugh.

"Take good care of your beautiful babies," I say as I take Bryony by the hand once more and bid everyone good night.

Dionne, with a mother's instincts, is too perceptive not to know there's something going on, but she'll never ask. It wouldn't matter if she did. Tristan's name has not been mentioned since that long-ago conversation with Leandro.

It's not about to be mentioned now.

*   *   *

We mail out the invitations and the neighborhood is instantly agog with excitement. Finally, they shall meet the mysterious Contessa! Snoop in the big house and explore the vast property! Drink her juleps and gossip! Welcome her to the wonders of King Henry!

Honestly, I'll never understand how the slightest standoffish-ness can create such a fuss. Perhaps it's that really stinking-rich people are not used to being shunned by one of their own. Or that they can't conceive of not getting their own way. We've already heard stories about some of these people, claiming to be descendants of Jamestown settlers. Descendants of English convicts is more like it. I'd like to throw them all in the dungeons for a splendid evening of meditation, but that's too easy. It doesn't matter how their families first procured their fortunes and social standing—fraud, thievery, slave labor, and cunning, I suspect, played a large part—as long as the money keeps flowing now. How very convenient is a memory ravaged by bourbon!

There's Osbourne Robertson, the mayor of King Henry—he's best known for his holiday parties, the eggnog at Christmas, the grog on Boxing Day, the champagne on New Year's, the Bordeaux (like our Lord's, he says) at Easter—and his wife, Dippy, as in just dipping into the snuff. There's Justin Blackwater, heir to a great cotton fortune, and his wife, Letitia, famous for her hunt parties and detours into local barns for some refreshment of a most unusual sort; Hubert and Muffy Leighton, the "steel people," with hearts allegedly made out of the same material; Col. Wade Robey and his wife Claudette, whose brother, Reginald Marriner, is the erstwhile police chief, who never seems to be found in his office unless it's to pick up his paycheck and the secretary's skirts. Reggie's sister Constance is married to one Rory Chesterfield, famous for shooting birds off telephone poles when in the passenger's seat of his Packard convertible, and not much else.

I would go on, but I find this list such a chore. Not that we've actually had the pleasure of meeting any of these charming folk. They can wait. Mother Hubbard and his brood in Tantalus House keep us apprised, and they have already made some wonderful suggestions about local investments in neglected businesses. It seems we already own a lot more of King Henry than our plantation. Bel-

ladonna merely nods her approval when we tell her what we're
up to.

Which is why I'm so surprised when she says she wants to drive
into town. She's been getting driving lessons from Templeton, and
is often found with him drag-racing down our long expanse of runway. So far, though, she's only ventured out onto real roads at
dawn, when there's even less traffic than usual. Templeton is as
pleased with his pupil here as Dino had once been with her at Ca'
d'Oro, smiling at her near-immediate dexterity with the clutch and
the gearshift.

I need to go into town with Jebediah to check on some rare
woods that have come in to the lumberyard, owned by Reggie Marriner's son, Cooper. The shipments had been dribbling in for
weeks, and we told Cooper to hold on to them until the entire pile
was there; we didn't want constant deliveries from inquisitive drivers coming up to the house. Baines didn't really want to go, but I
nagged him so much he finally relented. Now, he looks even more
uncomfortable when he sees "the nanny" getting ready to hop into
the driver's seat of one of our more dilapidated old Chevy pickups.

I don't ask Belladonna what's going on. Maybe she wants to see
some faces other than our own before having a big party. Maybe
she wants to practice her driving in the daytime. I've no idea. Trying to deal with the capriciousness of her moods is becoming a
nearly impossible task, even for one as perspicacious as yours truly.
So when Orlando, who's insisted on coming with us just in case,
bursts out laughing at the sight of her, I relax and figure we're okay.
She's clad in her gardening outfit of dirt-stained denim overalls,
grubby sneakers, and a red-checked seersucker shirt and shapeless
sweater. With her hair tucked into an old bandanna and cheap
wide plastic sunglasses, she looks like a poor cousin of Judy Gar-
land in *Summer Stock.*

It is a bright sunny day, smelling of springtime. We bounce
along in the Chevy, Baines and I in the back, and I feel like singing,
the wind soft in my face, the dark nights of the Club Belladonna a
seeming lifetime ago. My delicious mood evaporates instantly as
we hit Main Street and the avidly curious stares of the locals. Belladonna ignores them. I jump out of the truck as gracefully as I can
and signal to Baines. I want us to check the wood, then go right
back home.

"I can't go in there," Baines says.

"Why ever not?" I ask, frowning.

"Colored folk don't go in there," he replies.

Botheration. How stupidly thoughtless I am. No wonder he didn't want to come with us on this expedition, yet was too polite to remind me of reality. No wonder people are staring. We forget about things like this, locked in our own world. There, we don't judge people by the color of their skin. Only by the blackness of their hearts.

"Do forgive me, Jebediah," I say quickly. "I'm an idiot. I'll bring the wood out for you to look at here. You can see the grain better in the sunshine anyway."

Cooper is all but fawning when he sees me. He knows I'm from the Contessa's property, but not what my exact role is, so he's playing the southern gentleman role to the hilt. He's still all affability when I ask to take the wood out to the light, but his smile fades when he sees me conferring with Jebediah. In fact, his face undergoes a rather instantaneous transformation.

"I'll have to ask y'all to step back inside, sir," Cooper says to me. He's a blond, with pale white eyelashes that make him look vaguely gerbillike, and his cheeks are suddenly very pink. So is his bald spot, which he's tried in vain to cover up with long wisps of hair.

"Why?" I ask, smiling broadly. Two can play this little charmer game, and I know I'm better at it than he'll ever be.

"Y'all can't parade around town with his sort," he says.

"What sort is that?" I ask, all innocence. "You mean Mr. Baines here? Why, he is a valued member of the Contessa's staff. Her favorite sculptor, as a matter of fact. She depends on his judgment for all matters pertaining to wood."

"I don't rightly care what y'all say he's a valued member of," Cooper says. "He knows better than to show his face with white folk. Don'tcha, Baines? Y'all don't belong here, and I want y'all out of my sight. Every one, before I lose my temper." Two of his employees have come up beside him, and one of them hands him a two-by-four that he starts smacking menacingly in his palm. So much for southern hospitality, or any thoughts of sucking up to the Contessa's hired help. I look around, noticing that most of the shopkeepers on Main Street have come out to gawk, smelling blood.

"I beg your pardon," Belladonna says.

"I'm not talking to *you,* ma'am," Cooper tells her. "Mind your own business."

"But I, sir, am talking to you," she says, opening her door. "And this *is* my business. I don't take kindly to being ordered around. Certainly not from the likes of you."

"Well, aren't we the high-and-mighty princess," Cooper says with a sneer. "Don't y'all know what we do to nigger-loving princesses around here?"

"No, I don't," she says, taking off her sunglasses. Her eyes are practically spitting fire. "Why don't you illuminate me."

If he had a cell left in his brain that wasn't sozzled, he might have figured out who she is. But he hasn't. He's not used to uppity northerners telling him to stuff it.

"We put them in their place," he says.

"And what place is that?" she asks. "A place like the jail cell you may as well call your home due to your rather constant bouts of public intoxication? A place like the courtroom where your daddy's always bailing you out? A place of honor like the moose head you have over your fireplace?"

"How do y'all know about my moose?" He is furious. I'd be, too, if I were the moose. "Who the hell do y'all think y'all are?" Then he steps a bit closer, along with his good-ol'-boy employees, trying to look menacing. "Get out of my sight before I lose my temper. If I do, y'all'll be sorry."

"It appears you already *have* lost your temper," I reply. His constant *y'alls* are really getting on my nerves. "And we do as we bloody well please. Besides, we haven't chosen which piece of wood we like best." Decisions can be *so* annoying.

"Y'all just hush your mouth," he says, and whacks our Chevy with his two-by-four. Baines cowers and covers his head with his hands. Orlando slowly walks over to examine the dent. The look on his face is not a happy one.

"Y'all're asking for it, boy," Cooper says.

"*Non é un' ragazzo,*" Orlando replies.

"What did y'all say? Is that some Guido bull? Well, y'all go on now and take that Guido bull right back on the boat to Guido-land," Cooper says. His blood is really boiling, and I think his cheeks are going to burst.

Orlando looks at me and I look back at him, then at Belladonna. Before they know what hit them, all three of the South's finest have landed flat on their backs on the street.

Belladonna crouches down next to Cooper, who still doesn't know what hit him, and pulls the two-by-four out of his grip. She pushes her sunglasses back down so he can't see her eyes; she's not used to in-your-face confrontations without a mask on. "I thought you southern boys were full of grace and hospitality," she tells him very softly. "I guess I was wrong about *y'all.* Are you going to make me sorry, or are you going to go right back in your nice little store and get me the money to pay for this dent? Should I have a nice chat with your daddy about your public assault on my truck and your appalling lack of manners?" Her voice becomes more menacing. "Should I?" He tries to get up, and she puts one of her grubby sneakers on his neck. "I'm talking to you, and I haven't given you leave either to insult anyone in my company or to get up. No, I wouldn't try to get up now if I were you," she says. "I am going to warn you once, and only this once. If I ever, *ever,* hear language like that in front of any man, woman, or child, I am personally going to cut your tongue out and feed it to my pigs. And if you try to harm me or any of mine, I will come for you in the dark of night and slit your throat and leave you to bleed and feed *you* to the pigs and then bury your bones where no one will ever find them." She smiles sweetly. "Have I made myself perfectly clear?"

He can barely nod, he's so dumbstruck. He still doesn't know what hit him—a judo throw or a crazy lady, or both. All he can think about is the look on the crazy lady's face, and the calmly threatening tone of the crazy lady's voice. Spitfire anger he understands. Softly spoken intimidation he does not.

She neatly breaks the two-by-four over her knee and drops it near his face.

"I've so enjoyed doing business with you," she says.

The Contessa has arrived. Welcome to the neighborhood!

13

A Romp in the Hay

"*I*'ve written something wonderful. Do you want to hear it?"

"No," Belladonna says. "Leave me alone."

Botheration. Looks like it's going to be one of those days. We've been having a lot of those days lately, ever since Cooper was left lying in the dust. Unfortunately, that charming scene with him barely diffused the rage Belladonna hasn't acknowledged since our encounter with Sir Patty. This anger is percolating so madly—like the coffee in our newfangled electric pots—that I fear something larger than Krakatau is soon to erupt.

" 'Dear Laura,' " I plow on, undeterred, " 'I wish to thank you for all your letters, and ask your forgiveness for my silence. I've been—' "

"Enough," she interrupts, her teeth clenched. "What the hell do you think you're doing?"

"Writing to Laura, of course," I reply. "It's long overdue, I might add."

"No one asked you to add anything."

"I thought it might be a good-luck charm. First Laura came to the club, then June, then Sir—"

"Don't you dare mention his name to me," she says fiercely. "I only want to hear his name when you tell me he's dead."

"All right," I say. "Sorry." I suppose this isn't an especially propitious moment to tell her about June, the silly cow. She and her family have fled Kansas City in bankruptcy and disgrace, exactly as we'd planned. Back up to the frigid landscape of Minnesota, to the sheltering embrace of mommy and daddy, who don't know what to do about their daughter babbling about kidnappers and torture. Nor do they realize that most of their holdings are about to disappear as well. Can't imagine what'll happen to their fragile health then. I'm certainly not losing any sleep over it. It's a small price to pay for what they did to Belladonna, for negligence and disdain. For not ever trying to find her. For leaving her to—

No no no, we're not quite there yet.

"Tear that letter up immediately. I don't want Laura here, or anyone else," Belladonna is saying. "I want to get this stupid party over with and be left alone."

So I dramatically tear up the letter in front of her and go away. Except I forgot to tell her it was only a copy. After discussing the situation with Matteo and Jack, I'd taken the plunge and mailed the real letter a few weeks before—forging signatures is still one of my favorite pastimes—and had just gotten a reply, Laura thanking Leandro's wife for her kind invitation to come on an extended visit to Virginia. That she was filled with gratitude to have heard from her after all this time. That she would be bringing a friend or two with whom she'd been planning to travel, since the Contessa was kind enough to extend her hospitality to them.

She's arriving with them next week, and I know there's going to be a lot of screaming when Belladonna finds out.

I shall spare you the unpleasantness that ensued, because you don't need to hear the details. I'm not used to being on the receiving end of Belladonna's hostility; nor do I want to return to that place ever again. It took me several days to come out of my room and stop sulking. I often wish I could be more ruthless, as she is; it would simplify my life. But no, I am condemned to be what I am by the sweetness of my nature.

Belladonna finally sends Bryony up with a peace offering of an Utrillo snowscape I'd been coveting for my bedroom, so I relent. Besides, she needs me to sort out the details for our party. We thought at first to have a masked costume ball, but that is too reminiscent of the Club Belladonna, even though thousands of parties around the globe are still being based on our infamous theme nights. People are simply too lazy to think of their own ideas for entertaining.

Flattery from bores is like selling ice in the winter: useless.

So we're having a casual afternoon barbecue for the tenants after the Baineses get back from the christening. Later that night will be the grand, more formal buffet for all the neighbors and whatever assorted hangers-on they can try in vain to sneak past the additional security guards we're bringing in, colleagues of our regular employees, a few friends of Jack's who happen to be in the neighborhood. Mingling as guests in their trim white dinner jackets, frosted silver julep beakers in their hands, they'll blend in seamlessly.

"What should I call her?"

"You mean the Contessa?"

Laura nods. "I never really have talked to her, you know."

"I think Contessa is best for now. If she wishes something else, she'll tell you. She is a bit peculiar about names," I say, leaning forward to whisper that bit confidentially.

"I see," Laura replies with a small sigh of relief. "Thank you."

She is thrilled to be here; I can tell from the glow of her eyes, the same color as the cornflower blue sundress she's wearing as she comes down after unpacking to have a drink with us on the veranda. I swear, this woman is made for sundresses with tight-fitting bodices and full sweeping skirts over rustling crinoline slips. And I see that she still likes espadrilles, laced around her ankles. I open a bottle of *vin santo* we'd had shipped over from Tuscany, and she smiles at the sight of it.

"This reminds me of Leandro," she tells me.

"The wine, or the view?"

"Both. Is your brother here, too?"

"No, I wish he were," I reply. "He got married, and he lives with his family in New York."

"How nice," she murmurs.

"Yes, it is nice, but I miss him something awful."

"It's not the same without him," Belladonna says. She's come up from behind us, so silently that we both jump out of our skins at the sound of her voice. "Hello, Laura."

She doesn't extend her hand to be shaken; she still hates being touched. It is unusually hot and she is holding her glass, full of iced tea, against her wrist to cool down her pulse. An old southern ladies' trick, or so I've been told. Southern belles aren't supposed to sweat. Too dainty, or something ridiculous like that. How they manage to procreate and spawn the hideous specimens of the human variety we're to meet in three days' time at our party is beyond me.

"Hello, Contessa. Thank you for having me," Laura says, her cheeks flooded with color. She's terribly nervous, I realize, and I see no hint of her penchant for pouting. Belladonna, unsmiling and visibly stiff, hardly seems pleased to see her at all. "And thank you for inviting my friends. They're arriving the day after tomorrow, I believe."

"What are their names?" I ask, although I know them perfectly well. We must pretend that we don't know anything at all about Laura—at least not anything she might have told us in the Club Belladonna. "I know you've told us, but I'm afraid my memory isn't quite what it used to be."

"There's Hugh. Hugh Trevenen." She blushes; we know what *that* means. "And Guy, Guy Lindell. He's Hugh's best friend."

"We look forward to making their acquaintance," I tell her.

"Thank you," she says. "It means more to me than you know. We haven't been in America together for nearly a year, you see."

"Ah," I say, "and where were you the last time you met?"

"New York." She shakes her head slightly. "Guy took me to the Club Belladonna. It was a fantastic place in an appalling neighborhood, and the most extraordinary thing was that I met her, Belladonna herself. Afterward, when I thought about it, it was like a fanciful dream. She wore these amazing masks and costumes and gloves with rings over them. I was astonished when I received an invitation to her private office. It was almost as if she had been reading my mind, she seemed to know so much about me. When I told her my dream was to sing, she let me. In her club, can you imagine! Then she offered to send me someone in London who—" She stops, embarrassed.

"Ah yes, I'd heard that she helped women who needed her," I say. "In unusual or unfortunate circumstances."

Laura laughs sharply. "Yes, you might call my husband an unfortunate circumstance."

"You needn't speak of him," I say quickly. I look at Belladonna, who nods imperceptibly. "But you will talk to us of Leandro? It would please us very much to hear about him."

"Do you want to know how I met him?" Laura asks.

"We've been wanting to hear it for a long time."

"Really?" Laura looks dumbfounded. Belladonna has hardly said a word to her.

"Really," I say. "Take your time. We have nowhere to go and nothing to do but listen."

I see Laura visibly unwinding; she wants to please her hostess, yet she doesn't quite understand why. It's not about their shared past. It's as if she has instantly fallen under a kind of spell. Belladonna hasn't been welcoming; in fact, she's bordering on hostility. To tell you the truth, she's scary. It's the set, blank look on her face, as if she were wearing a mask of frozen politeness that is in reality covering a terrifying void. You want to do anything in your power to make that face change, or disappear to a place where it can't hurt you.

"It was because of my stepmother," Laura says, folding her hands in her lap and staring down at the perfectly manicured ovals of her nails, willing herself to stay composed. My heart flops, and I prepare to succumb with a happy sigh, any lingering doubts I may have had about her selfish petulance evaporating like the light in the evening sky.

"My mother died of blood poisoning after a difficult pregnancy," Laura goes on. "The baby died, too. Sophie, I called her, even though I wasn't allowed to see her. I was only seven and a half, but old enough to remember."

"It must have been hard for you when Beatrice died," I venture, thinking back to Laura's sarcastic comments about her friend at Merano, and wondering if she had forgotten what she'd said all those years ago.

"Excruciating, which made me bitter. Worse for Leandro, of course." She turns to look at me. "I never forgot what I said to you in Merano, Tomasino, because I was ashamed of myself." She takes a sip of wine, unaware that she is shredding a *biscotti* into crumbs. "Beatrice had fallen in love with a partisan who hid at Ca' d'Oro between trips to Rome, and she'd gotten pregnant. Some of the locals said he was a spy, a collaborator, but I know that was malicious gossip spread to hurt Leandro and damage his reputation. They couldn't bring him down, you see. Beatrice would never have allowed herself to be with a man who wasn't honest, of that much I am certain."

"So the lady Beatrice was actually a paragon of virtue after all," I say.

"She was a woman, for what that's worth," Laura says, biting her lips.

"You miss her," I say.

"Awfully. And it's nearly ten years, which I find hard to believe. Afterward, Leandro didn't like to talk of her. It was as if he closed his heart. Until he met you." She ventures a glance at Belladonna, who is rocking quietly, staring out at the sunset. "I'd get so angry at him—at her, too, for dying when she was so young and strong—that I almost hated her."

"And you lashed out," I say.

"Yes. Everybody lashed out at Leandro. He was an easy target, powerful enough and rich enough to have the kind of enemies who'd have done the Borgias proud."

"I wonder if he felt he was being punished," I say.

"Punished for what, exactly?" Laura asks.

"Punished for being ruthless, and successful, and fantastically wealthy. Karmic retribution, you know, for exceeding your station in such a manner."

"Daring to play God," Belladonna says to herself.

"I never asked him anything like that. It wasn't any of my business," Laura says. "Once the war was over, I went straightaway for a visit, but I felt myself such a useless reminder of Beatrice, of what he'd lost. When I found myself pregnant with Rupert, I needed to be back home. Mostly we wrote each other, after my son and then my daughter, Cassandra, were born."

"Where does your stepmother fit in?" I switch right back to the subject of the wicked witch. "When did your father remarry?"

"As soon as he could," Laura says, her voice bitter. "Four months exactly after my mother died. He gave up; he couldn't cope on his own. He knew nothing about children, and was grateful any woman would take him on with me and Spencer, my little brother. Instead of a new baby, he got a new wife. Except Viveca was as unlike my mother as any woman could be."

"The claws came out, I take it."

"Yes. She told my father either her or us, and so he chose her.

We were shipped off to boarding school in Switzerland the day after the wedding. If we were really bad, according to Viveca, when we came home during the school hols, we'd be banished to the nursery, where everything had been set up for poor dead Sophie. And then we'd be left there with nothing to eat and no one to care for us." Laura laughs ruefully. "Spencer and I would console each other that we'd grow older and escape somehow. The hardest thing for me to understand was how my father could abandon my mother's memory so completely. I thought they had been happy together."

We sit in silence for a while, Belladonna rocking and staring out into nothingness.

"When I was fifteen, Viveca tried to have me committed," Laura blurts out, then puts her hand up over her mouth. "I don't know why I'm telling you this. No one knows but Leandro."

See what I mean? Anything for an approving nod from Belladonna.

"What happened?" I ask gently.

Laura leans back and closes her eyes. The expression on her face looks surprisingly like Belladonna's, only for an instant. "Viveca said I was incorrigible. If they'd signed the papers I imagine I would never have been let out of that place," she says, her voice hard. "But I overheard them plotting. When I got back to school, Beatrice saw me in tears. I told her everything, and she went straight to Leandro. He called upon a friend, a judge in London, who had me adopted as a ward of the state until I could be emancipated. Then I went to Leandro's, until the war started. So you can imagine what he meant to me."

"A lot more than your own father."

"Leandro must have dug up something, either about my father or Viveca, to make them capitulate. I could never figure out what, and he certainly would never tell me," Laura goes on. "I believe the judge must have had some interests in shipping, or owed Leandro a favor, to have been so accommodating. Who knows what men like that got up to—I certainly don't. I can barely follow how and when they meet one another."

"Who indeed," I murmur. I look over at Belladonna, but I can't read the expression on her face in the twilight.

"But I got my own back," Laura says.

I'm not surprised. I'd always thought her a sly fox. "What did you do?" I ask.

"Beatrice did it, really. A classmate of ours was the daughter of a journalist, and Beatrice got to him, and he went to the clinic where they were going to have committed me, posing as the father of a troublesome child. He wrote an exposé about parents who dump their children—not naming names, of course, but causing immense embarrassment because everyone in our circle knew whom he was writing about."

"Viveca must have really loved you then," I tell her.

"Oh, the look on her face kept me going for years. Even more than the grateful look on my brother's. It was then I realized that the meek and the feeble *can* avenge themselves."

"If ever the powerless discover power," Belladonna says carefully to the evening stars, "they often realize that vengeance is deeply satisfying."

"Yes," Laura says. *"Deeply."*

The cunning little cow!

"Where is your brother now?" I ask.

"In Singapore. He's got his own family, and he's quite happy there, although we rarely see each other. It's better for him to be far away."

"And Viveca?"

"Still in Gloucestershire with my father, spending his money, hating me. The only thing that gives her pleasure is knowing how unhappy I am with Andrew."

"Andrew is your husband, I take it," I say. She nods. "Why, then, did you marry him, if I may ask?"

"You'd think I'd have learned, but I suppose I married someone who is like my father, really. Outwardly charming and loving, but underneath he's a, well . . ." She sighs. "I was such a fool. I found out through the journalist that I had quite a sizable fortune in trust."

"Sounds more like you married a Viveca type."

She pats a nonexistent stray hair, that familiar gesture. "On our honeymoon, Andrew said he wanted to take me somewhere special. Silly me, I thought it might be a swanky private nightclub, but it turned out to be the best-known brothel in Paris. There in the drawing room were dozens of half-naked girls, sitting on the sofas, laughing and chatting and flirting with the men, serving them drinks. I'd never been so shocked in my life. 'Monsieur Andrew,' the girls greeted him, 'where have you been?' I can't believe I was ever so naive."

"I once heard of a client who was so beloved in his favorite brothel that when he died, all the girls carried on the day of his funeral with their private parts draped in black crepe," I offer, trying to lighten the conversation. "Mourning as they knew best."

"Tomasino," Laura says, trying to smile, "you really are too much."

The sky is now a deep azure, and we sit in not-unpleasant silence. People are never what they seem. The selfish, bitchy Laura of Merano seems no more tangible than a dream. And although it is not yet apparent to Laura, with the telling of her tale in the balmy twilight, relaxing on a veranda that reminds us of Tuscany, she quite unwittingly allies herself with Belladonna's forays into the vengeful realm.

"Well," Laura says eventually, as if reading my mind, "no one compares with Leandro."

"No," I say. "No one does."

*T*wo days later, Belladonna is walking her horse back to the stables after a long ride when she hears noises. Noises of a particular sort, ones she hasn't heard in a very long time. That's odd, she thinks, not yet panicking that some interloper is on her property. She hitches her horse to a rail outside the stables and peers inside. She doesn't see anyone who should be there—not Frederick Firkin, the normally reliable stablemaster, or his son, Clive. They love the horses too much to let anything happen to them. Something must be going on. She quickly lifts one of the potted geraniums near the main entrance, pulls up the loose brick there, and hoists out a lovely little pearl-handled snub-nosed two-shot Derringer wrapped in a small pouch. She checks the gun and releases the safety. Like I said, you never can be too careful.

There are still noises in the stable. She creeps forward, pistol in one hand and riding crop in the other, not making a sound, to see what or who it can be. She peers carefully in each stall as she walks slowly toward the back wall, until she hears a man's deep voice laughing softly, and a woman's giggling in response. And then she sees them: the body of a man, his buttocks exposed, with bits of hay sweat-glued to them, his back bare and tanned and strong, a woman's arms around him as he leans close to kiss her again. Her hands are stroking his back and her nails are very red, just like Andromeda's.

The sight of those crimson nails infuriates Belladonna more than anything else. She tucks the crop into her belt and fires a shot into the roof of the stable. Its resounding explosion sounds louder than a cannon being fired on the battlefields of Manassas.

The couple start instantly. The man rolls over in a flash, and the woman beneath him quickly pulls her clothes up to cover her nakedness. The man hurriedly pulls up his trousers as his eyes slowly trail over Belladonna's body, and he smiles broadly, despite the pistol pointed at his face. His eyes are dark blue, flashing with pleasure at the sight of this equestrienne standing above him in all her glory: her hair curling into ringlets after the exertions of her ride; the well-worn leather of her boots, splattered with mud and molded to her legs; her snugly fitting riding britches and pale blue polo shirt; the clove-colored kidskin gloves holding the gun firmly; the fury blazing in her green eyes.

"Just who the hell do you think you are?" Belladonna asks.

"I'm Guy, of course," he says as he languidly buttons first his trousers and then his shirt. He has an English accent and an altogether-insupportable air of sexual confidence.

"Yes, of course. Silly of me to ask," she says between clenched teeth. "A Guy. How clever. Whatever could I have been thinking?"

"Guy Lindell, at your service, madam," he goes on, unabashed. "I have the great honor to have been invited to La Casa della Fenice by my dearest friend, Laura Garnett, along with my other dear friend, Hugh Trevenen, whom I believe is expected at some point this weekend." He turns to his lover, her cheeks still flushed with passion. Or embarrassment. "And this is my *other* friend, Miss Nancy Conrad."

"Miss Nancy Conrad. Your other *friend,*" Belladonna says. "I'm touched. Who, pray tell, invited you, Miss Nancy Conrad, onto this estate? Certainly not its mistress."

Nancy is much too flustered to answer. "I did," Guy says, as Nancy looks at him in consternation and finishes dressing, "and this impromptu, ah, *situation,* is quite my fault. We dropped our

bags at the house and were so entranced by the glorious surroundings that we took a walk. I alone am responsible for having taken
the shameless liberty of asking Miss Conrad to accompany me
here."

Belladonna frowns. "Surely Laura Garnett has stressed to you
that there are several rules that all guests of this estate are expected
to obey."

"Ah yes, she did." Guy pulls on his boots with a grunt. "But
are you the lord high executioner of King Henry, Virginia?" he asks
sarcastically, pointing to the pistol. "Or perhaps a mere slave to the
household rules? Let me guess, you're the governess, or the riding
instructor. No, wait, I've got it—you're an early-arriving guest, off
on her daily ride when she is unpleasantly surprised by the sounds
of pleasure in the stable. How *shocking!*" He stands up, brushing a
stray piece of hay from his trousers, and buckles his belt. "Do forgive me, but I suppose we must be going."

"Not so fast," Orlando says as he runs in, his own pistol in
hand. I am right on his heels, Stan and the barking bloodhounds
beside me. Nancy stifles a scream, and Stan hushes the dogs.

Orlando looks at Belladonna, and she signals nearly imperceptibly that she's all right. She hadn't pushed the panic button, after
all, but Stan heard the shot and summoned us.

"Certo?" he asks, and she nods.

"Oh dear," says Guy, immediately figuring out what he's done.
He's a clever one, this Guy. I remember him well from the Club
Belladonna, sitting on the banquette with Laura. Yes, Guy, who'd
come for the first time to the Ball of the Elements, with Peregrine
somebody and Celeste something, those fashion people. They'd
been talking about a sociopathic squire. Schultzie, his name was,
he of the lascivious lederhosen. Botheration. I'd meant to find out
more about Guy then, but I'd been distracted, the first time by
Annabeth and the second time by Laura herself. And the Pritch
had been instructed to follow up on Laura's husband, not her
friends. Double botheration. I must be slipping.

"I'm afraid I've offended my dear hostess," he goes on, bowing
with a flourish. "I do most humbly beg your forgiveness."

"Beg all you want," Belladonna snaps, "you won't get it. Even
if you are a friend of Laura's and invited here with my permission."

She hands her pistol to Orlando and pulls the riding crop from her belt. Nancy hides behind Guy, trembling.

"Where's Frederick?" I ask, looking around. "And Clive?"

"Several of the horses got loose, and they went out chasing them, I'm afraid," Guy says. "You are quite welcome to blame me for the horses as well, even though that is one incident for which I am not at fault. We merely happened upon the scene and took advantage of the, well . . . I accept all blame."

Belladonna ignores him and directs herself to Nancy. "Where do you live when you aren't intruding on other people's property?" she demands.

"In Richmond," she says. Her cheeks are no longer flushed, and she's as pale as if she'd seen a ghost in the stables instead of her handsome lover.

"And how do you know this"—a flicker of Belladonna's crop—"person?"

Guy's lips twitch, trying to repress a smile.

"We met a week ago, and we . . . and he . . . he invited me to drive up here with him," Nancy says. "I had no idea that—"

"How and where did you meet?" Belladonna demands.

"At a dinner at Bambi Simpson's. We're cousins of Dippy Robertson, your neighbor. That's where I'm going to be staying."

Belladonna glances at me. I'll be calling Dippy shortly, to confirm this. Only a woman named Dippy could have a cousin named Bambi.

"We will take you to the Robertsons," Belladonna says sternly. "I suggest you go with my driver now, or I shall be having an extremely unpleasant conversation with your cousins, and, I promise you, they will be most seriously displeased should I tell them the truth."

"I'm sorry," she whispers as her eyes fill with tears. Poor silly thing. She doesn't know that, in her own way, Belladonna is not really angry with her, that she's actually trying to protect her. Guy's the one who should be quaking in his boots.

At that moment, Frederick comes into the stables with two of the horses. Clive has untied Artemis and is leading her in. They look at all of us in surprise, and the dogs start barking again. "Is everything all right, ma'am?" Frederick asks as he tries to control the whinnying horses, rearing from the sound and smell of the bloodhounds. His eyes are round with worry.

"What happened?" Belladonna asks him, her voice curt.

"It's Hermes, as usual. In a right stroppy mood, he was, so I thought to take him out for a bit. I didn't mean to leave the stables untended, ma'am, but then Essex got loose as well, and, oh lord. It's just that they was acting so strange, spooked like, and I didn't want no harm to come to them. I shoulda left Clive behind. I'm terribly sorry." He is hanging his head in guilt and shame.

"It's my fault, ma'am," Clive says. "I know I shouldna left. It was wrong of me. Please, don't blame my father. We know better."

"There's no one to blame, Clive," she tells him, her voice so low that only he can hear it, and Clive tries to smile.

"Thank you, ma'am," Frederick says. "It won't happen again."

She nods and puts her crop briefly on his shoulder, then does the same to Clive, who is now anxiously rubbing down the horses after their impromptu gallop.

Stan and the dogs saunter off toward the garage to tell Templeton to bring the car up to the house. We show Guy and Nancy out, walking behind them on the flagstone path lined with hollyhocks and roses, up to the house. Guy has his arm protectively around a sniveling Nancy, but I can tell he's bored with her already. She probably thought she'd be having the romance of the century with this dashingly romantic Englishman when all she got was a romp in the hay. At least she's no spy, I console myself about this terribly embarrassing breach in our security. Of all the things for Belladonna to stumble upon, this is—

Suddenly, we hear children's voices shouting in the distance, and we all stop. It's Bryony, running around the trees with Susannah. They see us, wave, and run over. For some reason, I look over at Guy, and am surprised to see that his skin has gone deathly gray under his tan.

Bryony comes closer, laughing. "Guess what!" she says. "Susannah found a frog. Or a toad. He's so cute. Look!"

Susannah walks over with the toad cupped carefully in her hands.

"Can we keep him, Mommy? Can we? Please?" Bryony pleads with her mother. "Please oh please oh please?"

Belladonna crouches down. "Oh, he's a lovely toad," she says, her voice startlingly unlike what it had been with Guy only minutes before, "but don't you think his own mommy will miss him? And all his brothers and sisters? They're probably frantic right now, looking for him. Listen." She stands up and cups her hand to her ear. "I can hear them croaking from here. I bet they're telling each other that this little toad is missing. Quick, go put him back where you found him, before his whole family gets upset. Okay?"

Bryony and Susannah look at each other, burst into giggles, and run off. I glance carefully at Guy again, who regains his composure as we reach the house. Nancy points to her bags in the front hall, next to his. Blinken takes them, beckoning to Nancy to follow him. "I'm sorry," she says again as Guy kisses her cheeks good-bye.

"We'll see you at the party tomorrow," I tell Nancy, and her face brightens considerably. "Do tell the Robertsons we're looking forward to seeing them as well." I can only imagine the explanation she'll be giving Dippy about *this*. No doubt it'll be something gushy about our beautiful grounds and welcoming hospitality.

"Where's Laura?" Belladonna asks me.

"She must have gone for a walk," I reply. "Toward the rose garden." In the other direction, naturally. Had she been in the house when Guy arrived, Belladonna could have been spared this ridiculous encounter. Oh well, something will come of it, I tell myself. Something unusual.

"Where should we put Guy?" I ask, looking at his battered but still handsome suitcases.

"In the yellow room," Belladonna says coldly.

Guy looks at her strangely. "I've been called many things," he says quietly, "but never a coward."

"The yellow bedroom is my daughter's favorite," Belladonna says, her voice as frigid as the ice in our punch bowl. "Since she seems to have had such an extreme effect on you, it will no doubt please her that you're in it. She chose the wallpaper and the colors in the room."

Tucking her crop smartly behind her elbow like a soldier, my observant darling strides out of the house, and Guy's eyes do not leave her until she is too far away to see.

14

Left in
the Dust

When Laura sees that Guy has arrived her eyes light up and she gives him a swift hug, but her face crumples in disappointment when she realizes that Hugh is not with him.

"He's trying his best," Guy tells her gently.

Luckily for me, I have hidden myself in one of my favorite places during this interlude, tucked behind a large lacquered Chinese screen luridly painted with dragons hitched to chariots and other hideous scenes, in one of the little studies off the grand salon. It is perfect for peering from behind its hinges. Although when Guy and Laura sit down on the leather chesterfield with a slight whoosh, I have no idea I am about to be privy to such a tender scene.

"He has business in Washington; you know that," he goes on. "It's the only way he was able to leave London. He swore he'd do everything in his power to be here tonight. In the meantime, I shall try my best to entertain you."

"I hear you already entertained the household today," Laura says, her voice low. "Really, Guy, how could you?"

"Yes, I confess it was naughty," he says nonchalantly. "But my little romp wasn't premeditated, if that's what you're thinking. Nancy's a sweet young thing, and the stables were empty. You know me. If the flesh is willing, carpe diem."

"Yes, I do know you, which is why I'm so mortified that your flesh is so willing," she says, her anger growing. "This isn't our sparkling London set where everyone seems to be bonking everyone else. Do you have any idea who the Contessa is, or that I've waited for years to hear from her? That she's my only link to Leandro and Beatrice? I do wish you'd think of someone other than yourself for once."

I hear Guy swirling the ice cubes around in his drink, and he takes a while to reply. "I'm sorry, Laura," he says eventually. "Truly I am. I should never have been so thoughtless. And now our estimable hostess loathes me as well."

"Well, *I* certainly don't loathe you. You know no one can stay mad at you for long, unless it's one of the thousands of lovers you've sent packing back to their husbands. That's your problem—you always seem to be able to get away with everything, no matter what."

"Not always," he says. "I think I've met my match. Tell me about her."

"You mean the Contessa?" Laura says, and starts to laugh. "You can't be serious."

"Why not? She's attractive, rich, clever. More attractive, rich, and clever than nearly any woman I've ever met, in fact. But there's something about her I can't quite put my finger on. Something bubbling underneath the surface that's absolutely fascinating. Doesn't she strike you as unusual?"

"Yes, but in truth it's not so much unusual as terrifying. I barely know her; I'd only really seen her once before, when I was in Merano with Leandro, and I don't care to recollect that ridiculous incident at all."

"You were never ridiculous, dearest Laura," he says, ever the smoothie. "When were you in Merano?"

"Seven years ago. Yes, it was nineteen forty-seven. She was with her baby and two of the oddest men I'd ever seen. One of them is still here with her—Tomasino. You've met him, I'm sure."

"The fat one with the curly black hair."

"He's not fat. He's merely large," Laura says stoutly in my defense, and when she does, my heart flips over. I have quite forgotten that I ever disliked her at all. "Tomasino moves so gracefully I can't think of him as fat. And he's ever so amusing. The odd thing is that his twin brother, Matteo, was much more like the Contessa. Quite off-putting. He rarely spoke, as I recall. Leandro told me they'd both been tortured in the war, that something perfectly ghastly had happened, and that Matteo also had his tongue cut out.

When Tomasino told me his brother had gotten married I was ever so surprised; he always struck me as, well, *removed* somehow. Certainly not the type to fall in love. Not that Tomasino isn't; he merely hides it better. So does the Contessa."

"I see. Yes. That makes sense. I've barely spent any time with her, but already there is this feeling of something coiled inside her, something watchful and hard," Guy says thoughtfully. "Not fearful, exactly, but immensely wary. When we first met, when I was watching her in the stables, I had the sense that her anger wasn't so much directed at what I'd done—which was inexcusably presumptuous, I admit—but at the breach in her security on the estate. She doesn't like not being in control. That much is obvious."

"She learned that from Leandro, I'm sure. He had hidden security all over Ca' d'Oro. It's rather a necessity when you're that rich and that powerful. Nor is it just paranoia, being worried about spies and kidnappings and such things."

"Yes, but security can be used not only to keep people out but to be able to control them when they're in."

Oh ho, he's definitely a dangerous one, this Guy. Deftly perceptive.

"Perhaps. Tomasino would be the one to ask about that. Or Orlando," Laura says. "I remember him from Italy; he was in charge of security there."

"He's the way to get to the Contessa, no doubt. The merely large and graceful Tomasino, that is."

"I doubt that anyone can get to the Contessa if she doesn't want them to. Leandro always said she had a forceful will," Laura says. "Do you know, we had a long talk the other night; Tomasino asked me questions, and she sat on the veranda with us, in a rocking chair. Now that I think about it, she hardly said a word, yet I walked away with the impression that it was one of the most wonderful conversations I'd ever had."

"So you don't know how long she's lived here."

"I'm not quite sure. A few years, perhaps. She was in Italy when Leandro died, and that was three years ago. We lost touch until recently. Why do you ask?"

"Because she reminds me of someone."

"Who?"

"Belladonna. From the club. The enigmatic lady of the night. She certainly had a forceful will of her own."

"Yes, she did. I still wear colored kidskin gloves because of her."

"You sang in her club, didn't you?"

"Yes, darling Guy, but you weren't there that night, were you?"

"No, my angel, I wasn't; I had to leave town before you, remember."

"Chased out of town was probably more like it," she says fondly.

"Well, I'm surprised I passed muster with the dogs. Twice, as a matter of fact."

"Everyone was. No one more than I." Laura laughs softly. "I wonder whatever happened to the club. It shut down as mysteriously as it opened, didn't it?"

"That's what I'm thinking," Guy says, rattling his ice cubes. "I might be crazy for wondering it, but do you think your Contessa could possibly be Belladonna herself?"

There is a long pause. "I never thought about it," Laura says finally, "and I don't think I ever would had you not just mentioned it. And you know, I don't think you're right. The Contessa is quite—what's the word?—*retiring*. She's silent. She strikes me as someone who wants only to be left alone, who's actually terribly shy. Belladonna was much more confident and in control, at least with me. I should think it takes a tremendous amount of energy and self-possession to mingle with people in a nightclub. I don't see how someone who's shy and reticent could pull it off, do you? I know I couldn't."

"No, not really. I expect you're right," Guy says. "I mention it only because something doesn't quite fit. You said the Contessa already had her baby with her when she met Leandro."

"Yes, Bryony. She was quite tiny, only a few months old. The Contessa was with the baby and Tomasino and Matteo at Merano."

"So Leandro isn't Bryony's real father?"

"No, but he adopted her. I think that's one of the reasons they were married, so Bryony could have a father and his name. I don't know if Bryony even knows. But I'll never ask the Contessa about it, if that's what you're thinking. Her private life with Leandro is none of my business, and none of yours, either. I've said much more than I should already."

"You know I am discreet about such matters."

"Yes, but I also know that you're a prying so-and-so. And I must get dressed now, and have a good cry because Hugh's not here."

"I shouldn't give up hope quite yet."

"I have given up hope yonks ago, dear Guy," she says with some bitterness. "I love Hugh so much that I can allow myself no hope. Do you understand?"

"Yes, my dear. At least I hope I do."

"Do you promise to behave yourself tonight?"

"I shall try my best."

"Good. Come along now, and you can help me button my dress."

"With pleasure."

I hear the whoosh of the leather sofa's cushions as they get up, and their footsteps receding into the grand salon. My knee starts to throb with a sudden spasm. Hearing Guy compare the Contessa with Belladonna is worrisome, to put it mildly.

As if she already doesn't want him banished from her sight.

"Night, Mommy." Bryony gets up from the dinner table and gives her mother a kiss and a hug.

"Night, Bryony's Mommy," Susannah says shyly, and they run off. Susannah is much too terrified of Belladonna to venture close enough for a hug. The two little girls are on their best behavior, because Susannah's sleeping over in Bryony's bedroom tonight, and Belladonna told them that if they're good, they can both stay up late for the party tomorrow and then have a sleep-over at the Baineses' house. One less thing to worry about. They needn't know that our security spies will be posted outside Susannah's house during the night, just in case.

Rosalinda shoos them upstairs, and we move into the grand salon to relax over several different flavors of eau-de-vie. Guy has been perfectly charming, telling silly stories that had both children and adults enthralled. Now, naturally, the storytelling is going to develop a slightly more grown-up flavor.

"That was a lovely dinner," Laura says, and Belladonna forces herself to give a faint smile. I realize suddenly with a terrible frisson that I am feeling entirely alone, missing my brother something fierce. And Jack. Someone I know well and trust; another male presence. I didn't realize until we'd left New York how much I always relied on Jack's calm, steady demeanor. He never asked for anything; he did his job, and then wanted to do more.

All for the love of Belladonna.

Matteo and Jack, both far away, both inextricably entwined with our lives in New York. I'd invited them to this party, of course, practically begging, which as you might have guessed is not a trait that comes naturally to yours truly, but they both pleaded their busy schedules. The only bit of good news was hearing from Matteo that he thinks Jack has been stepping out with Alison, just as this matchmaker had hoped.

But there is no match for me, and I think a bit of my woe shows in my face. Belladonna touches my shoulder lightly as she passes by with a slender glass of Poire William, her favorite.

"I hope Matteo and Annabeth can come with the children this summer," I say, for lack of anything better. "But they'll probably want to go to a camp instead."

"What exactly is a 'camp'?" Laura asks.

"Summer camp," I explain. "For kids to spend the lovely hot weather, tucked away out of sight of their parents, in hideous little houses called 'cabins.' There, they are forced to endure ridiculous activities like arts'n'crafts and organized sports." I shudder in mock horror.

"One doesn't do 'camp' where I come from," Guy says.

"Oh, really?" I ask. "Where *do* you come from?"

"Most people say I come from hell," he replies. "Or at least that's where they're telling me to go."

Laura laughs indulgently. "You really are too ridiculous."

"Hardly," he says. "We don't 'do' summer camp, true. I suppose it's because nice little English boys and girls have been shipped off to what you Americans refer to as 'boarding school,' so their parents feel guilty in the summer and permit them to return home. Then these devoted parents will desert them again as they find their way to Europe or wherever they go after the season. But the children have been brought home; duty has been done." He can't keep a tinge of bitterness out of his voice.

"That kind of parents, eh?" I ask.

"Not my mother," he replies, twisting his ring. It is a simple wide gold band set with a Russian alexandrite. It's a rare, amazing stone that looks green in daylight and red in candlelight. It reminds me powerfully of Leandro's cat's eye, winking mockingly. "But she died when I was eight. I never got along with my brothers. I was the youngest boy, the least useful after the heir and the spare. In fact, if I tell you that we grew up hating one another, encouraged by our relatives to see one another as rivals and competitors, it would hardly be an understatement."

I notice he hasn't said anything about his father.

"My brother John Francis was extremely naughty," Guy goes on. "Addicted to opium, leaving the hookahs around for the maids to trip over. He usually hid most of his stash in some lovely gold Russian snuffboxes that had belonged to Rasputin, but got into terrible trouble when he left them at Sotheby's to be appraised for auction and forgot to take the drugs out beforehand." He swallows his drink and leans back, crossing his legs nonchalantly. I don't know if he's pulling our legs or not.

"Oh Guy, you do exaggerate so," Laura says. "To think that you expect everyone to believe the ridiculous things you say."

He smiles wickedly. "Only the thousands of women who've been in love with me believe them."

"Whatever do you mean?" she asks, laughing.

"Only this: It is no great matter of difficulty to entice a woman who thinks she's in love to believe anything her beloved says."

"And seducing these thousands of women is a gift of nature, one with which you have undoubtedly been prodigiously endowed," I say sarcastically.

"Yes, of course," he replies, tongue now firmly in cheek. Or so I hope. "Seduction is quite simple if the woman is willing. With very little difficulty, one can become rather instantly passionate and persuasive." He gets up to pour himself another drink. "If, however, she is *not* willing, seduction is quite like war. I learned several indubitable lessons from the skillful maneuverings of Napoleon Bonaparte. His seductions and battle plans were some of the few history lessons I bothered studying at school. Although, unfortunately, Bonaparte had great contempt for women. Unlike myself. He ordered these lovely ladies into his tent, told them to disrobe without bothering to look up from his papers, had his merry way with them, and sent them packing."

"But you never send them packing," I say, "or at least not until you've brushed the hay away."

"Touché," Guy says good-naturedly. "And you're right; I don't send them packing. They're usually all too happy to leave of their own volition."

He's joking, but there's some weird catch in his voice. I look over at Belladonna. She hasn't said a word, as usual, but is watching Guy intently. He knows it. I wonder for whom this conversation is intended, actually. Maybe he does want some sympathy and is trying to make Belladonna like him just a little bit. Or maybe he should just be stuffed and hung to dry in the Narcissus Room.

"That's because Guy uses a mummified monkey hand as a paperweight," Laura says with a shudder. "It is altogether hideous."

"The paperweight once belonged to Swinburne, the poet," Guy says. "He also used the hoof of his favorite horse as an inkwell, inscribed with its name and date of death."

"How masterfully macabre," I murmur. This conversation has gone quite far enough.

"Oh, don't let's talk about such things anymore. Not inkwells or Bonaparte or wretched summer hols. And certainly not the English aristocracy," Laura says. "I married one of *them,* and that's more than enough for me."

Belladonna stands up abruptly. "Good night" is all she says, and leaves the room.

"Oh dear," Guy says, his eyes once again following her.

That's an understatement. Against my better judgment, I am really starting to like this Guy, although I can't put my finger on what exactly makes him tick. At least not yet. I kick myself yet again for not telling the Pritch about him when I should have. Oh well, Guy's not going anywhere. Not until we've checked the family pedigree.

Yes, Guy is definitely an interesting addition to La Fenice. I imagine he can present himself as angelic and enthralling, full of humor and wit and tenderness, and then just as quickly become a devil, full of rage and cruelty.

Like Belladonna.

* * *

"**D**o you know what happened when I was a little boy?" Guy asks Bryony and Susannah. They're sitting on the veranda, the hills shimmering in the distance, eating their breakfast the next morning while he tells them stories. The girls are wide-eyed with delight. As long as they're of the female persuasion, Guy is able to charm them. I'll bet he could charm the shell off a tortoise.

"Well," he is saying as he downs his fresh-squeezed orange juice. "I was ill so often with nasty colds and nasty coughs"—here he pretends to have a coughing fit, which leaves the girls helpless with laughter—"that the doctor decided that my tonsils must be removed. At once!"

"I had my tonsils out already," Bryony announces, "when we lived in New York. In the hospital. I got to eat ice cream every day 'cause I had a sore throat."

Now Guy knows we lived in New York. Botheration.

"Did you have your tonsils out?" Guy asks Susannah. She shakes her head no. "You're lucky," he replies. "It can hurt a lot."

"Mine hurt, but Mommy said I was very brave," Bryony says.

"I'm sure you were," Guy goes on, "but I don't think I was very brave. I cried and cried because my throat hurt, and the doctor did the operation at home, where we lived in England. I didn't get to go to the hospital where the nurses could look after me."

"Who looked after you?" Susannah asks. "Your mommy?"

"Yes," he replies, "and some nurses who came when my mummy wasn't at home. But you know what happened? The doctor took out my tonsils and he put them on a plate, and one of the nurses took them down to the kitchen. And then my brother ran into the kitchen and he snatched them off the plate and he ate them!"

"Eeeuggh!" the girls say.

"He thought they were strawberries," Guy says. "What a silly boy! I don't think he ever forgave me."

"I don't ever want to eat a tonsil," Susannah says solemnly.

"Then you never will," Guy says.

At that moment, Susannah sees her mother, out walking with her little brothers, waving at her, and she dashes off to join them. "Can you come with me, Bryony?" she calls out, flying down the hill.

"I have to ask my mommy," Bryony replies, pouting, "but she's still asleep." Bryony knows better than to disturb her mother in the mornings. I choose that moment to venture out to join them.

"Can I go to Susannah's house?" Bryony asks. "Please, can I, please?"

Guy pretends to start crying. "You mean you don't want to stay with me?"

Bryony looks at him, then me, clearly torn between her old friend and her new one. "Why don't you stay with Guy for a little while, and then go to Susannah's for lunch," I suggest. "You can play with her all afternoon and then come back here together to change for the party. How's that sound?"

"Good," she says.

"Then hurry and tell Susannah and come right back," I say. "Maybe you can go for a walk with Guy and the dogs and show him the gardens. So go get the dogs, too, okay?"

"I'd like that very much," Guy says. So would I; this way, I can call over to Tantalus House and have Winken follow them and monitor their conversation. I quickly make the call and come back to the veranda, pouring myself a glass of juice.

"She's an amazing child," Guy says.

"That she is," I reply.

"May I ask you something?"

"Of course."

"Where were you stationed during the war?" he asks.

"How did you know I was in the war?"

"Soldier's instinct."

"I see." I sigh. "It was Italy. Near Lucca. But we weren't stationed," I say. "My brother and I ran off to join the partisans. Delusions of grandeur, that sort of foolishness. And you?"

"India. Ceylon. Bloody nightmare, but useful contacts afterward. I set up my business there. Tea. Import-export."

"Explains the tan." And the willing ladies, I'm sure, last vestiges of colonial wives swooning for him under the mosquito netting. "Why do you ask?"

"Just wondering," he says lightly. Oh sure.

"Wondering where I met the Contessa, you mean? It's a long story," I say carefully. "Too long for the morning sun." Too long for you, period. "And you've got a young lady who mustn't be kept waiting."

"Quite right," he says. "None of my business, I might add. I shan't ask again."

"Quite right."

Luckily, Bryony comes rushing out of the house with Basilico in her arms, the mastiffs lumbering after them, barking lustily. As they saunter away, I hear Guy ask Bryony if she wants to hear a silly song. She puts Basilico down, slips her hand into his, and he starts singing:

"Tallyho, tallyho, biff whack whack!
Chickens and fishes and the olde Union Jack
Tell me a story or I won't come back
Tallyho, tallyho, biff whack whack!"

"That's a good song," Bryony says, giggling. "You wanna hear one that I know. It's a song about spies."

"Oooh, spies, yum yum. Will you teach me the words?" he asks.

"Yes, I will I will I will," Bryony says, already starting to sing:

"Spies and spies and spies and spies and spies and spies and
    spies
Miles and miles and miles and miles and miles of spies
You can't buy anything
You can't do anything
Because there's
Miles and miles and miles of spies and spies
Miles and miles of spies."

Then she spins around and falls down, laughing. "You can do it about flies and pies, too, you know," she tells Guy.

"Oh, I see," he says. "But I like spies the best. Who taught you that song?"

"Tomasino. He was a spy. So was Uncle Jack. And Matteo. That's Tomasino's twin brother. He didn't move here with us 'cause he got married to Annabeth 'cause he was lonely."

"Did Tomasino *tell* you he was a spy?"

"He says he wasn't, but I know he was. When he wasn't so fat," she says conspiratorially. "I always know when he's lying. His pinkie starts to twitch."

This child has been picking up some very bad habits.

"Like this?" Guy crooks his pinkie and starts to waggle it. Bryony collapses in giggles. "Who is Uncle Jack?" he asks. "Is he really your uncle?"

"Un-uh. He works for Mommy and Tomasino and Matteo. He lives in New York, where we used to live, in our old house. He stayed with the dogs so they won't be lonely."

There is a lot of talk about loneliness in this conversation, isn't there? Don't think Guy hasn't figured this out already.

"Were they your dogs?"

"They're the house dogs, Mommy says, so they had to stay with the house."

"I bet I can guess their names," Guy says.

"Betcha can't."

"Hmm. Let me think. Missy, Prince, and Lady."

"No, silly, those are boring names," Bryony says. "Boring boring boring!"

"I agree. I once had a dog named Raymond. That's rather a boring name, but he wasn't a boring dog. He was a Jack Russell terrier, and he loved to bark."

"What happened to him?"

"He got very old and he died in his sleep. He was a good dog and lived a good dog's life, and now he's up in doggy heaven chasing rabbits and butterflies."

"Oh," she says, her divine little face bright with consternation. "My house dogs aren't dead. They had to stay in New York with Uncle Jack, and they're waiting for me to go back and visit them. I have new dogs here."

"Yes, I see," Guy says. "What's the little one's name?"

"Basilico," she says proudly. "That's the Italian word for basil. He's a miniature longhaired dachshund. And that's Casseopeia, and Hector, and Drizzlepuss. They're Neopolitan mastiffs. Come, come here!" she shouts at them, and they obey, running over to lick her face. Basilico runs around, barking wildly. He barely comes up to their ankles.

"I'll wager you named them yourself, didn't you?" he asks. "Those are the best names I ever heard for dogs. Much better than Missy and Prince."

"And Lady. What's a wager?"

"It's like a bet," he replies. "Were your New York dogs Neopolitan mastiffs, too?"

"Un-uh." She shakes her head. "Irish wolfhounds."

"Oh, I see. Did you give them nice names, too?"

"Yes I did: Froggy, Dromedee, and Tinkletime."

Guy laughs. "I think I know how Tinkletime got his name."

"Tinkletime is a girl, silly. Like Froggy and Dromedee."

An Irish wolfhound named Dromedee. That name sounds rather close to Andromeda, from a child's perspective.

"Oh, I see, I see." Guy's smile widens and his deep blue eyes are twinkling with pleasure. Yes, he suspected it yesterday when he was talking to Laura. The smug, perceptive bastard. He is certain he's about to solve the world-famous mystery of the nefarious Belladonna, and all because he is best friends with a man who is having an affair with a woman who was once befriended by a vivacious Italian girl named Beatrice. The twists and turns of this saga have led him to a perfectly innocent conversation with an adorable little girl whose dogs are romping around a plantation in King Henry, Virginia.

All our planning and plotting and careful preparations undone by an innocuous conversation about tonsils, dogs, and spies. Guy has gotten the idea in his head that Dromedee is really Andromeda. Botheration. I am right to be wary of Guy. He would have been a good spy; I'm now convinced his wartime exploits in India and Ceylon were not confined to scouting locations for his tea plantations. He's too much like Leandro and Jack, quietly persistent. And he's too much like me, prying in such a charming manner until he gets the answers he wants.

Too much like Belladonna. Cunning and patient.

My longing for Jack deepens, to pour my heart out, to ask his advice. I can't do it, though; it's not fair to Jack to talk about any of my worries of another man paying attention to Belladonna. Nor could I have such a conversation on the phone. But Jack would know what to do, how to handle Guy. Jack, overloaded with honor and integrity, we can trust. He'd never have tried to pry so openly, even though he was equally desperate to know everything.

I wonder what it is that makes two men, clearly obsessed and insatiably curious about the same woman, so much alike and yet so dissimilar. I'll bet Guy, filled with a voracious lust for life, would be willing to act out, push hard for whatever he wants, while Jack could not help but repress those same desires. Perhaps that's why Belladonna trusted Jack so much. She knew he'd never cross the line Guy has already breached.

What worries me is that she's curious about Guy in a way she's not been curious about any man since I met her. And it isn't only due to his odd reaction when he first saw Bryony.

You can't do anything
Because there's
Miles and miles and miles of spies and spies.

Guy has found out way too much in way too short a time. He certainly has to have sussed that all this information is invaluable, and he can afford to keep a stiff upper lip and wait. Then he can name his price.

I wonder what he's going to do. All I know is what I'm *not* going to do.

I'm not going to tell Belladonna.

I am admiring the cut of my snow-white dinner jacket for the party tomorrow when the telephone rings, and Winken tells me it's the Pritch. How splendid. Perhaps he has a momentous update for us. Nothing like a little bit of longed-for death to spice up a party.

"He's finally kicked it," Pritch says smugly.

"My heart is breaking," I reply, trying to contain my exhilaration. At least one of *them* is gone. How many more are left? I call to Winken to tell the Contessa to pick up the phone. "Ashes to ashes, dust to dust. Couldn't have happened to a nicer fella. What's the next step?"

"There's a funeral service at St. Martin-in-the-Fields in three days' time. Meanwhile, we have the preliminary cleanup crew in the house. Disinfecting the sickroom, if you know what I mean." Indeed I do. "The secondary crew is scheduled during the service itself."

"Pritch, you are too much," I tell him, laughing. "Not even I would have the cheek to snoop through a man's drawers during his funeral."

"What better time?" he asks. I can picture him shrugging. This is far too much joy for our wonderfully dedicated Pritch, looking for papers and bank accounts and diaries and letters to friends that Sir Patty forgot to burn before he left for his fateful trip to America. Why would he have thought he'd need to burn anything? "A select handful, including myself, will be amongst the mourners, of course."

"Of course."

"Should have an update for you soonest."

"Hello, Harris," Belladonna says. I realize she's heard practically the entire conversation without my realizing she's picked up a receiver.

"Hello," he says. "So lovely to hear your voice."

"So lovely to hear your news," she replies.

"Yes, madam. Anything else I can do for you?"

"Call me as soon as you have all the mourners identified."

"Of course. I already have extra manpower in place."

"Thank you," she says. "I appreciate it."

"Glad to be of service," he says, and hangs up.

We are creeping ever closer. But in the meantime, we have a party to throw. The house will soon be full of noisy strangers eagerly chugging mint juleps and dragging their paws over all our lovely things. I know Belladonna is dreading this evening. She's already told me she's not going to the casual barbecue after Ezra and Ezekiel's christening. I didn't think she would. She doesn't want to see twin boy babies. Bryony nicknames them "Eze" and "Zeke," and she asks her mother why she can't have a baby brother of her own. Belladonna merely smiles and says she'll think about finding one.

There will be no thoughts of babies tonight. Belladonna won't be wearing a mask, but one is already in place. Her nerves are like steel.

A steel trap, about to close on its prey.

15

Made for Each Other

*M*oney is wasted on the rich.

That's what I decide on this balmy June night as the guests start to arrive for their long-desired party to end all parties at La Casa della Fenice.

Fen-isse, they wrongly pronounce it. Rhymes with Venice. Of course if any of them had ever gone to Venice, they'd have seen the glorious La Fenice opera house there. But never mind. I'm quibbling. Why should they go to Venice to see the sights when all the sights they need to see are so lovely in King Henry?

At least these sights had been lovely earlier today, when I hosted a splendid cookout for the tenants. The kids dashed around, pausing between games of tag and kickball to chow down on barbecued chicken and ribs, and nibble on Bianca's peerless scones and *biscotti*. Guy was a special hit, playing games until breathless, showing off his ring which mysteriously changes from red to green every time he rubs it. The grown-ups were content to sprawl on lawn chairs and blankets and happily nurse endless cups of my special punch, spiked with bourbon and spices and a few herbs from the garden. All work was forbidden, except for feeding the animals, and we all pitched in to have the chores done with as expeditiously as possible. It was easy to laugh at the chickens squawking madly when there was a nice southern punch buzz going.

"That's what the guests are going to look like later," I announced to the henhouse and all assembled. "Just like our prize hens, grubbing around for worms."

When everyone collapsed for naps later in the afternoon, Laura and I retired to the second-floor balcony, relaxing as the verdant landscape stretched endlessly at our feet.

"Tell me how you met Hugh," I said. Belladonna had asked me to elicit the details, and this was a perfect time. "Conjure him up, so when he arrives later it'll seem more like magic."

"We met quite by accident," Laura said, leaning back, eager to talk of him. "At a house party in Devon, about a year and a half ago. I knew his name vaguely. Hugh Trevenen. And I knew of his wife, of course, Nicola, Lady Pembridge. Everyone in our 'set,' as we call it, knows of her."

"You mean how much she charges for her favors?" I rudely asked.

"No, how much she doesn't," Laura replied. "Andrew was too 'busy,' of course, so I went on my own. Nicola, too, was otherwise engaged. I had arrived a bit early, and went for a long walk before dinner. Then I went upstairs for a bath, and to change. This was a fairly enlightened household, mind you." She laughed. "They had en-suite bathrooms for most of the guest bedrooms. So I sat down on the bed and was taking off my shoes and stockings when I realized someone was already in the bath. I heard him humming, rather tunelessly." She smiled. "Terribly out of tune, as a matter of fact. I didn't know quite what to do, and just as I was deciding whether to knock on the door to the bath or find one of the servants, the door opened and out he came. Wearing only a towel, poor thing."

"Luckily he was wearing that," I offered.

"Quite." She was now smiling broadly at the memory. " 'Good Lord,' he said when he saw me. 'What? Who are you?'

" 'I was just about to ask you the same question,' I replied, 'and I rather think you owe me an explanation, considering that this is my room.'

" 'Good Lord,' he said again. 'There must be some dreadful mistake.'

" 'Or some dreadful practical joker.'

" 'I do beg your pardon,' he said. 'I'm terribly sorry. I had no idea—'

" 'You mean you didn't see all the girlie things in the bath?' I teased. He turned scarlet, so deeply mortified that I could hardly remain afraid or angry.

" 'I was so late I'm afraid I failed to notice . . . oh dear. I didn't think. Terribly clumsy of me.'

"He sank into the chair and I went to the bath and handed him my robe. He could hardly look me in the eye as he put it on. 'I shall dress immediately in the bath and find one of the servants to move my things,' he said. 'I can't understand why such . . . such a thing has never happened to me before. Please do forgive me.'

"Well, by this time I had quite gotten over the shock and was beginning to find the humor in the situation. Besides, he looked awfully adorable, and ever so forlorn. 'No,' I told him, 'I think it might be better if you dress here whilst I dash in the bath.' He looked rather stunned. 'Truly,' I said. I don't know why I was so bold. 'Since we're both already here, let's pretend that we've been doing this for years. Won't be a sec.'

"I grabbed my frock and things, ran the fastest bath of my life, hurried into my clothes, and threw some powder and lipstick on my face. I don't know why I was afraid he might be gone by the time I got out."

"But he wasn't," I said.

"No, he was sitting exactly as he had been, in the same chair, fully dressed this time. He looked up at me, still mortified, and smiled. 'You look lovely,' he said.

"I didn't know what to say, so I asked him to fasten my gown. Which he did, although his fingers were shaking. Then he sat down again as I fussed about with my jewelry.

" 'Do you know,' he said, 'I don't think in all the years I've been married that I've once watched my wife dress.'

"There was something about the manner in which he said 'wife' that went straight to my heart," Laura said, looking at me. " 'Do you know,' I said to him, 'in all the years *I've* been married, I can promise you I've not once watched my husband dress.' We both laughed."

"Too intimate, you mean," I said. "Something about the state of partial undress that is more provocative than the body itself."

"I tend not to think of *provocative* and Andrew in the same breath."

"Well, what happened next?" I asked.

"We snuck out of the room once we were certain no one was

watching. He suggested that it might have been someone trying to trip him up."

"For photographs of a potentially adulterous situation, you mean," I said.

"Quite. But we found out later that it had been an innocent mistake by the staff. Guy found that out, I should say."

"Is that when you first met Guy?"

"Yes, they're the best of friends, Hugh and Guy. He said he'd find Guy, that Guy could fix anything."

Oh ho, I'll bet he can!

"In the drawing room was a silver tray with envelopes on it, so that each gentleman would have the name of the lady he was to escort in to dinner," Laura went on. "I watched as the man who'd been in my room pulled someone aside; I figured that was Guy. I could see them both looking at me. I thought everyone else was, too." She blushed, and as usual her entire face and neck were suffused with a lovely pink glow.

" 'Ah, well, jolly good luck,' Guy told him. 'She's a corker.' "

" 'Yes, she is,' he said. 'But I don't know *who* she is. I'm such a sodding fool, I forgot to ask her name.' He told me this later," Laura added. "We both forgot to ask."

"Enter the rogue," I said. "The dearest Guy."

"He's not so bad once you get to know him. Truly he's not. He introduced himself, told me all about Hugh Trevenen and his wife, Nicola, Lady Pembridge, and said I was the best thing that ever could have happened to him. All this in five minutes before dinner. It was ever so ridiculous, but made me relax. Then Guy whispered that it wasn't quite such a good idea for us to be seated next to each other at dinner, just in case. 'Besides,' he said, 'dinners are always the most successful when you seat people who are bitter enemies right next to one another. A wife and a mistress, for example, or a dismal playwright and his least favorite critic. A touch of loathing quite improves the conversation.' " She laughed, again. "I still remember his exact words because they were so, I don't know, so *troppo*."

"And so true," I said. "What was the dinner like?"

"I hardly remember," she said. "Hugh and I were trying to keep our eyes off each other, but it was hopeless. All I kept thinking was that this wonderful feeling was some kind of warning, that there was something so expectant about Hugh, as if he were sitting down to a banquet while at the same time expecting the food to be snatched from his lips before he had a chance to take one bite. That he was haunted by the feeling that he would always be disappointed and unhappy. And then I realized I could have been describing myself.

"After dinner, all I could think of was Hugh," she went on. "How much I wanted to find him in my room when I went upstairs."

"Do you mind my asking if you did?" I said.

"No, of course not," she replied, her eyes dancing. "And no, I didn't. Not that night. I was frightfully sorry. But it was too dangerous. The last thing I could risk was someone discovering us together and gleefully relating all to my husband. Or to Hugh's wife."

"I think we should introduce Andrew and Nicola," I said. "They sound like a perfect couple."

"Indeed," Laura replied, sighing. "But I'm afraid it's not that easy."

"It never is. Do go on." I knew we were about to get to the really juicy bits.

"The next morning, I was lying on a sofa in the study, in front of the fire, when two of the guests came in and began gossiping about Hugh and Nicola," Laura said. "They'd no idea I was there, and I was wondering what to do when I saw Guy strolling in from the gardens. He took one look at me, one look at *them,* and took charge immediately. That's when I realized Guy was truly a friend indeed.

" 'Ladies,' he said as he sauntered in. Rather bursting with vitality, I remember. I could see it all in the mirror. 'I have a dilemma, which only you can solve. Should I go upstairs for a quick kip before lunch, or shall I return to the splendors of nature . . . in which case I shall rather desperately require the company of such adorable creatures as yourselves.' He kissed their hands. They, naturally, were giggling that they weren't properly dressed for an outdoor expedition."

"Guy's reputation preceded him," I said. "Was he born seductive?"

"I don't know," Laura said with a fond smile. "Those two certainly decided he was. He told them that if they could return in exactly seven minutes with their wellies on, they'd be off. They ran off, and Guy came to me, leaning over the sofa to say that Hugh was waiting, that his room was at the end of the hall, opposite the knight in shining armor. That's how it started."

"Opposite the suit of armor." I sighed deeply. I so hate unhappy romances. "What is to be done now?"

"I don't know," Laura said mournfully. "Belladonna, from the club, put me in touch with a detective in London, but he told me we must be absolutely certain the case is airtight. It's ever so difficult. For all his philandering, Andrew doesn't want a divorce."

"Could it be that he doesn't want to lose access to your money?"

"Yes, of course, but I've got to think of the children. As Hugh thinks of his."

"Does Andrew know about Hugh?"

"No, I don't think so." She patted her hair, as usual. "I'm afraid he'll find out and that will be the end of everything. It's why Guy is so special. I couldn't see Hugh without Guy poking his nose every which way, making sure everything is spit-spot. He really is terribly sweet."

She sighed again, and we sat lost in thought about the impossibility of love.

When the guests began to arrive, we had them park their proudly shined chrome behemoths in neat rows on the runway. Every license plate, already photographed by the hidden security cameras at the gates, is matched to its occupants on a cross-indexed list Winken and Blinken set up. Everything about this evening has been organized with military precision. We probably have more security people, dressed in white dinner jackets, carrying the ubiquitous silver beakers full of icy mint juleps, than guests. Such a vast estate and the people visiting it are not as easily controllable as the Club Belladonna, of course, which makes us slightly edgy.

But it can't be helped. And this one evening will soon be over.

Belladonna stands in the entrance hallway, a stunning portrait of serene elegance. A large ruby, complementing the color of her eyes, shimmers on a choker, and she wears matching pearl and ruby earrings. Her mass of chestnut hair is twisted in a chignon like Laura's, and her lips are stained a dark pink. She is wearing a most becoming pale green strapless dress of duchesse satin, nipped tightly at the waist and flaring out to her ankles, with matching elbow-length satin gloves so she won't have to touch anyone's hands directly. Not a single ring adorns her fingers, although many of her guests have imported the affectation of wearing them from the famous club they'd heard so much about.

Belladonna forces a slight smile, so her guests have no idea she is counting the minutes until they leave. She has already endured the gushing compliments of the Robertsons and their blushing houseguest, Nancy. She has an especially gracious greeting for the lumberyard's very own Cooper Marriner, who turns such a pleasing shade of puce when he sees his hostess that I have to pinch my wrist to keep from laughing. We've heard about the Blackwaters' hounds and the Leightons' decorating fiascos and how hard it is to manage all these, well, you know, *dreadful* people down here. The guests look askance at Bryony and Susannah, flitting excitedly from room to room, commenting on the fantastically overdone ensembles the ladies are wearing. The Contessa murmurs politely, refusing to rise to the bait. Why, she's become the talk of the neighborhood, how downright *friendly* she is with *undesirables.* Must be because she lived so long in Europe, they tell themselves. Those barbarians know nothing. We of King Henry, on the other hand, have all the answers. They come in a bourbon bottle, don't you know.

I guess it's because alcohol is a preservative. Keeps them all well pickled.

Belladonna shows no sign of weariness as the guests flow in, trampling through the house in awe, poking at the fish in the smaller dining room, trying to keep their fingers off the valuable objects in the other rooms—until they realize they're being watched by an unsmiling waiter with a tray of crabmeat canapes in one hand and a holster near the other. Off they trot to the over-laden buffet tables on the veranda, or to the bar for endless cups of punch or beakers of juleps. Then it's time for a whirl around the magnificent copper ballroom while the band plays Cole Porter tunes and all seems right with the world.

After an hour or two, Belladonna has had more than enough, and goes upstairs to the blue bedroom for a breather, leaving the door slightly ajar. There she finds a dejected Laura waiting, sitting in one of the two silver-blue leather wingback chairs she has turned to face the balcony running nearly the length of the second floor. They look at each other but say nothing. If only Belladonna could open up and allow herself a friend. If only she—

The door is flung open, and they hear the soft crinkle of satin skirts. There's a dull thud as two rather large bodies heave themselves down on the sofa nearest to the door. They have no idea anyone is sitting in the chairs facing the balcony.

"Did you *see* the chandelier?" one of the bodies says in a deep drawl. "I happen to know it cost at least forty-five thousand dollars. Maybe fifty."

"*No.* You don't say," says the other. "Just exactly how much money do you think she's got?"

"Buckets. Buckets and buckets."

"And how, may I ask, d'you think she got it?"

"The usual way. Flat on her back."

Laura frowns as Belladonna's eyes narrow. Actually, she thinks these two are about the most amusing creatures she's heard all night, but she's certainly not going to give them the pleasure of knowing that.

"Why, Shirley Marriner, you are a wicked creature."

"No more so than you, Letitia Blackwater."

"Thank goodness for that."

There is a short pause while Shirley and Letitia revel in their moral superiority. Shirley is stuffed into a bright teal blue taffeta frock with so many petticoats that you could hide an army in them; her ensemble is topped with a peacock-feather headdress. Letitia's endless loops of pastel ruffles make her look like a vast puddle of melted sherbet. Worse, their shoes have rows of rhinestones marching around the heels. The copycat rings and gloves and masked theme parties are bad enough, but the sight of Belladonna-inspired shoes at a plantation ball in King Henry, Virginia is too much for me to bear. Something simply must be done, with immediate dispatch!

"That heathen room with all those grotesque statues. Why, no honest Christian woman would have such a thing."

"Those revolting nudes in the salon. It's a disgrace."

"Those horrid little fish in the dining room. Ghastly."

"That horrid little girl, playing with the daughter. Can you imagine?"

"Not what I want my Melissa playing with."

"Or my Polly."

"No indeed."

"Dippy says she was married to some perfectly dreadful Eye-talian; that's why she has the airs to call herself a contessa. Why, she's no more a contessa than I am Mamie Eisenhower."

Laura bites her lip as Belladonna shakes her head and motions her to remain silent. Eventually, the overgrown debs heave themselves back up, sighing with happy maliciousness, and, after sticking their noses into all the other rooms on the second floor for a peek and a poke, wind their way back to the revels downstairs.

Belladonna is smiling broadly for the first time tonight. She gets up without a word, leaving Laura, finds me, and whispers an altogether splendid idea in my ear. I go off in search of Orlando, bring him back, and we straighten our bow ties as we approach Shirley and Letitia. They're standing near the punch bowl in the glistening copper ballroom, engrossed in their gossip. Bowing deeply, I leaning on one of Leandro's lion-topped canes for support, we ask for a dance.

With enough flutters and coos to stock a pet store, Shirley and Letitia drop into deep, creaky curtsies, thrilled and simpering that two men seen so close to the Contessa are singling them out. As they rise and I circle behind them, they remain oblivious to my sudden jab with my cane. A razor-sharp blade springs out and just happens to slice at a particular angle into Shirley's sparkling heels. Blink and you would have missed it. My point entirely.

Orlando whisks Letitia away as Shirley coyly bats her lashes at me. I hand my cane to the waiter serving the punch. "They say I'm the best dancer in the county," she tells me smugly as the music starts. She practically leads me all over the dance floor, making sure every guest in the room can see her.

"Then I am fortunate indeed to have chosen such a delightful partner," I reply, and her smirking smile deepens.

After only a minute or so of a breathless waltz, though, Shirley's heels break clean off, and she stumbles awkwardly into my arms with a sharp, ugly cry.

"Whatever could be wrong, dear lady?" I ask, my voice dripping with solicitous concern. "Are you hurt?"

"My heels!" she cries. "My beautiful Belladonna heels!"

She hasn't got it quite right. *She* is the heel and Belladonna is her hostess.

I help her limp off the dance floor, and she shrugs my hand away in anger when we reach the wall and she can stand without losing her balance. Everyone is staring at her with veiled amusement, and several ladies are tittering loudly. Shirley's mouth is set in a hard line as she takes off her shoes and stomps away to sit down in a chair in the hall to examine them carefully. Heels don't break like that. Not the custom-made heels of Shirley Marriner.

She feels a shadow fall on her peacock feathers and looks up, to see the Contessa regarding her with bland detachment.

"Forty-eight thousand six hundred and fifty-five dollars and twenty-four cents," the Contessa says coolly before turning to walk back to her guests. "But such a chandelier is worth it, don't you agree?"

Shirley pales and nearly swoons, her heels forgotten.

*A*s the party begins to wind down, we send Laura to the folly to wait for Hugh. That area of the estate is off-limits for our "guests," so she can mope in total privacy without worrying about the likes of Shirley and Letitia.

Belladonna moves to the balcony, so she can watch Laura find the path to the pool and the folly, her dejected shoulders slumping more with each step. The sky is a luminous, deep blue and the stars thickly clustered. The band is still playing and people are laughing, but Belladonna's heart is weary.

She stays out there, watching everything and nothing, until there is a knock on the door. I come in with another one of our guests. "I beg your pardon, Contessa, but I should like to introduce you to Mr. Hugh Trevenen," I announce.

So he made it after all. How splendid. Hugh smiles nervously, and his gray eyes are weary. He's slim and not that much taller than Laura would be in her espadrilles, and his sandy brown hair is thinning at the temples. There's nothing spectacular or flashy about his appearance—not like Guy's at all—but he seems pleasant and desperately eager to see Laura.

"I am most dreadfully sorry to be arriving at this late hour," he says. I notice that he has beautiful long fingers and doesn't wear a wedding ring. "Please do forgive this intrusion on your privacy."

I love how these upper-crusty Brits say *privacy*. It sounds like a clipped hedge.

Belladonna shrugs.

"There's no need to apologize," I tell him. "We're happy to have you. Guy will be happy, too, I expect. Wherever he's disappeared to." Probably nuzzling with Nancy in the hayloft. "But no one more so than Laura."

"You are too kind," he says, and he's so earnest I almost want to hug him.

"She's in the folly," I say. "I'll take you as far as the path toward the pool, and point you in the right direction. It's a little house with a thatched roof; you can't miss it. I expect Laura has locked the door, but the spare key is under the pot of pinks, just to the left of the geraniums."

Hugh doesn't move, a bit dumbfounded.

"Why are you standing there like a big lummox," I tease, "when she's been waiting for you all this time?"

I can't help but be pleased at the sudden shy happiness shining in Hugh's eyes and the transformation of his anxious expression. It is as if his entire face has been lit from within by love.

Hugh says good night and one last thank-you, and I drop him at the path, handing him a flashlight. He practically runs down the steps, then slows to a tiptoe when he sees the house. After only a minute he finds the key under the pot of pinks. Laura has flung herself facedown on the bed, sobbing her heart out, and she doesn't hear the door open softly or the tumble of the lock as Hugh secures it. She doesn't hear his quiet footsteps as he strides to her. She thinks she's dreaming when she hears her beloved calling her name. She still thinks she's dreaming when she sits up and then flies into his arms.

Back at the house, Belladonna is still standing on the balcony. She has seen Hugh hurry away, just as she had seen Laura walk with such dejection only a short while before. She doesn't know and she can't see him, but Guy is standing in the dark, hidden by the shadows of a great oak, watching her. From his vantage point, her face is clearly illuminated from behind, and he can observe a curious mixture of satisfaction mingled with an overwhelming melancholy. Weariness as well, he thinks, and resignation.

She hasn't moved when a few minutes later he knocks on the door Hugh had left open. "Would you care for a drink?" he asks when she turns to see who it is.

"No." She turns her back, clearly signaling her lack of interest.

"May I ask you a question?" he says. "About your daughter."

Oh ho, what a persistent bugger! He knows this'll get her attention.

She turns back, her face a blank.

"She asked me this afternoon if she and Susannah could call me 'Uncle Guy,' and I told her she'd have to ask your permission," he says, seating himself comfortably in one of the silver-blue wingbacks. "She said she already has an Uncle Jack in New York and wants to have an Uncle Guy in Virginia."

The expression on Belladonna's face doesn't change. "I don't mind," she says, "if it's what Bryony wants."

"I shouldn't want you to think there's anything untoward in my behavior toward her," Guy goes on, "given the circumstances of our first meeting. Yours and mine, I mean."

"Given those circumstances, I expect an answer to this question: Why did she startle you?" Belladonna asks, sitting in the other chair, her dress rustling softly.

Guy stares at his nails, buffed as perfectly as his shoes, for several minutes before replying. Belladonna doesn't move, or press him.

"She looked like my little sister," he says eventually. "Gwendolyn. My Gwennie." His eyes mist. "I rarely talk about her, you see. When I first saw Bryony from a distance, it was as if Gwennie had come back to life. It was a trick of the light, that's all. Wishful thinking, too, I suppose, for the more I come to know Bryony, the less similar she becomes. But the expressions on her face, the way she's always singing and dancing around, remind me so much of Gwennie. She died a long time ago, when she was nine."

"I'm sorry," Belladonna says, although her voice remains cold and detached. "How old were you?"

"Twelve," he says.

They sit in a fairly affable silence for a long while. He obviously does not want to talk about Gwendolyn, and she feels no need to ask. An occasional loud drunken laugh wafts up to the balcony. Some of the guests are obviously reluctant to leave, probably because they are too drunk to remember where their cars are. No matter—Winken and Blinken will be only too happy to steer them in the right direction.

"I'm glad Hugh is here," he says eventually.

"Tell me about him."

Guy, who's obviously an indefatigable sort, is only too pleased to be of service. "Hugh has perfect manners, which you may have noticed, but that is an amiable facade," he says. "His father was notoriously promiscuous. Once, during a drunken binge, he sliced his leg and his mistress's leg with a razor so they could bind themselves in blood. As if that weren't enough, he showed everyone the photographs of the event, and proudly displayed his scar to all and sundry." Guy shakes his head. "He thought that children should be seen as little as possible, and so, like most boys of our class—and I use the word advisedly, mind you—Hugh was raised by his nanny. His was a loving one; I think it's what kept him sane. Nanny would stretch his wool undies with a hairbrush so they wouldn't fit too tightly and itch. Nanny loved him and protected him from the world, and most especially from his father. His mother was busy entertaining, going to parties and fittings and teas and so on, so as not to be bothered with the frightful mess of either her children or her husband."

He can't help a tinge of distress from creeping into his voice, and his eyes are focused on the lights flickering in the distance. He's describing some of his own childhood, she realizes, the memory of the kind of neglect and pain that never goes away.

"When did you meet?" she asks.

"At school. He was eight and I was nine, so I'd already weathered a year of abuse. I think leaving Nanny for school's brutal realities is a shock from which part of us never really recovers." He's not saying this because he expects sympathy, only because it's true.

"What was school like?"

"You don't want to hear it."

But she does, forcing herself to sit calmly with him and ask these questions, tolerating his overwhelmingly male presence because he can answer some of the questions that have been plaguing her for years and years. She wants to hear him talk, because he knows about what formed them, the members of the Club. Belladonna can picture them at school, obsessed with punishment, thrilling to the sound of a good flogging to get the juices flowing. Reveling in and abusing the power of their rank, delighting in the misfortune and unhappiness of their peers.

"Tell me anyway," she commands.

"It seemed the premise of the public schools I grew to loathe was to forbid any activity once it seemed to give pleasure," Guy says. "Hence the bad food, bad beds, bad heating, bad masters, bad everything. God help any little boy who showed signs of weakness or despair. No one to ask for help, no one to turn to, no one protecting you."

He could be speaking of her. What they did to her.

"And not a female to be found, save the cooks, who brought Attila the Hun to mind rather than Nanny or mummy or the little girls you used to play with before they sent you away," he goes on. "After my mother, after—"

After his mother died, he means to say, but can't. This she understands instinctively.

"School made me hard. I became quite an enterprising little chap, expert at constructing a sort of lasso out of twine to catch rats as they poked their noses out of all their little holes in search of the cheese I'd baited them with," Guy goes on. "The other boys found it an admirable skill, and learned to stay in my good graces or they'd find a dead rat in their pockets or their beds. I learned this from one of my schoolmates. Landis, his name was. When Landis arrived, the boys planned their usual hog pile, jumping atop him, pummeling him into dust to show him who was boss. Landis, however, managed to outfox the bullies. When he installed himself in his room and began unpacking, everyone was astonished at the sight of his lovely monogrammed ivory hairbrushes, the kind you'd see on a lady's dressing table. One of the boys, who was at least eight inches taller and three stone heavier, grabbed them, thinking a good paddling was in order. Landis swung around and punched him full in the face. Down he went, covered in blood. Then Landis offered his hand, yanked him up, brushed him off, kicked his backside, and sent him on his merry way. Landis taught me how to fight, to defend myself. That was the only way to earn respect at school—with sudden, brute force. It wasn't so easy for Hugh, who was small and delicate." He runs his hands through his hair. "If school doesn't break one's spirit, it certainly leads one to believe in one's superiority for having mastered it. It makes one a glutton for love."

"For romps in the hay, you mean," she says.

Guy smiles. "Especially romps in the hay."

"And vengeance," she says.

Guy looks at her curiously. "Yes, quite. Hugh and I would lie in our beds at night, shivering with too much cold to sleep, and dream of our revenge."

"Did you get it?" she asks.

"Some of it," he says. "It takes planning."

"That I understand," she replies. "But tell me, what exactly does Hugh do?"

"He's at Lloyd's. Insuring my tea plantations."

"And his wife?"

"Ah yes. The *splendid* Nicola."

"I take it Laura is nothing like her."

"Quite right. Laura has a heart."

"Why did he marry her?" she asks. "For the same reason Laura married Andrew?"

"Pride," he says. "Stubbornness. Foolishness. But mostly to get back at his father."

"I don't understand," Belladonna says. "She's Lady Pembridge, isn't she, so it wasn't a disgrace to his family to have married her."

"Can I trust you?" Guy asks. "I've never told this to anyone."

"Of course," Belladonna replies. She wonders what he might be about to say, and I wonder why this conversation is even happening. It's more than her needing to know about men of Guy's class. Although, obviously, she does have a particular knack for eliciting confessions of the most intimate sort. It's the intense, quizzical, yet hard look in her dazzling green eyes, one that seems to dare a person, *Tell me, I need to know.*

But Belladonna is spending more time alone with Guy than with any man she's met since we came to America. This worries me, yet I still like him. I can't help it. He's a terrible roué, but funny and charming, devoted to Hugh and Laura as he nurses his own bruised heart. Maybe that's why she can tolerate him. He has asked nothing of her but to listen.

"I never trusted Nicola. Perhaps because I always knew she was an opportunist like myself," Guy says. "But Hugh was in love and I tried to be happy for him, although I knew something was—what's the word?—*off.* So I had her followed."

He looks at Belladonna, expecting to find censure, but she is merely watching him intently.

"I discovered something of a most alarming nature, and debated for weeks what to do," he goes on. "The wedding was meant to be one of the social events of the season, you see." He shakes his head. "But I had to protect Hugh. The night before his wedding, after a bit too much to drink, I took him for a walk to sober him up. His family had taken a suite, an entire floor, actually, at Claridges. We had adjoining rooms, so I could keep an eye on him. My idea, of course." He sighs. "By some great coincidence, our walk took us to his parents' house very late on the eve of his wedding."

"His parents who were supposed to be at Claridges."

"Precisely. Luckily, Hugh was drunk enough not to have sussed out my intentions, because I took him into the garden and pointed to a ladder I'd bribed one of the servants to place there for me, against the wall and leading to a bedroom window upstairs. I handed him a torch and told him to climb up, that he couldn't get married until he climbed up the ladder."

"So up he climbed and shined in the light," she says softly, "and whom did he see?"

"His father. And Nicola."

She frowns and looks away. *"Finita la commedia,"* she says.

"Yes," he says. "I'll never forget the look on his face when he climbed down the ladder. 'Do you have photographs?' he asked, and I nodded yes. He said nothing more as we found a taxi and went back to Claridges. I tried to apologize; I didn't know what to say, for once."

"They went through with it, obviously," she says.

"Yes. He pulled it off, too; no one suspected a thing—not Nicola, not his father—until they were about to leave for their honeymoon. Hugh asked his father to come into his room, and he handed him an envelope full of photographs, and he told him he was never going to speak to him again until the day he died, and that if he ever tried to touch his wife again he'd send these photographs to the papers and that his solicitors already had the negatives and family be damned.

"That evening, once the happy couple was ensconced in the marital bed and Nicola was preparing to surrender her prized virginity to her beloved, he handed her another envelope full of photographs, and told her he wasn't going to touch her until he had proof she wasn't carrying his father's child, and that then, if he so desired, she'd do whatever he told her to do, strictly for the purposes of producing an heir."

"She must have made quite a scene."

"Quite. The tears, the pleading, the apologies. He was adamant. She had no choice but to behave, for a short while at least. She wormed her way into his good graces, knowing that he still carried quite a torch for her. After she rapidly produced two children, she went back to her former bad habits. Except with more discretion. That's when he met Laura."

"I should think Nicola and Andrew would be a perfect couple," Belladonna says, waving her hand dismissively. "They seem to deserve each other."

Guy gives a little half smile. "You're right. I'm working on it."

"Are divorces that difficult in England?"

"Not extraordinarily," he says, "but should Nicola find any information whatsoever about Laura, Hugh would have a much more difficult time of it."

"I see," she says.

"You know," he says, "the way you waved your hand just now reminds me of a woman I met. Well, not *met* exactly. Made her acquaintance. In New York."

"Let me guess. Her name begins with a *B* and ends with a club."

"How did you know? Must be the eyes."

"Yes, I'm sure I'm the only woman in America with green eyes," she says sarcastically. "You're not the first person to have remarked upon it."

Guy smiles, for real this time. "Did you ever go to the Club Belladonna?"

"Do you mean, did I ever stand outside and wait to be chosen by a dog? No, I'm afraid I did not." She's not lying. Of course she never did. "I don't like being surrounded by people."

"Then why, may I ask, did you subject yourself to this party tonight?"

"To relieve my social obligations and give my tedious neighbors something to talk about," she replies, her voice cold once again. "Now that they've seen the house and my *eccentricities*—especially my mingling freely with what they consider social and moral undesirables—they'll stop pestering me with invitations to their ludicrous parties and drinking engagements and shooting expeditions and leave me alone."

Guy wonders for a fleeting second if he might be wrong. He knows she's telling the truth about wanting to be left alone. Perhaps Bryony had a dog called Dromedee, not Andromeda, and his suspicions are pure coincidence.

Perhaps not. She sits so still. She is so imperious. She listens with such powerful concentration. She has enough money to buy the Bank of England. There's an air of impenetrable mystery about her, and he knows he's falling in love.

He stands up, stretches, and says good night.

She nods. Her face has resumed its polite blankness, the same look he'd seen when he first came into the room and sat down in a silver-blue chair.

I know that look, Guy says to himself as he heads to his room. I have seen that look too many times before, staring back at me in the mirror.

16

Fathers
and Sons

"It was considered a great honor to be eaten," Hugh says. "That's what Guy told me about some of the cannibal tribes he met on his travels. If one ate the flesh of the fiercest and bravest enemies, that fierceness and bravery would enter one's own body and be perpetuated forever."

"I see," I tell him. "Thank you for imparting that valuable bit of information. I'll consider it next time I wish to roast one of our neighbors on a spit."

Hugh laughs, and Laura smiles. We're near the pool the following afternoon, enjoying iced tea—mine spiked with a healthy dollop of bourbon—and the relative calm after yesterday's excesses. Guy is off on what he called an "expedition" with Bryony and Susannah, exploring the maze and the paths beyond, so Belladonna and I are listening to Hugh talk about him.

Nothing like a healthy dose of lovemaking to loosen the tongue.

"There aren't any cannibal tribes in Ceylon, silly," Laura says, resting her head on Hugh's shoulder as he kisses her hair. It's lovely to see them like this, I decide, magnanimous soul that I am. Someone around here deserves to be happy.

"No, but there's a wildness in the jungle that suits him," Hugh replies. "Guy chose to escape the family shackles as soon as he could; to the manor born became all that sort of rubbish to him. His father was a bully and a tyrant; I rather think he made mine seem nearly human. It is a terrible thing for a child to realize he is both unwanted and unloved by his own father. It is almost more than one can bear."

We don't know what to say, and Hugh falls silent. That terrible truth we understand, I realize. All of us sitting with our silver beakers full of iced tea and mint on this lovely limpid afternoon. Bound by the tyranny of our childhoods.

"Guy's been disinherited, as well, which is quite a feat for the son of an English lord. But after his mother died, and then his sister, he wanted nothing but to escape. There was a monstrous fuss after he accused his father of killing both of them. His mother and his sister, I mean. Although his father didn't, of course, unless you consider deliberate neglect a form of slow murder. I know Guy did."

"Please explain," I say. "I don't follow you."

"Guy and Gwendolyn, his little sister, had always been exceedingly close. His mother was a delicate creature, completely at the mercy of her husband, and she never really quite recuperated from Gwen's birth. She loved Guy passionately—more than his elder brothers, I fear, which in part explained their antipathy to him—but was not able to supervise the household as much as she might have had she not been ill and often confined to bed. Guy was utterly devoted to Gwen, especially after their mother died."

"How old was he when his mother died?" I ask.

"Let's see, he's a year older than I am, so that was when he was eight. Gwen was four." He shakes his head. "I find it exceedingly difficult to believe Guy is going to be forty this year. Which means I'll be forty next year. Bloody hell!"

"You're not such an old bag," Laura says.

"Thank you, darling," he says, "for that vote of confidence. So when their mother died I believe Guy felt an even deeper responsibility for his sister. Their father was rarely home, thankfully, and showed no interest in his children when he was. As I recall, if the children wished to see their father, it was necessary to make an appointment with his private secretary."

"But why did you say Guy accused his father of killing his mother?" I ask.

"Because his father had gotten his mother pregnant again, explicitly against the doctor's orders. She was frightfully ill for months, and then lost the baby. Another boy. Why his father was so persistent in procreating escapes me. Perhaps he knew that he had spawned two of England's most useless bastards, and that his only worthy son loathed him and everything he stood for. I don't think I'll ever understand it. Nor will Guy." He shakes his head. "Whatever the details, the pregnancy and the death of her baby did Guy's mother in. She lingered a few months, then died. Guy never forgave his father for it."

"And what about his sister?"

"It was the measles, I believe, or mumps," Hugh goes on. "One of those childhood diseases we all catch and then usually get over. There was no reason for her to have taken so ill; certainly not to have died. Guy was at school and she was at home, and they thought she had flu or some such, a typical fever that children get from time to time, that sort of thing, and therefore her symptoms were neglected until it was too late. Nanny was a horror; she didn't believe in coddling her charges, not that one. Gwen was such a stoic little thing. She didn't want to complain or make a fuss around her father or Nanny. It was a senseless tragedy."

"Was Guy with her when she died?" Belladonna asks.

Hugh looks at her quizzically. "Yes, it's funny you should ask that. I think the bond between Guy and Gwen was almost tele-pathic, so that when she took ill, he knew something was wrong. I remember this quite clearly. We were at school, and he woke me up in the middle of the night and told me he was leaving, that he had to get home because Gwen was ill and she needed him. I told him he was daft, and that he'd be caned and sent down if he dared run away, but he said he didn't care and he'd already bribed one of the groundskeepers to give him a ride to the train, and he had to do it. I gave him what little dosh I had hidden in my socks, and off he went.

"He made it to his house, being Guy of course, and snuck in, up to his sister's bedroom. She was terribly ill, but I think she willed herself to wait for him so she could say good-bye. She told him not to be sad, that she was going to be with Mummy and their baby brother in heaven, and that she would always love him and be his guardian angel."

A tear rolls down Laura's cheek, and I'm afraid I am all choked up as well.

Hugh stops to catch his breath. "She died in his arms, which I'm sure was a small measure of comfort to him. But then the rage took over. He stayed with Gwen until she was cold. No one came in to see how she was feeling, not a soul. Then he snuck downstairs, using the servants' staircase, where his father was having a very important dinner."

"No one knew yet that Gwen had just died, or that Guy was there, in the house?" I ask.

"Exactly," Hugh replies. "So when Guy burst into the dining room, this furious young chap screaming at the top of his lungs at his father, pummeling his chest with his small fists the way his chum Landis had taught him, well, it was rather a scene. Well-bred young gentlemen did not indulge themselves in public outbursts; and most certainly not amongst prominent friends and colleagues of one's father. But Guy didn't care. He was screaming at his father that he'd killed his mother, and now his beautiful little sister as well, and that he was going to pay for it someday, that Guy wasn't going to rest until his father had been punished as the murderous bastard that he was. And then he told his father he never would speak to him again, that he would hate him forever, until the end of his days, until the day he knew he was dead and left to rot. It took nearly all the servants to subdue him and put him up to bed, he was so hysterical."

"Poor little boy. That's dreadful. I never knew all the details," Laura says softly.

"And do you know, it was particularly ironic that this was most likely the only time in his life that Guy's father was actually proud of his son," Hugh adds. "Guy's outburst proved to dearest papa that Guy had character and courage. That he was willing to fight for what he believed in. Threats and rage belonged to the kind of language his father used to intimidate all who met him. He was a man of imperious will and power. The one time I had the misfortune to meet him, he scared me half to death."

"What was his name?" I ask conversationally, trying not to look at Belladonna. Guy's father sounded exactly like the kind of man His Lordship might be. "Is he still alive?"

"He was the Earl of Ross and Cromarty." He laughs bitterly. "Such a name for such a man. But he died yonks ago. Before the end of the war, I believe. Guy told me he'd long gone to his just rewards."

Botheration. If he died during the war, the earl certainly can't be *him*. Of course it's not exactly realistic for me to think that every rich English bastard we hear about could be His Lordship himself. Why, if I keep this up I might as well suspect Hugh's father. Or Laura's. Or even the Pritch's. Double botheration. I must stop it.

"So the eldest son is now the earl," I say, keeping my doubts to myself.

Hugh nods. "John Francis. Utterly useless sod. The last I heard, he was drinking himself into insensibility. Most of the estate is gone. I don't recollect where Frederick, the second son, is. Probably off in the veldt shooting monkeys in the back for sport. He's that sort."

"Did Guy ever go back to school?" I ask.

"Yes," Hugh replies, "they took him back after the earl had a word with the headmaster. He came home with me for all the hols, and as soon as he was eighteen, he ran off. Since his brothers hated him as much as he hated them, they were glad to be rid of him. As far as I know, Guy went all over Africa and India, and we caught up again during the war. He was posted to India and so was I. Lots of contacts there. When the war was over, his business took off. Same 'useful' contacts, I expect. Gemstones and import-export and those tea plantations in Ceylon and Lord knows what else. I know Guy better than to ask for specifics."

"But he is a good friend," I say.

"The best," Hugh agrees solemnly. "Oh, I know he has a wicked way with the ladies, but he's got a good and passionate heart when push comes to shove. I wouldn't be sitting here, with the woman I love, without everything he's done for me. For us. And he asks nothing in return." He frowns. "I think Guy is a tad too proud about having such a will of iron. I've thought about this quite a lot, you know, because I feel I owe him so much. But I fear he treats his emotions much as an army treats its recruits. He is a master of concealment."

In that, he's met his match.

*H*ugh can only stay for another four days, and Laura is despondent, moping around the folly, once he's gone. She had been planning to leave soon after, but I convince her to stay for a few more weeks. Her children are traveling with their father, so there's no reason for her to go back to a lonely house. Next time Laura comes, I've insisted that she bring Rupert and Cassandra. It'll be good for Bryony, who is going to miss Guy something fierce once he goes. But that's been put off, too. Laura begged us to let Guy stay on as well, so they could travel back to London together. He's then planning to go on to Ceylon. Trouble with the tea is all he'll say. Been away too long already.

Much to everyone's surprise, Guy and Belladonna have taken to riding every morning. It had been Laura's idea to saddle up and keep herself busy, but she soon lost interest. Firkin watches them go instead, with a pleased gleam in his eye.

"Born horseman, that one," he says proudly.

"Though not like the Contessa," I retort.

"No one can charm an animal like she can," he agrees. "But he sits a fine horse, he does."

Belladonna doesn't discuss her morning rides with me, and I don't ask. Our routine is smooth and pleasant, perfectly suited to sultry July days. They get up and ride. I have a leisurely breakfast with Laura and let her talk about Hugh and Guy. We have grown to adore each other, and she doesn't ask prying questions about Belladonna. We putter around the house or read. I attend to my mountains of paperwork and Laura writes letters. We have a swim. We have a light late lunch. We often garden as the afternoon draws to a close, when it's cooler. Bryony plays with Susannah and the other children. I check in with Jack and the Pritch if need be. More of the same. Be patient. Plotting and planning.

Take a deep breath. Shoot steady. Aim for his heart.

After dinner, we sit on the veranda and watch the fireflies dance. The rest of the world seems so far away. It can't hurt us here.

That's what I keep telling myself. I'm waiting. Something is going to happen. Something soon. Belladonna is changing. There is some small part of her that is softening, and it's Guy's doing. She's fighting it, I can tell, but not as hard as she might once have.

"You seem fairly chipper," I say to her late one balmy night when the two of us are alone.

"What do you mean?" she says.

"I mean your chipperness may in part be due to Mr. Guy Lindell, he of the hay."

"Bryony is terribly attached to him," she says blandly.

"So am I, in my way. And Laura is, too, of course. He's an awful charmer. And he's nice, once you overlook his rather unfortunate libido." I smile. I can't tell her I especially like him because he's kept his mouth shut about his suspicious queries with regard to her true identity. "But I expect he's been a perfect gentleman with you."

I wait for her to bite my head off for saying that, but she doesn't.

"Yes, he has been," she says after an uncomfortable pause. "When we're riding we rarely talk. Or when we do it's about nothing important. He reminds me a bit of Jack. Only less upright. Still, I think they're equally honorable, in their own way."

"That's true. But Jack is an employee, and he knows a lot of things about you. We went through that—"

No no no, I don't want to remember Sir Patty. I shouldn't have brought it up.

"Anyway," I quickly say to correct myself, "I just worry about you, that's all. I worry that *you* might be worrying about him. Does that make any sense?

"No, it certainly does not. Did your knee tell you that?" she asks sarcastically. "Damn you, Tomasino, I hate it when you're right. But if it makes you feel any better, I can tell you that I honestly don't understand why I can tolerate him. And that's all there is to it on the subject of Guy Lindell."

Oh ho, what have we here?

You can't trick a trickster.

The trunks are packed and tickets bought. It is going to be very quiet around the house, and I'm prepared to indulge myself in a nice long sulk once Laura and Guy leave. I've gotten too much accustomed to their faces.

Their last night, Belladonna can't close her eyes, and she goes down to the library in the middle of the night in search of a nice boring book that once may have lulled La Pompadour to sleep. As she is walking back down the hall toward her room, she notices that Guy's door is cracked open, the light spilling like bright gold onto the carpet.

He, too, is restless.

Curiosity overwhelms her and she peers in. Guy is in his pajamas and a robe of hazelnut-colored silk, sitting on the bed with a small silver frame in his hands. He is staring at it so intently that he doesn't see her, and Belladonna knows instinctively that it must be a photograph of his sister and mother. His head is bowed, and there is such an expression of tortured grief on his face that she can't help feeling a pang of grave sadness stab her heart. It surprises her, and scares her deeply. She hasn't felt grief for any man, not in all the years since Leandro died.

She steps away from the door, then knocks.

"I saw your light on," she says. "Is everything all right?"

He has instantly wiped the melancholy off his face and put the photo facedown on the night table. He is, in fact, astonished that she's asked after him. She's never done that before; she doesn't like to talk about feelings, hers or his. She is not what he'd call a sympathetic sort.

"Yes, thank you," he says, looking up at her and trying to smile. "I like a woman in a man's pajamas."

"You mean you like a woman in no pajamas," she teases.

"Why, Contessa," he says, "if I didn't know you better, I'd tell myself you were making a pass at me."

Her face hardens imperceptibly. "I'm not," she says.

"No," he replies, "I didn't think you were. Would you like to come in? Or sit somewhere else?"

Without understanding why, she goes into his room and sits on a chair upholstered in pale buttercream-colored satin, drawing her knees up to her chest in a self-protective pose. "Bryony is going to miss her uncle Guy very badly," she says. "Will you write to her?"

"Of course," he says. "I'll send her telegrams from Ceylon."

"How long must you be there?"

"Not long, I hope. Until things are sorted out."

"I see."

"Most people would ask me what 'things.' "

"It's your business, Guy."

"I would tell you anything that you wanted to know."

"Would you?" she asks. "Like what?"

"Like how wonderful you are."

"I didn't say I wanted to hear that," she says flatly. "And I know I'm not wonderful. You don't know what I'm like at all."

"I know what I've seen. And I know what I want."

"What do you want?" she asks, her face arranging itself quickly into the polite blankness she uses as a mask with strangers. Except Guy is not exactly a stranger.

"You, of course."

"Why?"

Guy looks at her, puzzled. He's not been asked that by a woman before. "Why do I want you? Do you mean, why would I want you the way you are now?" he muses. "Do you honestly think you are such an ogre? Can you look me in the eye and tell me you're not interested in me, or any man?"

"Yes," she says, "yes, I can."

"I see." He doesn't tell her to look him in the eye and say it. He's afraid she might. "But I don't really believe you."

"It doesn't matter what you think or want, Guy," she says sadly, picking at the fuzz on a velvet pillow. "It has nothing to do with you."

"Whatever it was that happened to you. To make you this way, you mean."

She looks at him, startled.

"I know something happened to you," he goes on. "Something I'm assuming is too dreadful to talk about. It's like you're—I don't know how to say this—like you're *corked*. There's something stuck inside that's eating you alive. I wish I could help you with whatever it is," he says passionately. "How I wish you would let me. I wish you could believe you can trust me, and I'm willing to wait till you believe you do."

"I ask for no pity," she says. "I want none."

"It isn't pity I offer you," he says, his voice low. "It's love. You know I'm in love with you."

"You can't love me. I don't want you to," she says. It is exactly what she once said to Leandro. Does she remember that? "I am not capable of love. I have no heart."

"That's not true," he protests. "You love your daughter; you love Tomasino. Laura and Hugh and all the people who live here worship you, you know. They see the goodness in you, even if you don't."

"I've heard enough," she says harshly, standing up. When Jack talked to her like that, she made him swear he'd never say anything like it again. But Jack knew much more than Guy does. And Guy

means much more to her than Jack did. "I don't want you to say
that to me ever again."

"I think about it every day, what's wrong with me," she said to
Leandro. *"But I can't . . . I don't think I can, ever . . . I don't want to
be like this, but I don't know any other way. It's too deep in me to
undo."*

"I don't care," Guy says. "I love you like I've never loved any
woman in my life, and I'm not ashamed to say it. And if you ever
thought about anyone but yourself, you'd know how excruciating it
is for a man to declare himself to a woman he knows will spurn
him. But that hasn't stopped me, and I will not let anything you say
stop me, and I will go on loving you until the day I die."

"That's what Leandro said," she says, looking at the floor.
"That he loved me. That you can burn with hatred and rage for
one creature and yet still love another."

But Leandro was old enough to have been her grandfather. It
was different with him. Leandro saved her.

"I don't understand what you're saying," Guy says, standing up.
With a bewildered pang, it strikes him that, indeed, he doesn't
understand her at all. "Why shouldn't he have loved you?" He
sighs. "But you're right. I concede that point. I *don't* know who
you are, Contessa. You won't even tell me your name." He looks
up at her, his eyes full of anguish. "Why can't you trust me? Why
can't you tell me who you are? Who are you? Who *are* you?"

He takes a step closer to her, and she shrinks back against the
buttercream-colored chair, a look of panic so horrifying fleeting
across her features that Guy stops instantly.

"What is it? What did I say?" he asks desperately. "Contessa,
what's wrong? What?"

She no longer sees him, he realizes. He backs away from her
instinctively and then sits down on the bed, pulling the covers up
around himself.

She is still pressed against the chair, frozen in panic like a cornered animal. "I'm getting Tomasino," Guy says to her. "I'm getting up slowly and I'm going to fetch Tomasino, okay?"

He rolls off the side of the bed, opens the door wide, and runs
down the hall to my room. I am awakened instantly by his frantic
knock.

"I don't know what I said," he says to me, breathless.

"I'm sure it's not your fault," I tell him as we hurry to his door. "Wait out here. No, go get Orlando. His room's at the end of the hall, across from the grandfather clock." He nods and runs off.

I go in, murmuring softly in Italian, then sit down on the bed, waiting for her to snap out of it. I haven't seen her like this since we lived at Ca' d'Oro. I never thought I'd see her like this again, as she had once been. I thought her indomitable, like a steel trap. She has been hard and remote and unshakable for so long.

"I'm beyond understanding," she said to Jack when she spurned him. *"I am a creature of the imagination, nothing more . . . there's nothing I can do now to undo it but find them and make them suffer."*

I don't know what to do for her; I can't bear this alone. Oh how I wish Matteo were here. He could comfort her like no other.

Belladonna's gaze is fixed on some spot above Guy's bed. I don't want to touch her for fear it might trigger something worse. After a while, though, she shudders deeply and her eyes focus on me.

"Make him go away," she says, starting to rock back and forth. "Make him go away."

For an instant, a distinct picture of the long-forgotten damp forehead of Mr. Nutley flashes into my head. *"Make him go away."* That's what she'd said to him, in Merano, when he scared her so.

Who are you? Why are you here?

"He's gone," I say soothingly. "They're all gone. You're safe now. You're in your own house, in Virginia, and you're safe. Come on, it's bedtime." I look back and see Orlando's comforting bulk in the doorway. *"Cara mia,"* Orlando says to her. *"Avanti, per favore, cara."*

As if in a trance, she slowly gets up and walks out with him. They head for her room. He'll talk softly to her in Italian, his voice deep and calming like Leandro's, and stay with her until she falls asleep. And then he'll sit and guard her, watching over her until she wakes.

Guy watches them walk away, and when I put my hand on his arm he nearly jumps out of his skin. "I'm sorry, Tomasino," he says, running his hands through his hair. "I've no idea what I said that scared her so. I told her I loved her, that's all. Because I do." He looks at me, visibly shaken. "Do you know, I've never said those words before, and meant them."

"I'm glad you do, Guy, believe me. I'm on your side," I say soberly, "although I'll bet she wasn't exactly receptive to whatever it was that came out of your mouth."

"Quite right," he says, sighing and going back into his room, sitting down on the bed, his shoulders hunched. Lines of fatigue that I'd not seen before appear on his face. He seems terribly, terribly sad, and I wish I could say something to comfort him, too.

Botheration. I am feeling altogether useless tonight.

"Something horrible happened to her, didn't it?" he says, not expecting an answer. "I know it did. Some man did something horrible to her, didn't he?"

"You can't imagine," I say.

"I'd do anything to make it right," he says. "If she'd let me."

"I know," I tell him. "But the best thing you can do for her now is get on that plane tomorrow. She'll be herself again. I'll work on her."

He looks up at me and tries to smile. "You don't trust me, either," he says.

"On the contrary, dear Guy. I trust you more than you know." I want so much to tell him that he's right, that of course she's Belladonna, but I can't.

He looks up at me, and I think he knows. But he's too much the gentleman to say anything. I see a hint of the roguish charm seep back into his features. "I will get on that plane," he says. "But I'll be back as soon as I can. Will you say good-bye to her for me?"

"Of course. And don't forget a few cat's-eyes for the needy."

"You mean chrysoberyls? How do you know that they come from Ceylon?" he asks.

"Leandro wore one," I say. "A charm against evil spirits, he said it was. He willed it to me when he died, but I don't feel worthy of wearing it."

"Tomasino, you are a goose," Guy says softly. "What would she do without you?"

Oh ho, how I love a man who understands the value of a jewel, priceless beyond compare!

And I don't mean the cat's-eye.

*B*ryony is moping with a passion after Guy's departure—almost as much as Laura had when Hugh left—but she brightens considerably when the first telegram arrives a few days later.

"Darling Bryony," it reads. "Terribly hot. Terribly buggy. Terribly many tea leaves. Terribly lonely without you. Coming back ASAP. Love. Uncle Guy."

Then Bryony skips around the house, singing one of her nonsense songs, and draws pictures for him with Susannah and writes him sweet little stories that we send air mail special delivery.

September comes and Bryony goes back to school. And then another month; there is a distinct chill in the air when we till the flower beds and Belladonna pours honey water on the mandrake late in the day. She spends a lot of time alone in her garden, or riding with Orlando and Firkin. She apologized to me after that scene with Guy, and I told her I didn't know what she was talking about.

Every Monday just before dinnertime, the doorbell rings, and Bryony runs to answer it. There stands Jimmy, the telegram boy, allowed up the drive by Thibaud in the gatehouse, with his telegram from Ceylon for the little lady. We let Bryony sign for it and she reads it to herself a few times before deigning to share Uncle Guy's message with us.

And then comes a Monday when I wake up with a throbbing knee. There is no doorbell or Jimmy the telegram boy or phone call. Just the sound of the crickets and the occasional echoing cowbell at dinnertime. Bryony cries herself to sleep, despite Belladonna's trying to reassure her that Uncle Guy will be okay, that these things happen.

But Bryony's like me that way. She always knows when something's wrong.

When no telegram arrives the next day or the next week, I get on the phone to Pritch and ask him to find out what might be going on in Ceylon. We get Hubbard and Nod on the case as well, pulling embassy strings. I place calls to Hugh and Laura, but no one has heard anything.

It is as if Guy has fallen off the face of the earth.

So when the doorbell rings the following Monday afternoon, Belladonna herself answers the door, thinking it's Hubbard or Nod with an urgent message. It's pouring loudly with rain, the skies darkly threatening, thunder rumbling like my stomach when I'm hungry. The man standing there is soaked through; the hat pulled down over his face is sodden and his raincoat is dripping. He's leaning against the door as if it's the only thing holding him up. Which it is. He tries to straighten, to say something, wavers, and promptly falls down in a dead faint.

Belladonna cries out sharply for me, and I come running. We turn the man over, but I already know who it is. Guy, of course. And he looks like death.

"I'll call the doctor," she says, rushing into the hall and pressing one of our emergency buttons to summon help. "Bryony can't see him like this."

"Don't worry," I say. "She's at Girl Scouts till six."

Orlando and Hubbard come quickly, carry Guy upstairs to the yellow bedroom, take off his wet things, put him in pajamas, and cover him with blankets. He is moaning in pain and burning with fever. His skin is an odd color; his palms and the soles of his feet are bright red. He must have something dreadfully tropical.

When Dr. Greenaway arrives, he spends relatively little time with the patient. "It's not contagious, thank goodness," he says, "but he's very sick. It's dengue fever, I'm afraid. I spent a lot of time in Africa during the war, so I recognized some of the symptoms right away. The red palms and feet, a rash. It's dengue all right. It's often misdiagnosed as yellow fever or typhus. The wrong treatment could've killed him."

"He's not going to die, is he?" Belladonna asks.

"I sincerely hope not," the doctor replies. "We should know soon enough if his fever worsens. But if he was strong before he got infected, he has a fairly good chance of pulling through. Fifty-fifty, at any rate."

This is not very encouraging.

"Must we move him to a hospital?" I ask. "We'd much prefer to nurse him here. We can get round-the-clock help, whatever you say. Just tell us what to do."

"I suppose that can be done, as he should be moved as little as possible right now," the doctor says with a frown, not wanting to offend the infamous Contessa who'd practically financed an entire wing of Jefferson Davis Hospital, "but he must have skilled nursing, day and night. Constant monitoring and intravenous fluids. I'll make some calls."

"Thank you, Doctor," she says. "He'll get the best care. With your supervision, of course."

"Complete and absolute bed rest. Clear liquids, if he can keep them down. The nurses will advise you. He's going to be in terrible pain—dengue is often called 'break-bone fever.' I'll stop by first thing in the morning."

"I appreciate it," Belladonna says. "Everything you've done. We're lucky to have you."

He flushes, smiles, puts on his hat, and steps out into the rain.

The phone rings a few minutes later. It's Thibaud, from the gatehouse. "I hope everything's all right," he says, sounding worried. "The young gentleman asked for it to be a surprise, for Bryony, he said, so I drove him just past the second gates and didn't call up as I'm supposed to. He looked mighty peaky."

"Don't you fret, Thibaud," I said, "but he's pretty sick with a fever. We're going to need some of your famous gumbo as soon as he gets better."

"Say the word," he tells me, and hangs up.

So that's it. A surprise for Bryony, come from the jungle. I don't like the thought of jungles; they make me think of the woods in Belgium.

Of trying to conquer the unconquerable.

17

The Return of the Prodigal

"Bryony, my angel, I have some good news and some bad news. I want you to be very brave when I tell you what it is. Can you be extraspecially brave?" Belladonna says to her daughter after the first of our nurses has arrived, tended to Guy, given us cursory instructions, and installed herself in the next bedroom. "Which do you want to hear first?"

"The bad news," she says solemnly. "Is Uncle Guy dead like Papa?"

"No, darling, he's not dead. But Uncle Guy is very, very sick with a terrible fever. That's the bad news. The good news is that Uncle Guy has come here so we can help him get better."

Bryony's face is transformed. "He's really here?" she asks.

"He really is, in the yellow bedroom, just like last time. He has his very own nurses watching over him."

"Uncle Guy is here!" Bryony throws her arms around her mother. "Can I see him now, please? Can I? Can I? Please, can I?"

"Yes, but only for a minute. Do you remember when you had the flu in New York and you were so sick that you were crying all the time?" Belladonna asks as Bryony nods. "Well, Uncle Guy wants to cry because he feels so bad, but he can't. We think he knows he's got a high fever, but not how very sick he is. We can't let him know how bad *we* feel about it, so we have to try very hard to be cheerful. You see, Uncle Guy doesn't look healthy, like he did when he left. As soon as he gets better, he'll start to look like himself again."

"Do you promise? Truly? Cross your heart?"

Belladonna gets down on her knees and puts her arms around Bryony. "Yes, darling girl, I promise. He's *not* going to die. We aren't going to let him, are we?"

Bryony shakes her head. "Should I get him Sam to make him feel better?"

"Not just yet," Belladonna says. "I am very proud to have such a brave little girl."

"I'm going to make him get all better," Bryony announces. "Let's go, Mommy. Hurry. He needs us." Hand in hand, they walk slowly upstairs. "Now we have to put these masks on," Belladonna says, taking them off a table laden with supplies outside the room, "because we don't want Uncle Guy to get sick from our germs. He's very weak." She ties the masks on and pushes open the door. Bryony runs to the bed where Guy lies muttering and tossing about in his fever. The nurse frowns behind her mask but doesn't say anything when Bryony takes his hand.

"He's all hot and sweaty, Mommy." Bryony looks at her mother with tears in her eyes. "He doesn't know who I am."

"He will, as soon as he wakes up. It's the fever, darling. He doesn't know what he's saying or where he is or who anybody else is, either. We must be patient, and stay here quietly until he gets better."

"Can I stay with him every day?"

"Yes, for a little while every day, after school. You can do your homework here and we'll keep talking to Uncle Guy, and soon he'll wake up because he hears your voice. The doctor said that's the best thing we can do."

I think the nurse is about to have a fit when she hears this. Belladonna stares at her, eyes ablaze, until she turns her head away in embarrassment.

"That's a good idea, Mommy. Can Susannah come, too?"

"We'll have to ask Susannah's mommy about that," Belladonna says lightly. "Now give Uncle Guy a kiss so he can get better, and say good-bye, because we don't want to wear him out."

Bryony leans over the bed and gives him a kiss, then giggles. "His beard is all prickly," she says. "He looks like a pirate."

"You can tell him that when he wakes up."

"Now you give him a kiss so he can get all better, Mommy," Bryony states.

Belladonna has no choice. It is the first time her lips have touched a man's cheek since—

Since Leandro.

As Guy lays dreaming, looking like death, we sit in the room with the nurses recommended by Dr. Greenaway. Our favorite soon becomes the very proper yet slightly less crabby Nurse Sam, who usually has the late-afternoon shift.

"Her name is Nurse Sam, like your doll," Belladonna tells Bryony.

"Is she a boy under her dress?" Bryony asks.

Belladonna stifles the urge to laugh. "No, darling, her name is really Samantha," she replies. "And we have to listen to her, and do everything she tells us to."

Nurse Sam is rather square and stout, but capable and devoted to her feverish charge. I wonder who I can fix her up with. Templeton, the chauffeur, perhaps? Firkin in the stables? I am fixating on my matchmaking skills as a diversion, especially after reading a letter from Jack that Belladonna handed me earlier in the day. Jack's going to marry Alison in a few months, and he asks for our blessing. How splendid. Bryony can be one of the flower girls and I can get a lovely new suit.

"Are you glad?" I ask Belladonna. "I know I am. But he wasn't in love with me."

"He was in love with someone who didn't exist," she says wearily. "This is a load off my mind, Tomasino. Truly, it is."

"I understand," I murmur, waiting for more.

"He deserves a good woman who loves him. I'm happy for him," she says. I think she is protesting a bit too much.

"What about Guy? Is he a good man?" I venture to ask.

Her face sets in its familiar blankness. "I don't know," she says after a minute. "I hope so, if only for Bryony's sake."

"Hugh knows that Guy's a good man. As does Laura. Surely that means something."

"What are you getting at?"

"Nothing," I say, all innocence. She's clearly in one of her moods. Guy has always had a strange effect on her, and his presence in our house, even though he's still practically comatose, is a disruptive one.

For the first time in a very long time, you see, Belladonna doesn't know what to do about someone. Worse, that someone is a man.

She tells me she wants to be left alone, but she is spending more and more time in Guy's room, sitting with Bryony or reading in a rocking chair she's brought in from the veranda. She helps the nurses, and watches over Guy as if he were her own child. I can't describe how surprising and lovely it is, watching her watching him. She is softening because of Guy, the ramparts carefully constructed around her heart crumbling as each day passes, and it scares her almost as much as the thought of His Lordship does. Perhaps it's because Guy is helpless, burning with fever in the yellow bedroom as he calls out his dead sister's name in his delirium, and she doesn't have to fear him or talk to him. Perhaps it's because Bryony loves him so.

Or perhaps it's because Belladonna is tired of fighting, of planning and plotting. She doesn't talk to me about the Pritch's progress, not the way she used to. She is focusing instead on Guy's precarious health, especially now that he is, finally, starting to get better. He is still very weak, his muscles and joints aflame with achiness, but every day a bit more of his energy comes back, and we no longer have to burn his sheets and wear masks on our faces.

I am feeling very lonely.

Our routine changes in the ensuing weeks. Bryony comes home from school, flings her books down, runs up the stairs and into the yellow bedroom where her mother is already sitting. She tells Uncle Guy everything that's happened that day. Then she goes back downstairs for a snack, to see Susannah, to play outside. We have dinner on the veranda if the weather is warm. Bryony and Belladonna go back up to Guy's room, where Bryony does her homework, then switches roles and reads him a bedtime story every night. Belladonna pulls her rocking chair close to the bed, to listen. Guy's sitting up now, and eating more. Something's changing in him, too. I can no longer picture this gaunt, pale man romping merrily in the hay or holding court in the Club Belladonna. He used to talk easily and sarcastically, with a savage and trenchant wit about life and love. Now he says little. Doesn't that sound rather awfully familiar?

Sometimes I'd swear that he and Belladonna are courting telepathically.

One night, after Bryony has gone to bed and the night nurse is dozing in front of her television set in the next room, Guy stretches out his right hand to Belladonna. She looks at it for a moment as if it were some alien creature, then picks it up and peers carefully at his palm, tracing the lines with her nail. She frowns slightly.

"You have lines of restlessness, and of travel," she says. He smiles. What a surprise. "But you also have a very deep influence line," she says. "Deeper than your life line."

"What does that mean?" he asks. His voice is still rather croaky, which I think makes him sound unbelievably sexy.

"It means that the incoming influence will be a forceful one," she replies.

"What else? What about my heart?"

She looks up at him, bites her lip, then looks back down. "Your heart line starts high up, which shows an emotional vulnerability that is often masked behind a hard or callous exterior."

"Like Belladonna's," he says.

"What?" she asks. "What do you mean?"

"She always wore masks. Who knew what she was thinking?"

"Who indeed." Belladonna's frown deepens. "But why did you mention her just now? Do I still remind you of her?"

"You remind me of no one but yourself."

"I don't want to be myself," she says, without realizing what's slipped out. Nor does she realize that her fingers are still tracing the lines on his palm. She's never read anyone's palm before without her gloves on.

"Why not," he says softly. He encircles her slim fingers with his hand.

"I can't tell you."

They can't tear their eyes off each other. I don't know why, but for some crazy reason they remind me of Matteo practicing his silent magic tricks when we lived at Leandro's.

"Please," he says. "Try. Tell me. Tell me what's in your own palm."

"Treachery," she says. Her face shifts almost imperceptibly in the soft buttercup light, as if some strange transparent mask had wafted its way in and settled on her features. But it's not hard and cold like her habitual mask of frozen politeness. I can see through it, Guy says to himself. I can see through the mask to the other side, because I love her.

He won't let go of her hand, half-expecting her to start panicking, but she doesn't. She knows he hasn't got the strength to overpower her.

After a few minutes, he sighs and releases her. "I would never hurt you," he says. "You *saved* me. I owe you my life. I'd do anything for you, and not just to repay you for curing my fever." His cheeks are flushed. "Do you know, Laura once told me that Leandro wrote her, claiming that you said he saved you. And now you saved *me*."

"I haven't thought of it like that."

"Then why are you so afraid of me?" His voice deepens to an even raspier croak. "Do you know how it feels to be feared by a woman so dear to your heart?"

Belladonna shakes her head.

"Were you afraid of your husband? Did Leandro hurt you?"

She looks shocked. "Leandro hurt me? Of course not. Why would you ask such a thing?"

"Because you can't bear to be touched," Guy says. "Just now, it's the first time you've touched me."

"It's not because of Leandro," she says. "Laura will certainly tell you that, too. Leandro did save me."

Please, my darling Belladonna, please keep talking. Tell him everything, don't clam up now. He can help you; he can help us. We need him, he's so good for you, oh, *please.*

"Saved you from what?"

Belladonna starts laughing. It is like the laugh I heard the first time I talked to her, when I told her about Mr. Lincoln. A short, barking kind of bitter laugh, verging on the hysterical. It wakes up the dozing night nurse, who comes in, tells them to settle down and be quiet, then goes right back to her television.

"I've never met anyone as persistent as you are, Guy," she says to him when she quiets down. "You're like Casseopeia and Hector fighting over a bone."

Like Andromeda, he wants to say, but he doesn't. His eyes glisten as he bites his lip. "Must be my indisputably inquisitive personality," he says instead, trying to make a joke.

Oh ho, the clever boy is starting to sound like me!

"I doubt it," she says, and stands up. "It's time we both went to bed."

"I am in bed," he says in a sad, small voice. "You saved *me.*"

"I think you're confusing me with my daughter," Belladonna says. "She decided that you absolutely had to get well. Do you remember anything she said to you when you were delirious?" Guy shakes his head no. "She'd sit in here and talk to you for hours. She'd bring Sam—the doll, not the nurse—with her and have long discussions with him about all the things you were going to do together as soon as you got better," Belladonna goes on. "You're going to teach her how to ride, you know. And then you're taking her to Ceylon so she can squash all the bad mosquitoes infected with dengue fever with her flyswatter."

Guy suddenly looks like a little boy, waiting for his mother to kiss him good night. I think Belladonna realizes this, because before she can stop herself she leans down to brush her lips on his forehead. She's never done that before either, at least not when he was awake.

"Don't leave me," he whispers.

"Go to sleep, Guy," she whispers back. "You don't know what you're asking me to do."

"Yes I do." He is still whispering. "Promise me you won't leave me."

"You can stay here till you're well—you know that. For as long as it takes."

It is going to take forever, he wants to say, but he closes his eyes and pretends to sleep.

Weeks turn into months and Guy becomes as much a part of the landscape as the tenants and the animals. As soon as he can start getting up, Belladonna gives him an intricately carved walking stick I'd asked Baines to sculpt. Together, they go walking every day, at first only the length of the veranda, and then farther and farther. When he is stronger still, he starts gingerly riding our tamest nag, the mastiffs following and Bryony trotting beside him on Pablo, the latest addition to our menagerie. Pablo is the shaggy-haired pony

Guy bought his little darling, and he drives Basilico mad with jealousy.

I get over my funk, and Guy becomes a sort of Matteo and Jack substitute for me, the man about the house I'd been longing for. We talk for hours, about liars and lovers and the potions Pompadour liked to drink and all the places he's been. One chilly evening when Belladonna has gone to bed early with a headache, I find Guy, sit him down in the Meditation Room, and ask if I can trust him, *really* trust him. He regards me with a funny expression on his face, then tells me I have his word of honor, that he is forever indebted to my hospitality and is willing to swear on it.

"You needn't go quite *that* far," I say, trying to tease him.

"What's the matter?" he says.

"I have a story to tell you. An unpleasant story."

"What happened to you in the war—that story?"

Of course that story. It's easier telling it this time, though, without Matteo's stony face and Annabeth's tearful sympathy to distract me. Botheration. I really am getting much too maudlin in my pseudo-dotage.

"I am very sorry, Tomasino," he says when I'm through. "I wish I could do something for you."

I pour myself another drink. "So do I."

"I'd like very much for you to tell me how you met the Contessa, though. I know it's all tied together somehow, but I've absolutely no idea how."

"She has to tell you that herself."

"Ah, so you don't really trust me after all."

"But I do," I reply, "because you haven't told the Contessa that you're sure she's really the infamous Belladonna."

Guy's eyes widen in astonishment and he laughs heartily for the first time in a very long time. "Why, Tomasino, you sly devil," he says, pouring me a drink. "I salute your superior skills."

"What skills could you mean, kind sir?" I ask, beaming.

"I'd have been a rotten spy," he says. "I reveal myself too quickly. You, on the other hand, have a natural talent for . . . hmmm, what exactly? For *concealment*. Kindly do forgive me for saying so, but the Contessa has trumped you there."

"Couldn't agree with you more."

"Trumped about what?" she asks. As usual, she has appeared without a sound. Honestly, she really can be so vexing sometimes.

"Trumped about secrecy," I say brightly. "About all the dastardly secrets of Casa la Fenice."

"Ah yes," she says sarcastically. "We are a world-famous hotbed of intrigue."

"*My* bed is cold," Guy says. I'm glad to see he's back to his old self.

"That's not funny," Belladonna snaps.

Oh ho, what a state she's in. Time for me to make a swift exit.

"Is your headache worse?" I ask gently as I get up to leave.

"I'm fine, thank you," she says, her voice barely softening. "I'm just tired."

Tired of waiting. Tired of wanting. Tired of not knowing what to do about the man sitting before you with a heart as near to breaking as your own.

"Would you like a drink?" Guy asks as she sits down and nods. She still can't admit how much she wants to be with him. That he doesn't scare her anymore, even though it is nighttime and dark and they are together in the same room in her house.

He is careful not to touch her fingers when he gives her the glass. He never touches her, she realizes, as he sits down in the chair opposite her own. He won't touch her unless she asks him to. He loves her so much, he won't—

"Leandro is not Bryony's father," Belladonna blurts out suddenly.

Guy smiles at her with the utmost tenderness, knowing what this admission has cost her. "I know," he says very gently, to her amazement. "I know because Laura told me how she met you, at Merano, and you already had Bryony then. But thank you for telling me. You must—"

"What else do you know?" she cries, her mood instantly shifting. "Has Tomasino or anyone else said anything? Have they—"

"No," he says quickly, interrupting her this time. "Not a word, I promise you. He's a gem, Tomasino is, and on the rare occasion when I've asked him anything, he's always told me to direct all inquiries to you. Which I didn't dare, obviously. Did I?"

She doesn't reply.

"Did I?" he presses.

"No," she concedes. "But what else do you know?"

Guy remains silent for a moment; then he can't stand it any longer. "I know that you're Belladonna," he says.

"You've tried this already," she says, her voice resigned.

"I don't recall exactly when I was sure, only that I am," he goes on, ignoring her. "It's much more than your green eyes, of course, although I think they are the most extraordinary eyes in the world. Nor is it that you lived in New York and possess the wherewithal to have set the whole operation in motion. Or that Bryony talked about her Irish wolfhound, Dromedee, which sounds suspiciously like a child's version of Andromeda. It's the way you move and the way you hold your head and the way you listen. You must have listened to all those women who came to you for help in much the same manner."

"You don't know what you're talking about," she mutters.

"Perhaps not," Guy says, "but the dead giveaway was a few weeks ago, when it was unexpectedly hot. I had just gotten up from a nap and I came downstairs and you were on the veranda, fanning yourself. It was the way you snapped your fan shut that did it. Only one woman in the world could snap a fan in such a manner."

"Undone by a fan, am I?" she asks sarcastically.

"I know you won't lie to me," he says sadly.

"I don't want to lie to you, Guy," she says. "I never did."

"Can you look me in the eye and tell me you're not Belladonna?"

She looks at him and sees nothing but his melting tenderness mingled with a terrible fear that she is going to run away and never look back. She opens her mouth to try to speak, but she can't.

She was like that, speechless, once before, in Belgium. When we first met, when she couldn't—

Guy gets up and walks over closer, then kneels before her. "Upon my honor, I will never tell a soul," he says.

"Get up," she says, "I can't bear to see you on your knees."

But he doesn't move, and she no longer can control her hands, the very same hands that had snapped the fan shut in despair. She reaches out to trace the line of Guy's jaw with her fingers, and at the surprising touch of her skin his eyes fill with tears.

"What happened to you?" he asks, knowing not to expect an answer. "Let me help you, please. Please, please let me in."

"I never did to Leandro," she says to Guy as if in a trance. "I never did let him in, so I can never forgive myself because I couldn't give him anything, be a wife to him or love him, truly love him as a woman is supposed to love a man." Her voice chokes. "I couldn't, not even after everything he did for me. Not when he saved me and Bryony and loved me and helped me understand and—"

I don't know any other way. It's too deep in me to undo.

Her voice seems to be coming from some otherworldly place. "I don't know how to touch a man or kiss a man, Guy," she says. "It sounds so ludicrous. I haven't touched a man or kissed a man, really kissed a man because I wanted to, for nearly twenty years. *Twenty years.* Do you understand what I'm saying?"

He shakes his head slowly, tears spilling out of his eyes and trickling down his cheeks. Her fingers are still on his face, and she wipes the tears away as sweetly as Annabeth had done to Matteo when he thought she would disappear forever.

"I love you," he whispers. "I don't want to—"

She leans over and kisses him so suddenly, so deeply, that he thinks he must be dreaming. He puts his arms around her and kisses her back until he can no longer breathe. Then she pulls away, and he realizes she's trembling.

"What have I done? I can't do this," she whispers. "I can't do this to you."

"Don't go—"

"I can't do this to you, don't you understand? *I can't I can't I can't.*"

Guy is afraid to move.

"I need Tomasino," she says, a rising note of panic in her voice. "I need him, quickly."

"I'll find him," Guy says, fearful still of what happened the last time he came to find me after a confession of love. "Wait here and I'll find him. Do you promise me you'll wait here?"

Belladonna stares at him, her eyes wide and pleading, and he hurries off. I've been expecting him, I must say, so we're back in just a minute. "In the library," she tells me, her voice flat. "Pompadour's Bible."

I know instantly what she's talking about. What a clever girl is my darling Belladonna. A Bible's the last place I would have looked for it. I run as quickly as I can to the bookshelf, climb up the library ladder, pull the Bible down, and run back. Guy is handing her a drink, and gulping one down himself.

I don't need a drink. I need an entire distillery.

She gestures toward Guy. *"Certo?"* I ask.

"Give it to him," she says tonelessly, and gets up. "Then he'll understand." She looks at Guy, but she no longer sees him or me or anything in this house. I am suddenly terribly afraid. I can't leave her alone; she can't be left alone. I press the emergency button near the mantel, and Orlando soon comes hurrying in.

"Would you mind escorting the Contessa to her room?" I ask, keeping my voice perfectly conversational.

"With pleasure," he says, knowing I'll explain all as soon as I can. First I need to call Matteo in New York. He's going to have to drop everything and get down here immediately. Guy, in the meantime, is clutching Pompadour's Bible to his chest and looking utterly bewildered. Only a minute ago, the woman he loves was kissing him with a passion he'd dreamed of all his life, and now it's as if she's vanishing before his very eyes.

"Tomasino, help me," Guy says, sinking down into his chair.

"It's a diary," I say, trying to keep a tremor out of my voice. I pour myself a drink, spilling most of it, my hands are shaking so. I haven't seen the diary since I secretly copied it over for her in that house in Belgium. "Hidden inside."

"Did she write all of it?"

"Yes. She asked me to copy it so it would be legible, but I didn't change a word. It was written in the third person. It could only have been done that way. You'll understand afterward." I've finished my drink already, and pour myself another. "I'm not going to tell you anything else, except that no one's read it but me. I told my brother the worst of it. She gave it to Leandro at Ca' d'Oro; she begged him to read it, but he refused."

Guy looks pale and weary as he runs his fingers around the softly bound edges of Pompadour's Bible. I wonder if he thinks I'm being melodramatic. But I'm not.

"If you breathe a word of this to anyone, your life is forfeit," I say. "Agreed?"

"Agreed."

"Your word, as a gentleman."

"You think I'm a gentleman?"

I smile, glad that he can try to joke, because my heart is so heavy I think it is going to pull me down to the floor and I will never be able to rise again.

"I know you are, because of what you must have said to her."

"She *is* Belladonna," Guy says in some wonderment, knowing without doubt that his hunch is correct. He gets up, still clutching the Bible so tightly I think his hand is going to fall off.

It is the diary, copied over in my strong, sure handwriting, that is rattling my nerves. Triggering too many memories I'd rather forget.

There will be no sleep in la Fenice tonight.

PART IV

The Secret in Pompadour's Bible

(1935–1947)

18

The Diary of Despair

—*Who are you?*

*It was a man's voice, deep and calm. Not the man who said he
was going to slit her throat. Not Hogarth. Someone else. She didn't
know what to say. She was too terrified.*

—*Who are you? he said again. Who are you? Why are you here?
What shall you do? Answer me. Who are you?*

—*Isa . . . Isabella. She said it so faintly it sounded like Bella.*

—*No. You are no longer Isabella. That life is over. That Isabella is
gone from the world. You belong to me now.*

*His voice was getting closer. Closer and closer, and she felt him
very near. She tried to pull away but she was paralyzed with horror.*

—*Your life has been reduced to something very simple. Perfectly
simple. He touched her cheek with one finger. He was still wearing a
glove, and she couldn't stop herself from flinching in fear and disgust.*

—*Your life means nothing, except what I say it is worth. Your
world is my world, however I choose to define it. Your sole purpose
in this life is to please me. You have no other life but to please me.
His breath was hot on her neck. You are mine.*

—*No. She tried to shake her head. No no no—*

—*You're all alone in the world, and no one cares about you but
me. No one can touch you but me. You are mine.*

353

She felt him move away. Then she heard ice cubes in a glass. He must be pouring a drink. Then he laughed.

—I bought you for a rather ridiculous sum, don't you agree? A bit vexing, that outlay of capital. He didn't sound vexed at all.

His voice was coming closer again.

—Are you worth it? Shall you be worth one million pounds? That is the sum I must pay to you. Yes, you shall be allowed to have it one day. It is in the Swiss Consolidated Bank, account number one one six dash six one four. Can you remember that? Hogarth must have mentioned that to you already. Never forget those numbers. They are your future.

She felt him near her. He was staring at her. She could feel it even through the blindfold.

—Yes, your future, he said. But not your present. Your present belongs to me, and me alone. And so when I ask you who you are, the only thing you shall ever be allowed to say is, "I am yours, my lord." You are here to do what I say. For all the time that you remain here as my guest, you shall never be allowed to know who I am, or anything about any of the other members of the Club. You are forbidden to ask. You are forbidden to know what I look like. He pulled up one of her hands and held it briefly to his face, brushing her fingers so she could feel his mask. You belong to me now. I am your master, and you are my slave.

—I'm not a slave, she whispered. She couldn't help herself.

—But of course you are, my sweet. None of that American nonsense, if you please. There are millions and millions of slaves, all over the world. There always have been and always will be. From wars, from famines, from stupid bad luck. Working for slave wages as slave labor, chained, metaphorically speaking, to their masters. Most women think that of their husbands, you know. That he is the master of the household, who must be obeyed.

He was taking off his gloves as he said this. He traced the line of her jaw with them, then slapped her lightly with the smooth leather. She turned her head away, and he turned it back.

—Yes, obeyed, he said. I don't suppose you've seen the Kama Sutra, a sweet innocent virgin like yourself. Well, you will, trust me. Part of your training, my dear girl, most useful. For all of us. The members of the Club. Especially should one become bored with the usual.

He wanted to talk, she realized. He wanted to talk to drag it out and out and out and torture her more—

—The Kama Sutra says that if a man wanted to marry a girl who was unwilling, he merely had to ply her with drink so she would be unable to fight him off. Or, even simpler, he might kidnap her instead. Once the dear lady had been kidnapped, she was available for what those filthy moghuls called enjoyment. Her opinion of the whole matter, or of the man who'd drugged her with drink or kidnapped her, was of no importance whatsoever.

—I'm not for sale, she said.

—But of course you are, my dear girl. Every woman is, whether she likes it or not. All women are whores. I'm sure Hogarth's said that to you; he told me he did. That you rebutted him. Yes, my dear girl, most women are grateful for their degradation, to be treated like whores. It merely serves to confirm their own low opinion of themselves and their station. He laughed to himself. The sooner you admit it the happier you'll be.

—Happy? What? She wanted to kick out at him, to fight him off, to stop his horrible mouth and the horrible things coming out of it. You bastard. Who do you think you are?

—I am His Lordship, he said calmly. I am your master, and you belong to me.

—I don't! I don't! Let me go! Let me go! I'm not for sale! Let me go! She could no longer bear the thought of how they'd tricked her and what they were doing to her, and she started to scream at the top of her lungs, trying to get free, though she knew it was futile. She was struggling and struggling against the chains, until she felt him come up behind her, his arms pulling her close, too close. He was pressing insistently against her back. She could feel the outline of his body underneath the robe.

—One million pounds, he said. I bought you for one million pounds. Therefore, I have quite rightly assumed that you were for sale. He pulled away from her, just a little. He wasn't ready yet, not for that. The pleasure from talking to her and watching her struggle was much too intense to stop.

—You see, my sweet, nearly every relationship—whether between man and woman in the realm of the bedroom, or man and man in the realm of business—is based upon this struggle for power and mastery, and this alone. It is a simple barter system. A man such as myself has

very plain needs. Money, and the power it buys. Status, and the power he derives from it. And sex, of course—and the pleasure it gives him. Most men are foolish enough to be ruled by their sexual needs, and will do anything in their power to satisfy their lust. We, the members of the Club, have found a rather unique manner in which to satisfy ours.

He moved even closer, and she felt his hands on her body. No man had ever touched her like that. No man had ever. She started to shudder violently at his touch, his hot, dry fingers trailing up from her belly to stop on her breasts.

—A man who is ruled by his sexual needs demands his satisfaction, he was saying, and, most usually and most unfortunately, the lady he desires will balk. The man, thwarted in his conquest, must do something so that his needs will be satisfied. Bestow gifts upon her, such as jewelry or a house or cold hard cash. A wedding ring, and all that. These gifts give the lady an illusion of security, and then, quite naturally, she feels obliged to give in. The man takes what he wants, but soon is bored. She, in the meantime, has all the material satisfaction she asked for, and a grudging obligation to this man, her lord and master. He is free to find his satisfaction elsewhere, safe in the knowledge that she and any brats she might spawn are utterly dependent on him and his whims. Yet the more he wants, the more she demands in return. So he decides something must be done about this unfortunate situation, and he looks elsewhere for the pleasuring of his needs.

His fingers were cupping her breasts, and he began to trace lazy circles with them, holding her closer. Blinded and helpless, still she tried to struggle away from him, and he suddenly let her go. She heard what sounded like a belt being unbuckled, and then he was back, exactly as he had been a minute before. The more she strained to pull away the tighter he held her, and she realized he'd tucked the front of his monk's robe up into the belt. So she could feel him against her. Exactly as he wanted her to feel him.

—This is your new life, he said, and it has but one purpose: to serve me. Your life before, where you were free to be silly and stupid and lead a boring, sheltered, do-nothing existence, is over. Wouldn't you rather be privy to one of the great experiments in human behavior? My own experiment. An endless source of pleasure, tucked away from the world to serve me. Mine and mine alone.

His voice was so calm and conversational.

—*You are here to serve me, he went on, and to serve whomever I choose. It is a higher calling. I should think you would consider yourself fortunate to have been singled out so.*

—*What? Are you mad?*

—*No, not mad. Not mad at all, he replied. Mad only with desire to recoup my investment. Mad only to have you trained, and trained properly. The training will be long and slow and exquisitely sensitive.*

With that, he pinched her nipples so hard that she cried out; then moved one hand down to her belly. The other slowly drifted up to encircle her neck.

—*You see, my dear, only a man who is immensely clever and immensely rich and immensely powerful, such as myself, could allow himself such a luxury as yourself, he said in her ear, pressing his head close to her own. The rare luxury of possessing a woman to whom he can do anything, anything at all. To have found and bought his own slave, who with the proper training can become anything he wants her to be, and do anything he demands of her. Only a man such as myself could possibly afford to buy the silence necessary to procure her and make all the necessary arrangements. To keep her from the world, to do anything he wants to her and with her, for the period of time we must obey as members of the Club. The length of time is dependent on the sum paid, as you know. And as you have no doubt already realized, I am allowed to have you for a very long time. He sighed happily. He was so close to her. She couldn't breathe.*

—*Now, I ask you again, and if you are the clever girl I think you are, you shall tell me what I want to hear. Who are you? Mine, you are. You are mine. Say it.*

—*No.*

—*When I say, "Who are you," there shall be one reply, and one reply alone, because you are mine. You say, "I am yours, my lord." I am your lord and master. Understand that very clearly and you will understand who I am and why you are here. The servants have been instructed to call me Your Lordship, and you shall do the same. You shall refer to me either as my lord, or Your Lordship, or His Lordship. That is my name: His Lordship. I have no other. I am your master, and you are my slave, to do with as I please. I trust I have made myself perfectly clear.*

He let go of her again and got up from the bed. She could not *hear what he was doing. The carpeting was so thick it muffled his steps.*

No no no, he had come back and now was sitting behind her. His horrible hot, dry fingers were cupping her breasts above the corset, his breath in her ear once more. She was trembling uncontrollably.

—You see, my sweet, you cannot win. There is no escape, no one to save you. If you resist, then your struggle will enflame me, as you have felt it already. And if you succumb, then I shall bask in the pleasure of your complete capitulation. So you see, you have no choice but to do as I say. No one can hear you scream. No one knows where you are, that you are here, alone with me and all I desire. And if they did, would they care?

—June, she said in barely a whisper.

—June? That ridiculous little guttersnipe? That hopeless, foolish twit of a girl? He laughed sharply. No, my sweet, June will be on her way home, and soon. She will be ever so miffed when she receives the phone call from Hogarth and the letters from you telling her you're far, far away with a splendid specimen of manhood you met the weekend of a magnificent costume ball, when she was home with a stomach ailment. Yes, you've met the most wonderful man in the world, and you're madly in love and soon to be married. Hogarth will see to all the details. No, June will be quite put out, and will return stateside in a huff, and she will no longer be burdened by her more beautiful and more accomplished cousin with the dazzling green eyes. Nor will you have your dreadful cousin to worry about anymore.

A sudden rage of pure fury sprang out of her. She struggled violently against him.

—Just get it over with, she screamed at him with hysterical passion. Go on, do it. You bastard, you mad, revolting bastard. Go ahead, rape me. It's what you're waiting for, isn't it? You bastard you bastard you bastard—

—Ah, I knew it. He laughed delightedly. I knew it. You have pleased me very much. A fighter. One of his hands moved off her breast and trailed down her thigh.

She tried to kick out at him with the leg that was free, but he was too strong for her.

—You won't believe me when I tell you that you'll soon be begging for my touch. Begging for this. Begging for me, your lord and master.

He gave her a little shove to the side and got up, moving around to face her. When she heard his laughter yet again she screamed out wildly at him.

—But, my sweet, torturing you with anticipation is far too delightful. I was debating what to do, whether to take you as I pleased without a word, but now I know I have made the correct decision. Yes. Of course I am going to relieve you of your precious virginity. Although, naturally, I prefer to think of it as a ravishment. I should have thought you'd want to be well rid of it. Or at least that's what Hogarth told me, that you were not bound by convention.

—Hogarth's a liar, she screamed.

—Yes, I suspect he is. But he has not made a mistake about you. There is simply no denying that you are absolutely perfect. And I've been watching you for a long time.

—What?

—Oh yes, my dear girl, you have no idea who I am, or what I look like, nor shall you ever. But I have seen you, many times. Hogarth thought you might be suitable, and he was quite right. You have been chosen. You belong to me now, and you shall do whatever I say.

—Oh yes, you think you're just the man to do it, she said bitterly.

—Of course I am, and I have paid very dearly for the privilege. I am going to make you beg within an inch of your life for me to stop. And when I'm through with you, I shall start all over again. Again and again. Again and again, until you can no longer remember when your life was not about doing what I say, the instant that I say it. That your entire existence is dependent upon pleasing me, and nothing else. Nothing else exists.

He was speaking faster and faster, his deep voice darkening.

No no no—

—Your old life is over and finished. That girl is no more, he said, who she was, her body, her name. You have no name. If I call you anything, it shall be Doula. That is the Greek word for handmaiden. You are my handmaiden, my slave, and you exist only to please me. And, as I have said, soon, sooner than you dare believe possible, you are going to beg me to do whatever I wish to do to you. If I say to open your mouth, you'll open it. If I say to get down on your knees, you'll fall to the floor. If I say to spread your legs and beg, you will.

She started to laugh uncontrollably, as she had at the auction. She had never heard such things before, or imagined them possible. She was beyond anything; hysterical, and certain she was about to die.

—*You are completely insane,* she said, laughing like a madwoman in between sobbing. *Let me go let me go let me go*—

—*No, I don't think so,* he replied. *But knowing you belong to me and using you at will shall give me rather unbearable pleasure. If that makes me what you so kindly refer to as insane, I'm afraid it shall be your misfortune as well.*

She stopped laughing, but was still sobbing.

—*No, there is nothing you can say, except the answer to one simple question. Who are you?*

She said nothing.

He circled behind her and pulled her hair back, tilting her head up painfully. She bit her lip so as not to cry out.

—*When I say, "Who are you?" you say, "I am yours, my lord." And then when I say, "Why are you here?" you say, "To do your bidding, my lord." And then when I say, "What shall you do?" you say, "Whatever you desire, my lord." Do you understand?*

She shook her head. She couldn't stop her trembling. *Somebody come save me. Somebody, please. I'm only eighteen years old. I don't want to die.*

—*Three simple sentences. "I am yours, my lord. To do your bidding, my lord. Whatever you desire, my lord."* His hands were pulling at her and his voice was harsh.

—*Not so very difficult,* he told her. *You shall say them whenever I ask for them. You shall say them so often they will become a part of you.*

She could sense rather than hear the rage building in his voice, but she had no voice. She tried to open her mouth, but she couldn't do it.

He let go of her hair and moved away. She couldn't hear anything. She tried to sit up, but she was too awkwardly balanced, and she realized that he had shortened the chains fastening her wrists. Her arms were fixed in place. The shackle around her ankle felt so heavy. She was utterly helpless. Tears were rolling down her cheek from under the blindfold.

Help me, somebody, please help me, why am I here, don't let him hurt me, please, make him go away, what have I done to have been brought here, why why why, make him go away—

She felt him again, near her, and she instinctively tried to pull away.

—*Still fighting,* he said. *Very good.*

He put an arm around her neck again, catching her in a viselike grip. *Don't move,* he whispered. *I am preparing to cut off your blindfold. I want to see your face the first time. This is the only time you shall be allowed to look upon me. Keep your eyes shut or you shall be blinded.*

She heard several snips and felt hot, bright lights on her face.

—*Don't move,* he said, placing one hand over her eyes so that she was unable to see. She felt him moving about slightly. He was arranging several small soft cushions behind her and underneath her bottom, propping her up so she was nearly sitting up, just so. She tried to kick them away, despite what he'd just told her.

—*You have disobeyed me already,* he said, taking his hand off her eyes and laughing softly. *I am very pleased indeed. For this, you shall be punished.*

As her eyes slowly adjusted she saw that the lights were shining directly on her face from huge bulbs at the end of the bedposts. The rest of the room was shrouded in darkness. She turned her head and thought she could see vague forms, what might be the outlines of furniture. The chains attached to her wrists and ankle were made of golden links, attached to hooks in the bedposts. There were more than four posts; there were posts going all around the bed, holding up the canopy, as if she were in some sort of gilded cage. Then she looked up and saw the mirror. She started to whimper and closed her eyes. She didn't want to see him do it. She didn't want to watch him kill her.

For what seemed like ages but was only a few minutes, she lay there, her eyes squeezed tightly shut because she could not bear to look. The part of her that still wanted to fight knew that he was toying with her terror, inhaling every drop as if it were delicious nectar, and she felt herself flooded with hatred and rage.

Someday she'd get free, someday she'd find him and make him pay, someday she'd—

She felt him at the end of the bed, staring at her. She opened her eyes; she couldn't stop herself. From her helpless angle he appeared larger than life, that part of him jutting out from under the belt holding up the front of his robe. She had never seen a man's nakedness before, and she couldn't take her eyes off the hideous sight of it.

—*Do you like what you see?* He was laughing softly.

He was a hugely looming monster, and her rage melted into pure abject terror. He wanted to hurt her with that awful jutting part of him. He wanted her to struggle and scream. He wanted her to and he knew she would. She started to whimper in fear again, a cornered animal.

Let me go let me go let me go—

The hood of his robe was pulled over the black mask. The mask covered nearly all of his face, with two small holes for his nostrils and two large holes for his eyes. She could only see his mouth, his full lips smiling wickedly.

—This is the face of the devil, he said. Look carefully, because this is the only time you shall be allowed to see it.

He was coming closer, crawling closer on the bed, and she could see nothing but his mocking smile and two dark eyes burning behind his black mask.

He leaned over her. There was a flash of gold, a ring on his finger shining in the bright light. She was paralyzed. He spread her legs apart. She wanted to kick out at him with the leg that wasn't shackled, but her legs felt leaden and useless.

—Who are you? he asked, looming over her.

—No no no—

—If you are going to say no, you say, "No, my lord." His hands started to trace up and down her body, his nails sharp and raking her skin around her corset. There was no tenderness in his touch, only an insatiable desire to possess and leave his mark.

—Are you going to be sensible, clever Doula, he asked, or are you going to make it worse for yourself?

—Please—

—Please, what.

—Please, my lord. She could barely choke out a whisper.

This must be a nightmare, please, please let her wake up and be back in her safe little flat, June blabbing on the phone, please, please—

—Aha, he said, and he knelt between her legs on the bed.

She closed her eyes, whimpering, tears on her cheeks.

—Oh no, he said, you've seen it already and you are going to watch me take you. You are going to watch your own degradation. He leaned forward and placed his hands on her face, on her forehead, forcing her eyes open.

—*Do you see this?* he asked, *pointing to that thing jutting straight at her, huge and unthinkable. I know you can't tear your eyes away from its splendor. He laughed again. Do you see this? Do you? Answer me.*

—*Yes,* she barely whispered.

—*Yes, what.*

—*Yes, my lord.*

—*Yes,* he said. *I am your lord and master and you are my slave. You obey my commands and you worship me and me alone. You obey this and you worship this. He was practically on top of her and he whipped first one cheek, then the other, then her chin with that horrible hard jutting thing.*

At the vile touch of him she started to scream. The energy flooded back into her legs and she started to flail wildly.

—*Get off me get off me, you bastard, you bastard, stop—*

She was screaming and screaming but before she could think one more second, he moved down and suddenly was lying on top of her, and he forced his way into her with a savage push. The most ungodly pain was splitting her in two. She was screaming with the pain and terror of it. Behind her screaming was the sound of his laughter. He stopped for the briefest of seconds and then started moving again, the entire weight of him moving back and forth. She couldn't breathe, not with the pain of it and the pain on her chest, from him, from the corset squeezing her. He was going to squeeze the life out of her, moving with agonizing, leisurely strokes. Prolonging his pleasure and her agony.

—*Do you want me to stop?* he said.

She was screaming and screaming.

—*Do you want me to stop?* he said again.

—*Yes,* she whimpered.

—*Yes, what. He placed his hands under one of the pillows, pulling her up even closer. He was going to break her in two. He wanted her to die.*

—*Yes, my lord.*

She couldn't stop screaming, but the monster was still on top of her. She was choking, and all she felt was pain. He was suddenly pumping pain faster and faster and harder and harder inside her and still she heard that wicked laughter. He forced her eyes open and tilted her face and she saw his mask, the wicked curve of his lips as his hands came up to brace himself on her shoulders, to force himself in deeper.

She was going to die. No one could survive this pain and still be alive.

After one last savage movement he stopped. He didn't move. He stayed on top of her for what seemed like an eternity. She couldn't breathe. She closed her eyes to the horror of the mocking grin on his face.

—You are mine, he said. You belong to me.

His hands were on her face, forcing her eyes open yet again. He reached over to a small table behind her head, at the end of the bed, and picked up a glass of what seemed to be water, with ice in it. Drink this, he said, putting it to her lips. She was afraid to drink it, that it was poison and he would kill her now that he'd taken her, but she had no energy left to fight. It was cold and delicious.

He put the glass down when she was done and pulled slowly out from her. Then he crawled close to her face.

—So much blood, he said. How splendid. Now that you're blood- ied, the proper training can begin. He caressed himself and wiped the blood on her face, on her neck, on her breasts.

She was getting dizzy again, so sleepy.

—Welcome to the Club, he said.

She didn't know how long she had been unconscious. She woke up to complete darkness, still dizzy and aching all over, the blindfold wound back around her head. She was vaguely aware that someone was gently lifting her up, taking her to the bathroom, placing a cool cloth between her legs, wiping away the stickiness, putting her on the toilet, putting her back on the bed. Her corset was unlaced and taken off. Finally, she could breathe. She was too exhausted to struggle any- more, and fell back asleep.

When she woke up again, someone propped a rigid cushion be- hind her, then spoon-fed her soup and gave her something cold and slightly bitter to drink. She fell asleep once more. When she next woke, she had no idea what day it was, or how long she'd been there. She had been turned on her side. Both her hands were attached to chains on one of the posts on the side of the bed.

He was lying beside her on the bed. She was completely naked, and so was he, pressed up tightly against her backside. She could feel

*the length of him, his arms around her in a suffocating embrace. She
was too drained to be able to try to pull away.*

*—Who are you? he asked, whispering in her ear. She felt him hard
against her, parting her legs and slipping inside her. The pain was so
excruciating she cried out in agony. He laughed. The more she
screamed, the more he laughed.*

—Who are you? he asked again. I'll stop when you tell me.

She couldn't say anything.

Please oh please oh please stop—

—You belong to me, he said.

The pain was going to kill her.

—Are you very sore? Do you hurt very badly? he asked.

—Yes, she whimpered.

—Yes, what.

—Yes, my lord, she whispered.

—That's better. Do you want me to stop?

—Yes, my lord.

—Very good. Who are you?

—Yours. She could only whisper. Anything to make him stop.

—Yours, what. I can't hear you.

—Your Lordship, she whispered.

*—What you mean to say is, "I am yours, my lord." Like that. Say
it like that.*

—Please stop, please. Please, my lord.

*—You aren't listening, he said, but he pulled away from her
abruptly. You are not obeying. What shall be done with you? What
shall I do?*

—Go away.

*—No hope of that, my dear, he said with a short laugh. Particu-
larly in light of your continued disobedience.*

*He crawled over her so that he could lie facing her. He ran his
hands through her hair, twisting fistfuls of it into a ponytail. Then he
jerked her head up awkwardly so she cried out, and he kissed her so
hard she could barely breathe. The insistence of his mouth was worse
than the corset, stifling her.*

*—When shall you begin to realize that you belong to me? He
moved away again. Kiss it, he said, his hardness up against her lips.
Kiss it.*

She turned her head away. She wouldn't, not ever.

—You must learn to obey, he said, climbing back over her and shoving himself into her backside so suddenly that she screamed.

—Is this what you want instead?

—No no no—

—No, what.

—No, my lord. Stop, please stop, please—

He stopped and got off the bed, but was quickly back, smelling of soap, he was facing her again.

—Luckily for you, I am a fastidious sort, he said. Unlike most. Now do as I say. Open your mouth.

She tried, but she could barely open it. She was sobbing too hard. He pinched her nose shut with her fingers, so she had to open her mouth.

—I am your lord and master, he said savagely as he forced himself into her mouth. He wanted her to choke. This choking was worse than the corset. He wanted her to die. The tears were streaming down her cheeks.

Choking, choking. She was dead. Men didn't do things like this. This could not be happening to her. There was no end to the pain. Where was she? What day? What year? Who was she? What had she ever done to deserve this? Someone save her, please oh please oh—

She could breathe again and he was lying with his arms around her.

—Who are you? he was saying. Who are you who are you who are you?

—Yours, she whispered. I am yours, my lord.

—Why are you here?

She was so tired. Why could she not slip into a larger darkness and die?

—To do your bidding, my lord.

—What shall you do?

—Whatever you desire, my lord.

And on and on and on it went. She woke to darkness. Someone, not His Lordship, fed her and took her to the bathroom; he let her soak in a tub every so often. He brushed her hair and blew her nose. She thought it was the man who was going to slit her throat, and she was too frightened of him to disobey. He chained her back to the bed. Only her wrists. He took the shackle off her ankle. She couldn't move even if she wished to. She slept. She awoke to find him there, his arms around her, taking her at will.

Her body gradually became less sore. Adjusted, in its own way; capitulating because it had no choice. The will to survive fueled her body. Her mind had stopped working. She could no longer think clearly. Nothing made sense, in the darkness. This couldn't be happening. She was so dizzy. It was always dark and he was there, his hot, dry fingers devouring every inch of her body, that hateful voice muttering ceaselessly in her ear.

—Who are you? he asked.

—I am yours, my lord, she said. It was so much easier to say it.

—Why are you here?

—To do your bidding, my lord.

—What shall you do?

—Whatever you desire, my lord.

—I am going to make yours the most exquisite mouth in the world, he said one day. Or night. She had no idea where she was and how many days or weeks or months since the torture had begun. Perhaps there were windows in the room, but she could see nothing but blackness swimming in the blindfold.

—I am going to make your fingers the most sensitive, divinely caressing fingers in the world. He was in a talkative mood. I am going to mold you into the most pliable, sensual creature who ever touched a man. You, my sweet, you will be famous. Infamous, I daresay: the woman worth a million pounds to a member of the Club. The million pounds in the Swiss Consolidated Bank, Limited, account number one one six dash six one four. No one shall know who you really are or what your name really is or from whence you came. All they shall know is the ecstasy you provide, and how much it shall cost them. All they shall know is that you are mine. Mine alone.

He would not stop for hours and hours. Or perhaps it was days. Not until she begged.

—When you have learned to behave, the blindfold shall be removed, he said to her afterward. That was what she hated the most, the hateful sound of his calm, deep voice and the hateful feel of him lying beside her, his fingers idly caressing her when he was spent.

—You needn't wear it when I'm not here, he said. But when I am, you shall learn how to tie it on yourself, because you shall never see my face. Do you think me a monster?

—Yes, my lord, she said.

—Very good. Do you want to see my face?

—No, my lord.

—Should you forget yourself and try to see my face, the punishment shall be swift and more painful than you can bear. Do you understand?

—Yes, my lord.

—For you, I have no face. I shall never have a face.

—Yes, my lord.

—You are utterly at my mercy. Nothing interests me but my desire, and I answer to no one. You are quite alone. You are mine.

—Yes, my lord.

—This is your world, he told her. Your hands are placed where I choose to place them. Whenever I choose to place them. I rule this kingdom where the laws are mine and mine alone, and you are my faithful slave. There is nothing at all to restrain me.

He forced himself inside her, so relentless that she screamed.

—I want you to scream, he said. You are nothing. Nothing but mine.

And on and on and on it went.

He wasn't there for what seemed much longer than usual. Nothing was different; they fed her and cleaned her. She lay in the dark, dozing. She couldn't think. There was nothing to think about except him and what he had already done to her. What he wanted to do. It was easier not to think. Every time she woke, she was afraid that he would be lying next to her, his breath hot on her neck. Now she was afraid no one would ever come back for her at all.

Until she woke with a sudden start, with him on top of her.

—Did you miss me? he asked when he was through, lying sprawled on top of her so she could barely breathe.

—No, my lord.

—Ever the virgin, he said with a laugh. Who are you?

—I am yours, my lord.

—Why are you here?

—To do your bidding, my lord.

—What shall you do?

—Whatever you desire, my lord.

—Do you hate me?

—*Yes, my lord.*

—*Excellent. Now you shall have another reason to hate me.*

He moved away and she heard him pick something up off the small table by the bed, then unscrew the lid off a jar. Then he was back, rubbing a cream into her. It stung a little, and smelled faintly of cinnamon.

—*It should start to work its magic in a moment,* he said.

—*What, my lord?*

—*It's a present,* he said. *A surprise. Wait, and you'll see.*

In a few minutes, she felt as if she were ablaze. It wasn't that she itched, exactly, but there was a leaden fullness and a growing unbearable ache that demanded to be touched wherever he had placed the cream. The unbearable ache would go away only if she touched it. Without realizing it, she tried to rub her legs together. Anything to satisfy the fullness, that dreadful ache. She had to touch it.

—*What do you think you're doing? I forbid you to move,* he said.

—*What have you done to me, my lord?* she whispered.

—*A special potion,* he replied. *You've earned it.*

He got up and pulled on the length of chains attached to her wrists so that her arms were pulled over her head. Then he tied something around each ankle and attached them to the bedpost. She was spread-eagled, open and vulnerable and aching unbearably.

His fingers were moving up her thighs.

—*Do you want me to touch you?* he asked. *Do you?*

She wanted to say no, not ever, you bastard, I'll never want you, except to want to see you dead. But the words wouldn't come.

—*Yes, my lord,* she said instead.

—*Where do you want me to touch you?*

—*You tricked me—*

He slapped the inside of her thighs, hard. They stung terribly, but she barely felt them, she ached so.

—*I didn't ask for your opinion. Answer me,* he said.

—*Please.* She was being driven mad by the ache. It was spreading out from inside her, it seemed, into every nerve. It was seeping into her very pores. *Please, my lord.*

He tricked her again. He was tricking her into liking it. Into wanting him.

—*Bad girl,* he said. He was crouching over her, and pinched her nipples, hard. Then he rubbed some of the cream on them, and placed *something cold and excruciatingly tight on them, so they stayed hard. Nearly instantly they started to ache, too. She was desperate to stop the maddening itch.*

—*Where do you want me? he said.*

—*There, where you—*

—*You want me there?*

—*Yes.*

—*Yes, what.*

—*Yes, my lord.*

—*You want me to touch you. Really, do you?*

—*Yes, my lord.*

—*You want me to take you? His voice was thick.*

—*Anything. Anything, my lord. She was being driven mad.*

He got off the bed.

—*Come back, she said. Come back, my lord. She couldn't help herself. He had to do something. Anything.*

He was laughing at her.

—*You want me to come back, the man you hate, he said. The man who kidnapped you, drugged you, raped you, tortured you. Who shall continue to rape you and torture you at his leisure. How delightful.*

—*You tricked me, oh please—*

—*But you want me now.*

Her body has gone mad, every nerve on fire. In some small part of her that was still sane she knew it was whatever was in the cream he rubbed on her that made her say those words. That she still hated him and would never want him, never want him to come back to her, never ever, not till the day she died.

—*Who are you?*

—*I am yours, my lord. Yours yours yours.*

His hands were on her, stroking her thighs, inching closer.

—*Please oh please oh—*

When he touched her, she nearly swooned. She had never felt such pleasure in her life, not such physical release, waves and waves of it as he kept touching her. She had no idea a body could feel like that.

When he pulled back, she moaned.

—*No, come back, my lord, she said.*

—*My, my, he said. How quickly doth the lady change her mind. From a sniveling little virgin to a begging little slut. You astonish me.*

He sounded very pleased with himself as he untied her legs. Now you are going to fuck me properly, he said.

—My lord, come back, she said again. Some voice coming from inside her was begging. That small part of her that was still sane was appalled, but her body overruled it. She would truly go mad if he didn't come closer. Before she knew what she was doing, her legs were wrapped around him and she was moving with him.

—This is how it shall be, he said to her, slowing her frenzy so she thought she would scream only if he didn't touch her again, touch her that very instant.

—Soon you won't need the cream to make you feel this way, he said. You'll hear my voice, and that shall be sufficient.

He pulled himself out of her embrace.

—No, my lord. Don't go, please, my lord.

—I want to hear you begging, he said, tugging on the nipple clamps. She was going to die from the waves of pleasure, the heat that had invaded her body.

—Please, my lord, she said, please oh please oh—

And on and on and on it went.

Except now he had her body enthralled to his. He knew it.

He went away. She didn't know how long it was, but she begged him not to go. He soon came back, and as soon as she heard the sound of the lid being unscrewed from the little jar she was begging. She knew that was what he wanted. He made her beg. He made her—

[Note from Tomasino: Pages missing.]

—It shall be excruciatingly difficult to be without you for several days, or perhaps longer, but I have business that cannot wait, he said with an exaggerated sigh. Fortunately, your value to me shall increase in my absence. No matter where I am or what I do, my thoughts shall be of my Doula waiting for me, and when I am with you again, I shall be very pleased to hear you beg.

He kissed her and left her in the dark. She fell asleep eventually, and when she woke, something had changed. She was lying in the dark, but the blindfold had been cut off. When her eyes adjusted to the light, she could see the outline of Hogarth sitting in a chair near the bed. The cuff on her left wrist was still attached to a long coiled chain fixed to a bedpost, but she could sit up and move around on

the bed. She could cover herself with a silk robe she found near her
pillows.

—Greetings, my dear, he said cheerfully. I must say you are looking splendid indeed.

—Go to hell, you bastard. You sadistic bastard.

—Ah, you delightful child. Haven't lost your spirit, I see. You are
making magnificent progress. Indeed, you are everything I'd hoped
you'd be, and more. His Lordship is very pleased with his Doula, very
pleased indeed.

He was smiling happily.

—He is not difficult to please, you see, Hogarth said. Not like
some. His desire is like a tiger's for prey—to possess, to own, to devour. Especially that which is forbidden. Naturally, you will always be
forbidden, because you have been brought here against your will.

He picked up a book.

—Let me read something to you, Hogarth went on. I'm afraid it
was not conceived by a Frenchman, comme d'habitude, but is quite
apropos of the situation, nonetheless. Considering that it was written
about two hundred years ago, by a certain Dr. Benjamin Rush. "From
the day you marry you must have no will of your own," the good
doctor said. "The subordination of your sex to ours is enforced by
nature, by reason, and by revelation." Et cetera, et cetera . . . Let's
see . . . your husband "will often require unreasonable sacrifices of
your will to his. If this should be the case, still honor and obey him.
The happiest marriages I have known have been those when the subordination I have recommended has been most complete." A man of
considerable wisdom, this Dr. Rush, don't you think? Some considered him the father of modern psychology.

—I'm not married, she said.

Hogarth snapped the book shut and stood up, brushing the
creases of his jacket.

—If I were you, dear girl, I should tell myself that I have indeed
been married, albeit in a most unusual manner. That I have been
forced by my wicked family and unfortunate circumstances to marry
a man I didn't love, but I must submit because I have no other choice.

She did not know what to say.

—I think we should find you a ring. To bind this marriage. Yes, a
splendid idea. I shall propose it to His Lordship. He is extremely
generous, as you know. Hogarth walked around the bed, examining

her with a critical eye. Then he looked at the watch he wore on a fine chain.

—Well, he said, I am afraid I must leave you temporarily. I shall be back to check on you as soon as possible, I promise. In the meantime, I shouldn't worry about your cousin. June has long been informed that you are otherwise engaged, and she has sailed off to mummy and daddy, back to whatever godforsaken hole they live in. She has been gone quite some time, as a matter of fact. I should not be expecting a visit from your dearest June anytime in the foreseeable future.

Hogarth was gone. The room was empty and dark.

How long had she been here already? June, gone for quite some time. How long could it be?

No one knew where she was. No one in the world could help her. No one cared.

She thought she going to go mad.

They unlocked the shutters and let her sit outside on a small terrace sheltered by high, smooth walls. The air was warm and it often rained, but she didn't know what month it was or where she was or what was going to happen or—

Hogarth came back. He was sitting in the chair by the bed when she woke, fussing with the knot of his ascot.

—You need to move about, he said. We don't want you getting weak or out of sorts.

She started to laugh hysterically.

—Since when are you worried about my health? she asked.

—I always worry about you, in my way, he replied, whether you believe it or not.

From then on, when His Lordship wasn't there, they let her sit outside, or take walks after dark. She could see the hulking outline of the house, but they turned off all the lights so she was unable to see the shape of it clearly. There were paths on the grounds, snaking through woods. Hogarth walked with her, and someone else, behind them. She couldn't tell who.

She couldn't try to escape. She didn't have the energy, or the will. It was chilly at night, and they were everywhere, she thought. Watching her from behind the trees, men in monk's robes and masks, peering at her.

The room they kept her in was comfortable enough, and she was allowed to read. Sometimes Hogarth came and sat with her, reading.

—Here is a remarkable story, he said one day, looking up from the book he was holding, about a madam, one Theresa Berkley, who kept a house near Portland Place. She thought her girls were only as good as her tools. Hmmm. Too true. They kept the rods in water so as to remain green and supple. Chinese vases full of green nettles. Ox-hide straps studded with nails.

—You are hateful, Hogarth, she said.

—Her great invention, though, came in 1828, he went on, calm as ever. The Berkley horse, or chevalet, in the French. It was a sort of expanding padded ladder, adjustable to height, in which a willing client was tied so that his face projected through one part and his private parts through another. Whilst being whipped on his backside, one of Madame Berkley's girls would pleasure him in front. I say, those Victorians were eminently shocking.

—Why are you telling me this? she asked. Is this going to be His Lordship's newest toy?

—Only to expand your horizons, my dear child. So that you realize you are not the first to have succumbed to a realm of—how shall I put it?—fantasy.

—This is no fantasy, she said bitterly.

—The Marquis de Sade said that animals eat one another as we eat animals, Hogarth said, putting down his book and eyeing her carefully. That we human animals eat other animals without moral misgivings, because we consider the animals we do eat to be inferior to us; we rule them. Why then, the dear marquis reasoned, could not we humans use other humans for our own satisfaction, doing whatever we want to them? Is it not pure hypocrisy to pretend there is some absolute gap between human beings and cows?

—Is this some justification for what you've done to me? she asked.

—The dear marquis could have taught the world so much more, had he been able to exercise a tad more discipline upon his own nature, he went on, ignoring her. Unlike myself. Self-control makes the loss of control all the more pleasurable. Men are really very simple, you know. If you indulge them their desires, your value to them increases. Within reason, of course. He sighed happily. The marquis had the most splendid dungeons, in his château at Saumane. We have

dungeons here, you know. I shudder to think of you in them. But that is indeed where you shall go should you not behave.

He stood up and left her without another word.

She came back from a walk and His Lordship was waiting for her, his back to the bed, so she was unable to see his features. They quickly tied her blindfold on, then picked her up, threw her down on the bed, and chained her arms. His Lordship was in a foul state, as if some pulsating energy were coursing through his veins, making him insatiable. She thought he would break her in two.

Afterward, he seemed calmer, and started talking.

—According to the rules of the Club, the price of our guests is one thousand pounds per week, he said. Which means I am allowed to keep you for nearly twenty years. Does the thought of that please you as much as it pleases me?

No no no, she wanted to scream, but she was afraid not to lie.

—Yes, my lord.

—When you are set free, you shall have a splendid fortune waiting for you in the bank in Switzerland, compounding interest, naturally. I can release you early, should I tire of you, but I see no reason to assume that should be so. Your training has just begun, of course, yet I am very pleased by your progress. Perhaps I shall return you to the world when you've earned me back the million pounds I was forced to pay to buy you.

—No one forced you, my lord, she murmured. She waited for him to hurt her, but he didn't.

—Ah, but that's where you're wrong, my sweet. You did. My desire was worth the money. Understand this. You, your body, has been given a price tag. There are already many, many men who've heard rumors of the girl who was worth one million pounds to a member of the Club. They will beg and beg and name their price to have a taste of her. So I must be very clever and figure how best to recoup my investment in your training while enjoying the maximum return. The fees they pay must go to you. Those are the rules. The other arrangements, though . . . His voice trailed off.

She stiffened in panic at the sound of his calm, deep voice. First Hogarth, now this. What was he saying—

—As your training continues, you will learn how to perform certain services, no matter how distasteful you may find them. You will be-

*come as habituated to them as you have become habituated to every-
thing else thus far. You have no choice. You belong to me, and your
life is not your own. I suggest you console yourself with the knowledge
that you have been chosen, and that each time you submit might very
well be nearing you to the last time.*

*He got up. She heard the door open and someone come in, put-
ting some things on the table near the bed.*

*—You must be marked, he said. They must know it is you. Now
lie still.*

*He sat down behind her and arranged her carefully, so her head
was down near his lap and she could barely move. They were near the
edge of the bed. He picked up her left hand and held her wrist tight.
Someone else touched her ring finger gently, turning her hand over.*

—Exactly, His Lordship said.

*She heard a high-pitched whirring sound. Then a sharp pricking
pain, over and over on her finger. His Lordship's fingers tightened on
her wrist. She was sobbing with the pain of it, the sick whining whir.*

*The noise stopped. Her finger was bandaged lightly. His Lordship
let go of her wrist and got up. She heard noises, and the door open
and close. He came back.*

*—It is an altogether splendid tattoo, he said. Altogether splendid,
that needle in your flesh. And the sight of your beautiful blood. Blood-
ied for a second time. He laughed to himself. When it heals, they shall
be very pleased with the sight of it. I am very pleased indeed.*

*He put the cream on her so she became desperately aroused, and
took her over and over and over, until he could do no more and fell
asleep pressed tightly against her.*

*They woke her up and put the hood over her head although her blind-
fold was on. They laced her into the corset so she could barely
breathe. They unchained her from the bed and put the heavy thing
she remembered around her, lifted her up, and carried her, slung over
someone's shoulder, the blood rushing to her head. Through a hallway, into rooms, down a long staircase. She thought she was going to
be sick, she was so dizzy. They kept going down steps. Finally, she was
put down gingerly, and they took the heavy thing and the hood off.
She was sitting on the end of what seemed to be a comfortable wide
chaise, thickly padded. Her wrists were uncuffed and attached to
hooks on the wall. Then her head was pushed very close to the wall,*

near where her wrists were fastened, her forehead pressed into a padded headrest. A strap went around the back of her head so that it was
immobilized.

—Are you comfortable? It was His Lordship's voice in her ear,
and his arms around her. He'd seated himself directly behind her on
the chaise. Hogarth thought of it, he said. Don't move while we make
some adjustments.

After he got up, a panel lifted exactly where her face was. The air
was slightly colder on her face. She couldn't move. She couldn't
breathe. Fingers touched her face, the unmistakable feel of his hot,
dry fingers, caressing her lips. Then the panel came down.

—Excellent, he said. He was back behind her, arranging himself
so she was impaled on his lap. She cried out in pain and alarm. Then,
suddenly, he pulled away.

—Don't move, he warned again.

The panel went up and his face was there. He kissed her hard,
then pulled back. Open your mouth, he commanded. She opened
it. She had no choice. He forced himself into her mouth, until she
gagged.

He came back, his arms around her.

—Excellent, he said again to someone behind him, except we need
the hand. First they must see the tattoo; then the hand must be available.

He got up, and a few minutes later was back. She heard other
voices. Her left hand was unhooked and moved closer to the panel.
He was back on the other side, she realized, when his fingers came
through the hole in the wall and grabbed hers so she could fondle him
until he was hard again. Hard and implacable.

—Lovely, he said.

That was how it started.

On and on and on it went.

—You shall do as I say, he said. Each one of them has paid a king's
ransom for a caress from your lips. Each one of them. Perhaps they
are members of the Club. Perhaps not.

She lost count of how many times he made her do it. Dozens,
hundreds. Time had no meaning. She had no meaning. She was dis-
embodied; her hand, her fingers, her lips, there where His Lordship
touched her. As a person, she no longer existed.

Nothing pleased him more than what he made her do in this little room. To have her wedged tightly in his lap as other men abused her, her lips around them while he whispered in her ear, telling her what to do. Sometimes as she was being strapped in he put a tiny bit of the cream on her and went away, leaving her to go mad from the squirming until he returned and he heard her beg.

That always made him laugh with delight.

Then he started taking her out of the house. First they laced the corset tight, put the hood on her head, and wrapped a thick cloak around her so she couldn't move. Then she was carried through the labyrinth of hallways and stairs into a garage, into the backseat of a car. Sometimes the drives were so long she'd fall asleep. Sometimes they stayed in the car, waiting. The sound of gravel crunching, a driveway. The car stopping. There was no thought of escape. She had no clothes, no shoes, only the corset. They were all around her—they had to be. His Lordship was in the car; she felt him there, smelled him, although he never touched her. He wanted to wait. She was carried out, into a building. Through rooms, up and down, it made no difference. Their hands on her, the smell of them, the hideous feel of their bodies.

He was always there behind her, whispering in her ear.

—Who are you?

—I am yours, my lord.

One time, though, she snapped. The drive to the house had been bumpy and uncomfortable, and she was aching all over. His Lordship left her alone for a few minutes with a man who made her scream. She bit him, hard. She wanted to keep her teeth sunk into his odious body until he screamed worse than she had.

They took her away, back to the house where His Lordship kept her, but not to her room. A different room, down a long staircase and a narrow hallway. The farther they walked, the colder and more damp it became, and she started to struggle. It was useless. She heard a heavy door open. They dumped her down on a bed, took off the heavy cloak and hood, attached the cuffs on her wrists to chains in the wall, and left. She couldn't breathe in the corset. She couldn't see.

It was the dungeon he'd told her about. The dungeon down below. She heard awful animal noises, the harsh sound of her sobs.

She screamed and screamed, but no one came for her.

They left her trays of food, and things to drink, but she had no appetite. There was a pail for her to relieve herself in. Nothing else. No light, no sound, except the awful animals scrabbling.

They were going to leave her in there forever.

When His Lordship finally came, it was the first time she felt genuine gratitude for his presence. Another person, breathing and touching her so she knew she was still alive.

—You deserved to be punished, he said. You have made me very angry. Your mouth is meant only to give pleasure, not to inflict pain. Do you understand?

—Yes, my lord, she whispered. She had no voice left, nothing.

—Why are you here?

—To serve you, my lord.

—Did I give you leave to bite him?

—No, my lord.

—Will you ever bite anyone, ever again?

—No, my lord.

—Should you misbehave, you shall be left here in my dungeon for a very long time. Much longer than you've been here already. Is that what you want?

—No, my lord. She shook her head so violently he started to laugh. Then he pressed her down into the mattress and—

[Note from Tomasino: Pages missing.]

He didn't let her out of the dungeon for what seemed like forever. Often he came in with someone else.

—Do you want me? he asked.

—Yes, my lord.

—Do you want him?

—If it pleases you, my lord.

[Note from Tomasino: Half-page missing.]

Finally, they came for her and took her back to her room. Never had she been so happy to feel a warm bed and soft pillows and a bath. Clean space around her. Books to read.

They wouldn't let her outside, though.

He didn't return for a long time.

—Remember this? Hogarth asked. He came into her room, carrying what looked like a bundle of emerald satin. You looked particularly fetching in green.

—Why do you have those clothes? she asked.

—We're going to a very exclusive costume ball, he said.

He'd used those words before. Before everything, before they'd tricked her. Before, in her other life, when she could think.

Before, when she was still alive.

Hogarth smiled broadly.

—It's time, he said, putting the bundle on the bed, then pulling the emerald and diamond necklace out of his pocket and waving it languidly before her. It's been three years, my sweet. Time for another auction.

—It can't be, she said. That meant three years had gone by.

—And since you've been such a good girl, His Lordship has decided that you should keep this magnificent necklace. An anniversary present, of sorts. After tonight, of course.

Then he pulled a smaller box out of his pocket and blew an imaginary speck of dust off it. He opened it and showed it to her. It was a huge emerald, flanked by two slightly smaller yellow diamonds, on a thick band of gold.

—Your wedding ring, he said. Or had you forgotten? It will be fitted soon, when they are finished with you. Tonight, they must see the tattoo. Only you of all our guests have been marked. It is a great distinction.

He snapped the box shut and went away.

She was twenty-one, with millions in a bank somewhere in Switzerland and a magnificent emerald necklace and now a matching ring. It meant nothing. She meant nothing. She was nothing—

[Note from Tomasino: Half-page missing.]

She didn't know which was worse, the not knowing, or the certain knowledge of what they were going to do to her. She couldn't think, though. Her mind didn't work properly anymore.

There was the painted screen before her, the pole behind her, with its thick band pressing her up against it. The bright light in her eyes, the men in monk's robes and masks at her feet, looking up at her hungrily. Their paddles in their laps, waiting.

—Gentlemen, Hogarth was saying. Some or all of you may have sampled the delights of forbidden fruit in private, thanks to the graciousness of our most generous previous bidder. Tonight, as you may already have divined, two of you will have the most unusual and delightful opportunity to have our exquisitely lovely creature—she who is worth one million pounds—bestowing her favors upon you. The vote has been tallied, and it is unanimous. The two top bidders, gentlemen, the two top bidders will be permitted to take her here, for one hour. One hour only. The shy and inhibited amongst you need not apply, naturally.

There was a low ripple of laughter.

—I take it that none amongst you is shy and inhibited? Hogarth asked with a sly chuckle. Very well. The bidding begins at ten thousand pounds. Ten thousand pounds, sir. Fifteen thousand pounds. Twenty thousand pounds.

As before, they took off her bodice, then skirt and petticoats as the bidding progressed. She wondered wildly if His Lordship was bidding. What they were going to do to her, what—

—One hundred thousand pounds, Hogarth was saying. His gavel crashed. Excellent. You sirs, ninety-five and one hundred, may approach in five minutes exactly.

The screen was replaced and the blindfold wound tightly around her head. She heard furniture being moved. She was unhooked from the poles and pulled several feet toward where Hogarth was standing, then forced down on her hands and knees on a narrow, low table.

His Lordship was there. She could smell him, recognize the touch of his hot, dry fingers tracing a line down her spine, then farther down, where he rubbed a little dab of the cream on her. He dotted a bit on her nipples, then pinched them. She bit her lip not to cry out.

—You must do whatever they want, he said, whispering in her ear, his hands in her hair. You must do it because I am telling you that you must. You belong to me and you must do whatever they say and you must beg them not to stop. Because I say so. If you displease me, I shall throw you in the dungeon and leave you there to rot. Do you understand?

—Yes, my lord, she whispered.

He kissed the tears on her cheeks.

—Gentlemen, Hogarth said, she is all yours.

After that, she stayed in bed for a long time. Someone brought her bitter tea. It was always bitter, the tea they'd served her since she arrived, but they made her drink it. Eventually, she felt a little better, and His Lordship came often. He wouldn't leave her be. How he could keep at it, however old a man he was, she couldn't understand.

She only knew that he was insatiable. Sometimes they stayed in the room with the little panel in the wall for so long, one man after another, that they fell asleep on the chaise. Until he woke her and it started all over again.

On and on until Hogarth appeared one day and told her they were moving.

—There's a war coming, he said. We've been in one place long enough.

She didn't understand. She thought he was speaking in some cryptic code. Her mind was not working anymore. She couldn't remember anything from one day to the next, except the sound of His Lordship's voice in her ear and the feel of his fingers and the smell of the leather headrest he loved so much to strap her into so he could feel her and watch at the same time.

She ate the soup they gave her and drank the tea and a glass of cold, sweet water, and felt a profound lassitude overtake her. She could barely keep her eyes open as they bundled her up and carried her away, down to a garage and a car. They wrapped her in blankets in the back and she slept. They drove for days, it seemed. It could have been only a few hours. It didn't matter that they'd drugged her and were taking her away to hide her somewhere more remote. Nothing mattered.

She was dead to the world.

He was never going to let her go.

The new house was colder than the other, and it was foggy and windy and raining all the time. When they kept the shutters closed, she never knew if it was day or night. It didn't matter. It was always gray and wet. There was a long terrace outside the house, and they let her walk on it and the grounds nearby. She could see a high, smooth stone fence topped with barbed wire all the way around the property. The house was large and made of stone and seemed to have many rooms, but she saw none of them save her own.

His Lordship soon came and stayed for what seemed like longer than usual. At first, he installed himself in the room with her nearly all the time, which was unlike him. He told her she could keep the blindfold off if she behaved. He did paperwork at the desk, his back to her, while she read or dozed. Sometimes she sketched with sharp, hard pencils, trying to teach herself to draw. Once he stretched and she caught a glimpse of something flashing on his finger. His thick

*gold ring. She wondered idly where her ring was, the one Hogarth
had showed her. The one he'd said was her wedding ring.*

*Then His Lordship told her to tie on the blindfold and lie down.
He couldn't seem to get his fill of her. Over and over and over again.*

He stopped only once, when there was a knock on the door.

—Don't move, he said.

*He got up, and she heard voices. Then felt his hand tight on her
left wrist. Something cold was placed on her ring finger. Then she
heard a whirring. Not like the tattoo needle, a thicker sound. They
were doing something with the ring, but it didn't hurt.*

She didn't understand.

*He let go of her. The voices went away. He lay down next to her
and picked up her left hand.*

—You are mine, he said. You'll never take it off.

*He wouldn't let her up. Not for days and days and days. It didn't
matter. She was nothing. Nothing but what he wanted. She was lying
in the dark and he was next to her, on top of her, behind her. Savage
one minute, caressing her the next. She had no idea what time meant
any longer.*

When he was there, time stopped.

*Then he left. She woke up and he was gone. Her blindfold had
been snipped off and the shutters were open. She looked at her ring.
It was the huge emerald, flanked by two yellow diamonds. She tried
to twist it off until she bled, but it wouldn't budge. Then she saw that
there was a radio on the desk. She hadn't heard the radio in years,
she realized. There were voices on the radio. Real people. In a real
world. She could tell the time again. Five years since she'd heard a
radio.*

*The world was at war and she was locked away from it. She won-
dered what His Lordship was doing in the war. Something as horrible
as he was, most likely. And Hogarth. She could picture him in a crisp
uniform, shining his buttons.*

*She listened to the radio, day and night. She had no one to talk
to, so she talked to the radio. Her voice sounded odd, and far away.
The servants in the house who fed her and watched her did not say a
word to her. They worked for His Lordship—that was all she needed
to know. Matilda, that was the name of the woman. The squat, ugly
one who'd been stirring something, that night a long time ago. That
first night. Matilda, who laced her into the corset so tightly she*

couldn't breathe. Matilda gave her the bitter tea, and her meals on trays. The other servant was Markus. She'd heard Hogarth call him that one day. He was strong and he scared her.

She wondered if he'd been one of them, behind the panel. Or the man who'd said he would slit her throat.

They put piles of new books in her room, more sketchbooks, a palette of watercolor paints. One day they wheeled in a piano, and sheet music. Books that taught her how to read music, to play.

She almost felt like a person, sometimes, a person who was alive. She listened to news of the war and worried about the fighting and started to think again. Every day, she could think a little more. She started to try to write, with one of her sketch pencils, tiny, tiny scribbles, then words. Words turned into sentences. She wrote them on scraps of her watercolor paper, only a few at a time, because she was scared they were watching her, and then she tore them into minuscule pieces and swallowed them.

She was less fuzzy, wherever it was they were keeping her. Maybe it was the cold, wet air. Maybe it was because His Lordship hadn't come in nearly three years. Not once. There must have been another auction, but she wasn't taken to it. Maybe it was called off because of the war.

No one touched her. No one spoke to her but the voices on the radio.

Then His Lordship did come, waking her in the middle of the night, his hands all over her like a madman's. It was pitch-black in her room, but he had his mask on, as always. He held her wrists tightly and put her hands up to his face. He kissed her fingers. Then he stroked her fingers down his neck, down his chest, down down down—

—Did you miss me? he said.

—Yes, my lord, she said.

—You have become a wonderful liar, he said. I made you so.

He turned her over and took her with such ferocity, over and over again, till she pleaded with him to stop. He wanted to split her in two. He wouldn't stop till she was dead.

It didn't matter. When she was with him it was as if she were dead. She was nothing. She belonged to him. As soon as he arrived she started to forget how to think.

She couldn't think as long as he was there.

He put the cuffs on her wrists and the blindfold. He wouldn't let go of her for days, it felt like, weeks. She lost track of time again. They'd taken the radio away. Soon, he started to bring others in with him. She always knew when others were coming because they took her into a smaller room, made her lie on a soft bed with many small pillows, and attached chains to her wrists so they could arrange her any which way they wanted. They touched her ring in awe. His Lordship whispered in her ear and told her what to do.

Then he was gone again, and they brought the radio back and opened the windows. He had been there for only three weeks. She'd thought it was a year.

It took her months to feel better. To think as she'd started to think again. To be able to dare to write down a word.

Hogarth came. He told her there'd been another auction. Wasn't she a lucky girl, to be so far away. Only forty thousand pounds. Pathetic, wasn't it? Blame it on the war, he said, the shortages. She should be grateful His Lordship was busy with the fighting. But it will soon be over. He misses you.

He stayed for a while. He talked to her about the war. She asked him questions. She'd forgotten what it was like to have a simple conversation, to know how to talk. Hogarth was helping her to remember, she thought. Hogarth didn't want her head to be all fuzzy.

Once, Hogarth said something funny, and she actually laughed. She hadn't thought herself able to laugh anymore.

She didn't want to die. She was feeling much better.

She wanted the war to be over, but it was so confusing. When the war ended he would be coming back, and it would start all over again.

Hogarth was sitting at the desk when she woke up, a bottle of champagne in a bucket near a stack of papers.

—Drink up, he said. He looked very happy.

He handed her a glass. She figured the champagne was drugged, but she drank it anyway. It didn't matter—they'd make her swallow it, or worse, if she refused. Something was going to happen. Hogarth had that expectant look on his face.

—The war is over, and we're moving again, he said. It's a lovely house, and we have new servants. Matilda and Markus will still be with us, of course. But they can be such bores.

She was getting dizzy. Moving meant nothing, except another room to get used to. She had no idea where she'd been for ten years.

It couldn't be ten years. That meant she was twenty-eight. It couldn't be. It was only yesterday that Hogarth had tricked her.

She was still having a nightmare. She'd wake up and be eighteen and in London with her silly cousin June.

He had tricked her again. Her eyes were so heavy. They tied on the blindfold and snapped the cuffs on her wrists and wrapped her in something, that heavy thing, why that, not again, oh why—

It was cold and raining. She heard the rain, vaguely, on the roof of the car. She woke when they stopped moving. Someone carried her out into the damp, chill air, up several steps, and she was handed to someone else and laid down on her side, on a narrow bed. A thick belt was strapped around her waist.

She heard engines whining. It must be a plane, she thought. He was going to take her up into the sky and push her out.

There was a swift rush as the plane sped down the runway, up into the air.

His Lordship's fingers in her hair. Of course.

—Why are you here? he asked.

—To serve you, my lord, she whispered.

—Open your mouth, he said.

When he was finished, they raised her head and made her drink something bitter. She pretended to swallow, then turned her head away and spit it out. She didn't know why.

Nothing mattered. It was all starting again. He was there, his hands raking her skin under the heavy thing, shoving her onto her back, picking up her legs and wrapping them around his waist.

He was never going to let go of her. He was never going to let her go.

The plane was slowing down, descending. Her ears popped. They propped her up and made her drink something else, and this time she swallowed. It didn't matter. The plane hit the ground with a slight bump, and they taxied to a stop. She was so dizzy again. Someone unstrapped her and picked her up and carried her down the steps, into a car.

She woke up on a soft, comfortable bed. He was there; she felt him moving on top of her, but she was so tired, her legs like lead, that she didn't care. It was dark again.

With him there was nothing but darkness.

She woke again. His fingers were tracing lazy circles on her breasts.

—Welcome to your new home, he said.

—Where are we? she asked.

—What did you say? He pinched her nipples so hard she cried out.

—Nothing, my lord, she whispered. Forgive me.

—That's better, he said, but not good enough. Turn over.

He pushed her over before she could move. He took one arm, then the other, fastening her wrists so that her arms were pulled up over her head.

—You have forgotten much, I see. Shall we start your training over from the beginning?

No no no—

He was nuzzling her ear.

—I didn't hear you, he said.

—Whatever pleases you, my lord.

He didn't stop until he was satisfied she was too exhausted to keep screaming.

—It is indeed a lovely house, he said. Hogarth was right.

He would not take off the blindfold. It was still dark.

She had fallen off the face of the earth.

—If you're good, you will be allowed outside, he went on. There's a small garden that needs attention. Here in your room, you'll find an extensive library and a piano. There are additional servants. Moritz— he's a cousin of Markus and dreadfully unpleasant. As well as two others, twins who work for me. You shall want for nothing.

Nothing, except her life.

—I'm afraid I must leave you, but I shall be here as often as I can. The war is over, and you must not be allowed to forget that I am your master, and you shall continue to do as I say. Do you understand?

—Yes, my lord, she said.

She didn't feel well in the mornings. She was dizzy and tired. Matilda brought her tea and she threw up trying to drink it. She poured it away instead when Matilda wasn't looking. Matilda was preoccupied lately, looking after the new house and the new servants.

She sat in the garden and watched the new servants, the twins.

Belladonna comes from where?
Hiding in her secret lair
Locked away from days so fair
Brooding with the night's despair
Cruelly stolen, filled with lies
Belladonna left to die

They were both pudgy, with curly dark hair, but their faces weren't ugly like Moritz's. He patrolled the grounds with a shotgun under his arm. They were afraid of Moritz, too, she could tell. They were afraid to talk to her. She wondered what His Lordship had done to them that they were here. That they were so fearful.

She felt so odd. Weightless, almost. Her appetite was coming back and she was starting to put on weight. Matilda looked at her one day when she was standing by the window and nearly dropped the tray.

Hogarth was there soon after. He looked very upset.

—Matilda told me we have a little problem, he said.

—What do you mean? she asked.

—Your belly, I mean, he replied. She had never seen Hogarth flustered before. Your belly and what's in it. You are pregnant, are you not?

—I think so, she said. She felt flooded with calm. She was going to have a baby. She didn't know how it had happened, or why it hadn't happened before. It must have been in the plane, when she spit out the bitter tea. Matilda had been making her drink bitter tea ever since they'd stolen her away. There was something in the tea to stop her from getting pregnant. She'd been trying not to drink it for a long time.

—This has never happened before, Hogarth was saying. He was fussing with his cuffs. She was flooded with a sudden wave of intense happiness, because she was going to have a baby. Because the very idea of this baby had rattled Hogarth so.

Hogarth brought in a doctor. They tied on her blindfold before he came in. She thought he must be a member of the Club.

—Twins, the doctor said. She's going to have twins.

Twin babies. She was going to live again. She was going to start thinking, like she had when the radio was on. She was going to force herself to start thinking and she was going to escape. Escape from His Lordship and Hogarth and all of them, the members of the Club. She was going to have her babies and get away.

She was going to live. She was going to start to write again, on tiny pieces of her watercolor paper, and when it was dark in her room she would hide the tiny slips of paper in musty books no one ever touched. She was going to talk to the new servants, the pudgy ones who were afraid. She hated them, too, but she must try to talk to them. She needed to practice, to be able to talk to her babies.

—His Lordship must be informed immediately, Hogarth said to

the doctor. Then they said good-bye. Hogarth came back and untied her blindfold.

—*I am having these babies,* she said to him.

Hogarth didn't know what to say. For once.

—*Do you want to feel them?* she asked. *His Lordship would want you to tell him what they feel like.*

Hogarth looked at her in some amazement. Then, gingerly, he put his hand on her hard, smooth belly. She was growing larger every day.

She looked down at his hand on her belly. Hogarth was wearing a ring. A golden ring. He'd forgotten he was wearing it. It had an intricate design of a naked woman. It was the ring belonging to all the members of the Club, she knew.

She'd felt it on their fingers before, when they'd grabbed her hands.

Hogarth had forgotten, and she saw his ring.

She smiled at Hogarth.

One of the twins started talking to her. She was very surprised that he was an American. He asked her if she needed anything. She didn't trust him, or any man, but she needed someone. She had to get strong and get help, for her babies.

The twins would help her if she told them she was pregnant with her own twins.

He said his name was Tomasino Cennini and that his brother was Matteo. He said he was worried about her, and she didn't want to believe him in case he was a spy for His Lordship. Tomasino said they owed His Lordship their lives, that they'd been saved from certain death. That they were from Bensonhurst, in Brooklyn, but had been in Italy during the war.

His Lordship had told them to call him Mr. Lincoln, Tomasino told her, because he freed them from slavery.

That made her laugh so hard she choked.

Then he told her what had happened to them, and she felt sorry. It was the first time a man had made her feel pity in a long time, she realized.

At first, she felt pity only because she knew they couldn't hurt her. Not the way His Lordship hurt her. And all the members of the Club.

Then she thought about them, that they were as much prisoners of His Lordship and of Markus and Moritz and Matilda as she was. Only they didn't quite know it.

Or perhaps they did.

But they were young and they were strong, even if they were pudgy. She looked through the library in her bedroom and found some old books about their condition. She read them quickly, to see if they could still hurt her despite what had happened to them, and was satisfied when she realized that they couldn't.

When she felt brave and saw Tomasino, she gave him one of the books to read. He got a strange look on his face. He tried to make a joke, and she nearly smiled at him.

She would still be able to smile. She was still a person.

She would get her life back. The money was in the bank. The Swiss Consolidated Bank, Limited. The account numbered 116-614.

She decided she had to trust Tomasino. She had nothing to lose. If His Lordship found out she would be punished most severely, but she had to risk it. For her babies.

Tomasino and Matteo would help her. They were twins. Someday, she would give Tomasino the tiny pieces of paper that had become a diary and he would read it and tell his brother what they'd done to her.

His Lordship, and all of them.

The members of the Club.

[Note from Tomasino: Diary ends here.]

Guy finds me on the balcony outside the blue bedroom, where he had watched Belladonna in the dark during our grand plantation ball.

He hands the diary back to me, his face ashen, and I wave a bourbon bottle at him. He shakes his head. Nothing found in a bottle could dull this pain.

We sit together, not speaking, for a long time, listening to the sounds of the night. The rustling of the wind in the trees, the crickets buzzing in mindless chirps, an owl hooting in delight as it swoops on a mouse. The sky is alive with stars. Miles and miles and miles of stars.

"Don't you want a cigarette?" I ask him eventually. "I remember you from the club, and you were smoking then. Lit your cigarette from a necklace once upon a time, if I recall correctly."

"You do," Guy says. "But I gave it up. I didn't think she liked it."

"No, she doesn't." I sigh heavily.

"Can I ask you something?" Guy said.

"How did we escape? Where is Bryony's twin? Why no pregnancy before then?"

Guy nods.

"I think she was right—that it was the bitter tea Matilda gave her, with some sort of herb in it," I say. "I looked it up in some herb books. Maybe a touch of cedar oil, or frankincense. Just because doctors don't know about such potions doesn't mean they don't work. Surely the members of the Club had plenty of opportunity to experiment."

"Oh, Tomasino." His voice is so full of anguish I think my heart will break.

"I'll tell you the rest someday, Guy. Truly, I will. You need to know everything. But just not this minute. I'm very tired. You understand, don't you?"

"Yes," he says slowly.

Poor, sweet Guy. He must be bursting with curiosity. I'd be, if I'd just read a diary like that.

We sit in silence again, until my foot falls asleep. The sky is starting to lighten, with a rosy flush on the horizon.

"I'm going to London," Guy says. "As soon as possible."

I hand him a card with the Pritch's contact numbers on it. "He's expecting your call," I say. "He'll take good care of you. We trust him implicitly. Maybe some of the names will strike a chord somewhere. Or you may know one of them."

"I know men like them." Guy's mouth is set in a grim line. "They're the bullies in school who get their jollies from inflicting pain on anyone or anything that's weaker. My brother Frederick was like that. Except he preferred animals to women. Shooting them, I mean."

"Where is he now?" I ask. Anything to change the subject.

"Charged by a rhino in Kenya, he was. Gored to death. That he had to be buried down there gave me some small satisfaction. That he wouldn't be next to my mother and my sister."

"Dare I suggest it served the bloody bastard right?" I venture.

"It almost made me believe there is a God after all," Guy says bitterly. "But not quite."

"I wish it could be some other way," I say heavily.

"I know. She won't see me now, will she?"

"No. But if it makes you feel any better, I doubt she'll see me, either. She probably won't leave her room for weeks. Matteo is on his way down. He always had a special touch with her when she was feeling poorly. But she's never been like this. That's because—"

"Because no one else has read it," Guy says.

"Yes."

"I don't know how she found the courage to write that."

"I don't either," I reply. "I couldn't ask her. She asked me to copy it over so it was legible, that's all. She started writing on scraps of her watercolor paper when they thought she was painting. Sometimes she wrote on blank pages of books in her room, scribbling quickly in the bathroom or at night. Somewhere where they couldn't see her doing it. She was afraid they were watching her. Not all the time, but often enough. It's why we're a bit extreme with our security measures."

"You needn't justify anything to me. Truly you don't."

"I'm going to miss you, Guy. Miss you almost as much as the mint juleps I concoct with such delicacy." My feeble joke falls flat. This is not the time for joking.

"Thank you, kind sir. I'm going to miss you, too. And Bryony."

And Belladonna. More than—

"Find them, Guy. Please help the Pritch find them," I say. My voice is choking. I need to go lie down. "Find her baby. Find *him*. We're so close. I know we are."

They will come to you if they don't know who you are.

"I'll find him," Guy says savagely. "I won't rest until I find him."

Do not let the loneliness freeze your soul.

I want to tell him the dungeons are waiting, dusty, dank cells hidden behind the wine cellar. I want to tell him we've been waiting for this nightmare to end for nearly ten years. I want to tell him there have been so many times we have nearly given up in despair, certain that the members of the Club would forever elude us.

You will be forever captive to the vengeance if you let yourself remain obsessed by it.

I want to tell him that it's only the sheer strength of her will, planning and plotting, that keeps us going. "My mind will not be turned around," Belladonna once said to Leandro. "I will not succumb to the weakness. . . . And I *will* make them suffer."

Belladonna watch you die.

PART V

The Feverish Wanderings Toward Home

(1956–1958)

Belladonna has gone far
Malice shining like a star
Green orbs glowing in the sky
Sparkling teardrops in her eye
Belladonna watch you die

19

The Members of the Club

They stole her life. Now she's going to steal their future.

The call has finally come through from the Pritch, you see, with the name of one of the members of the Club. A colleague of Sir Patty, as we thought. "Took an awful lot of careful digging," Pritch tells me. "Had to have been absolutely spit-spot. Couldn't risk buggering a situation like this, going after the wrong man. Would've queered the whole deal."

He's absolutely, utterly certain, though, that he's found the right bastard. Trust our clever dick to do it.

"We bugged all the rooms, his office, the telephones," he explains to me, boasting only a little bit. He deserves a good gloat. "Easy as pie arranging entry, mind you; the servants are ever so deferential to uniforms. Phonemen, we said we were, imperative that we inspect the lines, thank you very much. Tell the maids they're sweet and take them out for a drink or two. Buy them a little trinket. Ply the schedule out of them, like candy from a baby."

And then break their poor little hearts, running off the way you did. Not nice, no, not nice at all.

I never said we were nice. Nice gets you nowhere.

We need only one, to put the fear of discovery in them. One leak to summon them and bring them all together for an emergency meeting of the Club council. It's risky, certainly, but they've got no choice. Not after a few hints have been dropped about Sir Patty's ignoble end.

We're counting on their arrogance. After all, hasn't their very particular organization run without a hitch, meeting once every three years like clockwork for hundreds of years? Even after Edward fell for that dreadful American and she threatened to spill the beans? Oh, perhaps one of the girls got a bit stroppy and needed a good talking-to; perhaps another went crying home to mommy and daddy and they filed a report with the police. But nothing ever came of it. Nothing is going to come of it now.

Pritch's team of trustworthy snoops has been plotting with military precision; in fact, the whole bunch haven't had so much fun since they were cracking codes during the war. I think the Pritch is the only one among us who's magnificently happy right now. Guy certainly isn't. He's laying low, staying in a suite at the Connaught, and he meets with the Pritch one dismal, dank afternoon for a walk around Green Park.

Pritch eyeballs Guy carefully, then starts to whistle a tuneless song. "Got under your skin, has she?" he says conversationally.

"I shouldn't think it that obvious," Guy says morosely.

"She has that effect on people," Pritch replies. "Mind you, I only met her the once. In Italy, when the Count was still alive."

"What was she like then?" Guy asks.

"Odd." Pritch pulls up the collar of his overcoat. "Never met a woman who could creep up behind you like that, without so much as a peep or a by-your-leave."

"She still can."

"I'm not surprised. Leandro told me his staff called her *'la fata.'* She was more ghostlike than human. I half-expected her to vaporize before my very eyes. Most odd." He looks at Guy again. "You're in love with her, I take it."

"Yes." Guy's face is as glum as the weather. "Is that so obvious as well?"

"That you're in love, or that you think it hopeless?"

Guy looks at the Pritch, surprised that such an unprepossessing man could have clocked him so clearly. He nearly smiles. She does have a knack for hiring only the best people, he realizes. He remembers having a conversation with yours truly about it, one balmy afternoon as we sat talking about everything and nothing on the veranda at La Fenice.

"She hit the jackpot with you," Guy tells the Pritch.

"It's been a pleasure," he replies, "to have been employed in the service of such a worthy cause."

"I'm here to help," Guy says. "To do whatever I can. I need to do *something*. Please, give me something to do."

"Righty-oh. Mostly the waiting game at present. Nearly there."

"I see." They walk on in companionable silence, both thinking about Belladonna.

"Might I ask you a question?" Guy says after a while.

"Certainly."

"Who is Jack? Bryony calls him her uncle Jack. He worked for them in the Club Belladonna in New York, didn't he?"

"Yes. Jack Winslow. A most honorable man; she allowed herself to trust him," Pritch replies. He knows exactly what Guy's getting at. "He was in love with her, too, mind you, before she closed the club. I heard it in his voice, and I pressed him one day, when we were chatting on the phone. 'She told me she has no heart' was all he'd say. Nearly did him in."

"But he still works for her, doesn't he?"

"Yes, but in a roundabout way. Coordinating whatever she needs doing in New York. He's married now. Settled down. A bit happier."

"I see."

"Well," Pritch says, tipping his hat, "I must be off. I shall be speaking to you quite soon, if all goes according to plan."

"Thank you, Mr. Pritchard," Guy says.

"Do call me Pritch," he replies. "Everyone else does."

They say good-bye and Guy walks slowly back to the hotel. The Pritch heads for the nearest pub to have a Guinness-inspired think. He's found their weakness—the way in, he calls it. It's via the son of one of the men, a certain Sir Benedict Gibson MP, who was at the funeral. How perfect; it gives us more room to ensnare the family and threaten a scandal. More room to call his bluff.

Sir Benedict spends his weekdays in the family's Eaton Square town house, and weekends at their country retreat in Gloucestershire. His son, Arundel, is not quite nineteen, on the cusp of being allowed a taste of paradise, we figure, and highly impressionable. Basically a sweet, decent boy, if a bit spoiled. Like most boys of his class, he worships his father as much as he loathes him, and feels tremendously protective of his mother and little sister, Georgina, conveniently off at boarding school. What works for our purpose is that Arundel often spends weekends in Eaton Square, playing hooky from Cambridge, with only the servants for company. His parents encourage these weekends, sowing the wild oats in polite society. He'll settle down soon enough.

Soon enough indeed.

We need only a few hours of Arundel's time. The Pritch will send in his best team, which will have no problem keeping the staff out of the way. We'll send them a few bottles of extra-special tipple, just in case. But they're always fast asleep by the time Arundel gets in from a night of partying, anyway. He's quiet, because he's a thoughtful young chap, and—who knows—he might want to sneak a young lady in someday.

We're even quieter.

The gumshoes have been following him for weeks, and tonight's the night. The only dicey bit will be when Arundel's in the club, when his friends are getting blotto. We must be sure he goes home alone, and not too terribly drunk.

Confrontations are always the most successful in the dark of night.

The key rasps in the lock; the door opens and as quickly shuts with the heavy thud of old money. Arundel Gibson drops his keys on the table in the front hall. He goes into the drawing room and throws his coat on the sofa, then walks over to the sideboard to pour himself a drink. We've heard him do this dozens of times.

"Lovely scotch, old bean," a voice says. "Single malt."

"Can't beat it," says another.

"Do join us."

"What? What?" Young Arundel spins around in a panic. The sound of strange voices in his parents' drawing room has startled him so profoundly he doesn't know what to do. Plus, he's still slightly befuddled from a pleasant evening of innocuous chatter and flirting and one martini too many. "Who on earth are you?"

"I'm Jay One," says the first voice. It's deep, and rough.

"I'm Jay Two," says the second. So is his.

"Just call us the Jaybirds."

"Who *are* you?" Arundel demands, starting to get his wits back. "How dare you?"

"We dare very well."

"It's our job."

"What are you doing here?" Arundel says, moving over to the desk and brushing his light brown hair off his forehead. He has eyes of a darker brown, is slender and tall, and has a determined look to him. "Breaking into my parents' home. I'm ringing the police."

"I shouldn't do that if I were you."

"Why ever not?" Arundel asks.

"The police know we're here," Jay One says smugly.

"The police sent us, as a matter of fact," says Jay Two.

"Encouraged this little chat."

"The police want no part of this mess."

"*Bloody* mess."

"I'll say."

"What do you mean?" Arundel says.

"Precisely what we said," Jay One replies.

"Why would the police know about spies like you?" Arundel asks, bewildered.

"Use your imagination, dear boy."

"We thought you were more clever than that."

"I don't understand," Arundel says. "Is my father in some danger?"

"Danger? No."

"Not imminently."

"*Trouble* might be a better word."

"Imminent trouble, yes."

"That's why we're here."

"To warn you."

"And to ask for your help."

"We're counting on you."

"My help?" Arundel cries. "What are you talking about?" Still, he is starting to let his guard down ever so slightly, lulled by the Jaybirds' singsongy speech and their air of relaxed ease in his parents' house. He takes a gulp of his drink. They seem more at home than he ever has, he realizes. "I thought *you* were the professionals."

"But you're family."

"He trusts you."

"*We* trust you."

"Are you trustable, Arundel Cyril St. James Gibson?"

"Lovely name. Posh all right," Jay One says confidentially.

"Ever so posh," Jay Two agrees.

"Bit of a mouthful, though."

"Quite. Right, then. Arundel Gibson, are you a man of honor?"

"Of your word?"

"To whom we may freely confide?"

"As a man?"

"As a gentleman?"

"Are you?"

"Are you?"

Arundel, being a little fuzzy from drink and shock, is thoroughly bewildered. "What do you mean about my father?" he manages to ask. "What the bloody hell are you going on about?"

"You haven't answered our questions," Jay One says sadly. They look at each other.

"No time to waste," Jay Two says.

"None whatsoever."

"He's not the chap we need."

"Afraid not, old bean." They stand up in perfect unison.

"Be seeing you."

"Righty-oh. Thanks ever so for your time."

"Terribly sorry to have startled you."

"Better luck next time."

"Wait. Wait! Don't go," Arundel says, putting down his drink and stretching his hand out beseechingly. "Tell me what you want. Something to do with my father. I won't tell a soul, I swear it. You have my word."

"My *word,*" says Jay One.

"I *say,*" Jay Two says.

"Well done, old bean."

"Just as we'd hoped."

"Yes. Better."

"Smashing job."

"I do believe this calls for a freshening of the drink."

"Don't mind if I do."

"You were saying," Arundel interrupts, exasperated, "about my father?"

"Yes, righty-oh. Your father."

"A nasty bit of business."

"Prepare yourself, old bean."

"Damaging, you know. Might ruin the family."

"Your mother. Won't take kindly to it."

"Counting on you, old bean."

"Counting on me for *what*?" Now he is completely exasperated. He pushes his light brown hair back off his forehead, where it flops endearingly.

"Could be a monstrous scandal," Jay One blithely goes on.

"That's why we're here," Jay Two explains.

"To stop it."

"Staunch the flow."

"Finger in the dam, that sort of thing."

"Prepare to get wet."

"Would you please tell me in plain bloody English what you're talking about!" Arundel cries.

The room falls silent, with the Jaybirds momentarily deprived of their squawking. Arundel realizes he can hear the clock in the hall ticking very loudly. He doesn't understand anything at all about men like these and their world, that they've got this act down to a science. Why should he understand that it works best on the young and impressionable, the hasty and the temperamental? He's done nothing in his short life to warrant this peculiar kind of confrontation.

"Your father," Jay One says eventually. "Has he ever mentioned a private club?"

"An exclusive men's club," Jay Two elaborates.

"Like White's, you mean?" Arundel asks.

"Not White's."

"We know he's a member there."

"*More* exclusive."

"A club one wouldn't discuss with one's wife."

"Or a little boy."

"Grown-up boy, yes."

"Only if he's discreet."

"A club for *gentlemen*."

"If you understand us."

"No, I—" Arundel says.

"Think, old bean, think," Jay One urges.

"Not a peep to you?" Jay Two asks.

"About where he'll take you when you're grown?"

"When you've proved your manhood?"

"When you've proved your discretion?"

"I don't know. I don't know!" Arundel says heatedly. "I can't think with all your babbling."

There is again a wonderful moment of silence.

"May I have another drink?" Arundel asks.

"You've earned it."

"Yes, I have, haven't I," Arundel mutters to himself. "Thanks ever so."

"Don't mind if I do." Jay One gets up and pours himself a stiff one, ignoring a quaking Arundel.

"Nor I." Jay Two mimics Jay One's movements exactly.

"Ah, Lagavulin," Jay One says, smacking his lips. "Hits the spot. *Manhood,*" he repeats.

"That it does," says Jay Two. "Although I prefer the Balvenie. *Discretion.*"

"A most *private* club."

"Only the lucky few are *members.*"

"Been in the families for yonks."

"Centuries, honestly."

"Edward the Seventh was a member, you know."

"A man of prodigious appetites."

"Not that son of his, though. A bit stodgy."

"Bloody horse."

"Fell on him in the Great War."

"Squashed his—"

"Well, *you* know."

"Dreadful accident."

"Every schoolboy knows that," Arundel says, exasperated again.

"Good old Georgie."

"Not his son, though."

"That Edward." Jay One shudders. "Peculiar tastes. No control, that one."

"With that dreadful Simpson woman." Jay Two shudders, too.

"Shameless."

"The only member to have been blackballed."

"In hundreds of years."

"Disgraceful."

"Shouldn't have told you that."

"Momentary lapse."

"Mustn't happen again." Jay One shakes his head.

"Never." Now Jay Two shakes his head.

"Know we can trust you."

"Can't we?"

"Of course we can."

"Strictly top drawer, one and all."

"All for one."

"And then some."

"Can't bribe your way in," Jay One says confidentially.

"Not for love or money," Jay Two says, equally confidentially.

"Certainly not for love."

"Here's the rub. Someone's about to snitch."

"Why we're here, old bean."

"But why are you telling me this?" Arundel asks. "Why don't you go to my father? He's the one who's meant to be worrying! I've not the foggiest idea what you're on about. My father's never told me about his clubs. I simply don't understand."

"He hasn't taken you yet," Jay One asks carefully.

"Hmmm," Jay Two says. "Not taken his only son."

"Very worrying."

"I should say so."

"Not even a clue?"

"Or a whiff?"

"No, nothing. I swear it," Arundel says. "I've been at school, and I rarely see my father. Only at holidays, really. He's terribly busy."

"No time alone with his nearest." Jay One shakes his head sadly.

"And dearest." Jay Two bobs his head as well.

"No place where he can be careful."

"Not overheard."

"Makes sense to me."

"Righty-oh, mate."

"I still don't understand why you haven't gone to him, if he needs to be warned about whatever it is you say he needs to be warned about," Arundel cries.

"Too dangerous," Jay One explains.

"Being followed," Jay Two says.

"That sort of thing."

"Could give it all away."

"You're in the safe house, old bean." Jay One winks.

"Bit of the lingo," Jay Two offers.

"Know we can trust you."

"So what am I supposed to do, then?" Arundel asks flatly.

"Tell your father you need to see him," Jay One suggests.

"Simple enough," Jay Two agrees.

"An emergency."

"An emergency about a girl."

"A girl in trouble, that always works."

"Like a charm."

"Tell him you need to see him."

"Most urgently."

"Tell him you will meet him in town."

"That he should stay for the weekend."

"But it's more private in the country," Arundel protests.

"Can't risk your mother, old bean."

"Nice and quiet here."

"So obvious no one'll think of it."

"Ever so 'Purloined Letter.' "

"Hide in plain sight."

"But what about the staff?" Arundel asks.

The two Jays cast their gaze slowly around the room. "Don't see them here, do you?" Jay One asks.

"All tucked in, nice and warm," Jay Two says with a smug smile.

"You haven't harmed them, have you?" Arundel looks quite alarmed. "If you have, I'll—"

"What do you take us for?" Jay One interrupts.

"Strictly professional, we are," Jay Two adds stoutly.

"Go see for yourself."

"Snoring away."

"Nothing to worry about."

"Nothing at all."

"If you ring your father and do as we say."

"Simple enough. A problem with a girl."

"Tell him it's urgent."

"When he's here, you give him this," Jay Two says. He pulls out a thick vellum envelope addressed to Sir Benedict Gibson in a thick slanting hand, sealed with a fat blob of crimson wax the color of a Belladonna cocktail. It is Sir Patty's seal, pinched from his desk during the cleaning after his untimely demise. "It explains all."

"Nothing to worry about."

"Nip it in the bud."

"Don't want a scandal, you see."

"Too messy."

"*Terribly* messy."

"Bad for business."

"Bad for the family."

"He'll be grateful, mark my word."

"But he *should* tell you about it," Jay One says.

"Time you were a member," Jay Two adds.

"Especially after this."

"Saving the family honor."

They smile broadly, pick up their bowler hats, and prepare to leave.

"That's it?" Arundel looks at them, aghast. "You barge in here uninvited, tell me this fantastic story about some private club and my father, and then get up to leave? What am I supposed to do?"

"You are supposed to do as I say, old bean," Jay One replies. His voice has shifted suddenly, and it is no longer light and breezy. Arundel's face blanches.

"We're not messing about," Jay Two adds. "This is serious business. Not for children. We suggest you do as we say, and let your father handle the consequences. Or wait for the consequences to handle you."

"But what if something goes wrong?" Arundel asks. He is crumpling, poor chap. The shock of having to make an important decision for once in his pampered young life is quite terrifying. Painful, even.

"What can go wrong?" Jay One's face softens very slightly in the shadows. "Here's what, though. Should there be a catastrophe, you might ring us at this number." He hands Arundel a tiny slip of paper. "Ask for Mr. Jay. If and only if there is a catastrophe. Have I made myself clear?"

"Memorize the number, then destroy it," Jay Two hastens to add.

"We don't take kindly to prying little boys."

"Not kindly at all."

"We know who you are."

"We know where you live."

Jay One pats Arundel on the shoulder, and he can't keep himself from shuddering at the touch. "Don't you worry. You're a good son. I'm proud of you, old bean."

"I'd be proud to call you my son," Jay Two beams.

"Righty-oh."

"Mum's the word."

"Sleep tight."

"Nighty-night."

With that, they saunter out, the heavy door closing slowly behind them. Arundel dashes to the window to watch them leave. There is no one to be found, not a shadow or a breath of wind in Eaton Square. He rubs his eyes to be sure, then looks around the room. They've even managed to pocket their scotch glasses. Not a trace of the fantastic Jaybirds remains.

Arundel falls back in a chair and closes his eyes. He's dreaming it all, that's it. He drank too much champers with his chums and then stupidly downed a martini, pretending to be grown-up and sophisticated, and he had a bizarre hallucination. Now he's woken up and can go to bed and forget all about it. Until his eyes fall on the large vellum envelope addressed to his father, still clenched tightly in his hand. Sealed with a thick blotch of scarlet wax.

When Sir Benedict Gibson MP sees the wax seal, his heart will skip a beat and the bile will rise to choke him. It is as if Sir Patty's hand has risen from the grave to drag him straight down into hell.

Oh ho, he wasn't dreaming at all.

There are only eight left, we found out courtesy of Sir Benedict Gibson's panicked messages to the other members, calling for an emergency meeting of the elder statesmen of the Club. Only the inner sanctum, unfortunately, not the junior members. Henley, Morton, Thompson, and Tucker have died. And Wilkes, of course—the dearly departed Sir Patterson Cresswell.

Rest in perpetual torment, you bastards. Consider yourself

lucky that you croaked before we had a chance to give you a fond farewell.

So far so good. We know where they'll be meeting. We'll be waiting for them.

Our scheme is perfectly elegant in its simplicity, if I do say so. Belladonna thought it up, of course, and relayed her meticulous plans to the Pritch. We'll have infiltrated the house where they're meeting, and we'll add some lovely tranquilizers to the drinks served by our solicitous staff, which will quickly help relax all the members into a pleasant stupor. Add to this cocktail a vaguely threatening demeanor, skill in weaponry, and a certain finesse in skullduggery, and you can pretty much arrange interrogations and other such diversions at your leisure.

First, before these men have woken from their stupor, we will be rifling through wallets and pockets, photographing and record-ing all necessary documents as our waiters had once done with Sir Patty in the Club Belladonna. We'll have the real names of the cowards, no longer able to hide behind the privacy of masks and the privilege of rank.

Next, we will arrange them carefully for a lovely portrait session. Photographs are so important for posterity! Or shall I say a *series* of photographs. In the first one, all the members of the Club will be seated in one cramped row, clad in their habitual garb—the hooded monks' robes and the masks and the gloves.

Smile for the camera.

Casual viewers, concentrating on the bizarre getup of this charming group, won't be able to see that, underneath their robes, these men have been rather uncomfortably *affixed* to their chairs. Casual viewers will most likely be wondering what exactly is going on, especially when they see the caption at the bottom of the pho-tograph: THE MEMBERS OF THE CLUB.

In the second photograph, only the face of the first monk on the left will be exposed. He'll look a little bit dazed and out of focus, but his features will be clearly recognizable. At the bottom will be the same caption: THE MEMBERS OF THE CLUB.

I want to add some words at the top: WHO ARE YOU? WHY ARE YOU HERE? But in this I am overruled by the Pritch. "Gives too much away, especially if His Lordship were to see them," he tells me. "Besides, how do we know His Lordship's pet phrases would

make any sense to the other members of the Club?" I am forced
to concede. Sometimes even yours truly must bow to the superior
judgment of professionals.

I'm sure you've figured out Belladonna's spectacular little
scheme by now. One by one, each photograph in this special edi-
tion will be released, until each dazed face is unmasked.

Who are you? Why are you here?

One by one, these photographs will be unleashed upon the public. Thousands and thousands of pictures of strange dark monks
sitting in a row, printed on flimsy white paper in smudging black
ink, will suddenly flood the blessed green isle that once sheltered
their sacred clubhouse. The photos will be found everywhere: fluttering like mad butterflies in the tube stations, plastered at crazy
angles onto billboards and scaffolding, shoved under windshield
wipers, taped securely to lampposts in the dead of night. They'll be
delivered in the morning post to select, socially prominent blabber-
mouths. They'll mysteriously appear on the desks of members of
Parliament, in the backseats of taxis, all over London's newsrooms.
Eager-beaver reporters will be begging to chase down the particulars of this most outrageous and unprecedented situation.

Why, several of the photos will even be slipped under doors in
Buckingham Palace.

How shocking!

All London will be agog, because every morning a new photograph will appear, until all of the members are unmasked. The buzz
will be even more deafening than the gossip that once surrounded
the secretive opening of the Club Belladonna. Who are they, these
members of the Club? What exactly *is* the Club? Is it for drunks,
or the very rich? Is it fun? Is it wicked? Is it shameless?

What must I do to join?

All this Pritch calmly explains to the members themselves several hours later. They are fully awake and still uncomfortably immobilized in their chairs, lined up in a neat row. There is a bright
light shining in their eyes and they squint in pain. Their heads are
throbbing, their mouths are dry, and their feet are numb. They are,
in fact, speechless. That's because we've gagged them with rough
rags. Not the kind of fine linen to which they are accustomed.

We prefer a silent audience at the moment. Besides, that's what they did to her. I imagine they are finding a taste of their own medicine distinctly unpalatable.

"Well, gentlemen," the Pritch is saying. He is clad as they are, in a monk's robe and a black mask. They have no idea who he is, but they know he's not one of them. His accent gives it away, for one thing. So do his ungloved hands and ringless fingers, and his quick movements. "We're ever so pleased you have come to be here with us tonight. All of you: Dashwood, Duffield, Francis, Lloyd, Norris, Stapleton, Whitehead. I have something, or rather, some *things* of an extraordinary nature to show you. I hope you will be as pleased with them as I am."

He goes over to a desk and picks up one of the newly printed photographs, then returns and shows it to them. It is the delightful group shot. Pritch silently displays it, pausing before each man and holding it up, putting it close enough to their eyes so they can figure out what it is even if they don't have their reading glasses. The sound of his footsteps echoes loudly in the room. There is no other sound. They could just as easily have died and woken up in a very hot and unpleasant place.

They are starting to get very nervous. The tension is, in fact, palpable, rising off them in churning waves. They can't make a noise and they can't move. They can't look at one another and ask for advice. This situation is most, well, most *unseemly*. They can do nothing but silently panic as the Pritch walks back to the desk, then picks up seven other photographs. One by one, he shows each member his mug shot, then the other six.

I should complain about the quality if I were a member. These snaps are not particularly flattering.

"Well, gentlemen," the Pritch says again. "I shall permit myself to make a rather broad assumption regarding your heretofore unassailably spotless record." He doesn't see any need to mention Sir Patty's small indiscretion. "If I were you, I should be wondering right about now if my beloved Club were to continue with its heretofore unassailably punctual triannual meetings. I should be wondering if this were indeed the end of hundreds of years of tradition. In fact, I should be wondering if I were going to be leaving this house alive."

He lets that last pithy bit of sentiment hang in the air like a kiss under mistletoe.

"Should you choose to cooperate with us, gentlemen, you have my word that you will be permitted to leave this house alive and well, in the same condition in which you entered it. Should you *wish* to leave, this will present itself as another matter altogether. Allow me to refresh your memory of the photographs you have just seen, the first of which will be released to the public tomorrow morning." He smiles happily, his lips curving below his mask.

"Now, we shall be engaging in a *private* chat with each of you, and I hope you will do me the great honor of cooperating. Indeed, should you cooperate, the interview process will be as *painless* and as *rapid* as possible. Should you not . . ." He shrugs. His smile deepens.

The lights go out suddenly in the room, and we take the added precaution of slipping hoods on over their heads. A tasteful little touch, don't you think?

We let them sit and stew for a nice long while, just to deepen their anxiety. Then the first of them is gently hoisted up and carried rather unceremoniously into a small room down the hall, where we're waiting for him, the tape recorder running. We fix him to another chair, take the hood off, then his gag. He blinks, then shudders. Standing before him are several clones of himself, monks who are not smiling. Unlike the Pritch, who is standing in their midst.

"Who are you?" the man says, trying to bluff and bluster. "What do you want?"

"We know who you are, Duffield. *Duffield,*" Pritch repeats. "Has a slightly different ring than Sir Horace Halliwell, doesn't it?"

"You won't get away with it," he says.

"Get away with what, dear Duffield? Or do you prefer Sir Horace? Which is the preference of your lovely wife, Lucinda? Your devoted children, Amanda and Christopher—do they call you Duffield or dear old dad? Your colleagues, I do believe, refer to you as QC. You, a Queen's Counsel, my word. A longtime member of the Club. My word, indeed. There once was a problem with a Duffield, wasn't there? In 1787. Was he related? Or were you the lucky inheritor of his name?"

Sir Horace says nothing. He is terrified into speechlessness.

"The punishment for unmasking is excommunication forever.

A fate worse than death," Pritch goes on smoothly. He's listened
to Jack's tape of Sir Patty so often he could recite it in his sleep.
"Is it not?"

Sir Horace nods slowly.

"Yet we have taken this pleasurable task upon ourselves,"
Pritch continues, waving a hand at the henchmen behind him.
"Therefore the rules no longer apply. The Club is finished. Finished forever. Such a shame, really, all those lovely secret assembl-
ies ending in such an unceremonious manner. All those charming
women. The thrill of the contact, the coded messages, the clandes-
tine meetings. And the bidding. Ah, the *bidding*. Silenced forever.
Undone by men masked as yourselves. Unknown. *Unknowable*."

He is standing so close to Sir Horace that he can see the pulse
ticking madly in his prisoner's neck.

"Are you prepared to die?"

Silence.

"Are you?" He gives the signal, and two of his henchmen move
suddenly closer to Sir Horace, who screams in unrelenting pain.

Too bad the walls of this house are so thick that the other members cannot hear his agony.

"We don't want you to die," Pritch says, calmly sipping from a
mug of tea. "At least not yet. Not until you've been exposed, and
told us what we want."

"Why me?" Sir Horace whispers when he stops moaning.

"It's always 'Why me?' with the likes of you, isn't it?" The
Pritch's voice is harsh with anger. "As if you're *blameless*. As if
we've singled out you and all the others for no reason whatsoever.
You fool. It's *over*. Do you understand? The Club is done with. But
we're not done with you. No, my dear sir, not with the likes of you.
You won't be able to escape us, the way the women you auctioned
weren't able to escape *you*."

"What do you want?" Sir Horace says.

"Louder," Pritch replies. "I can't hear you."

"What do you want?" he repeats, his voice rising in sheer panic.
"What do you want?"

"The eighth man," Pritch replies. "There are only seven of you
here. As for Henley, Morton, Thompson, and Tucker, well, we
know they have gone to the auctioneer waiting for them in hell.
And Wilkes, of course. I *do* beg your pardon. I meant to say Sir

Patterson Cresswell. Where is the eighth? *Bates.* Where is Bates? Is he dead?"

He's bluffing. What a pro is our Pritch. We don't yet know which one of them is His Lordship. We won't know until the tape recordings of all of them being interrogated are taken back to Belladonna by one of the Pritch's henchmen. She's waiting for them, with me and Matteo.

Waiting to hear the sound of that voice.

It's just a feeling the Pritch has all of a sudden, that His Lordship is the eighth man. The one who isn't here. The one called Bates. Catching him like this would have been too easy, even after all our careful preparations. He's too wily. He's probably been expecting an unmasking ever since her escape nearly nine years before.

"I don't know," Sir Horace says. He looks even more terrified at the sound of *Bates* than he has since we've started on him. "I don't know."

"Yes you do," Pritch says. "Either you tell us or you are going to live the rest of your days in excruciating pain and humiliation."

When Sir Horace is done screaming, Pritch asks him again.

"I can't tell you," Sir Horace says after what seems like an interminable time.

"Why not? Why are you protecting him?"

Pritch feels a thrill of nervous excitement run down his spine. He knows. He knows for certain that Bates is our man. Bates must have something, done something to blackmail them into silence. What? Pritch asks himself wildly. What could he have done to buy their silence?

Film, that's it. The particular and precise arrangements in a little room I vaguely alluded to once upon a time. His Lordship must have filmed them when he arranged their time with her. No wonder he had been so very pleased with his chaise and that sliding little panel in the wall, all those sessions with all those men when she was chained to the wall and his voice was filling her ear, telling her what to do to them. All the members of the Club.

Botheration. The Pritch needs time to regroup. He hands Sir Horace over to one of his colleagues, knowing he's gotten as much as he can out of this one. The story will be the same from every one of them, unless they tell us where Bates is.

Besides, you don't need me to tell you the particulars of our encounters with every member of the Club, do you? That would make you as sadistic as they are.

No, they'd rather risk public exposure from a group shot in a grainy photograph than the wrath of Bates and the more damaging photographs he possesses.

Well, we shall see about that.

The hired hands get to work. It is going to be a long night, printing up thousands of copies of the first photograph, paying off hundreds of people to distribute them.

Money, as I've said, is wasted on the rich. It works wonders on the poor when you've got a job to do.

I'm sure you remember the furor when the photographs began fluttering. Even the American newspapers report on the mysterious snapshots appearing all over England. Who are they, these members of the Club? Who has gone to such trouble of perpetrating such an elaborate charade?

Why, figuring out what might be going on is much more fun than a night in the Club Belladonna ever was. Unless, of course, you're one of the seven monks, gazing with such odd expressions at the camera.

Who are they? Why are they here?

All England is abuzz. Except for us. We're waiting.

After the thrilling spectacle of seeing five of the seven monks unmasked, the telephone rings in Pritch's office. "Speak to me," says one of his assistants, who answers the call.

"Is Mr. Jay there?"

"Who shall I say is ringing?" the assistant says.

"Arundel Gibson."

What have we here? If it isn't the honorable son himself. How delightful. Find their weak spot, Leandro taught us. Find the weak spot and reel them in.

"Hold the line." The assistant hurries over to Pritch and tells him who it is. Pritch's eyes light up like the diamond-studded heels of Belladonna, glittering with brilliant flashes as she walked from table to table in her club, waving her fan with assured languor.

"Mr. Gibson," the Pritch says, lowering his voice slightly. "I take it this is a catastrophe."

"Yes. God help me, yes, it is," Arundel says, sounding quite strung out. So on edge that he doesn't realize he's not speaking to one of the Jaybirds. "I need to see you right away. It's most urgent."

"I see," Pritch replies. "And how do we know you're to be trusted?"

"Bloody hell, man, I'm ringing you from a call box," he cries. "I *must* see you. No one knows I'm ringing. Certainly not my father. Even now. He'd have my head if he found out."

Or his inheritance.

"Hold the line," Pritch says. He puts the receiver down and lets Arundel stew for a moment. Then he picks it up again. "Meet us tonight at the Grey Fox. It's a pub in Aldgate East, on Old Montague Street. Eight o'clock sharp. Be on your own, or the meeting's off."

"Aldgate East—are you mad?" Arundel says. He can't help himself. This slum section of the East End is not quite the posh world of Eaton Square.

"Eight o'clock, old bean," Pritch says, and hangs up. Then he calls the Jaybirds and briefs them on what to do.

When Arundel shows up, flustered and nervous at eight o'clock on the dot, Jay One and Jay Two are already seated in a dark corner, their backs to the wall, nursing their scotches. In fact, a rapidly emptying bottle of Glenmorangie is on the table, along with a battered tin bucket of ice and a glass for their guest.

"Have a nip, old bean," says Jay One as Arundel sits down beside him, looking around anxiously and pushing his hair back off his forehead in the nervous gesture they remember. The lone table near theirs has already been claimed by a disheveled drunk, nursing pint after pint of Guinness. None other than Pritch, of course.

"Looking a tad peaky," says Jay Two, pouring him a drink.

"Shouldn't wonder," Jay One says.

"Bit of a strain."

"Rather overexposed."

"Terrible shot. Terrible."

Arundel buries his head in his hands, then gulps down his scotch.

"All alone, old bean?" Jay One asks.

"Of course I'm all alone. Who'd be bloody daft enough to follow me to this godforsaken hellhole?"

"Not quite what I meant," Jay One says softly.

"Knew we could count on you, though," Jay Two adds.

"Had you followed, just in case."

"Can't be too careful."

"Oh, you two could rouse the dead. If only for the pleasure of shutting you up," Arundel says in frustration.

"I say," Jay One sounds huffy.

So does Jay Two. "My word," he says.

They fall silent for a minute. Then Arundel blows his nose and sighs.

"A catastrophe," Jay One prompts.

"Urgent catastrophe," Jay Two says.

"We're waiting."

"Take your time."

"Bit of a mess," Jay One says confidentially.

"Not your fault."

"But it is my fault!" Arundel cries, then covers his mouth with his hand at his outburst. "I gave my father the letter, and look what happened!"

Oh ho, the passion of youth. He really is a sweet boy, after all. Much too sweet to have been inducted into the Club. They only wanted the nasty ones. Those bound by depravity to be enticed into bidding.

"Steady on," Jay One says sternly.

"Bit presumptuous," Jay Two says. "Not your fault at all."

"Listen, old bean," Jay One goes on, "and listen carefully. You are not to blame. We chose you because you are solely *without* blame. Because we knew we could trust you; that you are honest and forthright and, I daresay, still rather imbued with a sense of honor where the family name is concerned. If we hadn't chosen you, some other less praiseworthy messenger would have been sent in your stead. Do you believe me? Do you?"

He says this so earnestly that Arundel nods as his eyes fill with tears. Jay One had never before said so much in one breath.

"The fault lies with the members of the Club," Jay Two adds. "They and they alone are to blame."

"But what did they do that was so awful?" Arundel asks.

"What did they do?"

"What did they *not* do?"

"Trickery, old bean."

"Trickery and deception."

"But half the people I know are involved in some sort of trickery and deception," Arundel says.

Jay Two shudders. "Not what I'd call friends," he says.

"I didn't say they were friends," Arundel protests.

"Where'd they learn these tricks? I wonder," Jay Two goes on, ignoring him.

"Dear daddy, perhaps?" Jay One offers.

"At daddy's knee."

"Bent over daddy's knee is more like it."

"Surrogate daddy."

"Headmaster, you mean."

"And his switch."

"Paddle. Strap. Belt."

"Or school chums."

"Even Nanny."

Jay Two looks aghast. "Surely not the nanny?"

"Afraid so," Jay One replies.

"What *are* you going on about?" Arundel cries in frustration.

"What made them, of course," Jay One explains.

"Molded them," Jay Two adds.

"Warped them."

"Warped *whom?*" Arundel asks.

"The members of the Club, of course."

"Why they're so wicked."

"Why they must be stopped."

"But what did these members of the Club do besides trickery?" Arundel asks, clearly exasperated.

The Jaybirds look at each other, then at Arundel. The sick feeling in his stomach worsens into a painful, burning ache. His very own father is one of these perverted creatures the Jaybirds are going on about. His father is one of the monks, about to be unmasked for everyone in the world to see. His father knows all about whatever else the Jaybirds are going to tell him. His very own father.

"Can we trust you?" Jay One asks.

"Trust you implicitly?" Jay Two asks.

"Haven't told this to a soul, you know."

"Certainly not to one of the *children.*"

"I'm not a child," Arundel protests. "And you have my word. My word of honor."

The Jaybirds look at each other.

"I swear it," Arundel says fiercely. "I swear by the honor of my sister."

"They tricked women, old bean," Jay One says softly. His voice is kinder than Arundel has ever heard it. "Not even women, really. Young, innocent girls. Not much older than you are now."

"You mean they seduced these girls?" Arundel asks.

"No," Jay Two replies. "They didn't seduce them at all."

They fall quiet, and for the first time since their first unfortunate meeting, Arundel is desperate to hear them speak.

"But what exactly did they do?" he asks.

"They auctioned them," Jay One says.

"They tricked them, and they drugged them, and they auctioned them to the highest bidder," Jay Two adds.

"One thousand pounds per week."

"Once they'd bought her, they did anything they liked with her."

"They met every three years. In different houses."

"Have been meeting for hundreds of years."

"Tradition, you know. Coded messages."

"Secrecy was half the fun."

"Not as much fun as bidding."

They fall silent again. Arundel's skin has turned the frosty gray color of a winter sky just before a storm. He is willing himself not to be sick.

"My own father is one of them," Arundel says, his voice choking. "My own father did such a thing."

"Afraid so, old bean," Jay One says.

"Does my mother know about this?" Arundel asks.

"Surely not."

"Why ever would he do such a terrible thing?" Arundel asks. He is nearly in tears. "How could he want to do it? Did he ever buy—"

"Don't know," Jay One says. "Why would any man?"

"Power," Jay Two says.

"Power, and mastery."

"Wickedness."

"Am I going to become like my father?" Arundel cries.

"Not a chance, old bean."

"Not a whiff."

"How do you know?" Arundel asks.

"You're here, aren't you? Said it was a catastrophe," Jay One says.

"Haven't told us why yet, exactly," Jay Two adds.

"Because I know my father's in that photograph," Arundel says. They know which photograph he means. "And I want to know what I can do to stop it before he's exposed like all the rest of them. He hasn't been himself since the photos started to appear. He's been ill, and at home, you see, and my mother's frantic with worry. I don't want anything to happen to my mother, or my sister."

"Or yourself," Jay One says calmly.

"Rather ruin your reputation," Jay Two says, equally calm.

"What kind of person do you think I am? How dare you?" Arundel says in disbelief. "I'm not here on behalf of myself. Oh, I don't know *what* I'm doing. I think I'm going mad, that's what, and there's no one else to talk to. I know my father's done something. He's had many more visitors than usual, and—"

"We know, old bean," Jay One interrupts.

"Can't be too careful," Jay Two says.

"For your own protection."

"Oh God, help me," Arundel says, slumping and burying his head in his hands once more.

"No one helped the girls."

"No one at all."

"You can help them."

"You alone."

"What do you mean?" Arundel asks, sitting back up.

"Once they're all exposed, the Club will be finished," Jay One explains.

"Long overdue," Jay Two says.

"But there's one in particular."

"You mean my father?" Arundel asks.

"No. Not your father," Jay Two says.

Arundel sighs deeply and finishes his drink.

"The worst of all of them," Jay One says.

"By far the worst."

"Will you help us find him?"

"Will you?"

Arundel wipes his eyes. His mouth is set in a grim line. He looks an awful lot like Guy at this moment, as if he'd aged instantly from a self-absorbed young buck into a grown man facing the harsh realities of the world.

Welcome to the Club!

"I'll help you on one condition," Arundel says.

The Jaybirds pour themselves a drink and sit, impassive. They can wait.

Arundel takes a deep breath. "That you keep my father's face out of it," he says. "That, should he give me the information you need, you stop releasing the photographs. Or any that have his face exposed. It's not for my sake. Or for his, the *bastard*. It's for my mother and my sister. I don't care what happens to me anymore," he says.

"Or to your father," Jay One says.

"No. Not to my father," Arundel replies, his face paling further.

"You're a good man," Jay One says soberly. "I'd be proud to call you my own son."

"I'm my father's son," Arundel says bitterly.

"And your mother's," Jay Two adds.

"That is of no comfort to me now," Arundel says. His voice is weary. "Tell me what I'm supposed to do."

"Tell him Bates. Bates in 1935."

"Where Bates is."

"Bates will never know how we found him."

"We cover our tracks."

"Yes, you do, don't you?" Arundel murmurs to himself.

"The photographs will stop."

"The Club will be forgotten."

"If he can bring himself to tell his only son."

"Where Bates is."

"Otherwise, we offer no assurances."

"None indeed."

Again, they fall silent. An occasional laugh from the bar filters their way, but no voices are distinguishable.

"I've fallen down the rabbit hole, haven't I?" Arundel says eventually.

"The girls were pushed down the hole," Jay One says. His voice is again surprisingly tender. "And couldn't get out again."

"Would you like us to make a house call?" Jay Two asks. "Keep you out of it."

"Be a pleasure, old bean," Jay One adds.

"No thank you," Arundel says. He looks so forlorn and bewildered that I would have ventured to bestow one of my dazzlingly reassuring smiles upon him, had I been there, of course. My naturally sentimental disposition makes me turn to mush at times like this.

"You are a better man than he," Jay One says.

"That provides me with no comfort whatsoever," Arundel replies, then stands up to leave.

"Ring us whenever you're ready, old bean," Jay One says, handing him a tiny slip of paper with a new phone number. "We shall be waiting."

"You won't let us down," Jay Two says.

"You missed your calling, you know," Arundel says as he puts on his hat and buttons his coat. "You should have been performing in a music hall revue."

"Pulling our leg, are we?"

"Bit of a nipper, eh?"

Jay One stands up, then reaches over to clasp Arundel's hand. "You are a brave man, Arundel Cyril St. James Gibson," he says. "And I consider myself honored to have made your acquaintance."

"Likewise," says Jay Two, shaking his hand as well. "We won't let you down."

"Not now."

"Not ever."

Arundel squares his shoulders, then goes out to face the world, and his father.

We never do find out what exactly Arundel Cyril St. James Gibson said to his father. Or what his father said to the other members of the Club. All we know is that a few days later, Arundel calls the number we'd given him and says only this: Compton Bates. Marrakesh. Hasn't been seen in England since 1944, not in the flesh. But, somehow, he's kept in touch.

Oh ho, His Lordship's magic touch. His hot, dry fingers even hotter in the desert. Living the grand life in his own harem, no doubt, where women can disappear without a trace. Where secrecy can be bought for a lower price than willing flesh.

That's all we need to know.

One more time a member of the Club is unmasked, but then the photographs stop appearing as mysteriously as they'd begun. Who was the seventh monk? Everyone wants to know. Why did the Club exist? Who could have done such a thing? Who was responsible?

The six exposed Club members aren't talking. Their lives are over. Their reputations; their jobs, should they have them; their families; their exalted position and social standing in the world—all crushed and shattered, destroyed forever. Their future has been wiped out in as long as it takes for a flashbulb to explode. They deserve nothing less than utter ruin and humiliation.

Once we find them and grind them to bits, the members of the Club cease to exist. Their presence, so large and terrifying in memory, is now dwarfed by the reality of His Lordship. Frankly, we don't care about any of them anymore, no more than we care about June and her wretched family. They are discarded like popped balloons after a birthday party.

Our team is moving in for the kill. That's all that matters now.

The bribes are stupendous, but we pay them without question. The papers and fake passports are in perfect order. Compton Bates is a very sick man, you see. So sick that when we find him, he must be flown out of the country, strapped to a gurney, on private planes to his own cancer specialist in Washington, D.C. The planes have been chartered, the pilots on standby, their time bought. They're happy to wait by the pool of La Mamounia until the signal comes. First they'll be flying a fairly small plane to Lisbon, then transferring to a larger plane for the journey to Washington, D.C., then on to King Henry, Virginia, where they'll be landing on the private runway of a plantation.

We could have said their very important passenger was Nikita

Khrushchev himself and it wouldn't have mattered, not with all the baksheesh we've dispensed.

You don't want to know the particulars, do you? Not now. Not when we're so close.

Once we found him in Morocco, we kept watch. When we knew he'd been lulled into a sense of false security as six quiet weeks passed after the scandal of the monks, we snatched him. We drugged him heavily, and we blindfolded him, and we kept him in the dark.

Just like they'd done to her.

Then he was strapped to a gurney, trussed like a stuffed grouse, and flown off into the night sky, landing nearly a day later on our runway.

He is carried carefully out and then taken into the house. Down the steps, down down, past the wine bottles of the cellar and into the cell of the dungeon.

Perhaps, when he wakes, shackled to the rough brick walls, the dank, sour smell of the dungeons might strike a reminiscent chord. Then he'll know where he is.

Pritch removes the blindfold from His Lordship, motionless in his drugged sleep, and takes one last look. He comes back upstairs to the kitchen, where Belladonna, Matteo, who'd arrived late last night with Guy, and I wait. We asked Guy to sit outside Bryony's bedroom and make sure she doesn't awaken, and he grudgingly agreed. Bryony, who'd been missing him keenly, doesn't know he's here yet, and Belladonna won't acknowledge his presence. Ever since she'd gotten the tapes the Pritch had sent a few weeks before, she'd rarely left her room.

"It's a pleasure to see you again," the Pritch says to Belladonna. She doesn't seem to have aged a day, he tells himself in some wonder, wrapped as she is in that otherworldly aura. Only the faintest lines in her forehead and at the corners of her mouth show that she is harder and more brittle.

"Was my little boy there?" she asks. "Did you see a little boy in Morocco?"

He shakes his head no. "We've looked everywhere," he says. "Been watching *him* for weeks, mind you. Never saw him with a youngster. Not once. I'm keeping people on it, though. Just in case."

Belladonna sits down, shattered. "I know you've done your best, and I'll never be able to repay you. For everything," she says eventually.

We know it's him, you see. We have no doubts that it's His Lordship. Belladonna and I listened to the voices of the seven members of the Club on the tapes. I'd heard his voice infrequently, of course, but I'd never forget it. He wasn't heard on the tapes— but we have him now.

"Can't say it hasn't been interesting," Pritch replies. "Best job I ever had."

"What do you mean, *had?*" I ask.

"Must be off," he says calmly, looking at Belladonna. "I've done all I can, and now it's up to you. Only you know what to do."

"I understand," Belladonna says.

Botheration. Matteo and I exchange a concerned glance. I don't want to understand; I don't want to face His Lordship or Mr. Lincoln or whoever he is without the expert guidance of the Pritch. I don't want to think about the little boy. Please, Pritch, *please.* Don't go. You've been helping us for so long that—

"Guy will take my place," Pritch adds. "You need to let him help you. You must promise me that you'll let him help you. Now more than ever." He adjusts his fedora carefully on his head, pats his belly, and says good-bye. He insists on flying back to London tonight. I can't say I blame him.

I walk with Pritch to the plane, and he knows what I expect to hear.

"In my opinion," he says, "the boy is dead, or not to be found. I'll send a team to Belgium to explore the grounds, to be absolutely certain." We couldn't have risked it before, you see, in case our presence would somehow have sent a signal to alert His Lordship, and he would have known we were on to him. "It's going to take a while, I fear, if we don't know quite where to look, but once they know anything they'll be in touch."

"There's something Hogarth said about it just before he died. Something I can't recall exactly," I say. "I've been trying and trying to remember, but I was standing in the doorway and Hogarth was talking to Belladonna, not to me. It's no use asking *her,* because she's blanked the entire thing out."

"Stop thinking about it, and it will come to you," Pritch advises.

"Do you really think Tristan's dead?"

"Yes, I do. Wouldn't be retiring if I thought there was a hope in hell. If *he* had him or wanted him, the wee lad would've been in Morocco. My humble opinion, mind you."

"The very best opinion there is," I tell him. "I also want to inform you that a certain pub in Mayfair called the Witches' Brew has a new owner. The papers are waiting for you in your office. Keep you in Guinness till the end of your days, I hope. It's the least we can do. You certainly deserve a bottomless pint."

How I love the lady bountiful act! Even now, when our hearts are so heavy. Pritch thanks me, his voice nearly choking; then he's off. Who knows if our paths will ever cross again?

Belladonna is sitting in the kitchen when I come back, a mask on the table beside her. She's wrapped herself in a cloak to ward off the chill below, and her face is as gray as the leather of the gloves she's slipped on. She's staring off into some place awful I don't ever want to see. I sit beside her, and eventually Guy comes down with Matteo.

We're waiting for His Lordship to wake up.

Eventually, she stands and ties on the mask. Matteo and I get up, too, but she waves her hand impatiently at us, then walks down the stairs.

She wants to see him alone. She wants to be there when he wakes and realizes where he is and who is staring back at him in the dim light of the dungeon.

She is sitting there hours later when he stirs and tries to move. He realizes he can't, pulling on the chains, that he's trapped. His eyes focus and adjust to the dim light and he pulls on the chains again, trying to get up. A bright light floods the cell, and he turns his head away. Then he looks back at the light, his eyes adjusting, and her masked face floats into view on the other side of the bars.

He smiles at the sight. No mask could hide her from him.

"I've been waiting for you," he says.

She says nothing, just puts the lantern down near her feet.

After an hour or so more, we can stand it no longer, and all three of us walk gingerly down the stairs, down to the smell of fear itself. There is no sound but the echo of our footsteps and our ragged breathing. How could she have endured it? Guy asks himself. How could she not have been driven mad?

She is sitting on a small stool outside the cell, hunched and drawn, as she had been with Sir Patty. She is staring at His Lordship, as he is staring at her, that queer smile on his lips.

"Belladonna," I whisper, "let us see him."

She doesn't move or acknowledge our presence. I pick up the lantern so the light fills his cell. He squints, then recognizes me and Matteo. His smile deepens.

"Let me look at him," Guy whispers to me. He steps closer to the cell and looks inside.

His Lordship turns his head slightly and sees Guy. Then he starts to laugh. It is a laugh so horrible I quickly put the lantern down and instinctively place my hands over my ears to block out the hideous sound of it. The biting, strange cackle, bouncing back at us off the walls.

He won't stop laughing.

The light in the dungeon is so bad I can't really see Guy, but I swear his face is as white as it had been the first time he saw Bryony, when he turned pale under his tan.

I realize my knee is throbbing with pain. Belladonna abruptly stands up and walks out, past the wine bottles and up the stairs. We follow her quickly.

"You know who he is," Belladonna says to Guy once we're back in the blessed familiarity of the kitchen. Her voice is flat and expressionless.

"Yes, I know who he is," Guy replies. His voice is coming from a great distance, the same awful place she was staring at before.

"Tell me," she commands.

Guy looks at her and tries to smile. Then he tells her.

"He's my father."

20

The Unmasking Below

*T*hree little words: *He's my father.*

Three little words: *Who are you?*

"I thought your father was dead," she says in a monotone once we'd gotten over the initial blow. We're out on the veranda, where the night is alive with sounds and creakings and the natterings of animals on the prowl. I don't want to be in the house, knowing he's there below us. None of us do.

"I did, too," Guy mutters.

"Why did you assume he was dead?" I ask.

"I think I wanted so much to believe he was that I talked myself into it when he disappeared in 1944," Guy replies. "My brother John Francis thought at first he'd been a prisoner of war, because he'd gone to the Continent—I can't remember the exact year—and simply didn't come back. I couldn't believe he'd give up his world a minute sooner than he needed to. I don't know, though. I rather stay out of the way of John Francis."

"I looked him up in *Debrett's.* Your father, I mean," I say by way of explaining my ineptitude on this topic. Am I losing my touch? Was there some clue we'd all missed? After all this time, the miles and miles and miles of spies, to be undone by *Debrett's?*

After Hugh had mentioned the Earl of Ross and Cromarty, I remember going to the library, where I got down the fat red volume listing the lords and ladies of the realm and checked the entry. Four sons, it said, one deceased; one daughter, also deceased. That caught my eye, but the names were wrong. The eldest was Evelyn

J., followed by Clarence and Cholmondeley. William Dale and Julia were the two youngest, the deceased offspring. I remember shutting the book, pitying any boy named Cholmondeley, and thinking no more of it. "The names were all different."

"Yes, they would be," Guy says. His voice is nearly as stripped as Belladonna's, as if he were forcing himself to speak from an underwater cavern. "I'm sure my father insisted, just because he could. Only the first of the given names is listed, but we all had several names. That's what families like mine do."

"So John Francis is your elder brother's middle name, or something like that," I say.

Guy nods. "Evelyn John Francis, Clarence Frederick George, William Dale Arthur; those were my brothers' given names. Julia Claire Gwendolyn, my sister."

"You mean your name really is Cholmondeley?" I ask. If the situation weren't so devastating, I'd be rolling down the hills with laughter. He certainly doesn't look like a *Chumley*.

"Cholmondeley Horace Guy," he replies. "I've always preferred Guy, for obvious reasons."

"Where does Lindell come from?" I say.

"My great-grandmother on my mother's side. I didn't want a name that had anything to do with my father."

"I see."

We sit in silence for a while longer. I am trying to figure out the chronology in my head. His Lordship found us in Italy in 1943, and took us to Belgium. Belladonna was still trapped in the gloomy gray house where it rained—eastern Scotland, probably. We took our sweet time healing and renovating and dodging Moritz's stray bullets from target practice, and she was brought to us in the middle of 1946. Bryony and Tristan were born on February 10, 1947. Nearly ten years has passed since then.

What had His Lordship been doing when Belladonna was pregnant? Where had he been? Why did he never show up? What took him to Morocco? Was he planning to take her there? I wonder. Lose her in the desert where she'd never be found?

Botheration. All this feverish anticipation dissipates like fish food sprinkled in the aquarium in the dining room, while he sleeps way down below it. We have caged the monster, but it brings us no consolation. If anything, I am feeling a distinct letdown. Matteo turns to me briefly and I know he's thinking exactly the same thing.

Now that His Lordship's been found, we don't know what to do. Double botheration.

"I'm keeping him here," Belladonna says suddenly. "For as long as he kept me."

I am starting to get a very sick feeling. Not in my knee, but clenched around my heart. "What about Bryony?" I venture to say. "And everyone else? How can you keep a man like him locked in a dungeon in the house where you live for the next—"

"I'm going to tell her that I'm sick, with mono. First, we'll tell her that Matteo has come, and then Guy will arrive, to help me get better," she says, her voice flat. She doesn't look at any of us as she speaks, and I realize she's been plotting and planning this scenario for a very long time. "She'll become used to my unavailability, but she won't be unduly upset because Guy will keep her company. When school's over she can go to camp for most of the summer. Guy will tell her he has to go back to London for business, but he'll come back to see her on visitors' day. Then she won't mind so much." She is talking of months from now, of Guy as if he weren't there, staring at her blank features in dazed incredulity. "That's the way it's going to be. If any of you don't like it, or anything else I say or do, feel free to leave anytime."

She gets up and walks off without a backward glance. She hasn't said a word to Guy, whose eyes follow her until she is swallowed up by mist. Surely she must realize what he's—

Oh ho, she is *hard*. As hard and cruel and implacable as His Lordship. The living legacy of the members of the Club.

It is not quite dawn, but none of us is the least bit tired. I think back to Camp Minnetonka in verdant green Minnesota, when the Pritch first told us of June and her family. When we were sitting on Leandro's terrace, another lifetime ago. I can't bear it a second longer, so I hustle to the bar, pull a large bottle of bourbon and some glasses off the shelf, dump some ice in a bucket, then go back to the veranda and pick a few sprigs of mint from a pot near the window. I'm afraid that if I go to sleep, I'll hear the sound of his chains rattling my dreams.

"May I ask you a question?" Matteo says to Guy, and he nods. "Where did your family money come from?"

"In other words, how could my father afford the extravagant expenditure of one million pounds in 1935?" Guy asks bitterly. "Sugar cane in Haiti, opal mines in Australia, oil wells in Malaysia. Bribery, extortion, blackmail, I expect."

"Most men of his class didn't work, though, did they?" I say.

"No, working was beneath them—the gentry, that is," Guy replies. "My father was quite unusual that way. I don't know what drove him. I'll never understand what made him. I don't want to believe that any of this is true. If I can bear to think about it, I shouldn't wonder that I don't go quite mad." He takes a long swallow of his drink. "The only thing that keeps me sane is the knowledge that *she* survived it. Otherwise . . ."

"Why did your mother marry him?" I ask bluntly.

"I've no idea. I'm sure it was arranged, but my mother was gone long before I could have asked her the particulars," Guy says. "Her dowry provided much of the capital for my father's enterprises, I fear. She was only seventeen, and he was eighteen when they married. This was in 1911. John Francis was born a year later, then Frederick, and I was born in 1914. She never was meant to be pregnant after that. So many babies that quickly did her in. He never should have—" He buries his head in his hands. "I wish I'd never been born. It's been nothing but forty-two bloody useless years. And now this. I hope my father rots in hell."

Well, His Lordship is certainly about to find out what it's like to be left to rot.

"Perduto é tutto temp che in amor non si spende," I say, trying not to think about that for the moment. "All time not spent in loving is lost."

"Did Leandro teach you that?" Guy asks after a long pause, sighing deeply. "I wish I could have met him."

"I wish more than anything that he were here right now," I say fervently. "He'd know what to do."

"What I want to know," Guy says carefully, "is how you escaped from Belgium. You said you'd tell me, and I think this is the right time. You're both here, and I need to know."

I fill my glass and sip it slowly, conjuring the crumbling château in Belgium and the barbed wire hidden in the brambles tumbling down over the stone fencing. Here, in Virginia, we can breathe; there, it seemed we were encased in a forest so dense and silent it wanted to feed upon our very marrow. There we hid from the world and grieved for our shattered manhood. There *she* first appeared: Doula, Hogarth said her name was. A special companion to Mr. Lincoln. Keep out of her way, we were warned. Keep the doors locked. Or else.

Guy leans back and stares down at his hands, waiting for me to start talking. His slim, elegant fingers seem meant to caress a woman's flesh. His fingers so unlike his father's hot, dry touch. Those hands delighted in pain. Those hands meant to hurt.

Guy hasn't touched another woman since his romp in the hay.

There can be no other woman once you've fallen under the spell of Belladonna.

"We must escape. We must fly," I told Matteo one day in late October 1946 as we desultorily raked leaves off the garden paths. "We must save her. Do you know what's weird—I feel better just thinking about it. It's like it's given me something to focus on, a purpose. We are rotting away here; you know that. This is no way for the fearless Cennini twins to act."

"Once fearless," Matteo replied dully.

"We will conquer it," I said, scraping my rake on the gravel with an unpleasant rasp. "We survived, didn't we? We must be men again. We must think like men, like *them*. Be ruthless, like Mr. Lincoln and Hogarth and all the other ones. The members of the Club, she called them. Now we know what they're like, so we can outsmart them. We're smarter than they are. They think we're dumb and broken—but we're not. Are we?" I asked him hopefully.

Matteo looked doubtful, but from that moment on he seemed a bit more like his old self. We told her we were plotting, and her eyes widened in fear. "We're going to cross the borders, to Switzerland. I swear it," I whispered to her. "That's where the money is, in the Swiss Consolidated Bank Limited. After that, we'll hide out with the babies. Someplace where he'll never find us."

She looked shaky because she wasn't feeling very well, so we nagged at her to put her feet up and leave everything to us. I sounded much more confident than I felt. We needed clothes, transportation, passports, cash to pay for our journey to Switzerland. I assumed I could doctor the passports and identity papers once we pinched them from the three M's at least; my genius at forgery and counterfeiting a legacy of the Resistance. But the rest of it was the problem—a bit tricky when we didn't have timetables or a car or gasoline and we didn't even know the name of the village closest to this château. And there was no one we could turn to for help.

We needed a plan. To plan, and plot. Think, Tomasino, think. There's no time to waste. Maybe we could sneak off to the village and find someone there to help us. No, that wasn't possible. Wire cutters, maybe, so we could break free and clamber away under the cover of darkness. No, that wasn't enough, either. We needed more than wire cutters. We needed Markus and Moritz and Matilda out of the way.

Perhaps Hogarth was the key. Certainly he'd be here closer to her due date. His Lordship was nowhere to be found, and we were thankful for that. I didn't think she could take the feel of his horrible hot fingers right then; it might have shocked her into giving birth. No, Hogarth would never think we'd have the courage to challenge him.

For starters, we had to make nice to Matilda. Belladonna could do that without too much strain, because Matilda was showing markedly maternal tendencies. If the sight of this squat and taciturn peasant patting Belladonna's growing belly hadn't been so ludicrous, I might have laughed. Matilda was cooking nutritious soups and meals, and checking on the expectant mother so many times every day that I swore Belladonna was ready to scream. The mind boggled at the thought of Matilda sitting in the gatehouse at night, knitting booties and hemming diapers.

"But how are we going to get past the gatehouse?" I asked Matteo softly as we went for a walk one night. We'd already waved to Moritz, so he knew we were aware of him and he wouldn't have to shoot us. "It's the only way out."

"Slit their throats," Matteo said after an uncomfortable pause. "Like the war."

Yes, it still was like the war, and we were prisoners of the enemy.

"Except it might make a bit of a mess," I said, sounding a bit Hogarthesque. "Too much blood." I shuddered, and we kept on walking, our breath misting in the chill air as we pondered our few options.

Belladonna solved the dilemma for us the next day. Under the napkin on her tray, she slipped a slender tattered volume: *The Connoisseur's Guide to Poison*. "I found it in the library, hidden in another book," she whispered, her eyes huge and staring.

"How splendid. Now don't you worry about a thing," I whispered back. "You concentrate on making nice babies, and we'll take care of all the particulars."

The book was fascinating reading, and I hastened to the library to see if there was another book identifying which plants and mushrooms were what, so we could start poking around in the woods. A little oleander would be nice. One branch, a few leaves, was all we'd need. Or castor beans. They're terribly toxic. Except castor beans didn't grow around here. Potato sprouts—no, it was a bit late in the year for potatoes. Arsenic was foolproof, except I hadn't been able to find any here. Nor could I tell a toadstool from a truffle, so we'd have to skip the mushroom expedition. Besides, how could we feed the three M's mushrooms without them getting suspicious? I kept reading. There had to be something. Oh ho, autumn crocus. The entire plant is toxic; that'll do. Wait a minute—there's a section on botulism. *The Connoisseur's Guide* explained exactly how to grow the mold in little jars. Brilliant. We'd create our very own tasty toxic cocktail, and we'd hide it in the hollowed-out book where she found the guide. They wouldn't know what hit them. And then when the coast was clear, we'd gather their clothes and their money and their passports, which I'd tweak to suit our more pressing needs.

I refused to think of the further implications.

Quite soon after Belladonna's water broke, Hogarth showed up with the man he said was the doctor. I remembered this doctor from the examination when she'd first suspected her pregnancy. I didn't trust him any more than I did Matilda's maternal fussing, but I had to hope he was going to help Belladonna through the birth.

We had no choice but to trust him.

His Lordship was still nowhere to be found. His disappearance made me nervous, but he must have had his reasons for staying away. It was more than merely not wanting the birth to be disrupted by his presence. It was something else; I could feel it.

Once her labor started, it quickly became agonizing. I couldn't bear to hear her screaming so, for hour upon endless hour. "Can't you give her something for the pain?" I begged the doctor. He shook his head. He was very focused, which made me feel marginally better. Hogarth was pacing in the kitchen. The thought of all the mess was simply too much for him to bear.

Finally, a boy was born first, howling lustily. She called him Tristan. After Matteo and I quickly toweled him off, we couldn't help but notice Tristan's beautiful bright pink baby balls, whole and perfect. Of course I'd never seen any baby balls before, but his were disproportionately huge, it seemed to us. A violent wave of affection flowed from my fingers to the newborn's skin.

A baby girl slipped out with one final push from Belladonna, and we instantly fell in love with her, too, as we put her in Belladonna's arms, next to her brother. Belladonna could barely manage to kiss the tops of their heads before falling into a deep sleep of exhaustion. The doctor packed up his bags and Matilda swaddled the babies, clucking to them. She hadn't yet spoken to us, so I didn't expect to hear her crooning a lullaby anytime soon. We watched as she carefully put the babies in little cots lined with warm blankets, by the side of the bed, and then tiptoed out. Hogarth came in briefly to look at the babies, saw the rumpled, bloody sheets, and hurried out, practically green.

For the first time in a long time, Matteo and I felt nothing but pure happiness. We fussed over the babies; then we, too, fell into a deep sleep on the sofas near the piano.

I woke up first, and went, yawning, to check on the babies. Then I realized that Hogarth was sitting in the room, and my nerves tingled awake. He shouldn't have been there; something was wrong. I looked at my watch; late morning. The babies should have roused us by now, hungry for a feeding; that much I remembered from all the screaming infants who used to drive me crazy in Bensonhurst. I went to Bryony's cot first, where she was peacefully sleeping, then looked at Hogarth, frowning. "Matilda fed her from a bottle," Hogarth whispered.

This made me instantly cranky. Belladonna had insisted that she'd be breast-feeding—she was hoping that would make them let the babies stay close to her. I went to Tristan's cot, but he wasn't there. By then, all my nerves were jangling so loudly I was surprised Belladonna didn't wake from the sound of them. I shook Matteo's shoulders gently, and he quickly woke. The look on my face was enough to alert him that everything was not fine and dandy.

"Where's Tristan?" I asked Hogarth in a loud whisper, not wanting to rouse Belladonna.

"He's not well," he whispered back.

"What do you mean?" I said. I was ready to throttle him. He was lying; I knew it. Matteo came up beside me, and Hogarth actually stood up and backed out of the room. Oh ho, so we still could intimidate the enemy if we put our minds to it. This was reassuring. Or would have been, if I could have figured out what was going on. We couldn't do anything now. And we certainly couldn't try to escape with only one baby.

When Hogarth reached the safety of the door, where Moritz had suddenly materialized at his side, he turned back to us. "There's something dreadfully wrong with Tristan's chest," he said. "Matilda was worried about his breathing when she was feeding him. I certainly hope he'll be fine. The doctor's come back to take him to the village. Absolutely nothing to worry about."

How could we not be worried? "I don't believe you," I told him.

"I don't like your tone of voice, dear boy," he said, and strolled away.

This couldn't be happening. What was I going to tell Belladonna when she woke? They'd stolen her baby; I knew it.

When Belladonna stirred a while later and after we forced her to eat some soup, we handed her Bryony, who snuggled to the breast eagerly. She was so exhausted she fell back asleep with Bryony still nursing, so Matteo sat with them, keeping Bryony positioned perfectly. They almost resembled a happy family. Almost.

When Belladonna next woke, she was still too weak to get out of bed. "Where are my babies?" she asked sleepily. We brought her Bryony, who once again started to nurse like a dream. "Where's Tristan?"

I sat on the edge of the bed, and she saw the look on my face. "There's something the matter with his breathing," I said carefully, "and the doctor took him to the village for more care. He's going to be fine. Now you rest. Bryony needs you."

"No," she said, struggling to get up. "No no no—"

Bryony lost the breast and started to cry. Matteo tried to soothe

Belladonna, who was sobbing hysterically, and I ran off to the kitchen. Only Matilda was there; Hogarth was nowhere to be found.

"Where is her baby?" I screamed. "What have you done with him?" I was so angry that I was ready to pick up a butcher knife and stick it in Matilda's squat backside, when Markus came in. He shook his head, frowning, and I stopped screaming. There was no use. They looked as perplexed as we were. In fact, the newly maternal Matilda seemed positively sick with anxiety. Even though Matilda had been in His Lordship's employ ever since Belladonna could remember—was, in fact, the awful woman who'd laced her up so tightly the night of the auction that she couldn't breathe—she would never do anything to harm one of those babies.

Either Hogarth had stolen him away or he really was terribly sick.

All I knew was that her baby was never coming back.

"*I* want my baby," she whimpered like a wounded puppy. "I want my baby I want my baby my baby—"

She slipped into a desperate lethargy, weak and too unresponsive to breast-feed. Bryony was hardly fussy once we started her on bottle feedings. I didn't mind; it gave Matteo and me something to do.

Hogarth reappeared a week later and told me bluntly that Tristan was dead. That they kept him in the village for fear he was contagious, and still weren't sure what killed him. One of those dreadful things that could happen to newborns. They'll bring him back here to bury him, someday soon.

"Don't lie to me, Hogarth," I said wearily. How could a day-old baby catch a cough and be feared contagious? Why won't you let us see the body? I wanted to say this—I wanted to strangle Hogarth until the golden buttons of his bespoke waistcoat popped—but I didn't have the energy to fight. Besides, he needed to think we were weak and defeated.

But we weren't. We followed the instructions in our tattered guidebook. Jars filled with leftover food were tightly lidded and hidden in thick volumes of *Paradise Lost* and *Paradise Regained* in my room, sprouting a deadly mold. We'd snuck out in the night to dig up the crocus patch, then spent endless hours in the bathroom extracting the toxins.

Don't think I'd ever tell you how to do it.

Belladonna did not leave her bed. Without Bryony, I doubted she'd have kept going. Despite everything, Belladonna still had a mother's instinctive need to nurture her offspring. Bryony quickly settled down and was a remarkably good baby. She rarely cried, and slept well. She ate, pooped, napped, made faces, blew bubbles. She was altogether delicious, my little flower. It was as if she some-how already knew the circumstances surrounding her birth and was trying everything in her tiny power to ease her mother's situation.

Or perhaps I was just being ridiculous.

Hogarth left again, and we started getting ready to go, too. We rehearsed our every move. We didn't tell Belladonna, because she was too weak to care and would undoubtedly have protested that we couldn't go without Tristan. Matteo agreed with me, though. All that was keeping us here was waiting for her to regain a bit more strength. We had to fly before His Lordship returned from his prolonged absence. We had to.

We had no choice.

Sometimes we let Matilda hold and feed the baby, but only in Belladonna's room and under Matteo's careful supervision. We told Belladonna to ask Matilda for special things from the village, things that involved a longer trip, so we could get Markus out of the house. The day that Markus went on a shopping expedition for something big and bulky, so Moritz was obliged to go with him, was the day we'd been waiting for.

That day, I hurried into the kitchen at lunchtime to tell Matilda that Belladonna was desperate for her help with the baby, right that minute, and she almost smiled. She was only too glad to oblige. I offered to carry in the lunch on a tray, and she nodded.

I was surprised my hands weren't shaking when I put on my gloves. They still weren't shaking when I took the small glass vial out of my pocket and sprinkled a bit of poison in the sugar bowl and poured a bit of poison into the salt and pepper shakers. Then I spread a little on the bread of the sandwich Matilda had already made for herself. I spread a little more on the bottom of the loaf of bread Markus and Moritz would be eating for dinner. You are going to be a murderer, I told myself.

You are going to watch them die.

We'd already packed ourselves sandwiches and put them outside under a potted plant to stay cold and fresh. We weren't going to be eating anything that came out of this kitchen ever again.

I brought Belladonna her nutritious soup and Matilda her delicious ham sandwich on rye, heartily seasoned. Matteo and I watched her eat it. Botulism can take twelve to thirty-six hours to work, the guidebook said, but the crocus may speed things along.

By the time Markus and Moritz returned, Matilda was groaning upstairs in bed with a violent stomachache. She couldn't blame it on me, of course; no one touched the food but Matilda. Markus and Moritz banned us from the kitchen anyhow, and Markus told us he'd sleep in the house tonight, with Matilda, instead of in the gatehouse. Markus parked himself just outside Belladonna's door. Honestly, sometimes they could be so paranoid.

It wasn't easy to sleep. Matteo and I roused ourselves just before dawn, and the house was unnaturally silent. We trotted upstairs to find them. Markus had somehow managed to crawl up the stairs to the bedroom, where there was a terrible, indescribable stench, and we found him on the floor near Matilda's bed. Their mouths were open in agony and their eyes were staring, no doubt, at the fiery fires where they'd be burning for all eternity. We quickly covered them with sheets, and I would have said a prayer if I could have remembered any. Or if they had deserved one.

We took the keys from Markus's pockets and started emptying the drawers, looking for any useful papers and money and other things. Then Matteo hurried down to the gatehouse. He was going to gather everything else we needed, so that as soon as Belladonna woke up we could take off. We were going to prop her on a bicycle, Bryony snugly bound to her chest like a little native, and wheel her down to the village where we could hire someone with a car or a truck or some other vehicle that could get us to the nearest train station. Anything to get away, and quickly.

I was still upstairs, searching through drawers that were normally off-limits, when I heard a strange noise. No, the noise wasn't strange; it was just unexpected. A car. A car was driving up to the house. This was most unusual. No one ever came here, and Hogarth always parked down by the gatehouse. Who could it be? Not him. Not His Lordship.

Please oh please oh please, not him—

This couldn't be happening. Not now, not when we were so close.

I ducked down and peered out the window and saw Hogarth clambering out of the car and straightening his jacket and his few strands of hair with a frown. Hogarth must have found the gatehouse untended and opened the locks to the gates with his own set of keys, wondering what was going on. Matteo must have heard him and hid in a closet. Hogarth was by himself, thank goodness, and I pressed my hand on my chest to stop my heart from thumping. Focus, Tomasino, be calm. What was I going to tell him when he walked into the house and saw the bodies upstairs?

He wasn't going to be allowed to go upstairs. He wasn't going to do anything until he told us what really happened to Tristan.

Hogarth would come looking for her first, naturally, and he found Belladonna sitting by the fire, staring at the logs burning. She didn't move when she heard him. Bryony was sleeping peacefully in her cot.

"Hello, my darling," Hogarth said. "Where is everyone?"

She shrugged. "How should I know? Where's my baby?" She looked ghastly, her vivid green eyes dulled with pain.

Hogarth made a minute adjustment to the handkerchief in his pocket. Maroon-and-pine-green paisley, it was. Very subtle, very expensive.

"Your baby is dead, sadly," Hogarth said with only the slightest edge to his voice. "Your baby died and we buried him near the woods, on the other side of the carrot patch. Soon, we'll put up a gravestone and have a little service."

"You're lying."

"I wish I were, dearest," he replied. "Nothing would please His Lordship more than a son. But, alas, it was not to be."

That roused her from her stupor. "I should think he'd prefer only girls," she said bitterly.

"My dear, you astonish me," Hogarth said. "Now let me see the enchanting Bryony; then I must be off." He went over to the cot and watched Bryony for a few minutes, smiling a nasty little fussy Hogarth smile. I had tiptoed downstairs and was watching him from the doorway. Why would he have come only to peer in on

Bryony? Perhaps he had a message for the three M's. I was going to hate to have to be the one to tell him he was a little late for that.

He must be smoothing the path, I told myself. His Lordship was going to be here soon. I felt a dull thudding pain behind my kneecap. Perhaps he was on his way now, driving up to the house. What were we going to do? What—

I was thinking feverishly of all our options, waiting for Matteo to return from the gatehouse so we could overpower Hogarth and—

I saw a blur and heard a sickening, dull *thwack*. Hogarth made a mewing sound, then fell on his side. I heard another *thwack*, and another and another.

There was so much blood, seeping out of the cracks in his head. He was going to be very upset at the bloodstains on his collar and his handkerchief, I told myself, and then realized with a wild thrill that Hogarth was dead.

She dropped the poker and closed her eyes and wavered, and I caught her as she swooned into a dead faint. I carried her over to the bed just as Matteo ran in with Moritz's shotgun in his hands. He stopped short at the sight of Hogarth sprawled so unceremoniously on the carpet. Bryony was still fast asleep.

I didn't tell him that she did it. I told him that I did.

"Check his pockets, quick," I said. We were in luck. Another passport, a driver's license, a thick wad of money, and the keys to his car. This was too good to be true.

Except he was dead. They were all dead. And there was no one to tell us the truth about Tristan.

The beginning of our journey was fraught with nervousness.

We quickly packed some of Belladonna's clothes and the emerald necklace and Bryony's baby things and bottles of formula into small bags and suitcases, grabbed the suitcases Matteo and I had packed already, dug up the sandwiches we'd placed outside, and loaded everything into Hogarth's car. We gently carried Belladonna, who was still unconscious, and covered her with blankets on the backseat. I held Bryony in the front, and Matteo got behind the wheel. He drove like he'd been in a car just yesterday, speeding out the gate I quickly unlocked without a backward glance and into the village and down the road, till we found a larger village with a train station. Namur, it was called. There we stayed in a little hotel while I performed my magic on the passports. Belladonna woke up, and we told her we were going for a little trip, but she was still so deeply in shock that I didn't think she understood a word we said. She fell back into a deep sleep, and we debated which way might be safer, whether they checked your papers more closely in the train or at the border. We decided to risk the drive to France, because it wasn't that far. We didn't dare breathe until we were waved through customs by a bored guard. Besides, we still had the thick wad of Hogarth's money, and I could still smell a man in need of a bribe.

It was a scent you never forgot.

We drove on to the city of Nancy and booked ourselves into an innocuous hotel. We needed better passports, so I flexed my rusty muscles and pretended I was back picking pockets in Bensonhurst. It was easy once you got into the swing of it, like shifting gears in Hogarth's car. I followed unsuspecting tourists who looked vaguely like the three of us, and then helped myself.

I went off on my strolls while Matteo stayed with Belladonna and Bryony in the hotel, and I amazed myself with how quickly I readjusted to life on the outside. Despite everything, I was starting to have a good time, buying pastries and magazines and marveling at the clothes and the cars and the radio sets and the smell of cigarettes and yellow beer in the *tabac* on the corner. It was so much more pleasant to focus on innocent tourists than what we had left behind.

After two days we were ready to go, with all our papers in sparkling order. We decided to leave the car, and booked first-class passage on the train to Basel. It was much closer than Geneva. If His Lordship had arrived in Belgium—and we were living in terror that he had—he'd probably figure we'd be heading for Switzerland as quickly as possible.

Our train trip to Bern was mercifully painless. We checked in to a nice pension, recommended by our taxi driver. In the morning, we called the Swiss Consolidated Bank, Limited, and inquired about the status of account number 116-614. We were told the account holder must present him or herself in person, and we explained this to Belladonna, who didn't acknowledge us. This was the first time she'd been out in the world for nearly twelve years, but she did nothing but lie in bed in a daze.

I couldn't say I blamed her.

We couldn't afford to wait till she was better, so we sat her up and dressed her carefully, and we bundled Bryony up for the chill March air, and we took a taxi to the bank. Matteo stayed with Bryony in the vast outer lobby, and Belladonna and I were ushered into an office paneled in mahogany and presided over with somber solicitude by one gray-haired Monsieur Etienne de Saint-Soissons. We stated the account number and told him the first deposit had been placed in May of 1935. Monsieur Etienne nodded and disappeared to confer with someone else. Then he came back, sat down behind his desk, and slid a piece of paper over to us.

The account was now worth nearly 3 million pounds sterling—at least $12 million. A staggering sum in 1947. More than enough to buy our freedom, and then some.

Monsieur Etienne coughed discreetly and I braced myself for the punch line. Surely he must need some form of identification, and we had only bogus passports. Certainly nothing that said Isabella Ariel Nickerson.

Isabella Ariel Nickerson had been given up for dead a long time ago.

"You need identification," I said, trying to keep my voice calm. He nodded.

Belladonna, who appeared not to have heard a word he said, suddenly stretched out her left arm to the startled banker. Then she peeled off her glove and showed him the ring on her finger. The ring she could not remove. But if you looked at it very closely, you could see the slightest hint of something darker underneath. A tattoo.

Monsieur Etienne looked carefully at the ring and her finger, and then smiled.

"How may I be of service?" he said brightly.

The sky is a pale light blue and we have drunk all the bourbon in the bottle.

"I knew it wasn't you," Matteo says. "Hogarth, I mean."

"Thank you, *fratello mio*," I reply, but his words are scant consolation.

"Why did you go to Merano?" Guy asks. I thought he'd sound more shaky, but nothing we can say to him is going to lessen his love for Belladonna.

"We didn't want to go too far, because she wasn't up to another long journey," I say.

"We spoke Italian," Matteo adds.

"I overheard some tourists talking in a café, debating whether to go to the spa in Montecatini or Baden-Baden," I go on. "It made perfect sense to take the waters. We'd go to some out-of-the way spa in Italy where no one would think to look for us. I asked the night clerk at our pension about it, because I'd heard him speaking Italian with a northern accent I remembered from the war. He told me about several places, and that his cousin's wife's brother used to work at one in Merano. It wasn't too terribly far away; it was small and quiet and had lost its luster after the war. But he said the water was still good for the kidneys."

And whatever else ailed us.

"That's when you met Leandro," Guy says.

"Yes," Matteo says. "And he took us in."

"Whatever happened to the emerald necklace?" Guy asks.

"Ah," I reply, "that necklace." I look at Matteo. "I asked her about it just before we were to leave Bern for Merano. She asked to look at it, so I got it out from the sock I'd hidden it in, and she held it in her hands for a few minutes."

"The color of her skin was practically the same color as the emeralds," Matteo says softly. "Then she told us to get rid of it. She didn't want to think of it or see it ever again."

"I took it and went out," I continue, "with those beautiful bright stones sparkling in my fist. I wanted to throw them down the sewer, but I couldn't. I told myself something good should come of them, to undo the evil that had brought them to her. So I wandered around for a while, and found myself in a tiny little church. I don't know when the last time was I visited a church."

"Probably when they kicked you out for drinking the sacramental wine and trying to steal anything that glittered," Matteo says.

"Probably," I agree. "But as I sat there in this crumbling church I figured out what to do. I went to a hardware store and bought some very fine needle-nose pliers, and then I went to a stationery store and bought some envelopes. I sat on a bench in a park, tucked under the shadow of a large tree, and dismantled the necklace. Then I put the pieces of the necklace in the envelopes and dropped them in collection boxes in every church I could find. I couldn't risk the whole necklace being found and being gossiped about."

"Tomasino, you are too much," Guy says.

"There's one thing I did terribly wrong," I say. "I burned Hogarth's passport. I didn't think to write down any of the particulars, like his address, because we were in such a hurry to get to Switzerland. It could have been useful in the search, to help the Pritch."

"It probably was a fake name and a fake address, you know," Matteo consoles me. "And it doesn't matter anymore, does it?"

No, of course it doesn't, because we found them, all of them. The members of the Club.

"But what I'd like to know," I say, "is why His Lordship never showed up those last crucial months." What had His Lordship been doing when Belladonna was pregnant? Where had he been?

Guy and Matteo look at me, and I yawn to cover my stupidity. Botheration. I forgot for half a second.

I can go down to the dungeon and ask him myself.

21

The Root of All Evil

"Matteo!" Bryony shouts happily when she sees my brother that afternoon. Luckily, she doesn't seem too perturbed when he tells her that her mother isn't feeling very well and that he came to check on her.

"Mommy's usually in her room anyway," Bryony says, then turns away quickly and runs off to find Susannah.

Matteo looks at me, and I shake my head. I wonder how she'll handle what we're about to tell her once Guy leaves the room he's hiding in at Tantalus House and moves back into the yellow bedroom. She's too perceptive not to know then that something is really very wrong, but perhaps her joy with the presence of her adored uncle Guy will ease the impossibility of our situation.

And so when Bryony comes home from school two days later, Matteo and I are waiting for her as she flings down her books. "Darling girl, we need to talk to you," Matteo says. "We have some good news and some bad news."

"Is Mommy dead?" Bryony asks, her voice quavering, and I feel my heart near to bursting with the thought of who is sleeping down below, under her very feet.

"No, my angel, she's not. But Dr. Greenaway said she's got a virus called mono, and she's going to have to stay in bed for a very long time. That's the bad news. Are you going to be brave and help her get all better?"

Bryony nods, but her divine little face is so flooded with distress that I instantly smile brightly and say, "But don't you want to hear

446

the good news? Do you remember what happened the time that Mommy told you she had some good news and some bad news?"

"No," she says, her lips quivering. "I don't remember."

"Well, then," I say. "Go to the veranda, and you will." Bryony walks slowly outside. "Uncle Guy!" she screams, flinging herself into his waiting arms and bursting into tears.

"What's this?" he asks her softly, kissing her hair and holding her tightly as she sobs into his shoulder. "Don't cry, my scrumptious little poppet, don't cry. Mommy's going to be okay. I promise. After all, you and your mommy got me all better, didn't you?"

"Yes," Bryony says, her tears dissolving into hiccups. "Are you going to stay forever?"

"For as long as I possibly can. So don't let's think about it, because I only just arrived, and I missed you terribly, terribly much."

"How much?" she asks, delighted.

"As much as all the wags of Basilico's tail," he says.

"I'll go find him," she says, slipping away from his embrace and running off.

"Thank you, Guy," I say, sighing. "We've all become such splendid liars, haven't we?"

"What is a lie when the truth is unbearable?" he asks. I am spared from having to answer as Bryony comes flying back out to us, Basilico squirming in her arms, the lumbering mastiffs drooling behind them. She and Guy romp around with the dogs, and I wonder for an instant if His Lordship can hear them, even though I know full well that the walls are too thick for him to hear anything but the soft thud of approaching footsteps.

"Come along, Miss Scrumptious," Guy says after a while, looking at his watch, "I do believe it's time for us to pay a call upon your dearest mama."

He is not faking the enthusiasm in his voice, despite how she treated him just after he'd said those three little words, three days before. He has spent almost no time with Belladonna since she asked us to give him the diary, and that was months ago.

"Look, Mommy," Bryony says, running up the stairs and into her mother's bedroom, where the radio is playing softly. "Uncle Guy's here, and we're going to get you all better."

Belladonna forces herself to smile. She looks positively awful, I must say, her skin as colorless as the parchment shades of her lamps, and her manner drawn and listless. Only her eyes are madly, deeply alive, sparkling vividly green with a near-delirious distress. If I hadn't known she'd invented this illness, I'd swear she was truly stricken with mono and ordered by Dr. Greenaway to stay in bed and not get up a minute before he told her to.

"I'm sorry, my darling," she says, "but you needn't worry. But I'm just very tired, and I want you to know that if you ever come up and the door is locked, all it means is that I'm sleeping. I'm going to be fine."

"I know," Bryony says smugly. "Uncle Guy and I are going to take good care of you. Are we going to get Nurse Sam, too?"

Belladonna shakes her head. "No, sweetie, I don't think so. I don't need Nurse Sam when I've got you."

"And Uncle Guy," Bryony prompts.

"And Uncle Guy," Belladonna echoes, only to please her daughter. She still can't meet his gaze, although he hasn't taken his eyes off her for a second.

Bryony leans over the bed and kisses her mother on the cheek. "There," she says, "this will help you get all better."

"Thank you, my angel," Belladonna says wanly. She is fighting to keep her composure, and wants nothing more than to be left alone, but she can't very well say that to her daughter's face. She's lying enough as it is.

"Now it's Uncle Guy's turn. You have to kiss her and make her all better," Bryony tells him in a singsongy voice. "Kiss her kiss her kiss her better better better."

Belladonna's eyes meet Guy's at last, and they stare at each other, not knowing what to say. *Please,* Guy wants to say to her, please don't turn me away any longer. Please, I can't bear it, knowing who he is and what he's done to you. Please let me in. I hate him as much as you do, and he's my—

He leans over and brushes his lips briefly against her forehead, a gesture of ineffable tenderness.

"Please," he whispers to her, *"please."*

"Guy," is all she can say, mouthing the word without speaking it.

He lifts up her hand and kisses her palm, then smiles at Bryony when Belladonna doesn't pull it away. "Let's go play with the dogs some more," he says, summoning all his strength to keep his voice light and playful. "Tallyho, tallyho, biff whack whack!"

"Chickens and fishes and the olde Union Jack!" Bryony sings as she skips out of the room.

"Tell me a story," he says, looking pointedly at Belladonna, "or I won't come back."

We fall into a bizarre routine, as we have settled into so many others. Without fail, Guy, who has settled into the yellow bedroom, takes Bryony to school, and Belladonna gets up and goes down to the dungeon.

"Where's my baby?" she asks His Lordship in a dull monotone, sitting there in the dim light, the lantern at her feet. That's all she says to him. She doesn't ask him *why,* or anything about her captivity or the members of the Club. Day after day, she goes down the stairs to sit for hours on a little stool opposite his cell and ask about her child.

Guy knows she's down there, and in his frustration he often gallops around the plantation on Hermes, but he always meets Bryony when the school bus drops her off at the gate and Thibaud lets her in and gives her a praline, a touch of N'Orleans, he says. She and Guy go up to see Belladonna, back in bed, listening to the radio and rarely speaking. If it's a fairly good day, Bryony is permitted to do her homework in her mother's room. Then she goes out to play with Susannah or at another friend's house, or for an expedition with Guy. Belladonna stays in her room with only the voices on her radio for company, and the rest of us eat dinner on the veranda when it's not too cold, and we talk about everything and nothing, as if there weren't a man chained up behind the wine cellar, down below in the darkness.

We try to pretend that life is going on as usual. When she can bear it, Belladonna allows Bryony and Guy to read her a bedtime story, because it gives her daughter so much pleasure. Or sometimes Belladonna watches them play cards. Guy is teaching Bryony how to play gin rummy and poker, and she is showing a remarkable talent for bluffing her way out of a useless hand.

Sometimes, after Bryony has gone to bed, Belladonna gets up and goes down to the cellar once more.

Where's my baby?

It is her version of what he used to say to her.

Who are you? Why are you here?

Guy has so far refused to go down to his father. I can't say I blame him. Both he and Belladonna are locked in their own personal dungeons, battling the same monster.

Today I sneak down, tiptoeing as carefully as I can, and stand behind the door to the dungeon to listen.

"Your baby would be ten years old," His Lordship is saying to her. He'll say anything to torture her. He wants to hear the sound of her voice. "No longer a baby."

"Where is he?"

"Have you thought about our little meetings here?" he asks. He sounds perfectly calm, as if he were the master and she still his slave. "That you, by taking pleasure in my captivity, are no longer any different from me?"

"There is no pleasure in it," she replies.

"Is that so?" he says. "No pleasure in confronting the beast, in vanquishing the enemy? No pleasure at the sight of me, deprived of my freedom, utterly dependent upon your whims?"

"No," she says. "Nothing you say is going to make me let you go. You will stay here for as long as I stayed where you kept me, or until you rot. Whichever comes first."

"Is that so?"

"Yes, it is so," she says. "I want my baby."

"I'll tell you where your baby is," he says.

"I don't believe you."

"Who are *you*?" he asks. *"Who are you?"*

She opens her mouth. She nearly says, *I am yours,* but catches herself just in time.

He smiles. "I'll tell you where your darling baby is, if and only if you let me do to you what I want. You know what I want. You know very well indeed."

She gets up so abruptly that I have to scurry to hide behind one of the wine racks. Luckily, she doesn't lock the door upstairs, or I'd have been stuck there with him until Matteo came down with his meal on a tray.

I tell Matteo what I'd just overheard. The truth about Tristan is the only power His Lordship has left. That, and the memories of what made her.

Later that evening, I take His Lordship some books along with his dinner tray. Somehow, I can't call him Mr. Lincoln any longer, or the earl, or anything else. He retains his air of insufferable superiority, and looks remarkably well for a man of sixty-four who is being held against his will in a dank dungeon. He has no idea where he is, of course; all he does know is that he has altogether too much time to sit and fester and plan what hideous torments he is going to inflict upon her next.

His Lordship is not what I'd call a handsome man, because there is too much cruel authority etched into his features, but I imagine he was once seductive enough for ladies who liked a man with a penchant for inflicting pain. He is of medium height and slender; his fingers are long and thin, and he's wearing his famous gold ring. His eyes are a muddy dark blue, not sparkling with depth like Guy's; his nose is fine and thin, and he has surprisingly full lips. He has quite a lot of salt-and-pepper hair growing unkempt, and a slightly receding chin, now covered with a beard. That and the longish hair give him a bit of an air of an absentminded professor, until you look at him closely. There is no humor in his face, no joy. If he stares at you when the light from the lantern is shining, you want to cover your eyes and run away.

He examines the books, then gives a short laugh, like a coyote pouncing on a carcass. A horribly creepy, rasping sound.

"Lives of the Rakes," he says, reading aloud one of the titles. "How subtle."

"Yes, they're fascinating. I'll bring you all the rest of the volumes eventually. There's one about the founder of the Club's namesake, the first Dashwood," I say, picking up another volume and turning to a passage I'd already marked. I feel like Hogarth for a brief, awful second, always quoting from a book or a Frenchman. " 'When a man is born into a great position, is possessed of unbounded wealth and exercises widespread influence, and yet fails to show that he has done anything during a very long life except gratify his own inordinate desires,' " I read, " 'one cannot wonder that such a man, in spite of charm of manner and such like, is an encumbrance in any society.' " I close the volume with a dull thud.

"You are perfectly ridiculous, nothing but a fat fool. Even

though you may think you've done well for yourself. You and your pathetic brother," His Lordship says with a faint sneer. "And *her*. To have become *encumbered* with my son. To have *procured* such a fortune. Surely the fee I paid for her has long been expended in such a strenuous search."

I try not to show a reaction; I hate it when anyone calls me fat. "Why did you do it?"

"Do what, you fat fool? Save you from certain death? Or choose her for my pleasure? Why do you think? I thought you were the clever one."

"Because you could," I reply. "Because you liked it."

"Not bad, Tomasino. Close enough."

"Why didn't you show up when she was pregnant?"

"Foolish of me, wasn't it?" he says. "Foolish. I underestimated you." His face hardens. "Quite an error of judgment. Unfortunately, I was detained abroad as the war progressed."

"What you mean is, you'd been double-dealing so many Nazis and Allies that you feared for your safety, and you had to hide out someplace very far away from Europe so they wouldn't find you and hang you for the traitor you are."

"Perhaps," he says with a malicious smile, and I know I've nailed him on that one at least.

"Is that when you went to Marrakesh?"

"Do you honestly believe I'm about to disclose anything of importance to such a fat fool as yourself?" he says smugly.

"No," I say, "but I figure you first went to Malaysia, after the war, someplace where you already had your oil wells and connections and pots of money stashed away, and could bribe enough of the locals to keep their mouths shut when so many important people were looking for you. That way, when Hogarth's message finally got to you, you were so far away you couldn't get back in time for the blessed event. *Quite* an error of judgment, yes, I would say. *Quite*."

His smile has faded. Shoot steady, I tell myself. Aim for his heart.

"And then," I go on, "by the time you were finally able to wind your wicked way back to Belgium, you were greeted by a most unpleasant surprise. You hurried to the Swiss Consolidated Bank Limited, only to be told that account number one one six dash six one four had been closed a short while before and the trail had gone cold. You could do nothing but stay in your very particular kind of *touch* with the other members of the Club, hoping that your threat of blackmail would keep them wary, and that they'd alert you should they suspect anyone was looking for them. They, of course, would have no idea that your most beloved, prized possession had managed to escape."

I look away from him; I am afraid of the expression on his face, even though he is chained up and cannot place his hands around my neck to throttle it.

"Eventually," I add, "you decided Morocco was a suitable venue for your favorite pastime of abducting and torturing women. Baksheesh does wonders there, doesn't it? So do thick high walls and willing servants. Am I right? Or close enough?"

He says nothing.

"Don't you feel anything, knowing your own son is upstairs?" I press on.

"Why should I?" His Lordship answers eventually, hissing. He can't resist a dig about Guy. "He's a spineless fool like the rest of you. He always was a mama's boy, moping about."

I think for a minute about the boy in London who helped us. Arundel Gibson, the Pritch said his name was. That he gave up his father to protect his mother and his sister. I wonder if I'll ever get a chance to meet Arundel to tell him what a splendid thing he'd done for us. I doubt it. He's too far away, and I am having a hard time seeing anyone past the mist around my head. There is only this man with the muddy blue eyes sprawled as nonchalantly in his cell as if it were a drawing room in Eaton Square.

Who are you? Why are you here?

"Did you not wonder why you were caught?" His Lordship is saying to me. "Who it was who betrayed you?"

"Not really," I reply. "It was a long time ago. I can't undo the damage done."

"No, you can't, can you? The damage done to your precious manhood," he says, then barks his horrible raspy laugh. "But I know who betrayed you. Don't you want to know?"

"No," I say, but I hear my voice trembling.

"They told me who it was, when I was buying your freedom," he goes on. "If not for me, you'd not be standing here now, lording it over your precious captive. I shall tell you anyway. You need to know."

There is a short, uncomfortable silence. I am willing myself not to respond to him, but I can't help myself from asking who it was. The words somehow slip out before I have a chance to stop them, even though I know he is taunting me because he cannot bear to have me best him in a conversation. Now they are hanging in the air like a foul spray, a vague memory of what Moritz smelled like when he came back from his nightly patrol, shotgun tucked under his arm.

Who was it? Who are you? Why are you here?

He's laughing again. He sounds almost happy. The sound of his cackle is reverberating off the dingy brick walls.

"It was your own brother, you fat fool," he says. "Matteo betrayed you. Why do you think they cut out his tongue? So he couldn't tell you what he'd done. But they were incompetent, as usual, those Italians. Hopelessly incompetent." He is still laughing. "Not very nice, your dearest twin. Not nice indeed to have been so consumed by jealousy that he wanted you dead."

I feel a tremor start somewhere near my ankle and travel all the way up to my heart, where it is constricting me in a tight band, encircling me like a corset, its laces pulled so tight I start gasping for breath.

"Go ahead, ask him," His Lordship says. "I grant you permission."

This is how he does it, I realize. This is how he ruled them, the members of the Club. Why the servants were so cowed by him. Why *we* were; why we stayed in Belgium. He finds the weak spot and zeroes in for the kill.

Was Leandro ever that ruthless with his rivals? I wonder. Leandro would have been a worthy adversary. He would have known what to do, how to defuse this bomb before the explosion brings down the building with a catastrophic crash.

"I knew you were going to say that, but I don't believe you," I say eventually, trying to keep my voice neutral. I am not going to give him the satisfaction of knowing how much he hurt me. "The only power you have left is in your own tongue. And it's much more pitiful than you think."

I leave him, still cackling, and go outside to find Matteo. He's in the pool, swimming laps, perfectly rhythmical, back and forth, back and forth. I sit there watching until he pulls himself out of the water, shaking his curls like a dog's. Botheration. It's not fair that he has more hair than I. Marriage must be a hair tonic.

I'll never know about that.

"You're going gray," I tell him as he towels off.

"Likewise, *fratello mio,*" he says. His Lordship is having a bad effect on us. We feel like we're back in Belgium. "What's wrong? He's been saying things to you, hasn't he?"

"How did you know?"

"Because he's been saying things to me."

The heaviness around my heart starts lessening, bit by bit. "Let me guess," I say. We smile. "Why didn't you tell me?"

"I wanted to see if he'd do the same thing to you," Matteo replies.

"Thanks a lot, *fratello mio,*" I say.

"Age before beauty."

I kick my feet idly in the warm water of the pool. "What are we going to do?" I ask. "On the one hand, you want him to be trapped where he can suffer for years and years, but as long as he's here and alive then we'll be stuck, too, locked in torment with him."

"Leandro said that if we didn't know what to do, then we were not ready to do it," Matteo says.

Planning and plotting, he means. Plotting and planning.

"But this will help," he adds, picking up the leather-bound copy of *A Tale of Two Cities* I've noticed him reading, then opening it. Inside is stashed a tattered copy of a book I haven't seen since a cold winter's day in a house in Belgium: *The Connoisseur's Guide to Poison.*

"We really need to stop abusing the insides of books, you know," I say.

"I thought about making some more botulism, but it's too risky with all the people in the house," Matteo says, his voice so nonchalant that we could have been talking about picking Bryony up from school.

"I'm not doing that, or the crocus again," I say. "Not ever. I just can't do it."

"I understand," Matteo says. He closes the Dickens and we sit for a while, dragging our feet in the pool. Then he laughs. "What are we worried about?" he says. "It's right here at our feet."

"You mean chlorine?" I ask.

"No, _drogato_. In the garden. In the Hellfire Garden."

It takes a while to realize what he means, and when it finally dawns on me, I smile broadly for the first time in a long time.

"My darling big brother, you sly dog, you," I tell him, beaming. "What an absolutely wonderful idea. It did in that revolting ostrich."

"The dreadful Fluffy."

"Yes, the dreadful Fluffy. And it will certainly do in His Lordship."

Mandragora officinarum, he means. The divine mandrake, preferred talisman of spell-casters. Venerated root, symbol of manhood, gnawing its way through the earth as it twists into the very shape of sex itself. Growing here in her very own Hellfire Garden.

"Dig it up only at sunset," Caterina had said. "Do not tug violently on it or it will scream. Wrap it in a shroud and keep it in the dark."

"How will we find out exactly how to use it?" I ask Matteo.

"Pompadour must have had a gardening book with a reference to mandrake," he says. "If it's in Latin I'll ask Mother Hubbard to translate it."

"I'm going right now to look."

"Don't let Belladonna see you," he says.

_H_ubbard is only too happy to translate the section of the book I find, its vellum pages yellow and spotted with age but its message not diluted by time. "According to Madame de Lespinasse, the venerated author and sage of gardening of the mid-eighteenth century, the mandrake has two valuable uses," he tells me, his voice bland although he must be bursting with curiosity. Once again, I bless Jack for his sagacious judgment in the hiring of our employees. "As an aphrodisiac and as a poison. In other words, for arousal and for death. Madame de Lespinasse gives several different and fearfully explicit formulas for both these uses. Shall I write them down for you?"

"Oh yes, please," I reply, my voice equally bland, although I am practically trembling with excitement. "If you don't mind."

Hubbard's comments have helped me figure out what to do. An aphrodisiac, and a poison. For arousal and for death.

A whiff of a killer is a potent aphrodisiac.

We're going to make an aphrodisiac all right, a white cream in a little jar, smelling faintly of cinnamon, which we'll hide until it's needed. Matteo and I will sneak out one night when we know she's fallen into an exhausted sleep, and we'll dig up the mandrake root she's cultivated for years with honey water and whispered spells Caterina had taught her.

We will wait for it to scream, but will hear nothing but the screech of an owl, the squeal of a mouse, and the noises of the night.

We will wrap it in a shroud and then grate it fine and dry it to a powder. It will have the oddest, most pungent smell, and I'll be afraid someone will catch a whiff of it on our fingers even though we'll use fine leather gloves to protect ourselves. But we'll apply gallons of hand lotion every day, and no one will ever know.

And if things get worse, we're going to make a poison, slow-acting and irrevocably fatal. His Lordship will never know it's in his food. We'll keep feeding it to him until he starts to show symptoms, but the effects will be so gradual that it'll seem like nothing out of the ordinary and Belladonna won't get suspicious. And then when he takes a turn for the worse and can no longer spew his hatred, Matteo and I will whisper in his ear so he'll know what we've done to him. That he's being poisoned by the sorcerer's most potent symbol of manhood and there's nothing he can do about it. There is no antidote. We'll carefully regulate the dose, oh ho, how carefully we'll plan it down to the last scraping so he's choked by his own venom. And he is going to suffer in screaming, drawn-out agony until death will seem like a blessing, with no one to attend to his pain but the ghosts of his slaves.

I didn't say we were nice, did I?

Belladonna watch you die.

The only problem is in the testing. There's no one here we can ask to do *that.*

*A*nd on and on and on it goes.

"Where's my baby?" she asks him, and he taunts her.

Weeks go by, months. Belladonna's skin is as deathly ashen as

His Lordship's. Inside her, the little worm is snaking, gnawing at her distress and gorging itself on poisonous thoughts. She is finding it hard to talk to anyone, even Bryony, and it's as if we are watching her become a living wraith before our very eyes.

The vengeance will conquer you if you do not conquer it.

Matteo and I can stand it no longer, so one day when Guy is out riding and she climbs slowly up the steps from the wine cellar, we are waiting for her in the kitchen.

"He's winning, you know," Matteo says. "You can't let him win."

"Is this all you want to say to me?" she says coldly after clearing her throat.

"No," I tell her. "We merely want to remind you that you have something, here, of great value. Something that he doesn't."

"Is that so? Are you referring to my *freedom*?" she asks with deep bitterness.

"Not only that. Something else."

She looks at me, her eyes blank and unfathomable.

"Well, not a thing really," I go on. "A person."

"No," she says.

"Yes." I dare to plow ahead. "And I would venture a guess that His Lordship has a rather intense rivalry with this *person,* although he'll never admit it. In fact, I'd go so far as to speculate that the one thing guaranteed to torment His Lordship is the thought of you having any sort of personal anything with his much-detested offspring."

"I can't do that," she says after an uncomfortable pause.

"How would you know?" I ask. "Have you ever tried?"

She turns to me, her eyes suddenly blazing. She doesn't understand that I am trying to get her so riled up that she'll do something, anything, besides sit near His Lordship on her little stool in the blackness below us.

"I think Guy loves you so much that he won't expect you to do much of anything," Matteo hastens to add. "Don't you think His Lordship will have a fit if he sees a certain kind of ring upon your finger?"

He does have a penchant for rings, after all.

She looks at Matteo and then at me, and bites her lip before hurrying off upstairs. She tells Orlando that she is too unwell to see Bryony or Guy until further notice.

Guy and I are sitting on the veranda, watching the fireflies chase one another in the twilight. I am thinking of Italy, of the scent of the fields of sunflowers and the stream of hot gushing water at Saturnia, and I suddenly remember something.

"Leandro had a sculpted marble panel in his hallway, of Achilles on his way to Troy," I tell Guy. "He told us the myth behind it, that Achilles wounded the local king with his spear. The wound wouldn't heal, so Achilles went to an oracle for advice. She told him he would reach Troy only if the king he'd tried to kill would consent to guide him."

"Sleeping with the enemy, in a manner of speaking," Guy says softly.

"Sort of," I reply. "It turns out that the king had also consulted an oracle. *He* was told that he, the wounded, could cure what had wounded him."

"You mean, only the wounded himself could cure the enemy who'd wounded him."

"Exactly."

"Why did you think of this story just now? Is it meant to be about me and my father? Do you think he somehow can heal me? Should I venture down into his lair to mumble a few pithy words?" Guy asks me sadly. "Wish him a bon voyage to hell?"

"I don't know, Guy," I say wearily. "I don't know what to think or do anymore. I was just thinking of Saturnia, of taking the waters, and I remembered Leandro telling us that at such places even the most bitter enemies would lay down their weapons in order to heal."

"What did Belladonna say when he told her that?"

I think hard, remembering. "It was Matteo who said that he could never lay down his sword next his enemy's, I believe, and Belladonna agreed with him. And that's when Leandro said, 'They will come to you if they don't know who you are.' It's what gave her the idea for the Club Belladonna. I'm sure it is."

"I think what you're really trying to tell me in your very Tomasino way is that I must face my father, sooner or later."

"He's not going to be a happy camper when he sees the ring," I say.

Guy looks at his ringless fingers and then at me, venturing a ghost of a smile. He pulls a chain out from beneath his shirt. On it dangles the thinnest gold band. "Does anything escape your notice?"

"I should hope not," I reply smugly, trying to hide my hurt that he and Belladonna had excluded me from their wedding ceremony. Hubbard must have arranged everything at Belladonna's request—the paperwork and blood tests and the justice of the peace slipped, unnoticed, into Tantalus House. "Too bad Bryony wasn't there. Maybe there'll be a proper ceremony someday, and she can be the flower girl."

"I'm very sorry, you know. Terribly sorry, as a matter of fact, that you weren't there," Guy says. "But it couldn't be helped. It was done with in a flash, I'm afraid."

"She doesn't want you to wear the ring in case anyone catches on—is that it? Anyone except *him*."

"Quite," he says. "I keep it on a chain around my neck." He pauses. "If only Bryony could see it. She so desperately wants a papa."

"Yes, I know. But were you surprised that Belladonna, well . . ."

"I wish you could have seen my face. But she didn't actually come straight out and *ask*."

No, she wouldn't. Asking a man to marry you is not a very Belladonna thing to do.

"She knocked on my door, came in and sat all hunched up in the silk chair the way she used to, and didn't say anything for the longest time. I was happy just to be able to look at her, you know. Then she cleared her throat and asked if I would do her a favor," Guy goes on. " 'Of course I would,' I told her. 'I'd do anything.' I watched her grow paler and paler, as if she were having some private conversation with a demon only she could see. Then, suddenly, her cheeks flooded with color, and she asked me to get dressed, straightaway, and meet her in front of Tantalus House. She ran out of the room, and I threw on my clothes and ran after her. Hubbard and that odd chap named Winken met me at the door, and before I knew it, we were married. I was so astonished that I didn't have time to think. I took her to be my lawfully wedded wife, or whatever it is you say in this bloody country, and Hubbard gave me a ring." He sighs. "She closed her eyes, twisted off the ring she usually wears, then allowed me to slip the wedding band on before replacing her own ring. You'd never notice it unless you looked very carefully indeed.

"As we walked back to the house afterward, I gave her my word that I would never touch her as a husband touches a wife, unless she wanted me to," Guy adds. "She didn't say anything until we got to the staircase, and then she turned and looked at me, finally looked at me. 'Forgive me,' she said, and ran up the stairs."

His voice cracks, and my heart melts. I pull out one of Leandro's cherished handkerchiefs and blow my nose, sentimental softy that I am. Guy is not old and full of memories of a cherished love, as Leandro was. No woman has ever given Guy anything worth savoring, I realize, looking at the emotions flitting across his features. No woman ever threw her arms around him and loved him with the true kind of passion he deserves.

No woman is ever going to do that to me, either.

"He'll know she hasn't touched me," Guy says. "Oh, he'll know all right, the bastard. How long can he stand it down there?" He buries his head in his hands. "How can he stay so bloody calm?"

"He belongs to the darkness," I reply. "It's what spawned him."

"But *he's* what spawned *me*," Guy cries.

"Then let him be what heals you."

Guy takes a deep breath and stands up. "Bloody hell, I'm going down. It's got to be done." He pulls out the chain around his neck, unclasps it, slips on his wedding ring, and bids me good night.

I follow at a discreet distance as he slowly makes his way down the stairs, lights the lantern, and sits on Belladonna's little stool, his hands clasped in front of him. His father wakes at the sound, catches a glint of gold in the pale light, and laughs with his horrible raspy voice.

"I thought I would be spared the pleasure of hearing you speak to me again," His Lordship says. "Obviously, you are not a man of your word."

"That, I learned from you."

"Is she everything you'd hoped her to be?" he sneers. "You needn't be pretending to me with a ring around your finger. In fact, you could have asked your elder brothers what she can do, how well she's been trained to serve *me*. I lost count how many times they both had her."

His brothers, and all the members of the Club.

"You're lying, you filth," Guy says.

"Why should I lie about such a thing?" His Lordship says sarcastically. "It was one of my proudest moments, to have provided such temptation to my own flesh and blood. Why, Frederick had, on one splendid occasion, the opportunity to perform with her before an eminently distinguished group of gentlemen."

"At the auction three years after you kidnapped her and tricked her and bought her," Guy says bitterly. "Frederick was one of the two top bidders, wasn't he?"

His Lordship leans back and is silent, and Guy realizes suddenly that his father has no idea how much *this* son has been told about the members of the Club.

"I know everything," Guy says, his voice at that moment sounding astonishingly like the one he most despises. "Terribly sorry to inform you that she kept a diary, and she gave it to me to read. She wrote it all down on tiny scraps of her watercolor paper you so thoughtfully provided, and Tomasino copied it. They never caught her doing it; *you* never found her after she escaped."

His Lordship's eyes glitter, and he stands up. "How *touching*," he practically spits out. "I don't suppose she wrote down how much she enjoyed it."

I won't give in, Guy tells himself, *his words are his only power.* He finds himself staring, appalled beyond all reckoning, into his father's face, not knowing what to say or do. Then he suddenly blurts, "Why did you marry my mother?"

"Your mother? Because she was weak and passive and malleable. She worshiped me, at least until the first night of our honeymoon," His Lordship replies, "and by then it was rather too late for a girl of such heretofore-virginal innocence to go crying home to mummy, bleeding and soiled." He smiles and examines his nails. "But the truth, I must confess, was that she possessed an altogether-splendid fortune. How it must pain you to realize that your very own mother was in large part responsible for my having the wherewithal to have procured your very own *wife*."

"*My* wife came to me, and asked *me* to marry *her*," Guy says, lying only slightly, "which is not something *you* can boast about."

"Do you think your *wife* would have dreamt of marrying you had I not trained her properly in the first place?" His Lordship taunts.

Guy quickly backs away from the cell, hurrying off into the darkness before his father can manage to say another word.

*M*atteo wants to go home, but he knows it's not fair to leave me, not with everything so unsettled. Nor is it quite yet the time to give Belladonna our two wedding presents.

The first present is the result of a private counseling session with His Lordship, one he had to have known was coming, sooner or later. I'd judged correctly that Belladonna would not be able to face him quite so soon after the wedding ceremony, so we asked Orlando for help, to try to get it over with as quickly as possible. Orlando knows what to do that will be effective without leaving a visible trace that might make Belladonna suspicious.

But His Lordship won't crack, no matter what we do to him. When Orlando turns to us wretched hours later, lines of weariness aging his face, and shrugs, I'm afraid we must concede defeat. His Lordship is lying on his side, moaning and mumbling. Matteo leans over his face, then straightens up and leaves the cell.

"What was he saying?" I whisper.

"It sounded like 'carrots,'" he replies.

Carrots? What on earth could he mean?

We wind our way upstairs, shattered beyond all reckoning. I wearily climb the steps to my room, then collapse. "Carrots," he said. Something about carrots. "Stop thinking about it, and it will come to you," the Pritch told me. *They will come to you if they don't know who you are.* Was there ever a Club Belladonna? I ask myself as I fall into a deep sleep. Will there ever be peace?

When I wake up, I know what His Lordship meant.

Carrots. The carrots in the garden in Belgium.

"Your baby died and we buried him near the woods, on the other side of the carrot patch." That's what I could barely make out Hogarth murmuring to her, just before—

I call the Pritch's office immediately, and they promise to alert

the team in Belgium right away. Now, they have a specific place to
continue their digging.

I think I am about to crack, like Hogarth's head.

When one of the Pritch's team, someone who calls himself Jay,
calls three weeks later and soberly informs me that they'd found a
tiny skeleton in a plot of garden near the woods, and a pathologist
had confirmed that the remains were human, I thank him and hang
up. I tell Matteo and Guy, and we try to think of what to say as we
go up to Belladonna when Bryony is asleep and give her the news.
She sits in her bed, dumbfounded.

"I don't believe it," she says eventually. "I want my baby back,
and I'm keeping him here until he tells me where Tristan is."

"How can you go on with this when the child you *do* have is
suffering so?" Guy cries, and she turns to look at him with that
horrid blank expression. "If ever you bothered to think of any person besides yourself, you'd notice how Bryony's changed. She
never sings anymore; she's lost her exuberance, worrying about
you. She thinks she's done something wrong, something that made
you ill, and you're punishing her. It's a terrible thing to do to a
child."

Belladonna wants to ask him what he knows about children, but
bites her lip, suddenly remembering his sister, Gwennie. There is a
fleeting look on her face, as if she's about to crumple and give in
to him, Guy, her husband, who loves her and her child so profoundly. For an instant, her features change, and I realize I am
seeing her as she must once have been, when she was eighteen.
Before they found her, and tricked her. Before everything. And
then the mask reappears, and she is as brittle and hard as ever. I
blink, wondering if I'd imagined it.

"Besides, he told you already," I reply. "You're the only one
among us who doesn't believe the evidence. The Pritch himself
said to me that he wouldn't be retiring if he thought there was a
hope in hell of finding Tristan. And that if your son wasn't found
in Morocco, he wasn't ever to be seen alive. I don't think even His
Lordship could—"

"Could what?" she interrupts. "Could put the corpse of another baby in a grave and steal my own just to torture me? How do
you know? How will you know for certain?" Her voice doesn't rise
when she gets upset; it darkens and gets lower. So low, she is al-

most starting to sound like *him.* "Why did you have to kill Hogarth?" she says in a furious whisper, very nearly a hiss. "He was the only one who could have told us what they did with my baby. Why oh why did you do that to me?"

Oh ho, now she's done it. I feel that tight band of pain constricting my heart heat up like a branding iron, boiling my blood and leaving a searing image on my brain. In fact, I am so appalled at being falsely accused and of what our lives have become that I lose control.

"How dare you say that to me now?" I hiss back. Matteo places his hand on my arm, but I shrug it off and stand up so that my soliloquy sounds more dramatic. "How *dare* you? Do you think you've somehow got a monopoly on suffering that exempts you from concern about anyone else in the world, especially those who care the most? Do you think Matteo and I don't suffer every day of our lives because of what some man did to us? Do you think Guy doesn't suffer every day with the knowledge of who his father is and what that man's done to you, and that you used him by marrying him? Just who do you think you are?"

Who are you?

She is not used to confrontation, my darling Belladonna. She is staring at me with the horrid blank look that usually fills me with dread, but I ignore her and keep right on going. I can hold it in no longer.

"*You're* the one who killed Hogarth and conveniently blocked it out of your mind," I tell her, my voice dripping with sarcasm. "*You're* the one who suddenly decided to pick up the poker and whack him in the head. *I* was the one left behind to clean up the mess."

Then I realize what I've said, and I sit down so hard the chair squeaks in protest. I hunch forward and bury my face in my hands. Oh, Tomasino, how could you be so wicked? I'd sworn I'd never tell her *that,* no matter what.

The crickets outside her bedroom window don't care what we're talking about. They chirp on. A warm wind blows in from the windows and caresses the nape of my neck like the fringes of a white silk scarf Hogarth liked to toss over his shoulder.

"Is that true?" she asks Matteo, her voice sounding as if it's coming from deep underwater.

"Yes," he says with a sigh. "I would have done the same thing, under the circumstances."

She gets out of bed, turns off the radio, and goes to the dungeon, back down to where he is waiting for her, to torment herself with the knowledge that she killed the man who could have told her the only thing keeping her from plunging over the abyss into the shadows where His Lordship dwells.

After that, things are not the same between us. She is scrupulously polite when we see each other, but it is as if we have become strangers. I can't sense or anticipate her needs anymore, and I miss her terribly even though we are still living in the same house. Matteo speaks to her as I once had, but he is anxious to leave for a long visit to his family, and sits down with me by the pool the afternoon before his departure so we can figure out how he can give her the second wedding present we've concocted and then spooned carefully into a little white jar.

"You'll give it to Guy, without fail?" I ask hopefully at the end of our conversation.

"Yes, and if it hasn't started to work by the time I come back, I'm going to start making His Lordship's meals myself," Matteo says as he envelops me in a tight embrace. He is the only person I can bear to have hug me like that. He's nearly as big as I am, after all. "And I hope you know that I'm going to do my best to convince Annabeth and the children to move down here, when this is all over."

"Yes, it's a remarkably healthy environment," I say sarcastically. "Such a lovely, welcoming hostess. All that splendid fresh air down in the dungeon."

"I don't know why I put up with you," Matteo says affectionately. "It will be the best thing for all of us, for Bryony to have more children to play with, and then you'll have four other people to fuss over."

He knows how bad I am feeling about Belladonna's ignoring me, and I feel a sharp pang of jealousy. He was always the one who could manage her when she got in a state.

"Well, what are you waiting for?" I tell him, and he waves as he walks away toward the house, where he will find Guy and have a brief conversation. Guy will wait for her until she comes up after yet another fruitless hour with His Lordship. I am hiding in the bushes near the veranda, where he will sit her down. I need to hear what he's about to say.

"What do you want?" she says rudely when she sees him.

"Matteo's going home for a few weeks," he says as he motions to her to sit beside him. She does, eyeing him warily. "He and Tomasino asked me to give you a wedding present."

She turns her head away. "Don't," she whispers.

"I must." Guy leans back to soak in the fragrant night air, willing her to stay calm, to stay beside him. "Has my— Has *he* asked you about your ring?" he asks eventually, and she slowly shakes her head no, unwilling to meet his eyes. "Or why I'm here? Or how we met? Or how you found him in Morocco?" Her head is still slowly shaking from side to side, as if she's a marionette without strings. "Haven't you wondered—as I have—that it is more than slightly peculiar for a man trapped in a dungeon to have absolutely no curiosity about what brought him from his swank hidey-hole in Morocco to this place, Lord only knows where, hunted down and trapped by the very woman he'd lived to conquer? Why doesn't he care?"

She finally looks at him, her eyes a helpless, turbulent dark green.

"Because his needs are simple, and you give in to them every time you go down to his lair," Guy says softly, trying desperately to keep his voice steady. "He needs *you,* the sight of you and the scent of you, weak and faltering and silent. No ring on your finger, even if it was put there by me, his detested son, is going to diminish his pleasure with your weakness. Or at least not until he has proof that you've conquered it."

"No no no," she whispers. "I can't do that."

"I've not asked you to do anything," Guy replies, his voice stronger. "Have I? Although I am your husband, I would never dare to presume to tell you what to do."

If she could speak, she would. She opens her mouth, but no sound comes out.

"He has no clue what your name is, that it *is* Belladonna," he presses on, feeling bolder with every word. "He has no clue what you've become, because you haven't got the strength to show him.

Is that why you brought him here? To torture yourself for as long as he's alive? To destroy everyone who loves you? To be *afraid*?"

Her head starts that awful slow turning again.

Guy sighs deeply, then pulls a small unwrapped box out of his pocket. "They asked me to give you this. It's meant for both of us. A wedding present. Take it."

He presses it into her hands. She sits staring at it, not knowing what to do, so he sighs again in exasperation and opens the box for her, taking out a small white jar. Her face blanches when she sees it.

"Where did they get this?" she whispers, her voice cracking.

"Matteo told me they made it after reading through Pompadour's gardening books."

She holds the jar in her hands, then slowly unscrews the top and takes a whiff. The expression on her face changes abruptly, and she starts to laugh wildly, near hysteria, her chest heaving so that it almost seems that she's sobbing. She hasn't laughed in a very long time, Guy realizes. There is no place for laughter in her any longer.

"Have they tried it yet?" she manages to ask, still laughing madly. "Tomasino and Matteo, of all people. The eunuchs."

Weeks fly by and nothing changes, except that the mauve circles under Belladonna's eyes deepen into violet smudges. I tell Matteo to stay in New York until I summon him back, and he agrees without too much persuasion. I wake up and realize one day that Bryony's school is nearly out, and Guy will be taking her to a riding camp, driving up to the Poconos and then, he not quite truthfully telling her, getting on a plane in Philadelphia that'll take him to London for business. It can't be helped, he explained; he must go back. I think Bryony's relieved to get away from her pale, sick mother, poor darling, and is comforted by Guy's swearing on all the wags of Basilico's tail that he'll be back for visitors' day. That no, of course he will not go to Ceylon, where there are nasty mosquitoes full of dengue fever; and yes, of course he'll pick her up at the end of camp and drive her home again, too, because her mother's probably not going to be well enough to travel then, either.

He's already written out fifty-six postcards addressed to his scrumptious little poppet, one for every day of camp, and shipped them off to the Pritch's office. They'll mail them special delivery air mail every day, and Bryony can boast to all the little girls about her dashing uncle Guy in London while she counts the days till he returns.

When Guy and Bryony drive off, I am alone in the house with her, as unearthly as a ghost, and *him,* silent tormentor.

I can't ask her what she's going to do. She doesn't want to talk to me anymore, me, her devoted Tomasino, her masterpiece of ruined civilization. All I can do is try to stay out of her way.

I sit dozing on the veranda, moping with the unfairness of it all, and wake when I hear the ice cubes of a mint julep swirling in a cup near my elbow. Guy smiles wearily when I open my eyes.

"Yours are far superior, you know," he says.

"I'll make you another," I say, brightening instantly. "Is Bryony settled?"

"I suppose," Guy replies, "although I miss her fearfully already. Where's Belladonna?"

"I wish I knew," I reply. Guy nods, then goes up to bed. I stay out a while longer, listening to the crickets.

Every night is like the last; every day, every week a monotony of waiting and wondering. Guy goes to see Bryony for visitors' day and comes back again. We sit and drink juleps, or wander aimlessly around the plantation, where the mist is growing thicker and thicker around me.

Until the day when she is sitting on her little stool, asking him the same question she fears he will never answer, no matter how long she keeps him.

Where's my baby?

Even His Lordship is starting to look as awful as she does. Captivity takes a fearsome toll on a body, doesn't it? That, His Lordship ought to know.

Where's my baby?

"Is that all you can ask?" he sneers. "I shouldn't wonder that you'd come to me for advice about your *unseemly* lapse of judgment. No, the married state does not suit you. No doubt because you have already had a very particular kind of marriage, one far more suitable for your *particular,* though limited, talents." It is the first time he has alluded to the ring on her finger, and her heart starts thumping wildly at the sound of his asking questions she finally realizes he wants desperately to have answered. "Although I can't own to being surprised at your silence, considering the man you have had the misfortune to marry."

"You're jealous," she whispers.

He laughs. "Are you mad? Even if you were fool enough to marry my pathetic *son,* we both know that you cannot ever bear to have him come near you. The only man who can touch you is your lord and master. Surely such a well-trained specimen as yourself understands *that.*" His voice thickens and he stands up and comes close to her. She shies away, and he laughs again.

"Even if you give yourself to him, you still belong to me," he says. "You are *mine.* You'll always be *mine.* Say it. Say you are mine. *Say it!* Who are you?"

"No," she says, whimpering, *"no—"*

"Your life is nothing," he goes on, his horrible voice filling her ears as he strains to get close to her. "Without me, you are nothing. Nothing but what I made of you. Mine to possess. I own you. I shall always own you. You are mine. *Say it.*"

"I won't," she says fiercely, finding her voice at last.

"Say it!" he shouts at her. *"Say it!"*

"No no no!" she shouts back as she turns and runs out of the dungeon and up the stairs, into the kitchen and then upstairs to her room, slamming the door so hard it wakes me from a fitful nap.

I lie in bed, not knowing what to do, until I hear a sharp knock a few minutes later and, to my surprise, Belladonna herself hurries into my room. She is wearing a white chenille bathrobe, which puzzles me because it is so hot. She kneels down near my face, her hair wild and her cheeks flushed and her eyes dazzling emeralds of panic as she steadies herself on the side of the bed.

"Tomasino," she says, her voice a low beseeching, *"Narcissus."*

Me, Narcissus? What is she talking about? My eyes fill with tears, not only at her distress and her insult but, I must say, at the marvelous sound of my very own darling begging me for help. "What?" I say quickly. "What is it? What can I do?"

Her hands are trembling violently, I notice, as she hands me a heavy brown grocery bag that clanks in my hands. I spill out the contents on my bed and see four long chains, with leather cuffs attached to both ends, clasped with cunning little locks. There are also several long pieces of narrow black silk, and the little white jar, our wedding present. I have no idea how she's gotten these horrible chains, I tell myself wildly, even as my stomach lurches and I put everything back into the bag and fold the top so I won't have to look at what's inside. I know what she wants me to do.

She wants me to set it up.

Don't do this; it's not supposed to be this way, I want to say to her, but I quickly get up and run to the Narcissus Room, mirrored and golden. She has already heaped a pile of pillows on the floor. I tumble them up onto the bed, then attach the chains to each of the four posts, leaving them in neat coils. I place the white jar by the side of the bed, next to the silk blindfolds, and then wonder what to do next. I turn to survey the room and nearly jump out of my skin when I see her standing, wraithlike, in the door.

"Where's Guy?" I ask, trying to keep my voice conversational.

"I can't," she says. *"I can't I can't I can't—"* She turns and runs to her room, and I hear her turn the lock. I stand there for a minute, helpless yet again, then leave, shutting and locking this door as she had just done to her own.

She stays in her room all the rest of that day, and the next. When I bring her meals on a tray, as I used to do, I hear the voices on her radio, and see her pacing, back and forth, back and forth. She doesn't look at me; she doesn't speak and barely touches her food.

"You must accept the possibility that your plans may not end as you might wish them to," Leandro said.

The Narcissus Room is still locked, its chains untouched.

"Guy will take my place," the Pritch said. *"You need to let him help you."* She never told the Pritch she would when he said that, I remember. But now she must. She *must*. It is unendurable. No one can live through this and stay sane. Please, I beg you, *please—*

Belladonna goes to her closet as the sky begins to lighten, pulls out a box, and something inside of her snaps. She closes her eyes; she knows what she must do, can do it by touch alone. She picks up the gold brocade corset and places it around her waist, fastening it as tightly as she can without someone there to pull the laces taut. She runs her fingers over a pair of sheer silk stockings and steps into them, then slides on a pair of golden garters to hold them up. She feels for the thick white chenille bathrobe and puts it on, then opens her eyes, and the door to her room.

I hear her run down the hall, down the stairs, down to His Lordship.

Shoot steady. Aim for his heart.

She bangs on his bars to awaken him, and he sits up with a start. She opens her robe and lets it fall to the floor.

"Look at me," she orders, her voice ragged and breathless, "look at me! Fill your eyes with the sight of it, you bastard, because this is the last time you'll ever see it. I'm going to *him* now, your detested son; I'm going to him because I want to." Her voice is rising into near hysteria. "Do you hear me? *I want to and there's nothing you can do to stop me.*"

"Who are you?" he says viciously, even as his eyes feast on the splendid sight of the body he'd been dreaming about every night of his life since he'd been forced to leave her. "I forbid you, do you hear me?"

"You can't forbid *me,*" she says savagely. "I forbid *you.* He belongs to me now. You have *nothing.* You are *nothing.*"

"You whore! Impossible! You cannot. You cannot do this. You belong to me, and me alone!" he shouts, furious. "You are *mine.* Say it. *Say it.*"

"I'll never say that to you again," she shouts back. "Never never never—"

"You are here to serve me," he is screaming. "You are mine!"

She lets him shout and swear, eyeing him coldly and willing her breathing to slow so she can stand without wavering, until he stops abruptly. *He's afraid of me now,* she realizes in amazement. *He's afraid of me.* She pulls up her robe and steps closer to him, but even as he stretches out his hands to grab her she is beyond his reach.

"Open your mouth," she says in a loud, fierce whisper. "Open your mouth and I'll let you touch me."

He closes his eyes and opens his mouth, but she is already gone.

Guy wakes and senses that something is odd in his room. He opens his eyes and sits up, and thinks he is dreaming when he sees Belladonna sitting hunched in the chair and staring at him, wearing a thick bathrobe even though it is warm and sultry.

"What's wrong?" he asks in a panic.

She stares at him, and Guy's heart starts beating so fast he fears he will choke. He waits for her. He will always be waiting.

"Do you . . ." she manages to ask. "Do you love me?"

"Yes," he says soberly. "I do. I do love you."

"Why?"

"How can you ask me that?" he says to her with a vehement passion. "Why shouldn't I love you, as impossible as you've become? I do love you, that's all. I can't help it. I can't help believing in you."

It is what Leandro said to her, once upon a time.

"How can you?" she cries now, as she did then. "I'm not a *woman.*"

"That's not true!" Guy cries. "Why are you torturing me?"

She doesn't answer, just bites her lip as she looks down at her hands trembling in her lap, at the rings on her finger. Then she stands up, wavering. "The Narcissus Room. In five minutes," she says, her voice cracking as she runs out the door.

Guy looks at his watch until three minutes tick by, the longest three minutes of his life.

Three little minutes. Three little words.

Who are you? Where's my baby? He's my father.

No no no—

Let me in. I love you.

Guy gets out of bed and hurries to the Narcissus Room, waiting another minute before opening the door and locking it behind him. The shutters and curtains are drawn, and the room is nearly pitch-black. As his eyes adjust to the light, he sees a lump of white on one of the chairs—her bathrobe. Then thinks he sees her on the bed, something gleaming near her wrists and ankles.

What has she done to herself? he wonders, then steps closer to the bed. She is lying on a mound of pillows; she has wound the long black silk blindfold around her eyes; she has attached the chains to her ankles and wrists.

No no no—

"Do it, Guy," she whispers, and he hears the pleading and the panic in her voice. "Do it quick."

"Not like this. Not like him," he whispers back. "I can't do this to you. This is not the way it should be—"

"You must," she says, twisting her head from side to side. "You must you must you must—"

He moves closer and carefully sits next to her on the bed; he can't help himself. He leans closer to her face, close enough to kiss her, but he doesn't yet dare. Then he sees tears coursing slowly down her cheeks from under the blindfold. Belladonna, his most truly beloved, in tears. She, who never cried, weeping, imprisoned.

"I love you," he whispers, leaning over so that his lips can brush away the tears glistening on her cheeks. *"I love you."*

"Please," she says. "Say it, please."

Say what? Guy nearly cries, but he knows instead what she needs to hear.

"Who are you?" he asks.

"I am yours, my—" she says, her voice trembling, but stops when Guy puts his fingers gently on her lips.

"Never say 'my lord' again," Guy tells her, his voice soft as he keeps kissing away her tears. "I am not your lord and master, and never will be. I am your husband, and you are my wife. Now, I shall ask you again. Who are you?"

"I am yours," she says.

"Why are you here?"

"To do your bidding."

"What shall you do?"

"Whatever you desire."

"I desire you," Guy says, his voice choking as he thrills to the sound of her voice, the scent of her, her body so close to his. *She won't say it; she won't say "my lord," not ever again.* He can't stop kissing her neck, the swell of her breasts, the tip of her nose, her lips. He is kissing her, and she is kissing him back, deeply, as if she can somehow inhale the very life out of him so she can breathe again.

"Stop," she cries out suddenly, and Guy pulls away, terrified she will ask him to leave.

Not now, oh please, I beg you, not now when you're so close, oh please, don't stop—

"Open it," she murmurs, and he looks over to the table beside the bed, where he sees a small white jar.

"Is this what you want?" He thinks he sees her nod. "I won't hurt you," he says with the utmost tenderness. "I promise I won't hurt you."

He scoops out a bit of the cream and touches her where he knows she wants it, where no man has touched her since—

He sits beside her, waiting. He still hasn't taken off his pajamas. The room is stifling, but he is frozen, waiting. Waiting. *Please, oh please—*

"Guy," she says after a few minutes, and he sees her arch up, her legs moving closer together. *"Guy."*

"What do you want, my darling?" he whispers.

"You," she says, "I want you."

I bring their meals on trays and leave them outside the door, so Guy can pick them up. I stay out of sight, but I am in a much more pleasant state of mind than I've been in a long, long time.

Every day, Guy uses less and less of the cream. Gradually, he unfastens the chains, one by one; then he removes her blindfold, and, slowly, opens the shutters and pulls back the curtains.

His Lordship is in a fearsome state, and I call my brother, telling him everything, and he promises to get on a plane as soon as he possibly can.

The mist is starting to clear from my eyes. Especially when Matteo arrives and insists on preparing His Lordship's meals himself. We don't discuss what he's doing. I can't say I'm glad, exactly, but this saga must come to an end at some point, don't you agree?

Guy tears himself away from Belladonna only long enough to drive up to the Poconos to pick up Bryony, as he'd promised.

"Mommy's better, isn't she?" Bryony announces when she flings herself into Guy's arms and takes a good look at his face. "I can tell."

"Yes, my scrumptious little poppet," he says, "she is," and they sing nonsense songs all the way home. As soon as the car stops, Bryony jumps out and runs up the stairs to her mother. Belladonna is sitting on the chaise by her bed, reading, and she holds her arms out to her daughter and clasps her tightly.

"Do you still have mono?" Bryony asks fearfully.

"Just a tiny little bit," Belladonna replies, but she is able to smile for real, and Bryony bites her lip, a gesture so familiar it brings tears to my eyes. "Uncle Guy helped me get better."

Yes, she is getting better, but it is hard to heal when there is a man in the dark, muttering and cursing and pulling at his chains until the skin on his arms is raw and bloody. I can't go down there anymore; I am of no use to anyone. Each day, though, Matteo reports to me that His Lordship seems a tiny bit more lethargic. That is as we'd hoped, wanting him to sicken so gradually that nothing seems out of the ordinary. Considering where he is, of course.

Belladonna and Guy have not gone to the dungeon at all, not since Guy first went to her in the Narcissus Room. He has moved back into the yellow bedroom, but either she goes to him at night or he steals into her bed, then leaves before Bryony awakens. It is too soon to tell Bryony anything, even though she will be delirious with joy when that moment finally comes.

I think they are both afraid their happiness is too fragile to tempt.

*M*atteo tells me one October afternoon that His Lordship is starting to look much worse. I tell Guy that His Lordship seems to be unwell, and am not surprised to see him steal slowly down the stairs, hand in hand with Belladonna, several nights later. I've never seen her touch a man like that, I realize. It seems so natural, so right, even in the fetid air of this dungeon.

"Come to gloat?" His Lordship says sarcastically when he sees them. "You don't fool me."

"I don't recall asking for your opinion," Guy retorts.

Belladonna squeezes his hand and pulls away, moving closer to where His Lordship is staring at her. Then she smiles.

"Who are you?" she asks.

His Lordship is so astonished at this question that he takes a step back, but soon recovers his composure. "I am your lord and master, as you know quite well," he says, moving closer to her again. "You belong to me."

Belladonna turns pale, but she doesn't flinch. Guy comes beside her and kisses the nape of her neck. She turns her head toward his and for the briefest of seconds caresses his cheek with her left palm. The gold of her rings glistens in the light of the lantern, and, had she turned her face toward His Lordship's at that very instant, she would have shuddered at the savage expression on his features.

But by the time she turns back to look at him, not a trace of emotion remains.

"How sweet," His Lordship sneers. "I should hate to interrupt such a tender spectacle, but I do believe the *lady* and I have a bit of unfinished business."

Guy feels Belladonna tense, and as she starts to mouth *Where's my baby?* he kisses her so passionately that she can't help responding to him. Quickly, though, she pulls away.

"Let me go," she whispers, and Guy moves aside, leaving his hand resting lightly on her shoulder.

"I know where your baby is," His Lordship says matter-of-factly. "I have what you want."

"That is all you have left, you liar," she says fiercely, startling Guy. "You are nothing—*nothing*!" She turns and runs out as Guy calls out her name.

"Did I train her well?" His Lordship says, his laugh a horrible cackle. "Is she as pliable as you'd hoped, ever so responsive to your no-doubt insatiable demands? Obviously you aren't man enough to handle her."

"She's right," Guy replies, shaking with anger. "You *are* nothing."

"I expected rather more substance from a creature said to be my offspring," His Lordship says, sitting down and folding his arms as if he were a pasha conducting the business of state, instead of a man absorbing a few more shavings of poison with every meal, locked away from the world in hidden blackness. "But, frankly, I must confess that I am slightly *more* than nothing to you."

"Why ever did you have children?" Guy cries. "Was that the only way you knew to kill my mother and steal the remainder of her fortune?"

"You sniveling, useless *fairy*. Wouldn't you like to know?" His Lordship hisses. "It shall give me infinite pleasure to answer that question, though. In fact, I think I shall tell you on the long-awaited day when I inform your *beloved* as to the whereabouts of her precious baby."

Guy backs out of the dungeon, his father's laughter echoing in the darkness.

*   *   *

*H*is Lordship is having trouble breathing. He can barely speak; he can only croak for water.

"Should we get a doctor?" Guy mutters when Matteo tells him. It's not as if we can pick up the phone and ask Dr. Greenaway to make a dungeon call.

"Hubbard can probably sort that out, if we have to," I say dully, "but I don't think we should." It reminds me of something she said once, in the Club Belladonna.

Finita la commedia.

My brother and I look at each other. There is nothing more to say, although we thought a man of His Lordship's stamina would surely last a little longer. It has been less than a year, after all. Nothing close to the twelve years she spent, trapped and tortured.

No, we are not going to tell Belladonna or Guy what is poisoning his father, and who. Let them think that His Lordship is dying of natural causes, choking on his own thwarted, seething rage.

Malice shining like a star.

When Guy is upstairs talking to Belladonna, Matteo pulls me down to the dungeon so that we can quickly whisper a few appropriate words in His Lordship's ear, as he had so often whispered in hers.

"Who are you?" I ask softly.

"You are a dead man," Matteo explains.

"Why are you here?" I go on.

"To die a slow death by poison," Matteo adds.

"What shall you do?"

"You shall suffer unspeakable torments before you die."

He looks at us and tries to laugh, but it is too late.

We sit there, huddled in the corner, waiting for Guy and Belladonna. Eventually we hear them, and they slowly approach the cell, their hands clasped tightly yet again.

"Get up," Belladonna says to His Lordship, but then she sees the greenish tinge of his skin and drops Guy's hand to move closer to where His Lordship is lying. His breathing is labored and he is too weak to sit up, but his eyes are glittering with unspeakable malevolence.

Belladonna sits on her little stool, deeply shaken. "Where's my baby?" she asks, trying, and failing, to keep the panic out of her voice.

His Lordship's lips stretch into a wicked smile.

"You must get better—I forbid you to die!" she cries. "I forbid you to die until you tell me where my baby is!"

There is an awful stabbing pain in my knee, and I put my hand over my mouth so I won't cry out. Matteo cups his hand around my elbow, but this sympathetic gesture is scant consolation. It is too late to undo what we've done.

His Lordship can barely move, and we stay down there for what feels like hours. Finally, he tries to stretch his hand to her, his horrible hot, dry fingers. Belladonna gets off her stool and moves closer, kneeling, yet not close enough.

Who are you? His lips are moving.

Her own lips move to say, *I am yours,* but no sound comes out of them.

His Lordship closes his eyes, his body shudders, and there is a terrible rattle in his throat. She peers into his face, into his blank, staring eyes.

"No," she says, "no no no—"

His Lordship is dead, and Tristan is gone forever.

"We have to bury him," Matteo says to Guy.

"No, I don't want him in a grave. I want him here, so he can tell me where my baby is," Belladonna says, her voice rising into hysteria. "I want you to brick this up and leave him here in it until he tells me where my baby is!"

"Belladonna," Guy says, her words shocking him into action. "He's dead. You can't."

"I can!" she shouts. "I can, and I will! Get out! *Get out!* I'll do it myself, brick by brick. *Now get out and leave me alone!*"

Guy stares at her, appalled, then picks her up in a fireman's carry, slinging her over his shoulder. She tries to twist away, screaming and pounding him with her fists and heels, but she is too worn-out to fight him for long as he carries her past the wine bottles and up into the kitchen.

"He does not belong where we live and breathe. He will haunt this house if you leave him down there," Guy says sternly. "I promise you. I won't have it."

"But I want my baby," she says, and she sounds so brokenhearted that I have to leave the room and sit on the veranda. She doesn't see me leave. To her, I no longer exist.

"Come with me," Guy says as he picks her up again and carries her upstairs as if she weighs no more than Bryony. She buries her head in his neck. Matteo watches them, then beckons me to come with him.

We dig a deep grave in the woods that night, then wrap His Lordship in a shroud like the mandrake. We carry him up the stairs, out to the veranda, and place him in a wheelbarrow and take him to the grave. We dump him in and cover him with dirt and lye I had thoughtfully asked one of the gardeners to put in the shed for us weeks before. We pack it well, then place stones over the dirt and pack them in, too.

Wherever the path leads you, you must not give in.

Matteo leaves for New York, and the rhythm of our lives gradually returns. The mist before my eyes thins until it is barely visible, but I am looking decidedly wan. Botheration. Such a maudlin state does not suit my complexion. So I keep to myself and wonder what will become of me.

Until Belladonna comes to me one day as I sit reading one of Pompadour's poetry books in my bedroom. She shuts the door and locks it, and the expression on her face makes my heart skip a beat and the mist come crashing back before my eyes, as if I'd driven into a thick wad of fog. Then she throws a trowel on my bed.

"You dug up my mandrake and you poisoned him," she says.

I shut my book. I can't lie to her now. "Yes," I say, "because he was poisoning you."

"It wasn't up to you to make that decision for me," she says savagely. "How dare you? *How dare you?*"

I decide not to tell her Matteo helped me; I don't want the rest of his life ruined, too. Then she might not let him move in, and he and Annabeth have already sold their apartment and shipped all their belongings. In fact, they're taking a leisurely drive down from New York and should be here in a day or so. I've been counting the hours till my brother would be sharing the same house with me again, for good, and Bryony is thrilled to pieces that Marshall and Charlotte will be living here, too. She will be even more thrilled when Belladonna and Guy decide to announce their "engagement."

Her adored Guy will be her father as well as her brother.

"I don't know," I tell Belladonna simply, trying to defy her rage as my heart continues to thump wildly out of rhythm. "It seemed the only thing to do at the time."

"Now I'll never know about Tristan," she says. "I'll never find my baby because of you. I will never forgive you as long as I live." She unlocks the door and goes out, slamming it so hard the Utrillo snowscape she'd once given me falls off the wall.

"Forgiveness is a gift," Leandro told us. *"It is the only thing that can free us from the weight of hatred. . . . As long as we fail to forgive, we're holding the hand of our offender. That will always be the hand pulling us backward."*

Her words crack my heart harder than the poker on Hogarth's head. It shatters into splinters as dazzling as the diamonds on the heels of a woman's golden brocade shoe as she wanders around a nightclub, a trail of laughter in her wake.

It is altogether too unfair. She's given me no choice. There is only one thing I can do.

Belladonna watch you die!

PART VI

A Final
Little Ditty

(1958–1982)

Belladonna went away
Demons called her out to play
No one ever heard them cry
No one dared to ask her why
Belladonna watched him die

22

All Time Not Spent in Loving Is Lost

*J*ust because I am old does not mean I have forgotten about loving. Leandro said something like that once; I don't remember where. Botheration. I don't remember so clearly anymore. It all used to be so clear. Right and wrong and the dog outside the Club Belladonna. Planning and plotting and the sound of chains in a dungeon.

Leandro would talk to me in the twilight as other people walked around. Someplace near water, I think. The sound of the fountains tinkling sweetly.

There is a lovely fountain in Firenze, where I live now, in the Boboli Gardens. The Oceanus Fountain, surrounded by a moat and flowers. A little girl with strawberry blond curls used to run around it, laughing, looking for her wishing star.

"Close your eyes and make a wish," Hogarth said to Belladonna before he tricked her.

I close my eyes, but I can no longer wish. It is getting harder to remember. She is there and she is not there. A living ghost, that's what the Pritch said about her. He's gone now, too. He walked out of the Witches' Brew pub and slipped and cracked his head open. The wonderful balding head filled with clever ideas, scheming and conniving, broken and bleeding.

Or was it Hogarth? His head had been cracked open, too. It served him right, though, didn't it? Losing his hair and losing his head. He got no less than he deserved. Hogarth and all the rest of them, the members of the Club.

Concentrate, Tomasino, you have become a silly old fool. The quickness has left me. I'd had a goal for so long, you see. We all had. We kept moving and planning and plotting, and then we found him, and it was all over.

The secret of perpetual youth is perpetual motion.

Leandro said that, too, I think, but he died and left us before we were ready to do without him. I had to leave Belladonna. She wanted to blame me, and she didn't need me anymore. Me, her darling Tomasino. I was afraid she'd never forgive me, not ever, and then I'd have no reason to keep myself alive.

I clutch Leandro's cane with the golden head of a lion, and it keeps me from falling when I go out to walk. I used to walk with Matteo to the Boboli Gardens. He had stayed with his family at La Fenice until the children grew up and moved away. After Annabeth took ill suddenly and died, Matteo sent me a message via the Pritch's office, and after a while I allowed him to come find me in Italy. He, too, was not well, so we didn't discuss his pain or my own. All I told him was that we could not go to Ca' d'Oro—too many memories I was trying to forget. So we moved into a large flat with a wide terrace on the roof where we tended to pots of basil and sat in comfortable chairs to watch the sunsets. Italy was where it all started, after all. Where our lives ended and we were reborn.

I had called Thibaud down at the gatehouse, you see, and told him there was a family emergency, that he had to drive me to the airport and I didn't want to wake Belladonna. I left with only a few suitcases, several books from Pompadour's library, my lacquer fountain pens, my cane and cat's-eye from Leandro, and some small photographs. I couldn't take too much, or Thibaud might have gotten suspicious. Nor did I want to be encumbered; certainly not with the dazzling assortment of beautiful objects I'd accumulated, especially my Utrillo snowscape. I had plenty of money—buckets, actually. I could buy myself new things wherever I chose to go.

I flew to New York and called Jack, who met me at Idlewild. We sat in the airport lounge as weary travelers scurried by, and the story poured out. As he listened soberly, for some incongruous reason I thought of a conversation we'd once had in the Waldorf,

when I'd been so eager to share the details about the Club Belladonna. Then he told me he wished he could have been there to
help us, and I felt a little bit better. He asked me to accompany
him to Horatio Street to say hello to Alison, who was pregnant with
their first child, and keep them company for as long as I wanted,
but I declined. It was no longer my home. The tunnel leading to
the Club Belladonna had been filled in and the interior itself gut-
ted. Nothing remained of its former splendor; the scarlet door had
been bricked over. People spoke of that club as they would a ghost.
It was as if it had existed only in a fabulous dream.

I couldn't bear to see it.

Jack shot me a piercing glance and asked if I wanted to leave
anyone a message. I shook my head no.

"She'll call looking for me, at some point," I said. "But I'm not
telling you or anyone else where I'm going, not even my brother. I
know all your tricks, Mr. Winslow; the Pritch's, too. I won't let
myself be found."

"Please don't do this, Tomasino," he said.

"I must," I replied. "Just tell her I don't want to be found.
That, she'll understand."

He knew me well enough not to argue. After he tipped his hat
and walked away, disappearing into the passengers in the corridor
so seamlessly, I gave him a silent bravo, I got on another plane, and
then another, and flew away. You never can be too careful.

I checked in with the Pritch's office once in a while, just so
they'd know I was still alive and so my brother wouldn't worry too
much. On rare occasions I'd call him, but only after carefully setting a prearranged time, and never at the plantation house. Once,
he tried to tell me that he'd explained to Belladonna that he'd been
as culpable as his twin, and that she had forgiven us, but I hung up
on him.

I stayed for years in Madagascar, Tunis, Tasmania, Chile, Irian
Jaya. I asked tourists to mail my infrequent letters from their desti-
nations, so I was untraceable. I knew how to plot and plan to keep
one step ahead of all of them. After a while, I got used to moving
around the world, using my large assortment of forged passports. I
changed my name so often that I nearly forgot anyone had ever
called me Tomasino.

The secret of perpetual life—

Botheration. I am repeating myself.

It is hard to remember the particulars. I prefer to watch the people come and go, moving with supreme self-importance as I used to. The tourists' babbling can be very irritating, especially the Americans in their ugly blue jeans and long, dirty hair all over the place and short, short skirts. They are so sloppy and loud. Hogarth would have held his handkerchief to his nose in distaste at the sight of them. But Hogarth is dead, isn't he? His beautifully shaped balding head smashed like a hard-boiled egg cracked too hard on a plate.

Did I mention that already? I talk to few when I go out walking, over to the Museo Bargello, where I like the Della Robbia room the best. I squirm my bulk into one of the wooden chairs in the corridor because I am tired and it is so hot, then look down into the courtyard. It used to be an execution site. Do they have dungeons in the Bargello? I wonder. Industrious Americans with their dirty jeans and guidebooks and loud voices fill the courtyard with noise. Anyone left in the dungeon to rot, screaming for help, would not be heard above this din. I smile for a minute, and a tourist looks at me strangely. I, too, am an American, although I don't feel like one. I am getting so forgetful.

The worn patterns in the old stones are oddly pleasing.

Matteo used to love visiting this museum. When he had a good day and felt a bit like talking, I could leave him to sit with the guards, murmuring in his shy lisp with them like old friends. I would go visit one of my favorite churches, Santa Margherita de' Cerchi or San Lorenzo or Santa Croce. All those famous dead Italians buried behind grubby gray marble. I laugh to myself at the sight of all the enraptured tourists, who wouldn't be caught dead lighting candles in churches back home. It's always different when you are a traveler. There is more magic in the stones and the bricks around you.

Unless the stones and bricks are in a dungeon.

The tourists in the churches disappear behind a haze of indifference. Nothing really matters anymore. Whatever God there might have been had forsaken us a long time ago.

I light a candle in Santa Croce. I always count out the exact amount they ask for, or else it's very bad luck. The gods only understand rituals. Caterina understood rituals, but she is gone, too. They're all gone.

I kneel before the flickering candles and clasp my hands, staring down at the worn marble near the altar. I am kneeling on a tomb. Only a shadowed outline of it remains; it has been so well worn from thousands and thousands of footsteps that the letters have blurred and the features of the deceased have been erased. Smoothed and forgotten. All that's left are sleek marble lines etched into the floor.

I leave the shadows of the church for the brilliant sunshine, and the rancid reek of cheap leather baking in the sun in the market-place.

Wait—that's not quite right. I am still in the museum waiting for Matteo. The bell at closing time is ringing to kick us out. Doors slam shut and hurried footsteps echo down dark hallways. A child's whining changes to a shrill giggle after a promise of gelati from her grumpy parents.

Matteo and I walk to the Boboli Gardens, past the windows full of gloves and wallets and hand-painted platters, beautifully colored lacquer fountain pens and high-heeled shoes. The guards know us well and no longer charge us admission. They think our names are Tonio and Marcello.

Although Matteo told me she stopped looking when she knew for certain that I did not want to be found, old habits die hard.

I bring the guards lurid pink marzipan pigs and angels from one of the sweet shops, and they laugh. "*Ciao,* Tonio. *Ciao,* Marcello," the grocers call out as I pass by their stores no wider than my arm span. I raise my cane in greeting. "*Ciao,* Tonio. *Ciao,* Marcello," says the proprietor of the Bar Tabacchi.

Sometimes, in the Boboli, when I close my eyes and concentrate very hard, I can pretend that I'm back on the veranda of the big house in Virginia, the expanse of plantation stretching at my feet. A dog barks in the distance, a horse whinnies, a cowbell clangs with a melodious ding. The fields of grain are ripening in the distance. As the sun sets, gentle breezes finally start to blow, and I am holding a silver beaker filled with mint julep against my wrist to cool it down.

An old southern belle's trick.

I open my eyes. I am back in Firenze, sitting with my darling big brother on a bench under interlaced branches of the trees, arching over the pathways like desperate, creeping arms. I try to count the butterflies, but there are so many. Lizards and bugs crawling, too, full of purpose. They scatter when they hear the lumpen footsteps of shuffling old eunuchs.

On very hot days in the gardens, we sometimes don't see anyone for hours. I sit with my notebooks and a thermos of cold tea laced with whiskey. Matteo reads or has a snooze. There is nothing to say, really. I am nearly finished. It has been more complicated than I thought it would be, to keep it all in order.

I told you everything. I said I would.

I tried not to lie, but sometimes I couldn't help a tiny bit of exaggeration. You're clever enough to have figured that out by now, aren't you?

Don't try to ask me any picky questions, because my lips are sealed. We were the keepers of secrets, all of us.

I have told you enough.

*B*y the fountain down the cypress street is the wishing star. That's what Bryony called it. Bryony saw it and ran ahead, exhilarated, her strawberry blond curls flying, tugging Matteo along with her.

"Look, Matteo, this is our star. You have to stand in the middle, there. Stand on it and make a wish."

Then Bryony leapt off and ran down to the water, the moated garden on the island in the Oceanus Fountain. There were fragrant lemon trees growing in terra-cotta pots, each pot with a different design. *"Uno, due, tre,"* Bryony would call out as they ran races around the pond, laughing in pure joy. Bryony appointed me the timekeeper. She didn't need me, though, because Matteo always let her win.

"Make a wish," she said to the wind and the butterflies.

Make a wish.

I want to walk to the Oceanus Fountain one winter day, but Matteo says he is tired. There is a chill wind, too cold for moats and flowers. We go to our usual bench and Matteo falls into a light doze, his weight propped against my shoulder. I put my arm more firmly around him and ease his head down into my lap so he can sleep more comfortably. A worn light gray angora scarf that Bryony knit for him once upon a time is draped around his neck. He still has most of his lovely hair, curly and thick, even if it is nearly all gray. We kept our hair, and not much else.

I like the feel of my brother's warm heaviness against my own. He sighs in his sleep, and then his weight seems to shift. No no no. It can't be true. If I don't look at him, if I don't move, then it can't be true.

A little German boy brushes leaves and a speck of dirt off the bench opposite. He is a tidy sort, and the tentative shy smile on his face consoles me just a little before he runs off to join his parents.

Oh ho, I always was too sentimental.

I sit and caress Matteo's hair. It's still moving with each small breath of wind, still alive, rustling gently in the cold air. His color is a little off, but his skin is warm. He stays warm a long time.

If I sit here until dark, I know they will come to look for us, worried when they didn't see us pass by at 6:37 precisely, en route to our evening bowl of pasta at the corner trattoria, finished with a glass of vin santo and biscotti to dip in it.

A weary old gardener trudges by, his rake propped on his shoulder, and nods a greeting. He stops when he sees my face, and Matteo, unmoving. *"Per favore,"* I manage to say, *"per favore."* He drops the rake with an awful thudding crunch on the gravel and runs off, crossing himself as he disappears into the twilight.

I never do see that gardener again. I wonder what happened to him. I wanted to give him a token in remembrance. Perhaps he feels the sight of us was a bad omen, or maybe one of his nieces finally persuaded him to live in the south, where the warm weather will ease the aches of his rheumatism and he can tend his tomatoes in peace.

I don't know. I'll never know. It doesn't matter, I tell myself as I sit in the gardens and watch the butterflies. There is no peace.

Sometimes I try to write in my notebooks. I hold one of my beautiful lacquer pens, but the words don't come. I finished what I started, didn't I? I saw it through to the bitter end. I know I did. Botheration. It is getting harder and harder to remember. It is so hot.

I am nearly finished. And then?

Then I'll keep dreaming.

*   *   *

I am daydreaming on my bench. I finger Matteo's light gray angora scarf, the one he was wearing when he died. It was his favorite, that one Bryony knit for him years and years ago, the stitches all crooked and unraveling, the fringe uneven. Then I put it back in my pocket. It is too sweltering for scarves. I hear footsteps but am too tired to open my eyes.

I feel someone touching my sleeve, a ghost's touch. My eyes remain shut. Is this how it ends? I don't want to look.

Tomasino. I hear my name. *Tomasino, wake up.* I have died and it is my brother calling me. For that, I will open my eyes. Until I feel the lightest touch of fingers, drifting along my arm.

She never did like to be touched.

The wind rustles the drooping dry leaves and I catch a whiff of something. Hers, yet not hers. I must be dreaming. I have dreamt myself back to my dream's wishes; the wishing star that did it for me. Wishing as I was to hear that familiar, beloved voice.

Tomasino, I hear again. It is not her voice. Not hers, and not Bryony's. It is a ghost voice, come to taunt me.

Belladonna sounds so sweet.

For only a second, I am young again. Full of cunning and self-importance and a mania for conniving. I am a masterpiece of ruined civilization—she said I was as I sat by her side, masked and omnipotent in the Club Belladonna.

Oh ho, I was happy then, to plan and plot and watch them suffer.

I did it for you, Belladonna. I did it for myself. I'd do it again, if you asked me to.

I think I have died. Matteo is calling me. I felt the thrill of his ghost fingers tickling my arm. He needs me. I'm waiting for him here. This is where he left me. He's coming back; I knew he wouldn't leave me alone for long. He left me once before, when he got married to Annabeth. I was happy for him then, truly I was. But once she was gone, he said he'd never leave me again. He'll come back and we'll go for a walk the way we used to, me chattering and my darling big brother regarding me with fond, silent bemusement.

I open my eyes. I am not younger, and my brother is dead. I buried him near Leandro, on a hillside in Tuscany. But there is a little girl standing before me. She looks so much like Bryony, with sea-blue eyes, but her hair is light brown and very straight. It can't be Bryony. It is no more than a cruel trick of the hazy light of a sultry summer's day.

"Are you Tomasino? You must be Tomasino. You look like Matteo, except you're fatter," she says, then puts her hand up over her mouth and glances over to someone. I close my eyes, but I feel her tiny fingers tapping on my knee for attention, and I open them again. My knee doesn't throb anymore. It is as silent as I've become. "Tomasino, Tomasino," the little girl is saying. "I know you're Tomasino. I'm Angelica," she says. "My mommy sent me to look for you. Do you really have a lion on your cane?"

"Yes, a golden lion," I manage to tell her after clearing my throat. I don't want to disappoint a little girl who looks like Bryony. "But who is your mommy?"

She looks bewildered for a second, and then she laughs. She thinks I'm teasing her.

"My mommy is Mrs. Gibson. Her name is Bryony, like the flower. Bryony Bryony Bryony Gibson," she says in a singsongy voice, the same way Bryony used to. "I'm Angelica, like the flower. The Angelica flower. My daddy is Mr. Gibson. His real name is Arundel. Arundel means 'eagle valley,' did you know that? Arundel Arundel Arundel Cyril St. James Gibson."

Angelica, daughter of Bryony, who married Arundel Gibson. I can't believe I forgot all about them, that couple. How did they meet? Did Bryony ever know who Arundel's father was? Matteo told me; I know he must have told me. Did the Pritch set it up? Something about a Jaybird? Botheration. It was too complicated to write down and remember, I chide myself. No, that's not quite right. It was that they found happiness.

I had no room for happiness in my notebooks.

I smile at Angelica. Another beautiful little flower, a bright, sparkling child. And then I see Bryony herself, when Angelica runs to her and protests that I didn't know who she was. Bryony is as old now as Belladonna once had been, older even than she was when we first met her. Bryony looks so much like her mother, except her eyes are a brilliant blue-green and there is no hardness or fear in her face. No rage in her heart. She gives me a wobbly smile.

"I missed you so, Tomasino. All these years," she says as she sits down next to me on the bench, in Matteo's spot, and places her hand gently on my arm. "We found you only after they called us from Ca' d'Oro after your brother's . . ." Her voice falters. "After Matteo's funeral. That's when we knew you would let us find you again."

"Really?" I ask, pretending to be genuinely surprised. I don't want to talk about my brother. I'd rather drink in the sight of Bryony. She looks so much like her mother. I think I said that already; forgive me if I did. "You missed me?"

"You darling, crazy man," Bryony says, kissing my cheek. Belladonna never kissed my cheek. She didn't like to touch or be touched. And then I see that Bryony has tears streaming down her cheeks. Why is she crying? Do I look that awful?"

"Of course I missed you," Bryony says, wiping her eyes. "We all did, like crazy. My mother most of all, you goose. How could she not miss you? I thought for sure you would come for the wedding, and I cried all morning that you weren't there to see me in my flower-girl dress. My face is ridiculously puffy in the photographs."

"You did?" I ask, delighted. "But what wedding are you talking about?"

Bryony's eyes widen and she bites her lip, that gesture still so familiar I nearly cry out at the sight of it.

"My mother's," she says, her voice all wobbly. "My mother and Guy's." She fishes in her bag for a white linen handkerchief and blows her nose. "And then I hoped beyond all hoping that you might come to my own wedding. Even Matteo said you might."

"You always liked Matteo better," I protest. She laughs ruefully.

"We need you, Tomasino. She can't do without you; she never could, after all these years. No one comes close to you, not even Guy." Bryony sighs, then smiles sadly at me. I'm glad she didn't say "my father" instead of Guy. How much does she know? I wonder. What did they tell her?

That, I will never ask.

"Come with me, Tomasino," Bryony says. "I need to make a wish."

I shake my head no. I am too tired to get up. I am afraid I am still dreaming, and that if I move, the illusion will shatter and I will wake up alone.

"Please," Bryony pleads. "*Please.* Come with me to the wishing star. I need you."

Botheration. I never could refuse anyone who needed me.

Bryony pulls me up gently and links her arm with mine. Angelica is skipping ahead of us, kicking at the little pebbles on the path and singing nonsense songs, just as her mother had done. We are walking very slowly, and I try not to lean too hard on my cane. It is so hot and I am so tired.

"Tomasino," someone says. I shut my eyes. I have died, for real this time. We have all died, and this is heaven. Everyone I love is together with me, near the sound of a fountain in the bright light of a garden.

"Tomasino," she says. I know she is close by. I can feel her presence, unwavering, and the scent of her perfume, so delectable, so sweet, concocted from the essence of plants that could kill you with a single bite.

She always managed to materialize so quickly, when you least expected her. I never did figure out how she did it.

There is so much I will never ever know.

I open my eyes, and there is my heart's darling, my very own Belladonna, standing beside me. Her bright green eyes are shiny with tears, and she, too, bites her lip. She, the indomitable Belladonna, in tears!

Something must be very wrong.

"Why are there tears in your eyes?" I ask her, trying to sound nonchalant. "You aren't the crying type."

Her hair is twisted up into what is now an unfashionable chignon, and at first glance she doesn't look much older than the last time I saw her, when I disappeared from La Fenice nearly twenty-five years before. Her face is different, though. It's fuller, softer, more womanly. There is no hint of rage hardening her features into an impenetrable, terrifying mask.

But the softening doesn't mean she'll ever forget.

I had to go, I want to say to her now, I had to. You had Guy and my brother and all the rest of your lives together stretching before you and you didn't need me anymore. Every time you'd see me you'd remember what—

"I wanted to find peace," I tell her now.

"Oh, Tomasino," Belladonna says. "Come back to me, please. I beg you. I can't do without you. Truly, I can't. I *need* you."

Three little words.

This is how we ask each other for forgiveness. The words hanging unsaid, as if their echoes were shimmering in the haze like the wings of butterflies.

Like the echo of footsteps disappearing down a hallway in a dungeon, receding forever in the darkness.

Belladonna isn't real; she never was. She will remain forever untouchable, implacable, a mysterious goddess presiding over the dark realm below.

As I will remain forever her Tomasino.

And then I see Guy, leaning against the railing encircling the fountain. He is still dashingly handsome, although his face is deeply lined and his hair is streaked with more gray than mine. I was right about Guy all along, I tell myself smugly. He has the same air about him as when I'd first snooped on his conversation in the Club Belladonna, laughing about a sociopathic squire and lighting a cigarette from a woman's necklace. Guy beckons to a slender man with light brown hair flopping over his forehead and a somber look. He reminds me of Hugh, I decide, what Hugh might have looked like when he was younger. Arundel Gibson, he says, introducing himself. Bryony's husband and father of Angelica.

So I get to meet him after all, the man who did such a splendid thing for us once upon a time.

Bryony can't be old enough to have a husband and a child. Why, it was only yesterday when I left, wasn't it?

"Come home with us, Tomasino," Guy says. "We need you. *I* need you. The maid took down all of Pompadour's books for a proper dusting and left them in a hopeless jumble. *Please* come back. Hugh and Laura are arriving soon for a visit. They want to see you, too. *Please.* Besides," he adds with a naughty wink, "no one can make a mint julep the way you do."

Pompadour's books, Pompadour's Bible. The secret in—

Belladonna is smiling at me through the tears in her eyes. Her hands close over mine, on the golden lion's head of Leandro's cane.

Angelica is running around the wishing star, her hair streaming behind her. "Make a wish," she calls out, laughing.

Make a wish!

We stand there in the sunshine, watching her running races with her father. He lets her win every time. Just like Matteo had done with Bryony.

I catch a whiff of something pungent wafting by me on a puff of wind. *Nerium oleander,* I think, the flowers so delicate, so fragrant. No no no, that's not quite right. *Atropa belladonna,* it must be. Lovely red flowers shaped like bells, berries black and shiny as a cocker spaniel's coat.

How could it be anything but Belladonna?

Oh ho, the sweet sweet poison!

Acknowledgments

Much grateful appreciation is owed the indefatigable cheerleaders: Eve Parkes, *la plus belle du monde,* and her husband, Gerald, for years of boundless hospitality and kindness; likewise the splendid and scrumptious Sebastian Scott; Sally Ann Lasson, storyteller and faxtresse extraordinaire; Candace Bushnell, who always knew of fresh outrages to make me laugh; W. S. Merwin, for the *bastide* in Loubressac, where I found the musty volumes of *Lives of the Rakes;* Aniko Boehler, who took me to Saturnia; Maggie Alderson, for encouragement from halfway around the globe; Janis Altman, for much-needed advice; likewise Martha Haffey; the two Christophers; Demeter Fragrances, my favorite noses; George Andrews and Desmond Gorges, divine arbiters of taste; Bill Adams, my severest critic; Madeleine Morel, who believed in me way back when; ditto Marjorie Bramon; Joanna Doniger, who bought eleven copies of my last novel; Josephine Fairley, for mascara; Fontini Dimou, for style; Eddi Reader, whose voice really could melt a glacier; Andreas Wisniewski and Kim Lansdale, for *vin rouge* in Lacam; Annie Hansen, for the Elixir of Life; Tom Johnston, for the house in Cushendall; Eduardo Machado, for writerly discipline; K. C. Landis and all the Squares, who dragged me out of the house; Lucy Wauchope, for Cadogan Square; Santo and Margaret for all that paper; Marsinay Smith and John Aherne, the two most brilliant assistants in the universe; Alex Kingston, who knows about matters of the heart; Gloria Moline, fearless reader; many more assorted Molines; Harvey Keitel, who taught me about the journey; and Peter Gleason, who showed me how to shoot.

Special thanks for the cherished daily encouragement of two extraordinary, and endlessly amusing writers: Lynn Geller and Judy Green. My thanks and love to Eleni Lambros, healer and all-around wonderful woman; and Deborah Feingold, who knows me best.

This book took shape under the deftly perceptive counsel of my agent, the marvelous Suzanne Gluck, and my equally marvelous and insightful editor, Jamie Raab, to whom I am profoundly indebted.